NeWest
PRESS

Library and Archives Canada Cataloguing in Publication

Innes, Roy, 1939-, author
        The extra cadaver murder / Roy Innes.

Issued in print and electronic formats.

ISBN 978-1-926455-72-3 (paperback) 978-1-926455-73-0 (epub) ISBN 978-1-926455-74-7 (mobi)

    I. Title.

PS8617.N545E98 2016   C813'.6   C2016-901689-7   C2016-901690-0

Board Editor: Don Kerr
Cover & Interior Design: Greg Vickers for GVD
Author Photo: Gottfried Mitteregger
Anatomy images courtesy of Creative Commons. Anonymous/Publication/Public Domain.

NeWest Press acknowledges the support of the Canada Council for the Arts, the Alberta Foundation for the Arts, and the Edmonton Arts Council for support of our publishing program. This project is funded in part by the Government of Canada.

NeWest PRESS
201, 8540–109 Street
Edmonton, Alberta | T6G IE6
780.432.9427
www.newestpress.com

No bison were harmed in the making of this book.

We are committed to protecting the environment and to the responsible use of natural resources. This book was printed on 100% post-consumer recycled paper.

1 2 3 4 5 18 17 16 | Printed and bound in Canada

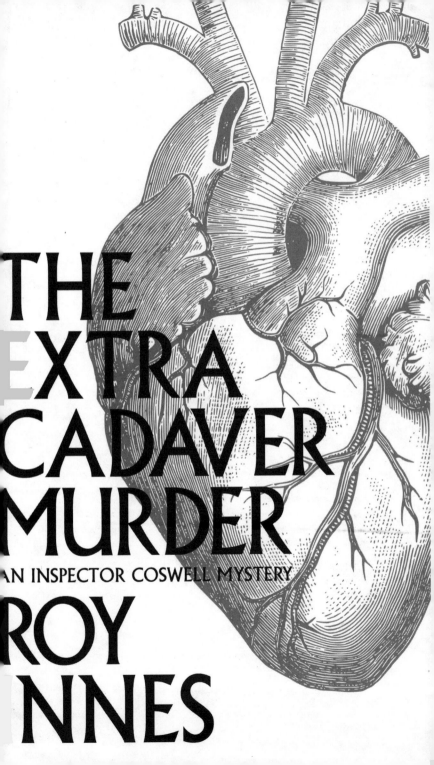

THE EXTRA CADAVER MURDER

AN INSPECTOR COSWELL MYSTERY

ROY INNES

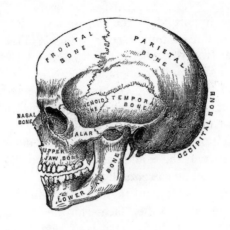

CHAPTER ONE

Monday, Sept. 7th

Fred Porter looked forward to the first day of anatomy class each year, despite the fact that he had been present for over twenty of them. The ceremony varied little—fresh-faced medical students gathered around ten gleaming, stainless steel coffins, six students per coffin, old Professor Dietrich standing imperiously on a small platform at the front of the room.

"Good morning, ladies and gentlemen. Welcome to what arguably could be called the most important subject that you will study in your entire four years at this institution."

Fred stifled a snicker. The word "arguably" coming out of the old tyrant was a joke. He failed more students in their first year than all the other medical disciplines combined, fanatical in his belief that without an intimate knowledge of anatomy, one could never be a true physician, ignoring the fact that those other disciplines—pathology, therapeutics, public health, and so forth were far more important in the day-to-day practice of real medicine. But Anatomy reigned supreme in the minds of first-year students, whether by mystique, history, or the professor's intimidating persona.

Fred, the lab custodian, however, benefited from the hatred, at least at the beginning of the term. The students feared anything and anyone related to anatomy, including him, but it didn't last. Eventually, handed down from the senior students, he would be debased from "Mr. Porter" to "Fred," and then eventually, "Igor."

But at this moment there was nothing but trepidation written all over their faces—for the lab, the instructors, and most of all, for what lay inside those steel coffins. Many had never seen a dead human being before, and to be soon cutting into one? He contemplated a few sphincters barely holding on.

"... respect for the generous men and women who have bequeathed their bodies...."

Dietrich droned on. Fred tuned him out, choosing instead to admire yet another perfect set-up thanks to Fred Porter, master embalmer.

A flurry of activity jolted him from his reverie. The students were about to open the coffins—always a letdown for Fred. All they would see were figures totally swaddled in burlap, reminiscent of Egyptian mummies. Lesson one: the forearm. That's all that would be exposed. No great trauma there.

Most got at it right away and pulled open the steel clamshell lid with false bravado, but one group appeared to be deciding just who among them would do the actual deed. When they finally opened it, Fred's wish that someone would faint almost came true—there wasn't a shred of burlap to be seen. Instead, lying face down on the steel slab was a deceased male, totally nude. The room's fluorescent lights gave the body an eerie blue-grey hue. Pandemonium struck.

Dietrich's voiced boomed out, "Close that

immediately!" followed by, "Fred!"

The students quickly swung the lid shut with a deafening clang.

Stunned, it took a moment for Fred to obey his master's summons. He cursed his gimpy leg as he hobbled as fast as he could to where Dietrich stood, arms crossed, eyes blazing.

"I ... I ... I ..." Fred stammered.

But before he could go on, Dietrich ordered the students out of the room: "A short recess."

Fred stood, mortified. But why? No way had he missed wrapping all of the cadavers. And then he knew—some son-of-a-bitching medical student getting back at them.

Dietrich gave him no time to object.

"Do your job—correctly this time," he said, and then abruptly left the room.

Two lab instructors remained behind: foreign physicians, one from Ireland, the other from England, both fully qualified surgeons in their own countries, but who required a year of resident training to obtain Canadian certification. This included time in a basic science, anatomy being the obvious choice for surgeons. Assisting in the dissection labs was one of their more demeaning duties.

Their amusement quickly changed to sympathy when they saw how disturbed the custodian had become, the poor man's hands shaking so badly he was having trouble opening the coffin.

"Hold on, Fred," one said. They hurried over to help. "We'll give you a hand and don't take it so hard, we all make mistakes."

Fred shot back, "I didn't make a mistake. Somebody did this."

With the lids dropped down, all three stood for a moment and observed the body.

"This didn't come from any of my coolers," Fred said.

"Smell it."

"Right," the Irishman said. "No formaldehyde."

The other bent down to get a look at the corpse's face.

"Good God!" he said. "It's Doctor Kelly and he's been garrotted. I can see the mark."

"The professor of surgery? Murdered?" Fred said.

The Irishman confirmed it.

"It's him all right. In the flesh. Dead flesh, unfortunately."

Fred whistled.

"This is terrible," he said. "The boss needs to be informed like right now."

He maintained an expression of deep concern as he hustled across the lab to Dietrich's office, but inside, a song played in his heart. *Not my fault, you old bastard, not my fault. Eat crow.*

Dietrich almost swooned when he saw the body.

"It *is* Patrick! He was at my staff party yesterday evening. This is terrible. Call the police, Fred."

Fred fought back the urge to smile. How quickly the tables had turned. He watched the rattled old bird hastily exit the lab, headed no doubt to the Dean's office. Fences needed mending.

The call to Inspector Mark Coswell's office at Vancouver's "Q" Division headquarters from the officer in charge of the University of British Columbia RCMP detachment didn't come through until mid morning. His assistant, Corporal James, fielded it.

"Inspector Coswell is engaged at the moment, Sergeant McMorran. May I be of assistance?"

Actually, Coswell was sitting on his ample ass three feet away, coffee cup in hand, trying to decide which of the Tim Hortons donuts that James had brought in would accompany it. Interrupting him would necessitate a significant issue—not likely forthcoming from the

THE EXTRA CADAVER MURDER

detachment considered no better than an R and R posting by officers in the crime-rampant districts elsewhere in the province.

This time, that assumption was wrong.

"Yes, Sergeant. I most certainly will un-engage him. A homicide on campus? A professor garrotted? My, my."

James held the receiver at arm's length, counted to ten, and then handed it to Coswell.

Much to James' disappointment, the sergeant's presentation was met with silence from Coswell—no questions, and then abruptly cut off with: "We're on our way. Don't let anyone leave the building. I'll arrange forensics."

Unlike most senior officers whose subordinates did the driving, Coswell invariably took the wheel. The heavy police cruisers had a tendency to rock like a boat when cornering. This triggered his motion sickness, an affliction he'd been cursed with since his boyhood. Holding onto the steering wheel effectively blocked it.

"Do you want me to turn on the flashers, sir?" James said. "We can make better time."

"No. The victim isn't going anywhere and it sounds like the situation is well in hand. We don't need to hurry."

Out of the corner of his eye, he caught James' quizzical look, but he ignored it. He needed some time to prepare himself for what he was about to face—not the murder scene, but rather the man in charge at the university detachment—Sergeant McMorran.

As he expertly manoeuvred through Vancouver traffic, Coswell blessed his luck that Corporal James had been assigned his partner. James was intelligent, orderly to the point of being obsessive, a non-complainer, and, best of all, a keen observer with a photographic memory. He had only two faults, the first being of no consequence to

Coswell, save possible interference from the right-wing faction of the Force: James was gay. The second was the corporal's propensity for non-stop chatter, which started up the moment they pulled out of the headquarters parking lot.

"What is this world coming to when professors are murdered? It had to be a student, don't you think?"

As usual, James required no response. He rattled on.

"But then again, maybe another professor committed the murder. I hear that university politics are brutal, constant infighting for advancement, grants, perks and all that. Garrotting, though? That's just so non-academic, more a professional hit man's technique. A paid assassin? Yes, could be."

The theorizing continued unabated. Coswell only half listened to him. He would have tuned him out completely, but James' sharp mind had a way of suddenly striking to the core, something that had happened more than once before with cases mired in complexities. A degree in Criminology from Carleton University added to his credibility.

Coswell had a degree as well—Law, UBC, Class of '81, which had proved useful to him ... in an unusual sort of way. Firstly, it settled his father's concerns about his eldest son's penchant for seeking out the pleasures in life and avoiding anything approaching hard work and commitment. The old man, one of BC's wine barons, earned his position in life with those very qualities. He dropped out of school at an early age and virtually clawed his way to success. Academia held little respect in his eyes. He considered it the easy route, but in his son's case, it appeared to be the only route ... if only he would stick it out.

But sticking it out was not a problem. The young Coswell thoroughly enjoyed university life. He cruised through the courses and exhibited a definite gift for public debate. He was a hit in the classroom, his fraternity, and the students' pub.

But a summer job with the Justice Institute of BC ultimately turned his career choice well off track. The time he spent with policemen, especially homicide investigations, stimulated him like nothing in his academic life. Even the courtroom sessions, which his fellow law students found fascinating, were, to Coswell, more often boring than not. As a result, with the ink barely dried on his law diploma, he made formal application to the RCMP.

When he received his acceptance letter along with the date for him to appear at the RCMP Academy, Depot Division, in Regina, the news had to be broken to Coswell senior. It was not well received. Nowhere did *policeman* fit in the ambitions his father had for his son, and even years later, when Coswell eventually made inspector, father never got over his disappointment.

From RCMP headquarters, just off Kingsway and Main, the shortest route to the university is Twelfth Avenue— virtually a straight line. But at Burrard Street, Coswell made an abrupt right turn.

"It's a beautiful day," he said. "Let them all wait a bit. We'll take the scenic route."

"Sergeant McMorran won't be pleased," James said.

"Bugger Sergeant McMorran."

"Thank you, sir, but I've never even met the man. Do you think he's my type?"

Coswell gave a coarse laugh.

"Definitely not ... in more ways than one."

James waited for elaboration but it was not forthcoming. Curious, he probed.

"I understand that he's a bit of an icon in the Force— always gets his man. Our motto at one time, I believe."

"Our motto, James, is 'Maintain the Right.' There's a big difference."

Again, nothing more from Coswell. James pushed on.

"It seems odd to me that with his reputation for success, Sergeant McMorran ended up in such a low-key post."

Coswell sighed.

"All right," he said. "It's all very confidential but maybe you need a little clarification of our motto."

Coswell took a moment to gather his thoughts. Finally, he spoke.

"It goes back a long ways actually, even before you were assigned to homicide. Chief Ward volunteered me to sit on an internal review committee dealing with our Sergeant McMorran."

A pause.

Fearing that Coswell had changed his mind, James prompted.

"A grave matter, no doubt," he said, "but I can assure you, although you may be surprised, I can keep my mouth shut when told to do so."

Coswell smiled at the thought of James keeping his mouth shut. He took a deep breath and carried on.

"Okay. It was serious all right. His fame started when he was part of a raid on a drug smuggling operation out of Steveston that used commercial fishing boats. A couple of the perps got shot during the takedown for reasons never made clear. McMorran was the shooter. He claimed self defense."

"Claimed? I gather there were questions," James said.

"One of the surviving smugglers said McMorran virtually assassinated them."

"No witnesses, I guess. His word against the smuggler's."

"You've got it, and with the glowing reports of his superior performance from fellow officers, good riddance to bad rubbish dominated the thinking at the time."

"He made sergeant, though," James said. "The brass must have been favourably impressed as well."

Coswell chuckled.

"One of the reporters who covered the takedown bypassed our official spokesperson and cornered McMorran, who was only too willing to talk. He came out the big hero even though he was well down the chain of command at the time. The reprimand from above was a feather tap."

"Did you have any dealings with him?"

"After the fact, so to speak. By the time I got notified, the bodies were in the downtown morgue."

"Steveston not a crime scene, eh?"

"Clean as a whistle," Coswell said. "I went out there but it was a waste of time. I insisted on an interview with McMorran, but that was an even bigger waste of time. His story was tighter than a drum. I can still remember the sneer."

"Oh my," James said. "Do I detect a little animosity?"

"More than a little. We clashed a couple of times after that. His promotion to sergeant came right after the Steveston incident and he got put in charge of a squad of undercover guys in the downtown Eastside. Their arrest record shot up like a rocket."

"Not a good thing?"

"Some pretty flimsy cases among them. The stings were more like entrapment. Even junior legal aid lawyers were getting dealers off."

"How did you get involved? Narcotic cases aren't in your bailiwick."

"But dead bodies are, and they started to pile up. The Steveston takedown scene began to reappear in the downtown Eastside, and the dead men all had one thing in common—they were repeat offenders."

James whistled.

"McMorran doing the judge, jury, and executioner thing?"

"It appeared that way to me," Coswell said.

"But to no one else?"

"Yes. Deputy Chief Constable Wilkinson, head of the Vancouver City Police homicide unit. We compared notes and then approached our respective seniors, but we got the same directive—'lay off McMorran.'"

"So how did he end up getting put on the internal review hot seat?"

"He finally made a mistake. His unit tracked a buy-sell operation to an upscale West Vancouver residence belonging to an engineer-type who specialized in building pulp mills in Malaysia, meaning he and the wife were out of the country for long stretches."

"Leaving the house empty?" James said.

"Yes, but they hired a home security firm to keep watch on it. Trouble was that they had a daughter supposedly living in residence at UBC. Common story— rich kid who picked the wrong boyfriend. She snowed the security company and moved back home with her drug-dealing lover."

"Oh dear," James said. "I can just picture the raid. Little resistance, was there?"

"McMorran the twit, barged into the middle of a house party, guns drawn, flak vests, the works. Unfortunately, one of the party types had a video camera. The daughter did the wildcat thing, spewing lip and clawing away, but she picked the wrong target—McMorran. He laid her out with a fist to the face. Bust her nose all to hell. The camera guy caught it."

"I take it Daddy wasn't a happy camper."

"And Mommy even less happy, but the kid's father was sharp. He gave instructions to his lawyer to bargain the girl off charges in exchange for keeping the nose busting quiet. No problem there. Neither he nor the Force wanted their reputations besmirched."

"I'm surprised that the video didn't go viral or that the media didn't pick it up?"

And risk having one of your high-class friends shown

up at a drug bust? Not a chance. A solid code lives amongst the offspring of the affluent."

James gazed pensively out the window towards the North Shore of English Bay where North and West Vancouver merged.

"One has to have a little sympathy for the sergeant's attitude towards re-offenders. Even I get angry sometimes with the revolving door legal system in this province. And you must, too, after all your years on the force watching criminals get off with wrist slaps."

"Not a bit," Coswell replied. "I've never confused my job with the judicial process, and I highly recommend that you do the same. Our duty is to apprehend the perps, not punish them."

He thought for a moment before going on.

"You know, even from my earliest days on the force, I got as much satisfaction out of catching a thief the tenth time as I did the first. In fact, I got more satisfaction, because on occasion the odd one got smarter after each arrest—ergo more of a challenge to me."

James laughed.

"I'll remember that advice. We're hunters, right, although it would be nice sometime to be the shooter instead of the guide."

Coswell glanced over at him.

"Now there's a metaphor I'd never have expected from you, growing up a city boy in Ottawa."

A smile from James.

"Not all gay men play with dolls and do embroidery. I went on many a hunting trip with my father, and if I must say so myself, a good percentage of the game in the family freezer was thanks to me."

Coswell's father had taken him hunting as well, but he hated every minute of it. He loved venison but only when it appeared cooked to perfection on his dinner plate.

"Next, you're going to tell me you were an all-star

quarterback for your college team."

James giggled.

"And take that snap from the centre's lovely behind? No. Hockey was my game—goalie."

Road construction slowed them down on Cornwall. Coswell was tempted to swing up to Fourth Avenue but Point Grey Road and the views of the Beaches—Jericho, Locarno, and Spanish Banks drew him on. Once past the short business district on Cornwall, all of English Bay appeared: a dazzling expanse dotted with freighters, pleasure craft, seaplanes, and far across on the North Shore, a continuous row of high-rise apartments that extended almost to its northwestern tip where the Point Atkinson lighthouse stood guard.

On the near south shore, dinghy sailors and windsurfers launched their crafts from sandy beaches. Above them on the paved seawalk were walkers, runners, cyclists, mothers pushing strollers, and in the park, Frisbee throwers, picnickers, and people sitting on benches gazing thoughtfully out at the vista before them.

"Impressive, isn't it," said Coswell. "Beats the hell out of Ottawa, I'll bet."

"Not totally," James replied. "We had the Rideau Canal. Great for jogging, walking, whatever, and in the winter you can skate from Carlton University right up to the Parliament Buildings."

"I prefer sailing."

What Coswell meant was that he preferred *watching* people sail. The mere thought of bobbing up and down in the ocean waves made his stomach turn.

Once past Spanish Banks, whether from a feeling of guilt or not, Coswell abandoned the scenic route and turned left onto Westbrook Crescent, which quickly led to Westbrook Mall, a major route through the UBC campus. Coswell knew where the medical school complex was located, but he would have been sorely pressed to find the Department of Anatomy housed in a modest structure completely surrounded by more imposing buildings. James had the campus map downloaded on the cruiser's inboard computer.

"Best to park in a designated lot," he said. "There's one just past the Faculty of Dentistry. It's a short walk from there. Otherwise we can end up going round and round out here. This place is a visitor's nightmare."

"No adjacent fire hydrants? Tsk, tsk. The life of a policeman is a hard one."

Coswell wasn't about to argue, however. James was usually right in these situations, but when he pulled into the lot, it was full. Among the parked vehicles were two RCMP cruisers.

"Didn't leave us a parking spot, the bastard," Coswell said. "Deliberate, I'll bet."

James consulted his computer again.

"There's another lot close by," he said. "Hospital visitor parking."

"No need. We'll park here."

With that, Coswell drove in and swung the cruiser perpendicular to the bumpers of the RCMP vehicles and stopped, effectively blocking them off.

"Don't want to obstruct the civilians from getting their cars out, do we?" he said.

James just shook his head.

CHAPTER TWO

A bored RCMP constable stood guard at the front door of the anatomy building, a cigarette dangled from his lips. When he saw Coswell and James appear around the corner from the parking lot, he quickly tossed it into the shrubbery, but not quickly enough. James lit into him immediately.

"That's not just a bad habit, Constable, it's a disgrace to your uniform. You look like some B-movie extra taking a break."

Coswell said nothing. His own plainclothes attire was beginning to look a little seedy, especially when contrasted with James' sharp, three-piece suit and perfectly knotted tie. The inspector's double chin did not get along well with knots, hence were always loosened and often askew.

"Sorry, Corporal," the constable said. "I am trying to quit." And then he quickly changed the subject. "Sergeant McMorran is waiting for you in lecture hall B. Would you like me to escort you there?"

"No," Coswell said. "We'll find it. You stay here and don't let anyone enter. It sounds as if the crime scene is cluttered enough as it is."

But inside there was no sign of clutter. In fact, the place appeared deserted, not a soul to be seen in the foyer, the hallway, or even in the offices on the main floor.

"What the hell is this all about?" Coswell said. "You don't suppose McMorran has everyone herded up in that lecture hall do you?"

"Crude, but effective, I suppose," James said, looking up at a board that had a diagram of the floor layout posted. "There it is. Second last room on the left."

The seating in the lecture hall was arranged in steeply sloped tiers, like a European opera house. The room was filled with individuals, most of whom wore white lab coats. All were looking down to the front where an RCMP sergeant and a corporal sat. The corporal stood up immediately when Coswell and James entered, but the sergeant remained seated.

"Ah, Inspector Coswell. Glad you finally got here," he said. "Any longer and I would have started the interviews without you."

Coswell bristled.

"We didn't take all that long, McMorran," he said. "And starting without me would not have been a good idea."

McMorran merely smiled but there was no humour in his eyes. He slowly got up from his seat and handed Coswell some sheets of paper.

"We passed these around the room. They have the names, duties, and times of arrival this morning of everyone in the building.

"Fine," Coswell said. "Now you two are dismissed. Corporal James and I will take it from here. We'll call you if we need your assistance."

McMorran didn't move for a moment. One could almost hear his teeth grinding, but then he turned abruptly and stomped out of the room, the corporal at his heels.

For a moment, the assembled appeared stunned by the exchange. The sergeant most likely presented himself to them in all his uniformed glory, and seeing him dismissed like that by a balding, overweight man in a rumpled suit coat and shapeless trousers would have seemed decidedly incongruous.

One member of the audience, however, recovered quickly—a tall, gaunt man in a white lab coat sitting dead centre in the first row. He stood up and looked down at Coswell.

"This has become ridiculous, holding our entire staff here like this. We have an educational and research centre to run. It's time we got on with it."

"Dr. Dietrich, I presume," Coswell replied, debating whether or not to take a hard line with the man.

"You presume correctly."

"You are quite right," he said, opting for the diplomatic approach. "No need to interrupt the progress of medical science. You may all return to your duties, but before doing so, it would be helpful if you added to this list exactly where we can find you this morning."

Another white coat put his hand up, a young man with shocking red hair sitting in the very back row.

"Yes?" Coswell said.

"Some of us have duties later this morning at the VGH. When will we be free to go there?" The man spoke with a broad Irish accent.

"Right after we interview you," Coswell replied. "But put an X beside your name. We'll do you first. Anyone else in the same position can do likewise."

Everyone began to file out, led by Dietrich who was about to bypass the list but James stopped him.

"You, too, Professor," he said with an impish smile.

Dietrich scowled.

"My secretary knows where I am at all times," he said. "You can check with her."

James put his finger on the list.

"Please," he said. "Your secretary may be on coffee break."

Dietrich stopped just short of objecting. Instead, he leaned over and scribbled something beside his name.

"That looks like doctor script," James said. "I can't read it. Perhaps you could print it for us."

"It says 'anatomy lab.' You print it."

Coswell stepped in.

"Ah. Not the anatomy lab just yet, Professor," he said. "It is, of course, a crime scene and will be for some time. I suggest you alter your lesson plans to accommodate that."

Dietrich struggled for words but finally spit out, "I'll be in my office then."

A woman's voice called out. "What about classes, Dr. Dietrich?"

"Obviously cancelled for today, thanks to our inspector here. I presume that we will be able to resume tomorrow morning?"

"Most likely," Coswell said, and after a pause, "If everyone cooperates."

As the professor swept out the door, a stooped, older man appeared beside them. He wore a white coat which bore a number of yellow stains and exuded the unmistakable odour of formaldehyde.

"I'm Fred, the anatomy technician," he said to Coswell. "I can show you around the lab if you like. I've run it now for twenty years and there's no one who knows every nook and cranny like I do."

"All right," Coswell said. "That will be most useful, but we'll wait until Corporal James finishes with the whereabouts list."

Waiting for his corporal served a purpose: James could take in details at a crime scene as well as Coswell himself and would store them in his photographic memory bank. Coswell's bank was getting a bit overdrawn recently.

The anatomy lab was at the end of a long corridor on the main floor. They paused at the entrance door while Fred punched in numbers on a keypad.

"Who has this code, Fred?" Coswell asked.

"Just about everyone in the building."

"Students as well?"

"Yes."

"Then who does it prevent from getting in?"

Fred gave a shrug.

"Waste of time, I guess," he said.

The electric lock snapped open. Just inside was another set of doors, each with a viewing panel, and beyond them the lab, a huge room bathed in natural light from windows on three sides, augmented by banks of fluorescent ceiling fixtures.

"Goodness," James said. "I'd need sunglasses to work in here."

They went over to the body and gazed down at it. Coswell bent over and perused the victim's neck.

"McMorran was right," he said. "Garrotted for sure. You can barely see the mark."

"Bruises on the back of the neck where the killer hung on tight," James added, and then leaning closer, "and one on his back from a knee, I'd say. The garrotter most likely bracing himself while he pulled on the wire. No other bruises, though. Not much of a struggle it seems."

He stood up.

"Why nude, do you think? A little sexual deviance?"

"Or to humiliate the man," Coswell said. "Pretty demeaning, lying there with your hairy ass facing the spectators."

"A hate crime? Interesting."

Coswell turned to Fred.

"I see elevator doors over there," he said. "What are they used for?"

"It's a service elevator direct to the basement. Our specimens are stored down there. Professor Dietrich would be horrified if bodies were wheeled anywhere that the general public might see them."

"And what is the security in your storage?"

"Old fashioned lock and key," Fred answered. "And nobody goes in there other than me."

"Who cleans it?" James asked.

"Me. No cleaners go in there. It's kind of my private office."

"There must be extra keys," Coswell said, "if for no other reason than fire access."

"Oh, yes," Fred said. "There's a master key for the firemen in a lock box outside, and one in Dr. Dietrich's office."

"In a lock box?"

"Well, no," Fred admitted. "It's just kept with all the other spare keys."

"Spare keys to what?" Coswell said. "I noticed that the front door had a standard lock. How about the rest of

THE EXTRA CADAVER MURDER

the outer doors?"

"Keys," Fred said. "But the whole building is alarmed."

"Yes, I saw the alarm pad just inside the front door. Who gets the code to that?"

"Only staff members, along with a front door key."

And, after a moment's thought, "And students can sign out a key if they want to come in after hours or on Sundays."

James let out a sigh.

"In other words," he said, "people can come and go in this place like water through a sieve."

"I'm afraid that's true," Fred said.

"See if anyone signed out a key for yesterday, James," Coswell said, "and collect the whole bundle for fingerprinting."

A knock at the door interrupted their conversation.

"That will be our forensics squad," Coswell said. "Let them in, Fred, and then I'd like you to wait outside. We might as well start our interviews with you. And don't, by the way, go down to your office. Everything within dragging distance of that elevator needs to be gone over by the forensics unit."

Reluctantly, Fred did as he was told and held the door open until all four members of the forensics squad had entered. They were wearing white jump suits, booties and toted equipment in what looked like hockey bags. Fred watched them for a moment and then, with one forlorn backward glance, left.

RCMP Sergeant Charlotte Jacobsen was in charge of the squad, a pretty, thirty-something, brunette, with deep brown eyes. She greeted them with a bemused smile and casually waved a roll of yellow crime scene tape at them.

"Your boys not using this any more?" she said. "What happened to 'forensics first?'"

"Sorry," Coswell said. "James and I just got here. Sergeant McMorran was first on the scene and I guess he didn't think of it."

A trace of a smile tugged at her lips but she didn't comment further. Instead, she tossed the roll of tape to James.

"Here," she said. "You don't seem to have come equipped."

James caught it easily and made no effort to control the big grin on his face. Seeing Coswell put on the spot was a rare treat.

Charlotte turned back to Coswell.

"Any requests, Inspector, before we get started? If not, I hope you two are about to leave."

"Just a couple, Charlotte," Coswell said. "I want that service elevator back there gone over thoroughly. Unless our nude corpse was murdered right here, and I doubt that, he had to get into his coffin somehow and the service elevator is an obvious choice."

Charlotte sniffed.

"Everything we do is thorough," she said. "Just give us the boundaries of the crime scene."

"That will be done directly by Corporal James," Coswell said. "We haven't checked the basement yet, but the trail probably extends at least that far."

"Okay. Anything else?"

The look in those brown eyes made him forget anything else.

"No," he said. "I'm sure you'll cover everything."

He and James turned to leave, but Charlotte had one more request.

"There's a box of booties outside and disposable gloves. Until I give the all clear, anyone putting one foot inside the crime scene is to wear those. And, I want prints—shoes and fingers of anyone who has gone through there in what ever time frame you think the killer might have done the same."

"We don't have that yet," Coswell said, "but we will

THE EXTRA CADAVER MURDER

have after we've done some interviewing. A ballpark time of death from you would be a help, though."

"I don't do ballpark," she said. "You'll have to wait."

Back in the hallway, Coswell grumbled out loud.

"Wouldn't have hurt her to make an exception this time."

"Got to admire her, though," James said. "Professional with a capital P."

"For her personality a capital A would describe her better," Coswell said. "But off you go and get that lab attendant, Fred whatever. I want to take a quick tour downstairs before we interview. He'll be our guide."

Actually, Coswell led the way after Fred pointed out the staircase to the lower floor; all obediently wearing gloves and booties. Fred followed behind Coswell, and then James, who stopped from time to time to string up some of the tape from the roll he carried. A door with a small window in it separated the stairs from the lower hallway. Coswell stopped in front of it and turned around.

"Before we go further, Fred, I want you to tell me your exact movements from when you left here yesterday to when you arrived this morning."

Fred was a bit unnerved by the inspector's intensity but he thought back carefully and answered.

"I spent all afternoon yesterday getting the cadavers up to the lab and in place. I finished just after four. I got my coat and hat from my office, locked it and then took the elevator back to the lab. I like to have one last look before I leave to make sure everything is just right for opening day."

"And then straight home?"

"No. I popped into Dr. Dietrich's office to let him know that all was ready."

"You spoke to him?"

"Well no. Just to his secretary."

"Okay. And how did you spend the rest of your evening?"

"Home with the wife. We ate supper, watched TV and went to bed early. I was tired. Moving ten bodies around takes a lot of effort and I'm not getting any younger."

"All right. Now take us through this morning."

"I arrived here quite a bit later than usual. Slept in. No time even to go down to my office. I went directly to the lab. The two assistants were already there and the students were starting to gather outside."

He shook his head.

"It's all too bad. If I'd gone into the lab earlier and done one last check," he said, "I would have discovered Dr. Kelly's body. A lot of fuss could have been avoided."

Coswell mused that Fred was far more upset by the fuss than about the chief of surgery being murdered.

He pushed open the door and they entered a long, wide corridor. Again, he brought them to a halt.

"Now, Fred," he said. "Tell me what I'm looking at. Start with that door on the left."

"That's a security and fire exit door. It opens only from the inside. There's one just like it at the other end of the hall."

"And your office?"

"Half way down on the left."

"And what else?"

"Mainly storage, the mechanical room, janitor's closet ... oh, and the practice room."

"Practice room?"

"It's usually residents who use it, but occasionally one of the senior hospital staff comes here to experiment with some new technique."

"How do the bodies get here?"

"Through this fire door."

Coswell gazed along the corridor floor, illuminated by the bright ceiling fluorescent lights, and caught the unmistakable arcs left by a big, rotary polisher.

"Looks like the janitor did a job here last night. What time would that be, Fred?"

"I don't know. I've never seen any of the cleaning crew, but then I don't stay much after five."

"Another job for you, James," Coswell said. "Find out who cleaned down here last night, and when. Hopefully it was early rather than late and we have some footprints to analyze."

He began to move down the hallway keeping well to the side. Fred and James followed his example.

"That's my room there," Fred said, pointing.

"Give Corporal James your key," Coswell said. "He'll open it."

Fred pulled a set of keys from his lab coat pocket and handed them to James, first isolating one of them.

"This is it," he said.

James put the key in the lock, turned it, and then used his elbow to hold the door open for the others.

The room reeked of formaldehyde. Coswell marvelled that anyone could stand being in that atmosphere for any more than a few minutes, but Fred obviously could. A large desk and a well-padded secretarial chair occupied one corner of the room. On the table were a telephone, a radio, an ashtray with a couple of butts in it, a crime novel opened face down, and a giant economy size bag of nacho chips, half empty. A Mr. Coffee machine and a mug emblazoned with the Vancouver Canucks logo sat on a shelf above the desk.

"Cozy," Coswell said.

The rest of the room was the picture of neatness and efficiency: straight ahead, two rows of sliding, morgue-style body containers and below them, glass doors through which could be seen funnels, beakers, syringes, shears and a trays of what looked like surgical instruments. Above were shelves laden with numerous large, opaque plastic containers labelled FORMALDEHYDE and beside them stacks of heavy burlap material in rolls. To the right, an L-shaped steel work table, the long arm of which had a shallow, concave surface and a drain at one end; above it was a shaded light that reminded Coswell of the type hung over pool tables. The short arm of the table had a lift-up lid that attracted James' attention.

"What's in there?" he asked.

"Leftovers," Fred said. "When the students finish mangling the bodies, we save parts to use in spot exams."

"Lovely," James said.

Coswell stood for a moment, deep in thought.

James quickly became impatient.

"Do you want to check for Fred's missing body in one of those coffins or, and I hope not, amongst the leftovers?"

"No. We'll leave all this untouched for the forensics crew and I doubt if it's in this room anyway."

"Why not? Haul the murdered man up to the lab, make the switch, and put Fred's cadaver back in here."

"Time. The killer didn't want to waste a second. He would have used a gurney, and if you noticed, there isn't one in this room. Cadaver and gurney I would suggest are tucked away somewhere out of sight."

"In the elevator?"

"Not there either. Think about it. This whole scenario is looking more and more like hate *was* the motive, and unless Charlotte finds something to the contrary, I suggest we keep that possibility up front. Doing away with our victim wasn't enough for the killer; he wanted the unveiling to go just as it played out. Fred, here, could have spoiled it all by noticing the switch when he came in this morning."

"Well then, where is Fred's cadaver?"

Fred gave them the answer.

"Probably in the practice room down the hall where the gurney's kept."

"Right," said Coswell. "Let's go have a look."

"Makes sense," James said. "And that tells us a lot, eh? The killer had to be very familiar with this building and its workings. An inside job for sure."

They both looked at Fred.

"Whoa," Fred said. "Not me. I've only had anything to do with Dr. Kelly a couple of times, once when he came out to give a talk to the students in the lab on surgical incisions—an incentive kind of thing. Anatomy can be very boring. I set up the demonstration for him."

"And the other?"

"He was one of the oral examiners here last fall. Bitched about the specimen I gave him. 'Ratty' he called it. Like it was my fault the students had butchered—"

He stopped and looked apprehensively at the two officers.

"It pissed me off all right, but not enough to kill him."

"No, I'm sure it wasn't," Coswell said. "Now how about any gossip or personal information you might have heard?"

"Nothing. But I'm not exactly anyone's confidant around here. Just one of the lowly working stiffs."

As opposed to the dead, non-working stiffs which he dealt with daily, Coswell mused.

CHAPTER THREE

The practice room was two doors down on the same side as Fred's office and was locked. The same key opened it and James used his elbow technique again to push it open.

"Uh, oh," he said, with his first glance inside. "This place is crowded."

Fred's cadaver was there all right, completely wrapped in burlap and lying on a gurney. But a second body lay face up on a steel table beside it, also wrapped in burlap except for the abdomen which had been exposed.

"What's this?" Fred said. "No one told me about any practice session yesterday."

He looked down at the floor. "And what a mess!"

A tray lay upside down under the gurney and surgical instruments were scattered about.

"The murder site, gentlemen," Coswell said. "We will stop right here. Look but don't touch."

He turned to Fred who still seemed pained about the mess rather than impressed that it was the murder site.

"I want you to go back up to the lab, Fred, and ask Sergeant Jacobsen to come down here ... via the stairs, of course."

After Fred had left, Coswell turned back to James.

"Turn on your internal camera, my good man, and take it all in. What happened here?"

James' camera didn't take long.

"Our victim was either about to practice himself," he said. "Or came upon someone who was."

"And?"

"Very little sign of struggle. Just the tray and instruments on the floor. I picture the victim facing the cadaver on the table and the killer sneaking up behind him with his garrotting wire, doing the deed, and then his victim slowly sinking to the floor."

"Meaning?"

"This door has a self-closing mechanism which is not exactly quiet. Our victim would have to have been deaf not to hear someone come in. And, given any warning at all, he would have put up considerable resistance. He was a big man."

Suddenly, the door burst open causing both men to jump.

"Jesus, Charlotte!" Coswell said. "Couldn't you have knocked first?"

A big smile when she realized how startled they were.

"This place giving you the heebie-jeebies? I'm surprised, two fearless homicide men like you."

Coswell ignored the jibe and quickly related to her the scenario that he and James had worked out.

"Okay," she said. "That will be taken into consideration when we do this room ... after the lab and elevator are done, of course. Don't want to break routine."

"God forbid," Coswell said. "Now, can you give us any idea of time of death? I promise not to hold you to it."

"All right then," she said. "Midnight, plus or minus an hour or two. Rigor mortis is pretty well maximum and body temp's down a dozen degrees."

"Thanks, Charlotte. Anything else you can tell us?"

"Nothing you don't know already. You'll have to wait, I'm afraid, and it will take a while."

"Not pushing," Coswell said. "But call me the minute anything turns up. You have my cell number?"

"Yep. Right up top on my contacts list."

"Doesn't speak well for your social life."

"Bugger off."

Sergeant McMorran's corporal was waiting for them when they returned to the main floor. "I'm sorry to bother you, sir," he said, "but there's a problem with your vehicle."

Coswell fished the cruiser's keys out of his jacket pocket and tossed them to him.

"Be careful jockeying those vehicles around. I don't want any scratches. You can leave my keys in Professor Dietrich's office."

"Yes, sir," the officer said, and then quickly turned and ran down the stairs to the front door.

"Time to move on, James," Coswell said. "Let's go talk to some people."

They used lecture hall B for their interviews. Fred rejoined them, having left to check in with his boss re duties for the rest of the day.

"The professor's told me to help you out any way that I can."

"That's very kind of him," Coswell said.

"I don't think it was kindness," Fred said. "More like—do your bit to get things back to normal—pronto."

"Right. Then what I'd like you to do is to start fetching people. Who's first, James?"

"The names marked with an X as you promised. Only two of them, a Doctor Tynan and a Doctor Debas."

"They're the lab instructors," Fred said. "I saw them go into the coffee room. I'll get them both."

When Fred left, James gave out a groan.

"There are over a hundred names on this list," he said. "Even if we fired them through at five minutes each, that's over eight hours. We'll never make it."

"Sampling, my good man, sampling is what we are going to do, and we'll soon break for lunch. My stomach is grumbling. Tim Hortons just didn't do it."

"And how do we do this sampling?" James said.

"I want you to go to wherever the medical students are holed up and do a survey. Find out who the class president is if they have one, or barring that, get a frat man or sorority type. They're always up on who's who on campus and did you get the names of anyone signing out the front door key for Sunday?"

James gave a little sniff.

"Of course I did," he said. "There were three students, one female and two males; names, Frank Hoffmann and Wing Chu. The female left early so I just added the other two to the list. We can do them right after the lab instructors so they both can get back to their studies."

"Okay and when you've done all that, let the rest go."

"And the staff members?" James said.

"I'm afraid we'll have to interview them all but I'll decide in what order after I've spoken to the two

Xs and your students."

The two Xs weren't of much help, their stories almost identical. They described Doctor Kelly as a stern but good teacher, and if they knew any gossip, they weren't about to pass it on. Both had alibis for the likely hours in which Kelly was murdered. They were on emergency call at the hospital.

"They're not taking any chances," James said. "No bad-mouthing anybody until they get their Canadian surgery tickets."

"I agree. I haven't met an underling yet who was totally enthralled with the higher-ups."

"Me excluded, of course," James said.

Coswell grunted.

The students, Frank Hoffmann and Wing Chu, weren't of much help either. Coincidentally, they were roommates in one of the campus residences. They saw nothing unusual and left the lab when the cleaning staff began to arrive. Both said they then went straight back to their residence to cram for an anatomy spot test coming up.

James did find the class president—Sally Chetwynd, a chubby young woman who looked more like a German barmaid than a prospective doctor but she was just what Coswell wanted—a real talker. The mere mention of the victim's name got her going at full speed.

"I'm just first year," she said, "so we don't do much in the hospital, but I'm rooming with a fourth year and I've heard plenty about Doctor Kelly."

She paused for effect and was rewarded by the obvious interest from the officers.

"He was an absolute tyrant in the OR. Threw instruments around and treated the nurses and assistants like dumb servants right from the moment he arrived. You'd think he would have behaved better, being the new man and all. His so-called private life reads like a cheap tabloid: an eye for anyone wearing a skirt and probably an affair or two because his wife divorced him three months after they arrived from Ireland. He was a real embarrassment to her. Loved boozing it up in some downtown Irish pub."

Taking advantage of a millisecond break in her chatter, Coswell interjected.

"That doesn't sound like someone this esteemed institution would keep on as head of a major medical school department."

Her voice lowered.

"Rumour has it that he got the position only because of his wife. She's famous. World authority in neuropathology. She gave UBC instant status when she came on board. That's why they put up with her jerk of a husband, and I'll bet he negotiated an iron-clad contract with them—instant tenure and all that."

"Who do you think might have killed him?"

She finally slowed down.

"Well, I can't really say. Murder is pretty extreme, even to someone like that."

When she finally left, Coswell exhaled loudly.

"She was really something," James said.

"Yes, but most useful. As I have told you many times, murder always comes down to greed, fear, or hate. The nude body element points to the latter."

"A vengeful wife?"

"Right up there, wouldn't you say?"

"Possible, but only if she had an accomplice. I still feel that the physical effort involved suggests that the killer is a male."

"Well, enough for now," Coswell said. "I am badly in need of lunch and it's almost two. We'll do the Pit Pub. A little nostalgia for me."

Coswell needed no directions. He headed off at a brisk pace that surprised James. Their route took them past the old, now defunct, outdoor Empire Pool, a leftover from the 1954 British Empire and Commonwealth Games. Beyond it to their right was the massive, modern Aquatic Centre, and to their left the new Student Union Building. But Coswell's eyes were fixed straight ahead.

"I bless that old tree-hugger David Suzuki for being the spark that got the pub going back in the early '70s. There was a lot of resistance to it from the over-eighty who forgot that they were young once."

Once inside the pub, the din was overwhelming.

"Not a good choice, sir," James said. "It appears that the entire first-year medical student body is lunching here today. I recognize them."

Before Coswell could agree, a shrill voice broke through from somewhere in the midst of the mob.

"Yoo-hoo, Inspector. C'mon over here. There's room at our table."

Sally Chetwynd, their garrulous interviewee.

"Great," Coswell said. "We're in luck, James. Let's go."

"Uh, sir, I'm not sure—"

Too late. Coswell was well on his way, bumping through the crowd. James had no choice but to follow, giving belated apologies as he went. "Excuse us, excuse us please."

Ten women were seated around a table meant for eight. Somehow they squeezed together to make room for the two officers. Sally, obviously, was in command.

"Girls, these are two of our finest—Inspector Coswell and his partner Sergeant James. They're going to find out who did in old Kinky Kelly."

"Sally! For heaven's sake. A little respect. What will these officers think?" The speaker was a small, mousy-looking woman sitting to Sally's right.

"Well it's true, Jenny," Sally retorted. "Loved to do

a little erotic leaning up against his female assistants during some of those long OR cases I've been told and I suspect that these officers are shocked by very little. Am I correct?"

James was having none of this. He remained silent, his discomfort obvious.

Coswell, on the other hand, appeared to be enjoying himself. He sat beside Sally at the head of the table. Before he could answer her, a waiter with a tray of empty glasses tried to pass by their table unnoticed. Sally grabbed his free arm, almost unbalancing the poor fellow.

"Chuckeee, my man," she said. "Bring us a pitcher of Canadian and two orders of nachos. You will have our undying love if it comes quick or our witches' curse if it doesn't."

"And the tab to me," Coswell interjected. "Our treat."

James gulped as he calculated the cost, hoping "our" didn't include him.

"Well, thank you," Sally said. "Such generosity—rare among the males around here I can tell you. Class of women haters."

That last comment, despite the surrounding din, carried over to at least one of the adjacent tables. A male student with his back to her turned and fired back.

"Shut up, Sally, you talk too much."

"Oh, my, if it isn't Frank the Wank. Go drown in your beer."

The man didn't respond. He turned his head away and made some inaudible comment to one of the others sitting at his table but Coswell recognized him as Frank Hoffmann, the student he and James had just interviewed.

Sally leaned over and spoke in a low voice.

"Now there's one suggestion for you, Inspector. Frank failed anatomy last year and should have been out on his ear. That's the rule: fail anatomy in first year and you're gone for good but somehow he got to repeat. Must have big clout somewhere. I heard that Dietrich had a hissy fit over it."

"But what has that got to do with Professor Kelly?"

"Frank spread it around that Kelly did him in at the orals. Never heard the other side, but according to Frank, Kelly was showing off by humiliating him with impossible questions."

"Surely these orals aren't one-on-one," Coswell said. "That would be grossly unfair."

"No, the examiners are in pairs, and you're right, both have to agree on failing a student. The truth, I'm sure, is that Frank just didn't know his stuff."

Coswell, wondering whether the man could overhear their conversation, glanced over at the him. Body language said that he had—tense shoulders and a hand grasping the handle of his beer mug, white-knuckled.

Coswell realized that to carry on a conversation with anyone other than Sally or her mousy friend in all that noise was hopeless. He was also anxious to get another point of view, one closer to the action than Sally.

"Is your fourth-year roommate one of the ladies at this table?" he said.

"No. Fourth years spend most of their time at the hospital. Marilyn, that's her name, is on the general surgery rotation right now."

She chuckled.

"I can see where you're going. Right from the horse's mouth, eh? Enough of rumours?"

"You got me," Coswell said.

"Her last name is Hawthorne, but you'll have to find her at the hospital. She stays over a lot in the med students' room at the doctors' residence. Gets her in on those middle of the night cases in the OR. She ultimately wants to specialize in general surgery and she certainly has the right personality for it."

"Personality?"

"Skin of a rhinoceros and blunt as a Mack truck, eh, Jenny?"

The mousy woman rolled her eyes.

"Not sweet and sensitive like you, Sally. That's for sure."

Coswell's good mood continued on their walk back to the anatomy building.

"Now that's the way to spend a working lunch hour, don't you agree?"

"I hope you got a lot more out of it than I did," James said. "Nothing but shop talk from the women around me. I sat there like a bump on a log."

"You probably don't give off an aura that would cause them to discuss anything else, James. But the beer and nachos were great, eh?"

"A different lunch for me, all right. Thank you for paying, by the way."

"The Force's treat. That was a legitimate work-related expense."

"Yielding what?"

"Two names. Marilyn Hawthorne, fourth-year med student who spent time in the OR with our deceased and is the source of our friend, Sally's, gossip."

"And the other?"

"That Frank guy. Worth putting on our suspect list. Label him disgruntled med student who blamed Kelly for failing him last year.

"Frank Hoffmann," James said. "So what's his motive? Kelly didn't succeed in getting him dumped from med school."

"Humiliation, James, humiliation. Haven't you ever failed anything? It can be a powerful motive in the hate category."

James thought for a moment.

"I don't think I ever have, at least in school. Seems a

pretty flimsy motive for murdering someone."

"Maybe not. There are a lot of warped minds in this world."

"Jack the Campus Ripper?"

"Be serious, James."

CHAPTER FOUR

They began their afternoon interviews with Professor Dietrich. He was not a happy man when Fred led him into lecture hall B, likely feeling that his interview should have taken place in his private office. Coswell, however, pressed his advantage. He and James sat side by side behind the table. Dietrich's only choice was a single chair moved a full pace in front. The only thing missing was a naked light bulb over his head.

Before he sat down, he handed over a sheet of paper to James.

"You are the list keeper, I believe," he said. "Here are the names of all the guests who came to my party yesterday evening. That should save us some time."

Coswell smiled.

"Thinking like a policeman," he said. "That's good."

Dietrich gave him a suspicious look, seemingly weighing whether that was a compliment or an insult. Obviously deciding the former, he carried on without a prompt.

"I doubt if I can help you any further. I hardly knew the man. He rarely came out to the campus."

"You invited him to your staff party, though," Coswell said.

"My secretary invited him. He took a small part in our teaching program so his name was on her list."

Coswell picked up immediately on the hint of annoyance.

"Would you have invited him if you had sent out the emails?"

Dietrich tilted his head back and gazed at the ceiling as though the answer were coming from on high.

"His attendance created an awkward situation. Doctor Montgomery was there, of course."

"Doctor Montgomery?"

Dietrich's head came level and he looked directly at Coswell.

"Doctor Kelly's ex-wife. I would have assumed that you knew that."

"It's still very early in our investigation. We haven't got around to her yet."

James interrupted.

"That name is not on the list we got this morning, Professor. Where might she be at this moment?"

"She's giving a paper at a conference in Edmonton."

James had his notebook out, pencil poised—all for show, since hours later he would be able to recall every word from memory.

"Now, Professor," Coswell said. "I think you can be of great help to us at this point. With your scientific powers of observation, your replay of last night's party would be very helpful to us. Put your spotlight, if you will, on Dr. Kelly, starting with his arrival."

Back went Dietrich's head again, to gaze at his "screen" somewhere on the ceiling.

"He arrived early, much to my surprise. The invitation read: cocktails at six, dinner at seven, and he appeared a few minutes before six."

"All right. Take it from there. Mood? Conversation?"

The head came down only momentarily and then back up again. "He seemed cheerful enough in that Irish sort of way, but I detected some tension. I offered him a glass of wine but he asked for something 'more substantial' which I presumed meant whisky. I brought out a bottle of good scotch and poured him a reasonable amount but he held his glass up to the bottle and didn't say 'halt' until it was half full—a good three ounces, I'd say."

And all the while thinking drunken Irish lout, Coswell guessed.

Dietrich continued.

"Other guests began to arrive at that point and so I didn't pay him much attention until Dr. Montgomery arrived."

"What time was that?" James said, notebook poised.

The head came down and stayed this time.

"Just before seven. I remember because there was no time to serve her a drink. We sat down for dinner promptly at seven."

"What was her reaction when she saw her ex-husband there?" Coswell asked.

"Surprise initially, and then a curt nod to him when he raised his glass to her from across the room. I had them seated well apart during the meal, of course, which ended shortly after nine."

"Was Dr. Kelly active in the table talk?"

"Very much so and I'm afraid to say he was a bit of an embarrassment in that regard. He made some outrageous statements in a loud voice, the scotch no doubt loosening control of his tongue."

"What sort of statements?"

"Oh, mostly about the superiority of European medical practice and the relative backwardness of ours here in Canada. You can imagine how that went over with the others. Dr. Montgomery looked especially embarrassed."

"And after dinner?"

"We returned to the living room where I served liqueurs to those who wanted them. Dr. Kelly seemed to find my cognac acceptable."

"Did he continue with his outrageous remarks?"

"Indeed he did. Moved on to the lowering of standards for admission to our medical school. Unfortunately, he had a point there. Our provincial government has dictated that we turn out more physicians to meet an increasing public demand. He did have some support among our staff, but Dr. Montgomery obviously felt that my party was not the time to bring it up."

"Did she say anything?"

Finally, a smile from Dietrich.

"Yes. She said, 'Patrick, you'd best be quiet. You, I believe, are the latest addition to staff. One might infer that the standards dropped a bit there, too.'"

James coughed.

"Ouch," he said. "And what happened after that?"

"Dr. Kelly more or less slinked off into a corner and didn't say a word so far as I could tell. He left shortly after that, saying he was going over to the practice room at the lab to prepare for a case on Monday."

"What time did he actually leave?" James said.

"Approximately nine thirty, I'd say."

"Did he come to your home by car?" Coswell said. "He must have been close to .08."

"No. He would have left it at the anatomy building and walked over. Our place is only a few blocks away. I did hope that he would have sobered up some before he drove home. He lives across town, near the hospital, I believe."

"And so, other than the sparks between him and his wife during liqueurs, did you see them in conversation at any other time?"

"No, and I think that exchange cut off his intentions to do so, which I'm sure is why he attended the party."

"Not a very good venue for a private conversation, I would think."

"Once their divorce came through, a private conversation with Dr. Kelly would not have been amongst Dr. Montgomery's desires," Dietrich said, and then quickly,

"Or at least that's what I have heard."

"What time did Dr. Montgomery leave your party?" James said.

"She left early, too. Around ten, I think. She had a very early flight out to Edmonton this morning and wanted to get a good night's rest."

"Did anyone else leave around the same time as Dr. Kelly?"

"Not that I noticed, but then my wife and I were busy hosting. Most left shortly after eleven, all in a bunch. We were helping with coats and saying multiple goodbyes."

"Would you ask your wife that question, please? It is important as I'm sure you can understand."

Dietrich nodded and then, suddenly, as though he were just aware of the time, looked at his watch.

"Now, gentlemen, I have much to do before this day ends and I think I have been more than patient."

"You have, indeed," Coswell said. "And thank you for your cooperation."

When the door closed behind Dietrich, James turned to Coswell. "Are you thinking what I'm thinking?" he said. "Odd choice of phrase—Dr. Montgomery's desires."

"Yes," Coswell replied. "He does seem to know a lot about the lady's personal life. I'm looking forward to meeting her."

The rest of their interviews added nothing significant. Kelly obviously had little to do with the people based on campus. Their versions of his behaviour at the party matched Dietrich's.

It was just after three o'clock when they ticked off the last name on their list. Coswell leaned back on his chair and stretched his arms above his head. James yawned.

Coswell chuckled.

"Getting a little bored are you?" he said.

"Boredom, I've discovered," James replied, "is a large part of our job."

"Okay, let's liven things up. We'll go and bug Charlotte. She should be close to finishing the forensics by now."

When they stepped out into the hall, Fred was sitting on a chair he had dragged from somewhere. He jumped up the moment he saw them.

"Sorry, Fred," Coswell said. "I should have let you go when you brought the last person to us. You've had a long day. Thank you for all your help."

"When do you think I can get back into my office and the lab?" he said. "I really need to straighten things out before I go home today."

"You have quite a work ethic," Coswell said. "Well then, come along with us and we'll find out for you."

Fred lit up like he'd won the lotto. He left the chair he'd borrowed and followed along beside them. James took the opportunity to ask him one more question.

"We expected to interview Dr. Montgomery's secretary, but no one on our list answered to that description. Does she not have one?"

"Oh, yes," Fred said. "From day one. Dr. Montgomery is a full professor. She gets all the perks and her secretary is a dandy."

Fred put a cupped palm to the side of his mouth and in a low tone added, "He's gay."

James couldn't contain a laugh.

"Gay! How droll. Where is he?"

"Took the day off, I was told. Dr. Montgomery's away at a conference somewhere."

They had almost reached the lab when the doors burst open. Charlotte and her crew emerged with all of their equipment and collected samples.

"We're done," she said when she saw Coswell. "The crime scene's all yours. I've called the coroner's office. Their wagon should arrive shortly. I presumed that you've seen all you want to see."

"Yes," Coswell said, "but—"

She held up her hand.

"No, I don't have much worth telling you other than we didn't find the murder weapon or the victim's clothing. We also went over his vehicle, which you forgot to mention. It's an old Triumph sports car with the top down, thank goodness, so we had complete access. No key in the ignition."

Coswell winced. He hadn't forgotten; he didn't even think of it. Slipping.

"I'll be in touch," she said. "No time to waste right now. We're off. Toodle-oo."

And without a backward glance, she left.

"A brief summary wouldn't have killed her," James grumbled.

"I didn't hear you say anything, though," Coswell said. "Afraid of her bite?"

James smiled.

"I was waiting for your legendary charm to persuade her."

"Fat chance of that."

"Where to now?" James said when they returned to their cruiser. "The hospital?"

"No, Kelly's apartment. He probably has maid service and I don't want anything disturbed until we get a look at it."

Coswell started the engine and shifted into reverse.

"What's the address?" he said.

James swung the inboard computer around.

"Just a second. I'll look it up."

"Didn't you get it from Dietrich's office?"

James shrugged his shoulders.

"Sorry," he said.

"That's okay. Forget things myself, occasionally."

In fact, Coswell was getting forgetful at a rate that

alarmed him. One didn't expect senility at age fifty-eight.

Obtaining Kelly's home address turned out to be a problem for James. A cell phone call to the Department of Surgery general office got him nowhere. "We are not allowed to give out personal information to anyone, I'm afraid," the secretary informed him.

Coswell chuckled at James' futile attempts to intimidate the woman.

"Are you surprised?" he said, when James finally gave up. "You could have been a reporter for all she knew, conning her with the RCMP label. Better hoof it back to Dietrich's office and flash your badge."

"I don't have to go that far," James said. "I see Kelly's Triumph still parked over there in the staff lot. The licence number will do."

A quick call to motor vehicles did the trick using his RCMP code number and then back to his computer to bring up Google Maps.

"It's just a block east of Twelfth on Ash."

"Okay," Coswell said. "We're off."

"Shouldn't we get a warrant first?"

"No. We're just going to go and have a little prelim look-see. Ash Street, that's just before Cambie, right?"

"Yes."

James' head was still buried in the computer.

"Google Street View shows a rather modest neighbourhood. I'd have expected something a lot more upscale for a professor of surgery."

"He's coming off a divorce," Coswell said. "Maybe wifey cleaned him out."

"Not likely," James said. "She's a professor, too. Probably makes as much money."

The address was an older three-storey apartment building surrounded by more elegant modern condominiums.

James scanned the row of call buttons opposite

apartment numbers—no names. The only label was for the manager in 101. He pushed the button and waited. No answer. He pushed it again and then heard Coswell rapping on the front door. Momentarily, it opened and a man dressed in blue coveralls appeared holding the nozzle of a vacuum cleaner, the machine still roaring away behind him.

They both showed their badges. The man switched off the vacuum and held the door open for them. The musty smell of old carpeting and the hint of stale tobacco smoke assailed their nostrils when they stepped into the foyer.

"Is it about those two women on the second floor?" the man said. "I knew they were up to no good. Coming and going at all hours. Different men. Hookers, eh? Told me they were nurses."

"No," Coswell said. "We're investigating a homicide. Doctor Kelly, one of your tenants."

"Well, I'll be damned. Who killed him? Where?"

"Can't give you any details right now," Coswell said. "Now if you'll just show us to his apartment."

Disappointed, the manager tried to prolong what was likely going to be the highlight of his day.

"Well, I don't know," he said. "Shouldn't you have a warrant or something?"

James couldn't hold back a smile.

"Inspector?" he said.

Coswell frowned at him before speaking to the manager. "None needed when a murder is involved and if you don't cooperate, you will be impeding a police investigation—a punishable offense."

"Okay, okay," the man said. "Don't need to throw threats at me."

The foyer smell continued up the stairs and into the corridor of the second-floor. Kelly's apartment was halfway down.

The manager unlocked the door with a key from a

ring of at least a dozen others.

"I guess I'll get back to my cleaning then," he said. "The door will lock behind you when you leave."

"No," Coswell said. "I'd like you to come in with us. We won't be long and you can attest to the fact that we haven't removed anything."

The man didn't object. In fact, he looked almost eager.

The apartment was a small one-bedroom affair. A few clothes were scattered about but generally all looked neat and tidy. No dirty dishes in the kitchen sink.

"He must have maid service," Coswell said, thinking of his own bachelor habits.

"He does," the manager said. "Balked a bit at the cost but took it on anyway."

"What does he pay for this—rent plus the maid service?"

"Seventeen hundred a month. Didn't want underground parking. Gets it free at the hospital, I guess."

The manager noted James and Coswell glancing at one another.

"Yeah, I was surprised, too. Rich mucky-muck surgeon living here. It ain't exactly the Taj Mahal."

James picked up on his tone.

"Not a very lovable type, I gather."

"Didn't like him one little bit. Breezed by me like I was a fixture of some kind, unless he wanted something, like clearing the empty booze bottles out of his apartment when they piled up too high."

He went on.

"And sometimes he was really slow getting his rent check to me."

"Did he have anything to do with his neighbours here?" James asked.

"Not bloody likely. He was a noisy bugger, coming in late at night singing some stupid Irish songs. Neighbours complained ... except for the two hookers, of course. He just laughed when I told him to tone it down."

A complete walk-through of the apartment yielded nothing of interest—no correspondence, no photographs—nothing. It was as though Kelly's use of the apartment was equivalent to an overnight hotel stay.

"Not even worth getting forensics in here right away to dust for prints," Coswell said, relieved that he didn't have to call Charlotte back so soon.

"We'd appreciate it if you would keep this door locked in case we need to go over it again."

"Can't show it?" the manager said.

"No. And keep the maid out."

"Well, that was hardly worth the trip," Coswell said on the walk back to the cruiser. "His office at the hospital should be a different story, though. He had to keep paperwork somewhere—checkbooks, bills."

"We did get another picture of the man's personality," James said. "And his living in that less than luxurious apartment has to have a reason behind it."

"True. And let's not forget what our talkative med student told us—Kelly was randy as hell. Maybe the two handy hookers are worth an interview. Tuck that away in our to-do list."

The Department of Surgery secretary was no less careful in person than she had been on the telephone to James when he tried to get the doctor's home address. She looked closely at their shields before leading them to Kelly's office.

"I've been told that a warrant is not required but I will caution you not to go through any patient records. Those are confidential, even to the police."

"Unless we do get a warrant," Coswell said. "But we'll keep our noses out of anything about patients at this visit."

He wondered if she would stay and watch them but

she merely waved her hand.

"Fine," she said. "Now I have a lot of work to finish up and it's late."

"You go right ahead," Coswell said. "This won't take us long."

But before she could leave, James spoke up.

"I'm sure Dr. Kelly's sudden death must have put quite a load on you," he said. "He would have had surgeries scheduled and patients to see. I presume you would be the one dealing with the rescheduling. Who, may I ask, will be taking those over?"

"The answer to that is yes. It's been a real scramble. Fortunately, Doctor Struthers has kindly agreed to cover all of Doctor Kelly's commitments."

"His assistant?"

She almost snorted.

"Doctor Struthers is a full professor in the department. He was acting head before Doctor Kelly was appointed, certainly not his assistant."

With that, she turned and swept out of the room.

Coswell smiled.

"Hit a nerve there, eh, James? There's got to be some juicy gossip around that reaction."

"Not likely going to hear it from her."

"Right, but I'll bet our class president's friend, the fourth-year student can fill us in. What was her name again?"

"Marilyn Hawthorne."

"Right. Now let's get at this place. We'll find Marilyn after."

Five minutes later, Coswell threw up his hands.

"I don't believe it. Not a goddamned thing and there isn't a single locked drawer or cabinet. Where did he keep all his personal stuff? There's nothing here that isn't hospital or university related. There isn't even a date calendar."

THE EXTRA CADAVER MURDER

"It's an electronic world, I'm afraid," James said. "I'll bet he had everything on his phone."

"Which disappeared along with his clothes, damn it all."

James smiled at his senior's frustration.

"No problem," he said. "I'm sure that either the hospital or the university supplied him with the cell phone. His secretary will have the number and the name of the provider. We can at least get a list of his calls, and if we're really lucky, he might have done some texting."

Coswell knew he should have thought of that himself—just one more reminder that he was falling behind in the modern world.

He had attended the lectures on information gathering from cyberspace given by one of the police department IT guys and knew how important it was, but the technical aspects threw him. He was strictly a two-fingered typist, both on the keyboard and in his brain. Another reason James was such an asset.

The secretary gave them the number readily enough.

"You can do us one last favour before we leave," Coswell said. "We want to speak to one of the fourth-year medical students—Marilyn Hawthorne. Can you tell us where she might be at this moment?"

The woman consulted her computer screen and then picked up her cell phone and punched in a number. A few seconds later, she spoke into it.

"Hold on a moment, Marilyn," she said. "There is a policeman here who would like to speak to you."

She handed the phone to Coswell.

Taken slightly aback by the abruptness of the contact (he was expecting her to be paged over the hospital intercom) it took him a second to respond.

He was saved, however, from explaining his call. Like everyone else, it seemed, she was aware of Kelly's demise.

"Sally told me you'd be calling," she said. "I'm having an early supper in the hospital cafeteria right now. Got a scrub coming up. Can you come over here?"

"On our way," Coswell said.

Just as they turned to go, the secretary handed James a printout.

"This is a copy of Dr. Kelly's schedule for the month. I can give you all previous months, too, if you wish."

Not so hard after all, Coswell thought. She would be worth interviewing later.

CHAPTER FIVE

They attracted many curious glances as they walked through the hospital corridors on their way to the cafeteria. Amid the swirl of white coats and green scrubs they stood out like two sore thumbs.

"We might as well be wearing our uniforms," James said.

Marilyn Hawthorne was sitting alone at one of the tables in the sparsely occupied cafeteria—too soon for the supper crowd and well past coffee break. She waved to them when they entered but continued to work away at a hamburger and side of potato chips when they walked over and introduced themselves.

"Don't mind me," she said. "But I need to get some calories in before the case I'm scrubbed in on—two hours likely and I don't want to pass out."

"By all means, keep eating," Coswell said. "In fact, the corporal and I could use a few calories ourselves. It's been a while since we had anything to eat."

He turned to James and just missed the eye rolling.

"Couple of coffees and something to go with them, eh?"

"The cinnamon buns are your best choice," Marilyn said. "They get them from the Whole Foods Market on Cambie. Scrumptious."

Coswell looked a little doubtful.

"That's a health food place, isn't it?"

"Don't worry," she said, noting the strain on Coswell's shirt buttons, "They're as gooey and sweet as anything you'll find elsewhere."

Big smile.

"Sold," Coswell said. "Bring them on, will you James? I'll reimburse you later," Coswell said.

Another eye roll but James went over to the counter to get them.

Coswell eyed the young medical student. She appeared to him like some gangly teenager dressed up in doctor's greens. Even hunched over her hamburger, she was obviously tall, and rail thin, auburn hair cut short, almost butch, he thought, freckles across the bridge of her nose. But the look in her eyes was anything but childlike. She regarded him with a self-confident, bemused smile.

"Sally said you'd want all the dope on our beloved, recently deceased Professor Kelly," she said.

"Yes," Coswell said. "She implied that he had an affinity for the female gender perhaps a bit too overt for his position."

She laughed.

"You mean he was horny as the proverbial toad?"

"That's another way of putting it."

"Confirmed. His surgical hands didn't always stay attached to scalpels."

"Were there any official complaints laid?" Coswell said.

"No. He was very careful to pinch only the bums of women who couldn't afford to fight back, me included."

"Was bum-pinching as far as he went?"

"Add groping, penis-rubbing, breast-poking, the works. I don't know how far he went with others, but I got cornered in dictation booths a couple of times. Fortunately, I'm a good ducker."

"How on earth did he get away with such behaviour? Surely that soon became common knowledge."

She smiled and looked him in the eye.

"Men," she said. "Particularly big, Irish, life-of-the-party, rugby types who treat everything like that as one giant joke. There are probably a few like him in the police force."

He couldn't deny it. She was absolutely right. Sergeant McMorran popped into his mind.

"Do you know of any actual affairs that he had? Anyone on hospital staff?"

"No. He was such a boor with women that anyone would be instantly labelled "slut" if they bent to his ... charms."

Coswell mulled that over. The man obviously had a considerable sexual appetite which would require filling somewhere.

James arrived with two coffees, the decadent cinnamon bun and a fruit cup.

"No bun for you?" Coswell said. "It's from a health food store, for heaven's sake."

James set everything down.

"Right," he said. "I'm sure it's very healthy, but I don't want to spoil my supper."

"What are you having—tofu surprise?"

No response.

"You carry on, James," Coswell said. "Easier for you to talk between bites of that delicious fruit than me. This needs my total attention."

Marilyn smiled and turned her attention to James.

"So far, we've established that Dr. Kelly was over-sexed and underfed," she said.

"Maybe you could tell us about his role as head of the department of surgery," James said. "Was he respected? Enemies? Anyone with a reason to want him dead?"

She laughed again. Coswell, munching away, was

beginning to warm to this girl—lots of spirit and a good sense of humour.

"You mean besides me?" she said, and then quickly, "Just joking. I learned a lot from the man. It was worth the odd grope."

She wiped her fingers with a napkin, took a drink of water and sat back.

"I'd love a coffee, too," she said, "but I can't afford having to take a pee break during surgery, being that I'm the retractor holder usually."

Coswell tried to imagine holding a retractor for two hours.

She went on.

"Kelly was a gifted surgeon. Just watching him in action was a learning experience, but as a teacher, he was superb, both in the OR and on the wards. He used the Socratic Method—questions and answers. Not terribly kind about it, mind you. Your questions and answers had to be good, but if they were, he made you feel like a colleague not a dumb student."

"And if your questions and answers weren't up to par?"

She frowned.

"He dumped on the poor soul without a shred of mercy."

"That must have generated some hatred," James said, "at least among the students."

"No doubt about that, and to a few staff men as well."

"Staff men? You mean fellow surgeons."

"Yep. No one was spared Dr. Kelly's barbs if he deemed their performance unacceptable, and he had no qualms about doing it in public."

Coswell interjected, having wiped his fingers on a napkin after finishing the cinnamon bun.

"Can you give us some instances ... names, too, if you would? Especially anything recent, say within the last month."

She thought for a moment.

"Last surgical grand rounds he and Dr. Struthers had a real set-to about complications after surgery on a staff patient with a hiatus hernia."

"Staff patient?"

"A charity case. Downtown Eastside derelict."

"I didn't think we had such a thing in this province," James said. "We're all on Medicare, aren't we?"

"You'd be surprised how many don't even bother to apply for it. They just end up in emergency or at the hospital walk-in medical clinic without a number."

"And become teaching cases."

"You got it."

Coswell interrupted again.

"Interesting," he said. "But carry on, please. We don't need medical details, just the mood. Looks to kill and all that. Other instances."

"Kelly shot Struthers' excuses down in flames. Grand rounds are held in one of the big lecture halls. Everyone attends—nurses, students, interns, residents, anyone on surgical staff. Terribly embarrassing to be shown up there."

"Dr. Struthers not as good a surgeon?"

"Not quite as talented as Kelly, but no slouch either, that's for sure. I wasn't there, but an intern friend of mine was assisting on the case. He said that the resident who performed the actual surgery didn't do such a good job. 'Herky-jerky' were his actual words."

"Where does Dr. Struthers come into this story?"

"He was there, supervising."

"Buck stops with him sort of thing, I suppose," James said. "But surely Dr. Kelly had the occasional failure himself in similar circumstances. You'd think he would be a little more sympathetic."

"Struthers is the complete opposite of Kelly. He's kind

to a fault, in my opinion. He protects his residents like a mother hen."

Coswell suspected that Dr. Marilyn Hawthorne, when her turn came, would be more the Dr. Kelly type.

"I understand that he was acting head of the department before Dr. Kelly's appointment. Was he not in the running for the position himself? Sounds like he would be a popular candidate."

Marilyn gave him a suspicious glance.

"I can see where you're going, but I'd scratch Dr. Struthers off your suspect list. The man wouldn't hurt a fly."

Coswell smiled.

"'Who knows what evil lurks in the hearts of men,'" he said. "A quote that good policemen live by."

"Shakespeare?" she said.

"No, but close. *The Shadow.*"

The puzzled look in her eyes reminded Coswell just how old he'd become.

"An old radio program," he said, lamely. "Please continue."

"Yes, a lot of people here were disappointed when Dr. Struthers didn't get the position, but in my opinion, heads of departments should come from elsewhere. There's a tendency for complacency otherwise."

Coswell couldn't help thinking that a similar philosophy might improve the efficiency of the justice system.

"Anyone else who would either want or gain from Dr. Kelly's death that you can think of?"

She pretended to be deep in thought for a moment and then shook her head.

"Sorry, but with a 'who do you think killed him?' sort of question like that, I'm at a dead loss for any suggestions."

Damn, he thought, this girl is just too intelligent. James bailed him out.

"Quite understandable," he said. "But speculation and gossip, no matter how ill-founded, can be tremendously helpful to us. Could you think a bit more and, if you can, tell us what you might know about his personal life away from the hospital?"

She smiled.

"My father's a criminal lawyer. He'd be horrified if he knew what had come out of his baby daughter's mouth already. I don't relish sitting in a courtroom over any of this ... or anything else that takes me away from my studies for that matter."

"Just a little hint, then. Can you, anonymously of course, point us toward someone else who might help us in this way?"

"Like my roommate, Sally, you mean?"

"Someone like that would be perfect."

"Try Mabel Pucket. She's the day shift aid on the staff medicine ward. There's nothing that goes on in this place that she doesn't eventually hear about and she's the Queen of Gossip. An interview by you would make her day."

She rose from her chair and picked up her tray with its empty dishes.

"Now I really must go. Nice to meet you, Corporal James, and you, too, Inspector. Good luck with your investigation."

Both men stood up but there was no shaking of hands. Marilyn was not going to waste time putting her tray back down again to do so.

They both watched her walk swiftly to a conveyer belt where she deposited the tray and then disappeared out the cafeteria doors.

"God, but she's tall," Coswell said. "What do you think? Six feet?"

"You notice the strangest things," James said. "Although I thought she looked very masculine."

"Even stranger. Now let's go find Mabel."

Unfortunately, Mabel's shift was over for the day. She'd gone home which according to her replacement was far out in Surrey.

"No way am I going to drive to Surrey at this hour," Coswell said. "Bumper to bumper, time-wasting, commuter traffic. We'll interview her here tomorrow."

"Where to then?" James said, but the ring of his cell phone cut off Coswell's reply. He glanced at the number in the display.

"Uh-oh,"he said. "It's Chief Ward. Why would he call me and not you?"

"Because you always answer it right away. Now, find out what he wants ... or ignore it. Your battery could be run down."

James answered the call which lasted all of five seconds.

"He wants you to come to his office ... now."

Coswell grunted.

"It's always 'now' with him. Someone's probably leaning on him."

"The media, do you think?" James said.

"Most likely. Kelly getting killed would attract them like flies. People like to read about doctors involved in anything sensational—being murdered almost as good as being the murderer."

"I wonder how we managed to miss the press horde out on campus. We were certainly there long enough," James said.

"Yes, I wondered about that, too, and I have a nasty feeling I know why."

"Why?"

"We were inside but you-know-who was outside."

"McMorran? He wouldn't dare."

"Wouldn't he? I'm willing to bet you that he gave out a few words and managed to get himself in front of the TV cameras. By the time we came out, the show was over.

To be repeated on the noon hour news no doubt."

"You are to wait here with Corporal Bostock," Ward's secretary said to James the moment they walked into the office. "He wants to speak with Inspector Coswell first."

"First?" Coswell said, glancing at a female uniformed officer sitting in one of the waiting room chairs. Her corporal's stripes caught his attention, but before he could contemplate her presence further, Chief Ward's voice boomed out.

"Get in here, Coswell. I haven't got all day."

His office door was slightly ajar. Obviously he had heard them come in.

Coswell took a deep breath and entered the inner sanctum of Chief Inspector Ward, the supreme commander of RCMP Q division, whose greeting was terse.

"Sit."

There were two chairs placed side by side in front of Ward's antique desk. Coswell walked over and settled into the one he thought slightly farther away.

Ward usually started off their meetings by making derogatory remarks about Coswell's rumpled appearance—in sharp contrast to his own spit-and-polish uniform; gold braid glistening, neatly trimmed moustache, and a full head of white hair—brush cut. But on this occasion, he got right to the point.

"I am assigning Corporal Bostock as your new partner," he said. "She's been transferred to us from D division. Just arrived, in fact."

Coswell's stomach fluttered. The female officer in the waiting room. No way.

"What about James?" he said. "We've really developed an excellent working relationship and—"

Ward waved his hand.

"I know, I know," he said. "But I've been put in a delicate position and hard decisions had to be made."

Coswell's mood plunged. What would he do without James?

"Corporal James, by your own words, is future inspector material."

Coswell cursed himself. He had said that when Ward prised the fact out of him that James was gay and he feared that the young man's career might be in jeopardy.

Ward went on.

"I've put a lot of thought into his new posting."

Oh, no, Coswell thought, James promoted to sergeant and sent to some redneck unit in the hinterland.

As though reading his mind, Ward said,

"I realize that the usual posting would not be wise in Corporal James' case. Instead, I'm creating a new position that he will fit into very well—RCMP liaison with the coroner's office. His degree in criminology makes him well suited for the job, and time with that unit will sharpen his skills as a future homicide inspector."

Coswell almost slumped in his chair. How could he object? It was a great opportunity for James.

Ward immediately caught the slight movement of resignation in Coswell's shoulders.

"Now that we have that settled," he said. "We'll move on to Corporal Bostock."

He looked down for a moment at a folder lying open in front of him and then quickly closed it before continuing.

"She comes to us from rather strained circumstances, which I'm not at liberty to discuss with you at this time, but I can say that she has allegedly been ill-treated by some members of our force."

It didn't take a crystal ball for Coswell to guess what defined "ill-treatment" when a female officer was involved. Sexual harassment wasn't exactly a new entity in The Force but its reporting in recent years was. But why him?

Again Ward read his thoughts.

"You appear to have an aptitude when dealing with situations like this, hence my assigning her to you. I trust you have no objections?"

Coswell felt so completely bowled over, all he could say was, "When does she start?"

Ward smiled.

"In about two minutes."

He reached over and pushed the intercom button on his desk phone.

"Send Corporal Bostock in," he said, and then turning to Coswell. "We'll get the introductions out of the way."

Coswell rose from his chair when she came in and took a more critical look at her this time. The uniform took away most of her femininity but she had a pretty face—a young Elizabeth Taylor came to his mind and when she removed her service cap, her jet-black hair was neatly drawn up in a French braid. But it was the look in her dark brown eyes that impressed him most—the complete opposite of Marilyn Hawthorne, the fourth-year medical student. This lady's eyes reflected nothing. She stood stiffly at attention with her hat tucked under her arm in front of Ward who hadn't budged from his seat.

"Corporal Bostock," he said. "Meet your partner, Inspector Mark Coswell."

She didn't crack a smile, even when they shook hands. Her grip was completely neutral—neither soft nor firm—careful. He was pleased to see that she was at least an inch shorter than him.

"Now be seated," Ward said, his gruff command voice back again, and he fixed Bostock with steely grey eyes.

"I'm taking a chance with you, Corporal," he said. "I could have assigned you to an office job, but I've gone over your record and see that you were involved in some more lively affairs during your constable years."

Coswell hoped there would be some elaboration of the "lively affairs" but that wasn't forthcoming.

"I am therefore throwing you into the homicide ring, so to speak. Inspector Coswell heads up our unit in Vancouver. You may have heard of him."

"Yes, sir, I have," she said. "And I consider it a privilege to work with him."

The "with" caught Coswell's attention. And the flattery was just air time. He wondered what it was based on. She hadn't been in Vancouver long enough and he doubted that his fame had spread to D division in Manitoba. Politicking?

Ward continued.

"This campus murder is very high profile, as I'm sure you can appreciate. I've already received some unwanted attention from the case."

Coswell groaned inwardly. How had word travelled so fast? He hadn't reported it yet. McMorran was the likeliest source via some of his redneck contacts, although it could have been more direct. Ward played golf with half the university brass; the Dean of Medicine most likely one of them.

His speech to Corporal Bostock ended abruptly as he turned his attention back to Coswell.

"Any questions, Inspector?"

Coswell had finally regained his composure. He made one last try. "Would it be possible for Corporal James to continue a bit longer with this case? He has already opened up some leads for us and—"

Ward cut him off with a resounding "No. Corporals aren't exactly in great supply as you surely know. One is all you get. Now both of you get to work."

Coswell reached the door first and held it open for his new partner. She hesitated for a moment but then went ahead. Before Coswell could follow, Ward called after him.

"And I want you to work with Sergeant McMorran. He did a good job handling that TV interview this morning."

Coswell bit his tongue. How come the old bugger had

time to watch the news during work hours?

"Yes, sir," he said and pulled the door shut behind him.

When he turned, James was standing and staring at him with a look of absolute bewilderment. Ward's secretary would have told him nothing, but perhaps Bostock had said something while he was in with the chief.

The buzzing intercom cut off any conversation.

"Chief Ward wants to speak to you Corporal James—now," the secretary said. She quickly moved from behind her desk and pulled the door open for him.

As he passed by, Coswell whispered to him.

"Gino's."

Bostock was standing backed up against one wall of the waiting room. For a brief moment, Coswell felt sorry for her. She looked like some lost orphan in a stage play, but then he got mad.

Damn Ward. This was all so unfair. Saddled with someone who had nothing more than "some lively affairs" to bring to his homicide unit. How the hell was he going to solve Ward's high priority case with her as his partner? Somehow he had to stay connected with James.

"I need a coffee," he said to no one in particular, but his new partner heard.

"Is Gino's a café?" she said.

He was about to tell her to go to her apartment and finish moving in, but her question caught him unprepared. He didn't think she'd heard him whisper to James.

"Er, yes," he said. "But—"

"Could I come, too? I didn't have much of a chance to talk to him."

Coswell took a deep breath. What the hell was he doing? This mess wasn't her fault and the pleading look in her eyes did him in. He forced a smile.

"Of course you can," he said. "We're partners, right?"

A trace of a smile ... forced.

CHAPTER SIX

Coswell liked the little coffee shop just a block away from RCMP headquarters for a number of reasons: excellent cappuccinos, the no-nonsense service, and the total absence of RCMP staff that preferred a Tim Hortons to which they could drive, park, and drink non-yuppie coffee with their cream-filled donuts.

On the walk to Gino's, Coswell quickly realized that Corporal Bostock was the exact opposite of James—she spoke only when spoken to—surprisingly annoying to him. He'd become accustomed to James' babbling and took it as a form of relaxing white noise. The silence from his new partner was painful, but his thoughts were on James. How had he become so attached to him, and then—how had he become so dependent on him? The answer to the first question he knew—working with James was comfortable; the answer to the second—a worry. Too close to his sixth decade, he wondered if the years had dulled his faculties that much.

The only customers in Gino's were two young hipsters sitting on stools chatting with the on-duty barista, a girl with purple-streaked hair and the usual complement of body-pierced adornments. All three turned their heads and stared at them when they entered. Coswell realized why—Bostock's uniform. Another damn. He had never been taken for a Mountie in all the times he'd been there before.

The barista, one of the regulars, who usually regarded him with a blank look, showed considerably more interest on this occasion. She faced him over the counter.

"What will you have ... officer?" she said. "The usual?"

"Yes, and a peanut butter cookie."

She nodded and then cast her gaze on Bostock standing at his shoulder.

"And for you, Ma'am?"

Coswell couldn't be sure but both the barista's look and the tone of her voice rang as insolent to him.

"Just a coffee for me," Bostock said. "Small."

"I've got it," Coswell said. "Why don't you go over and grab that table at the front?"

Normally, he and James sat on stools at the counter. The cafe was in the shape of an andiron, with floor-to-ceiling windows facing the massive intersection of Kingsway and Main. The tables occupied the entire prow section of the cafe. Parking one's butt at the counter, back to the street, prevented the sitting-in-a-fishbowl feeling. It was not conducive, however, to a party of three.

James arrived just as Coswell carried his cappuccino and Bostock's coffee to their table.

"Grab my cookie, would you James when you get your latté?"

He set the two cups down on the table.

"Thanks," she said. "Next time, I buy."

He sat down—to more silence. She picked up her coffee, took a sip, and then set it down without comment.

"How is it?" Coswell said.

She looked up at him as though he'd awakened her from a trance. "Oh," she said, and then obviously embarrassed, "It's very good."

He hoped James would hurry up. The barista was chatting him up as usual. He thought women had the innate ability to spot a gay man but this one obviously couldn't. Finally, she gave him his latté and he came over to their table, cup in one hand and Coswell's cookie on a plate in the other.

Coswell expected a jibe from him about the cookie so soon after the cinnamon bun, but James wasn't in a jocular mood. He cut off introductions immediately.

"Corporal Bostock and I have already met," he said. He set the cookie in front of Coswell, pulled out a chair and sat down so abruptly he spilled some of his latté on the table. Coswell handed him the napkin that came with the cookie.

"I'm just sooo frustrated," James said. "One second I'm number two man on division Q Homicide and the next I'm a glorified courier for the coroner's office."

The presence of Bostock didn't slow his rant one iota.

"What on earth happened?" he said. "Our almighty Chief Ward gave me virtually no explanation. Just said it might be a step towards a promotion. Bull! Do I make sergeant material by running errands? No way. He's punishing me for some reason."

Coswell tried to interject.

"No, I really think—"

But there was no stopping James.

"I'll bet it had something to do with McMorran. The jerk couldn't get back at you so he blackballed me instead."

"Because taking you out would incapacitate me?" Coswell said.

That finally halted the rant.

"I wasn't thinking that," James said.

Coswell didn't know how to continue at that point. He wanted to tell James that they could still work together, albeit unofficially. The nebulous job that Ward had created could easily be bent time-wise. The problem was discussing this with Bostock present. She would obviously take offense. He regretted giving in to her request to come there.

Silence followed—James because he was embarrassed, Coswell at a loss for words, and Bostock who apparently preferred to remain mute. Surprisingly, it was she who spoke first.

"I can understand your frustration, Corporal James," she said. "I've been parachuted in and broke up what sounds like an excellent partnership. The only experience I've had with homicide boils down to vehicular and a couple of knifings when I was a constable in Winnipeg."

Coswell looked at her, astonished. Admitting weakness to colleagues just didn't happen in the Force, especially by a corporal. She had to have been a star at some point to be promoted, and stars usually had larger than average egos.

She went on, her voice a weary monotone. "I don't know why Chief Ward unloaded me onto you. I expected, in my situation, to be stuck in some dungeon filing old, useless reports. I guess I should thank him for giving me this chance, but I do want to be of use to you."

James looked at Coswell.

"Harassment," Coswell said.

James understood immediately and started to laugh ... and laughed until tears ran down his face. The barista and her two friends gawked at him, mouths open, and then they began to giggle. Bostock looked shocked. Coswell, disgusted.

James finally got under control and wiped away the tears with his hand.

"I'm sorry, Corporal Bostock," he said, "but this is just too funny." He leaned across the table, nose inches from Bostock's face, and said in a low voice.

"I know just how you feel, honey. I'm gay as a rainbow. The inspector inherited me to avoid a harassment problem, just like you."

He sat back again in his chair and continued.

"Chief Ward thinks our good inspector has a special aptitude for such problems. Either that, or we're revenge for some past unnamed transgressions."

Coswell had pondered that very point himself on more than one occasion.

"That probably explains my new assignment as well," James went on. "The coroner's crew is predominately female. Pretty safe company for a gay man. Ward has thought of everything."

Coswell had no argument. He knew that Ward was as

homophobic as anyone else in the department, and word was out that he considered women officers poor field candidates, their appropriate place being in office-type positions. Someone way up must have directed him not to apply that bias to Bostock's new posting; make her happy and avoid any adverse publicity. It was all about image.

Anger gone, James was now off and running at the mouth as per norm.

"Let's drop the "Corporal" tag," he said. "We'll do like the boys in the locker room—last names only. I'm James and you're Bostock. Sir of course will be Sir, or Inspector. We must maintain some formality."

Bostock began to smile.

"Fine with me, James," she said. "You'll be interested to know that the same protocol goes in girls' locker rooms, at least the ice hockey ones."

"You played hockey?" James said. "Me too. We must chat about it some time, but let's settle this homicide thing first. Am I totally off the Kelly case? Ward implied as much although I didn't ask him directly."

Coswell took a deep breath. He still didn't know how to deal with Bostock. She saved him the trouble.

"I don't know what Chief Ward told you about me," she said. "But I'm willing to work in any capacity with both of you—officially or otherwise. Anything to get the job done."

Coswell wasn't yet convinced of her sincerity. She had to have been a troublemaker to some degree at least. Best to be careful with her. He needed to get a look at her file.

James, however, was more than a little enthusiastic.

"We could be the three musketeers," he said, and then pleased with himself, "I've always wanted to be a swash-buckler. What do you think?"

Time to jerk James' chain.

"I'd suggest that we each need to think of our careers here," Coswell said, with the sternest voice he could muster. "I, for one, plan to keep this job until it's pension time."

The gaiety ceased so abruptly that Coswell backed off.

"There is nothing, however, to prevent you from keeping in touch with us, James, and vice versa. Your position with the coroner's office may, in fact, facilitate things for us."

James cheered up immediately.

"Righto," he said. "All aboveboard for sure."

Bostock said nothing. She'd lapsed back into herself.

The coffee shop meeting had been most unsatisfactory to Coswell, True. It had been successful in one way—James had given a summary of the Kelly investigation par excellence. He literally brought Bostock up to speed faster and more effectively than he could have done.

He chuckled inwardly at the word "speed." So far there was nothing speedy about his new partner. She took in the whole report without a word. James, in the same position, would have been full of questions, comments, and half a dozen theories, interrupting at will.

They returned to headquarters in Coswell's cruiser.

"That's probably enough for today," he said as he pulled into the parking lot. Without looking at Bostock, he said, "Why don't you go on home? I'm sure you have some settling in to do."

Yes," she said numbly, and then after a brief pause, "Thank you."

As she got out of the cruiser, he added, "Civilian clothes tomorrow. That uniform makes some people uncomfortable and please don't worry about regulations. I don't foresee anyone complaining."

Back in the office, Coswell sat in his chair and absent-mindedly fished a donut out of the Tim Hortons box as he spoke to James.

"Well, what do you think of her?"

James pulled over one of the visitor's chairs, reversed it, sat down and leaned on the back.

"I don't know," he said. "I did get a little rise out of her but it certainly didn't last, did it?

"You got that right."

"What do you know about her? What did Ward say?" Coswell shook his head.

"Other than the harassment business and that she'd been transferred from D division not a bloody thing."

"All hush-hush, no doubt. Harassment will do that all right. I'm surprised, though, that you haven't been taken into the brass's confidence."

"Me, too, but maybe it will be forthcoming."

"Or maybe it's so big that the upper echelons have issued a gag order."

Coswell thought that over for a moment.

"You could be right, so how do I get around that? I'll be damned if I'm going to work with someone and not know what I'm dealing with."

"Well, you managed with me all right and I doubt if you were terribly informed when I got assigned to you."

Coswell laughed.

"Actually I was informed ... in Ward's delicate, round-about way."

"And you accepted me without a moment's reservation. I'm touched."

"Don't be. There was a moment or two."

He swallowed the last of the donut and brushed the crumbs from his lap.

"Now think, James," he said. "Where can I get the story on this lady? I don't know anybody in the whole goddamned province of Manitoba."

"Her records from back there would have been forwarded," James replied. "Everything is Ward's problem now, not theirs."

"And buried in one of Jane's file cabinets."

Coswell thought for a moment.

"Hmm. She probably would have glanced over it first," he said. "Good old Jane. She has a soft spot for me, you know."

"She certainly doesn't have one for me. I couldn't get a thing out of her when Bostock was in with you and Ward."

"You don't have my charm. It takes years of grooming to perfect it."

James got up and pushed the chair back to where it was.

"Well, good luck with that," he said. "Now I'm off to see the coroner in beautiful downtown Burnaby. I'll give you a call later and let you know how it went."

Coswell watched him leave and felt his mood plummet. The thought of Corporal Bostock at his side rather than James filled him with dread.

His cell phone buzzed. When he looked at the call display, his mood fell even lower—UBC RCMP. McMorran. He was tempted to ignore the call, but then would risk a complaint to Ward and so he answered it. His teeth ground as the sergeant's familiar gung-ho voice came through.

"I've made a break in the Kelly case," he said. "Eyewitness. Saw the killer sneak away from the anatomy building last night at eleven o'clock. I have a description of him and the car he took off in. I've notified Vancouver PD. They are alerting all their units."

Coswell was speechless for a moment and then, aware of McMorran's cowboy attitude to policing, began to quiz him.

"What brought the witness forward?" he said.

Pause.

"I took the liberty to have the student radio station send out a plea for information."

"When did you do that?"

"Shortly after you and James showed up on campus. I saw no point in waiting."

Coswell fought to control his anger, although he had to concede that the idea was a good one. But McMorran knew better than to move on a homicide investigation without consulting the lead man. Being exiled to the UBC post had obviously not lessened his arrogance. Ward's backing no doubt added to it.

"All right," Coswell said. "Now let's hear some details. Who is the witness? What exactly did he or she see? And, as an aside, what else have you done that I should know about?"

McMorran didn't skip a beat.

"The witness is a third-year arts student. Her name is Gladys Sawatzky. She and a friend were coming back on a city bus from some film festival at the Ridge Theatre."

"Okay. Go on. What did she see?"

"A man walking very quickly along the path that cuts across the green space behind the faculty of dentistry building to the parking lot. You will recall that the Anatomy Building lies just beyond that."

"Yes, yes. I know. What else? Description?"

"He was over six feet, hatless, and wore a dark, seaman's type coat. The car he got into was a compact hatchback, dark in colour."

"Which proceeded to go where?"

"Couldn't say. Her bus had moved past."

Coswell exhaled loudly into the phone.

"Sooo. Your witness on the far side of Westbrook Mall, two lanes each way with a grass median between, glancing out the window of a north travelling city bus, gets a what—two second look at your supposed perp and comes up with all that detail?"

McMorran wasn't the least bit cowed by the sarcasm.

"She is a bright, observant young lady. The man's

pace was suspicious enough to hold her attention and there were very few cars in the dentistry parking lot at the time. I think you'll have to agree, that could very well have been our killer."

Coswell did have to agree, reluctantly ... but he wasn't going to say it out loud.

"How do we get in touch with the student?"

"Is that necessary? I interviewed her here at the station, report's all typed out."

"It's necessary. Where is she staying?"

"Gage Towers."

"We'll find her. Now, anything else?"

Coswell could almost feel the gloating.

"Not at the moment," McMorran said. "But we'll keep working at our end. I understand that this case will be a team effort."

Coswell was about to say that he had all the team he needed but Ward's dictum to work with McMorran still rang in his ears.

"Fine," Coswell said, and abruptly broke the connection.

He sat at his desk for a few minutes trying to mull over the facts in the case so far, but his mind wouldn't cooperate. He felt only fatigue, unusual for him at that time of day when he looked forward to his evening repast. He could blame the cinnamon bun and the Tim Hortons donut, but he knew it wasn't that. For once in his life, Inspector Mark Coswell had to admit to himself that he was depressed.

When James left the precinct to keep his appointment with the coroner, his thoughts were not that dissimilar to Coswell's. He did not wish their partnership to be broken up and he sensed that his contribution to their work was increasing with every case, especially the recent ones. He had put this down to his own growing experience, but over the past several months he noted that the invincible Inspector Coswell was showing a few cracks.

The career advancement carrot that Ward had dangled held no appeal to James. His corporal stripes got him to exactly where he wanted to be—working homicide and partnered with an icon, an incredibly tolerant one. And he had no desire to be in any form of command, well aware that a gay officer giving orders to the typical macho rank and file members would not be well received. He had meant to let Coswell know this many times but compliments were rare from the inspector, and being considered advancement material was a compliment worth letting ride.

Bostock was a problem. With all the fuss she had created, her partnership with Coswell, if it worked out, could be permanent. What could he do about it?

Deep in thought, midway between two intersections, he missed seeing the pedestrian crosswalk signal lights flash on, blocked in part by the back end of a massive delivery truck in front of him. When the truck driver braked and came to a stop, James' reaction was a full second slow, and he barely managed to stop in time to avoid a rear-end collision. Unfortunately, the screech of his tires garnered considerable attention from bystanders and adjacent motorists. He was grateful that he'd signed out an unmarked vehicle.

When he pushed open the heavy glass doors of the coroner's office, James was immediately intimidated—rich carpeting, plush chairs, classy art work on the walls, and an immaculately dressed receptionist sitting behind a modernistic desk with a huge glass top. He likened the office to that of a very successful lawyer or architect, a sharp contrast to the no-frills environment of Q Division headquarters. Tim Hortons donuts would be out of place here.

He checked that his tie was straight and was about to introduce himself but the receptionist beat him to it.

"Corporal James," she said. "Right on time. Just hold on a minute and I'll let Dr. Prudhomme know that you've arrived."

She spoke into an intercom on her desk, and before James could even contemplate sitting down, a door directly to her left opened and a man stepped out, hand extended. He was the antithesis of Chief Ward—short, muscular with long, wavy silver hair and a full, well-trimmed moustache. Put a hat with a feather in it on his head and he could have posed for a Swiss chocolate ad. But perhaps the greatest difference was his broad smile and welcoming gaze. His handshake was firm without being bone-crushing.

"Very good of you to come by, Corporal," he said. "I can imagine how busy you've been with this awful Dr. Kelly business."

James struggled to hide his surprise. No way had he expected this kind of reception.

"Come in, come in," Prudhomme said. "We'll have a little chat."

The chat lasted all of seven minutes but at no time did James feel he was being rushed. When it was over and Prudhomme walked him out to the waiting room, James felt that he'd joined an exciting team of people and that he would be a vital link in its function.

His feelings of inflated worth disappeared quickly, however, when he returned to the waiting room. There was one more person for him to see, and from the hard turn the secretary's mouth had taken, he was not feeling good about it.

"Dr. Lockie will see you shortly," she said. "I've let her know you are here."

That was the name that Prudhomme had dropped during their conversation, the Associate Coroner and the actual person with whom the new liaison officer would be working.

It took fifteen minutes of leafing through boring

magazines before the secretary spoke to him again. Prior to that she was totally occupied either typing or answering the phone. No time for idle talk, much to James' disappointment.

"Dr. Lockie will see you now," she said, receiver in hand, "Her office is next down from Dr. Prudhomme's, on your right."

He knocked on the door and was greeted by a sharp "Come."

Dr. Lockie was seated behind a desk cluttered with folders. She was a big woman, middle aged, grey-blond hair cut short and wearing a well-tailored business suit. She waved him over to a single chair tucked in a corner beside a large filing cabinet—an oddity in the age of computers, he thought.

She took him in with a deep, intelligent gaze that made him feel slightly uncomfortable. There was no smile.

"Prudhomme just informed me of this new position—RCMP liaison officer," she said. "I've got to tell you, I think it's a load of crap and a waste of taxpayers' money. You should be out catching crooks or whatever it is you usually do."

James let her go on as he contemplated just how he was going to respond. Despite his feeling that she was treating him like some schoolboy called into the principal's office, he refused to be intimidated. She was an underling after all, albeit an important one obviously, but really no better than him.

"Now what, exactly, am I to do with you?" she said, continuing to fix him with her beady stare.

He smiled at her.

"I have no idea," he said. "Your boss didn't go into particulars with me. Did he not discuss it with you? That's strange, don't you think?"

She blinked. He had struck home. An opportunity to

go on the offensive.

"Chief Superintendent Ward didn't discuss it with me, either," he said. "So I guess that puts you and me in the same boat."

She blinked again, perhaps because she was imagining being in a boat with him.

He tilted his chair back and put his hands behind his neck, elbows out, and gave a stretch before continuing.

"We could pretend that we were working this liaison thing in name say, but in reality you could carry on as you have before and ditto for me. That way we'd both be serving useful functions and, in my case, I can tell you I'd be much happier doing so."

She pulled off her reading glasses and dropped them on the desk in front of her.

"That's dishonest," she said.

"Why is it dishonest? No one has really defined the job for us. We're free to make it whatever we want."

She pondered this for a moment and the hint of a slyness crept into her eyes.

"We could have daily meetings," she said. "That's probably all our superiors expect."

James laughed.

"Absolutely. We could even do that by telephone. I'll leave you my card. It has my cell number. A simple 'How are you, I am fine' will do."

A huge smile transformed her face this time into the visage of a favourite aunt of his when he was a small boy, a jolly lady who kept him supplied with candy.

"Corporal James," she said, "you and I are going to get along just fine. Let me see you out."

And see him out she did—right to the front door, past the secretary who watched them go by her desk, her mouth slightly agape.

CHAPTER SEVEN

Janet Louise Bostock, age 26, career RCMP officer, a success story and inspiration for the new wave of female officers, pushed open the door to her newly let West End sixth-floor bachelor apartment, walked in, and immediately began to cry. She let the door swing shut behind her and then, purse still in hand, made her way to the lone easy chair and collapsed into it. Her chest began to heave with sobs so violent that they hurt. She couldn't stop and, worst of it all, she couldn't think of a specific reason why she was doing this.

She removed her hat and threw it at the hall closet. It bounced off the bifold doors and landed upside down on the floor. She got up, put her purse on the kitchen table, and went into the bathroom. She was about to pull open the medicine cabinet above the sink but stopped, hand on the knob, and looked at the wretched face staring back at her from the mirror. God, she thought, is that really me? Pathetic.

Angry now, she jerked the door open. There they were—her "anti-stress" pills—two bottles of them. There had been a third medication used in the beginning but the side effects were terrible—dizziness, loss of balance, tremor. She stopped taking them after just a few doses. The second prescription worked but it made her feel like a zombie and her brain functioned like a snail. She'd stopped those, too. The third bottle contained fast acting anti-anxiety pills. They worked and seemed to be the best of the lot, although they, too, had side effects—drowsiness and lassitude which lasted for several hours. She used them sparingly, although she did keep an extra bottle of them in her purse.

The instructions on the label said one tablet twice to a maximum of four times a day. She shook two of the yellow tablets into the palm of her hand and returned to the kitchen where she got a glass out of the cupboard, half filled it with tap water, and swallowed one of them. The other she put under her tongue and went back to her easy chair. The under the tongue one, she had discovered, worked much faster and gave the other time to kick in.

It took only ten minutes for the drug to act, but in those ten minutes her mind filled with anxieties. The attacks were becoming more frequent. How would she handle one on duty? Six months of stress leave had spared her that problem, but now? Taking the pills regularly would probably prevent them but she knew she couldn't possibly function at top level doing that, and Coswell was certain to notice.

Inspector Coswell so far, was an enigma. He had let her come to the coffee shop and meet with James, but his reluctance was obvious and she felt that he remained guarded toward her the whole time. She would definitely be on trial with him from the start. Could she break down the barrier? So far in her career she had been a total failure in that regard—dealing with senior staff.

Finally, relief. She kicked off her shoes and leaned back, savouring the calming effect of the drug. What had her psychiatrist said? Think positive thoughts, happy thoughts. James popped into her mind. Now there was a happy thought. She smiled and then went promptly to sleep.

Coswell decided to walk home to his condominium in Chinatown, a mere three kilometres away—from Twelfth Avenue straight down Main Street—a scant five minutes by cab. Sunset wasn't until almost nine and it was a beautiful fall evening. He hoped that the walk might stimulate his appetite. Food always elevated his mood.

Unfortunately, he had never done this before. He hadn't owned a car in years and took taxis everywhere, including to and from work. This, according to statistics, saved him thousands over a year, as well as avoiding one giant hassle—trying to park on the street in front of his condo. The Resident Parking Only signs were totally ignored by the hordes that shopped and dined in the area.

The first few blocks were easy; a gentle downhill slope and Coswell began to feel invigorated. He remembered his basic training in Regina, the marching, and began to swing his arms. Not bad for a man his age, he thought. The noisy, exhaust-spewing traffic beside him was annoying but he paid it little heed. He was in a rhythm and moving well. By Sixth Avenue, however, he started to slow down. His feet hurt. Leather brogues did not make for long-distance walking comfort.

Science World was coming into view on his left, as well as the high-rise buildings downtown and the North Shore mountains in the background, but the scenery wasn't giving him any relief. The sight of the Main Street Sky Train station dead ahead, however, helped. It didn't look too far away and just past it were Thornton Park and the Pacific Central Railways Station. He could rest there for a minute or so. His condo was just a few blocks further on.

He didn't even look up when he passed under the glassed-in Sky Train station; his eyes fixed on the green of the park. The first rest stop he came to was a three-seater at a curbside bus shelter, but all three seats were occupied. Reluctantly, he turned into the park and made his way over to the first available bench at the edge of the pedestrian roundabout. He sat for a moment to catch his breath and then leaned over and untied his shoe laces, ignoring the pigeons and curious gazes from one or two panhandlers who worked the railway station.

He savoured the ecstasy from releasing the pressure on his aching feet for a full five minutes before lacing his shoes back up again, this time more loosely. He took a few tentative steps—too painful. He looked over to the line of taxis in front of the big station building. Yes, enough of a workout, he decided and hobbled over to the lead cab.

"Jackson Street?" the cabbie said. "Whoopee. Finally I make it to the head of the line and I get a fare to Jackson Street. I can throw a stone that far."

Coswell pulled out his wallet and flashed his shield.

"Police business," he said. "Now hurry."

If the driver wondered what police business there was in a luxury condo on that gentrified section of Jackson Street he didn't comment, and a five dollar tip sent him away slightly less morose.

Coswell waited until he saw the cab turn left at the end of the block onto Keefer Street before he climbed the stairs to the porch of his condo. Once inside, he shut down the alarm system, kicked off his shoes without unlacing them, and went directly to his wine cupboard where he quickly found a bottle of vintage Zinfandel. In less than thirty seconds, he had it uncorked and a generous amount poured into the biggest glass he could find, a seventeen ounce brandy snifter. He knew that a sommelier would have used a proper eight ounce tapered glass for such a good wine, but it would breathe faster in the brandy glass and he didn't plan to wait around.

The red light was flashing on his land line phone in the kitchen but he ignored it. Anything important and the caller would get him on his cell.

He had actually splurged and hired an interior decorator to do up his condo when he bought it. He gave the woman only one condition—there had to be a La-Z-Boy chair installed somewhere. Although she had turned up her nose slightly, she did as asked and stuck it into as non-feature an area as possible—a corner to the right of the entrance door, blocked from a visitor's view by an ornate, free-standing coat rack.

Glass of wine in one hand, bottle in the other, he made his way to the chair and settled in with a great sigh, first placing the bottle on the end table beside him. He had no sooner taken his first swallow of the nectar when his cell phone buzzed. Damn! Fortunately, he hadn't yet removed his jacket and so didn't have to get out of his chair to answer it. He put down his wine glass, pulled the phone out of his pocket, and looked at the call display—James.

"Where have you been?" James said. "They told me you left the station just before I got back. What did you do—walk home?"

The implication that this was an impossible event prompted Coswell to respond.

"As a matter of fact, I did," he said, "and it was most pleasant."

A pause as James considered whether or not he was being had.

"Right then," he said, doubt still lingering. "Well, I had my meeting with the coroner people and good news; I'm going to have a very loose rein there. I'll be able to help you out with the Kelly case."

"That *is* good news," Coswell said. "But don't risk getting into trouble for my benefit."

James gave a villainous chuckle.

"No risk whatsoever. The associate coroner and I are now bosom buddies."

"Lockie? I've met her. You've got to be kidding."

"Not a bit. You told me to use my charm and I did. It's really not so difficult."

James meant it as humour, of course, but Coswell couldn't help feeling a twinge—another advantage down the drain.

"Well, let's hope it continues tomorrow morning when we have to rattle Charlotte's cage. I have heard not a word from her since she left us at the anatomy building."

He was slightly embarrassed by the grumpiness in his voice; James picked up on it immediately.

"Tomorrow's another day, sir," he said. "And I've got a feeling it will be a good one."

Coswell sighed.

"I hope you're right," he said. "Now why don't you go home. You've done a good day's work."

"And you, too, sir. Have a good evening."

Coswell gazed at the display on his phone for a moment, watched it turn itself off, and then set it down on the table beside him.

He picked up his glass of wine and took another good gulp, holding it his mouth for a few seconds to let the essence linger on his palate before swallowing. He thought of getting something to eat but he still had no appetite. Maybe it was the adrenalin from his unaccustomed exercise.

He switched on the elegant floor lamp beside his chair, a sensually curved stainless steel marvel of artistic engineering—and hellishly expensive, as he recalled. It did give an excellent reading light, however, and light for reading seemed to be more and more critical for him lately.

There were two library books on the table beside him; he still abhorred the dependence everyone seemed to have on computers. E-books were alien to him. He read books that could be held in the hand, and real bookmarks that marked his place. One of the books on the table—*Living with Alzheimer's*, he had no intention of reading, but the other—*Alzheimer's Disease: Signs, Symptoms, and Early Treatment*, he did. For once the librarian had been too helpful. She caught him leafing through the signs and symptoms book. To offset any notion she might have that he was worried about himself, he simply said, "My poor mother," leaving out the fact that she had died many years back. The librarian then recommended *Living With Alzheimer's* and so he signed them both out.

Ten pages in and he was sure that he had inherited his dear Mom's disease. This distressed him so much that he ultimately finished the whole bottle of wine. At that point he didn't give a damn about anything and went promptly to bed.

Tuesday

He woke Tuesday morning with a splitting headache, a rarity for him. He knew why, of course—26 ounces of fourteen percent Zinfandel on an empty stomach. This was also a rarity for him since his credo was that wine should always be paired with food, not only to enhance the flavour of both but to give the brain some decent protection. His bedside clock read 7:45—an hour past his usual waking time.

He staggered into his bathroom and discovered that he didn't even need to empty his bladder. Dehydrated, obviously; another contributor to his headache. And everything was too loud—the medicine cabinet door, the tap splashing in the sink, even the noise of his motorized toothbrush.

Fortunately, the cabbie who drove him to headquarters looked as hungover as he was, and so, aside from honking horns and ambulance sirens screaming their way to the Vancouver General Hospital, he made the trip in silence.

When he walked into the office, James and Bostock were standing side-by-side looking at the large case board that James liked to keep. He had started one on the Kelly murder. Victim, suspects, and other pertinent data were chalked up in neat compartments.

Bostock was wearing a long-sleeved dark dress and black loafers with a raised heel. He wondered if walking in them would be any better than his brogues. They both turned to face him when they heard him come in. Bostock's face registered nothing; James raised one eyebrow.

"Not feeling well this morning, sir?" he said.

Coswell ignored the question, took off his jacket and hung it up behind the door. He desperately needed a coffee, but didn't want to admit it. The two big glasses of orange juice that he drank before leaving home hadn't done a thing. So much for the dehydration theory; his headache had gone unabated.

He went over to his desk and sat down. James and Bostock were still standing, waiting for him to say something. He pretended to show interest in the case board but his brain just wouldn't snap to attention. One name on the suspects list, however, did jump out at him.

"Who is Frank Hoffmann?" he said.

James gave him a puzzled look but answered quickly,

"He's the sour fellow from the campus pub. Don't you remember?"

Coswell barely remembered and it irked him. Best go on the offense.

"Of course I do. 'Frank the Wank' but he had a solid alibi, cramming with his roommate at their residence for some exam. His roommate, a Chinese fellow, Wing something as I recall, confirmed it. You should have pushed him out of your mind, too."

James shook his head.

"The man's name was Wing Chu and they may be more than just roommates," he said. "They may be bosom buddies covering for one another or even in on the murder together."

He was right, damn it. Routine police procedure.

"Pretty far-fetched," he said and then hated himself for saying that.

Bostock's inscrutable stare was starting to bother him. What was she thinking about all this, and was she beginning to question her "I consider it a privilege to work with him" statement to Ward?

"And what are your thoughts on all of this, Corporal Bostock?" he said.

She jumped and he realized that he had almost growled at her.

"Er, I don't really have any at this point, sir," she said.

"But James has been going over the case with me and his suggestions sound very good."

"I see. Well I think it's time for us all to huddle and think up a game plan."

James broke into a big smile.

"Oooh, a huddle. I've always liked huddles," he said.

Coswell saw Bostock's deer-in-the-headlights look disappear. James' comedic interjection had taken the heat off of her. He wondered how deliberate it was. Hard to tell with James.

"We'll go to Gino's," Coswell said. "It's probably not good for you to be seen hanging around with us, James. Ward sees more than we often give him credit for, and I can tell you that anyone not following his orders to the letter is in trouble."

Whether they saw through his motives or not, he didn't care. Only a drug addict in withdrawal would understand how he felt at that moment. He didn't just want a coffee; he needed one—along with something to eat. The orange juice hadn't cured his headache but it sure as hell boosted his appetite.

"Correct dress, by the way," he said to Bostock. "Uniforms just put up a red flag to Joe Citizen."

James winked at her.

Business was booming at Gino's. There wasn't a seat to be had and there was a big lineup at the counter. Coswell glanced over at the prow table and noticed the occupants getting ready to go. There was only one chance of reserving it.

"Bostock," he said. "You go over and save that table for us. I'll get whatever you want and James can help me carry everything over."

She looked momentarily peeved.

"It's my turn to buy," she said.

Oh, oh, Coswell thought. Sensitive, but why should he

have to tip-toe around her?

"You can buy lunch," he said, struggling to keep the annoyance out of his voice. "Maybe we can do the campus pub. It's a great place."

"If you like seal wallows," James said.

She seemed content, however, with the lunch promise.

"Just a coffee, please—black," she said. "I had a good breakfast."

Coswell watched as she moved quickly to the table, and then even more quickly when she saw two male business types headed for it as well. She won the race and smiled sweetly to them as she sat down and pointed to him and James. They nodded and looked elsewhere to set down their trays.

James outmanoeuvred Coswell in the lineup.

"You go ahead," he said. "I had breakfast, too. Just order me a latté—single shot, skim."

"I'm buying, I presume," Coswell said.

"Your generosity is appreciated, sir."

It seemed ages to Coswell before they got their order. In reality, it was only five minutes. He asked for a large cappuccino and two squares of something that reminded him of his mother's oatmeal date cakes, except that these were filled with a cream cheese icing and obviously contained a ton of sugar. Necessary carbohydrates and everyone knew that cream cheese was healthy.

"We can share these," Coswell said when he and James set everything down on the table, hoping neither would take him up on his offer.

"No thank you," Bostock said.

"Ditto," said James, looking askance at the decadent squares.

Coswell took a spoon and skimmed some of the foam off of his cappuccino along with the chocolate flakes that he had sprinkled over it.

"You start off, James," he said, popping the spoonful

into his mouth.

James took a deep breath.

"Greed, hate, or fear. That, Bostock, is the Coswell triad of motives for murder. You'll hear it a lot. He's left out love, but I suppose that is just another form of greed."

"Get on with it," Coswell growled. The first square was almost gone.

"Okay then. First, greed. Who will benefit from Kelly's sudden demise? Only one name so far—Dr. Struthers, who is now the head of the surgery department. Kelly, it appears, wasn't flush with assets, so money couldn't have been the reason. Insurance? The wife might still hold a policy on him but it doesn't sound like she needs any more money than she has now. Second, hate—"

To the amazement of both men, Bostock interrupted.

"Love," she said.

They both stared at her.

"Maybe he was having an affair and a jealous husband killed him."

"That would fit under hate," Coswell said.

She blushed and quickly started to sip her coffee.

"Not so quick," James said. "That's a good suggestion. Maybe Kelly was ruining someone's life and a loved one wanted to save her by doing away with him—a father or a grandfather."

"Humph," Coswell said. "Unlikely, but go on."

"Hate then. In that category the list is long and growing. People he belittled: doctors, nurses, medical students, people he embarrassed: his wife, Dr. Montgomery, and God knows who else."

"And fear?" Coswell said, both squares gone now and three quarters of his cappuccino.

"Can't think of anything in that regard," James said. "Can you?"

"He almost ended that medical student what's-his-name's career. Maybe there were others worried that they were about to be picked off."

Coswell downed the last of his cappuccino.

"Time to get going," he said. "We've dilly-dallied long enough. It's damn near lunch time."

"It's only nine o'clock," James said.

"Never mind."

CHAPTER EIGHT

Whether it was the caffeine or the sugar jolt Coswell couldn't be sure, but he suddenly felt a surge of energy. He actually set the pace going back to their office, despite his sore feet, and was happy to see that both Bostock and James had to hustle to keep up with him.

"We'll split up here," he said when they neared the parking lot. "Bostock and I are going to head out to the campus this morning."

James made no effort to hide his disappointment.

"Don't tell me I have to sit on my lovely glutes here all day," he said, "I'll be bored out of my gourd."

"No. I wouldn't wish that on anybody. What I do want you to do is to get in touch with Charlotte in forensics. Her crew should have some results from the crime scene by now. See what you can squeeze out of her. And Kelly's autopsy will be some time today. You can be my eyes and ears at that."

James was genuinely surprised.

"You're not going?" he said. "That's a first."

"I have complete faith in you and besides, being with the coroner's office now, autopsies should be your thing."

He didn't wait for James to comment.

"Come along, Bostock," he said, "Time's a-wasting."

The fact that Bostock and James had started working a good hour before he arrived didn't enter his head. He was congratulating himself instead for remembering to drop the *"Corporal"* when he spoke to her.

There was a mild hiccup at the cruiser. He foolishly held the door to the parking lot open for her and she got to the unmarked vehicle first. She walked around to the driver's side but Coswell stopped her.

"It's okay," he said. "I'll drive. It'll take you a while to get used to Vancouver traffic."

She got into the passenger's side, but a flicker of annoyance passed across her face. She probably interpreted his taking the wheel as a man thing—subliminal harassment but he wasn't going to risk his queasy stomach to her driving and then he congratulated himself again for not thinking *woman driver*.

He initially planned to take the direct route to the campus along Twelfth Avenue, but at Arbutus he turned left. Bostock had returned to silent mode.

"We're going to take a bit of a roundabout route," he said. "The route that McMorran's witness took the night when she supposedly saw our killer."

Just before Sixteenth Avenue, he pointed out the Ridge Theatre to her.

"That's where she and her friend were Sunday night."

He turned right at the stop light.

"Sixteenth goes all the way out to the campus and connects with Westbrook Mall," he said.

"I know," she said. "I grew up in this city."

"For heaven's sake. Why didn't you tell me? I suppose you went to UBC as well."

"I presumed that Chief Ward told you all about me, but yes, I lived here until I was sixteen—in Dunbar. I saw a lot of movies at the Ridge Theatre. My father got a position in Winnipeg so we moved and I went to the University of Manitoba, not UBC."

Silence again.

"Anything else you'd like to tell me about yourself?" Coswell said. "Ward didn't say much of anything to me.

No time, I guess."

"Not much to tell," she said. "Joined the Force seven years ago. First posting was in Weyburn, Saskatchewan and then back to Winnipeg. Ended up in the major crimes unit. Now here."

Silence, and then Coswell laughed. He couldn't help himself.

"Thank you," he said. "I always like to know who I'm working with."

She continued to look straight ahead.

"You wouldn't be interested in the personal stuff," she said. "And it won't affect my work, I can assure you."

Yep, Coswell thought, this is going to be some partnership.

Silence again, until they came alongside the University Endowment Lands, and then whether prompted by nostalgia or to make amends for being so abrupt, she spoke.

"I used to walk the family dog in there."

"You'd want to walk a really big dog in there now," Coswell said, "or be with someone. It's not safe for women."

He was going to mention the recent attacks on female joggers but thought better of it—another touchy subject, no doubt. Too bad there hadn't been a few men mugged there as well.

Westbrook Mall was a wide boulevard with lots of green: trees and grass verges. There wasn't much of interest in buildings—mostly playing fields on their left and low rise condominium developments on the right, including the RCMP precinct, a mundane two-storey structure with cruisers parked in front of a chain-link fence. It caught Bostock's attention, however, and she glanced over at Coswell when he passed by it without looking in that direction.

"We'll bump into McMorran soon enough," he said. "I'm sure he has his men keeping an eye out for us. This case is as high profile as it gets, and profile is the name of his game."

Bostock didn't comment and he regretted venting his hostility like that. James would have been another matter, but no James so he'd better suck it up much as it irritated him. He stayed in the far left lane and when they neared the Dental Building parking lot he said, "Okay, now pretend you're sitting in a city bus at eleven o'clock at night and look to your left. I'll keep up my speed. What could you see?"

She leaned forward and looked past him.

"The lot is well lit," she said. "The witness could easily see a car, even at the back."

"And the murderer?"

They were past now and coming up to the intersection at University Boulevard. She settled back in her seat before answering him.

"Difficult if his car was parked farthest from the street," she said.

"Or her car."

"Yes, or her car."

The light was green.

"We'll swing round," he said, "and I'll give you a tour of the crime scene."

He made a swift U-turn and entered the southbound side of Westbrook. He was in the process of changing to the curb lane, intending to turn into the Dental faculty parking lot, when he heard the siren behind him.

"You made an illegal turn, sir," Bostock said. "Did you not see the 'no left turn except for buses' sign?"

"Of course I did," Coswell lied. Actually he didn't, concerned only with cutting into southbound traffic.

"We're on official police business, for crying out loud. A shortcut is justified. Saves time. And what Dudley Do-Right stops a fellow officer? With a siren no less. Ridiculous."

"We're in an unmarked car, sir, and we're wearing plain clothes."

"Damn."

He pulled over to the curb. The cruiser drove up and parked behind him, leaving the red-blue lights flashing. The officer didn't get out of his vehicle right away.

"He's running our licence plate. What a waste of time," Coswell grumbled.

"Routine, sir, and I'm sure he will soon know the situation."

Indeed he did, but instead of waving them on, he got out of his cruiser and came around to Coswell's side. It was McMorran's corporal.

"Sorry, Inspector," he said. "I should have recognized your vehicle."

"Yes, yes," Coswell said. "Now you've had your bit of fun, so go back and turn off those damned lights and let us get on with our work."

"Certainly, sir, although I'm not exactly sure what to do with your infractions: illegal left turn, illegal U-turn, and a lane switch without signalling."

"I could tell you what to do with those infractions, but there's a lady present. Now bugger off."

"Well I—"

The rest was lost in the sound of the revving engine and the squeal of tires as Coswell accelerated forward ten metres and then swung into the parking lot. Only Bostock saw the officer standing where they'd left him, grinning from ear to ear.

The Anatomy Department was completely back to business when they entered, at least as far as the offices were concerned. There weren't any students to be seen.

"Probably all in the anatomy lab," Coswell said.

This was confirmed by Dr. Dietrich's secretary.

"I hope you're not going to disturb them," she said.

"The professor was so upset about everything being cancelled yesterday. He's in the lab giving catch-up lectures."

"We're just going to do a brief walkabout," Coswell said. "We won't disturb anyone."

Bostock gave him a sidelong glance as they walked along the hallway.

"Except Fred," Coswell said.

"Fred Porter, the anatomy technician? He was well down on James' list as I recall."

"You recall correctly, but as a source of information, he's way up there."

Coswell stopped at the door to the lab and looked at the keypad for a few seconds. Was it 3162 or was it 6231? Damn. Where was James when he needed him? But he wasn't going to embarrass himself by punching away. He knocked instead.

Nothing.

He knocked again, louder.

The door clicked open and they looked directly into Fred's frowning face.

"Oh my God," he said. "You're not going to interrupt, are you? The old man is in a bad enough mood as is."

"Who is it, Fred?" Dietrich called from the end of the lab.

Coswell stepped inside, gently pushing Fred out of the way. "Inspector Coswell, Professor," he called out. "I just need to borrow Fred for a few minutes. Is that all right with you?"

"A few minutes only," Dietrich said. "He's needed here and we've been more than patient with your intrusions."

"You have indeed, sir. Most appreciated," and aside to Fred, "C'mon, my good man, let's get out of here before I lose my patience and haul the old bastard off his pedestal and down to the station."

Fred smiled. He appeared to relish the thought.

Coswell introduced Bostock: "My new partner," he said. "She's taking over from Corporal James. Fresh eyes. I want her to see the whole scene."

And to Bostock, "I don't know what techniques they use in Winnipeg, but here I want you to turn into a camera and replay our murder. When you've filmed everything, you can play it back to me."

A look of confusion flashed briefly in her eyes, and then determination.

She paused at the foot of the stairs and looked through the small glass window of the door into the hallway. Satisfied, she pushed it open and stepped forward. A quick glance at the fire door and then down the hallway.

"Could we see the practice room now?" she said.

"No need to see Fred's office?" Coswell asked.

"No. I don't see the killer going in there."

Coswell just shrugged his shoulders.

Fred opened the practice room door with his key.

"I've cleaned it all up," he said, "but the gurney's still exactly where it was—minus the cadaver, of course."

"No matter," Bostock said. "There will be plenty of photos coming from the forensics people, and Corporal James gave me a very good description."

She stood, gazed into the room for only a few seconds, and then turned away.

"Thank you, Fred," she said. "And now may I see the elevator?"

Fred led her over and pushed the button to open the elevator doors. She glanced first at the margins and then inside. She thanked Fred again and then turned to Coswell.

"Okay," she said. "I've got it."

"Go ahead," Coswell said. "Let's see your movie."

She crossed her arms and began.

"If the killer followed his victim to the lab, he would have entered the hallway after him through the fire door.

I see a man, by the way, and not a woman. Too physical for the latter."

Coswell thought of a few Amazon females he knew in the Force, but kept quiet. Bostock continued.

"Or, he might have known that Kelly would be in the practice room," she said, "and preceded him here, waiting in the stairwell for him to pass by."

That thought hadn't occurred to Coswell, much to his chagrin. His assumption was that the killer had come through the fire door.

She went on.

"He lets Kelly get set up in the practice room and then either sneaks up on him silently or announces his presence. The former explains the bruise in the back more easily. James felt it was from the killer bracing his knee. If Kelly knew his killer, it becomes more complicated. Either he had complete disdain for his visitor and turned away from him, or he was actually about to show him something on the cadaver—teaching."

Fred blurted out, "A student. I knew it. A miserable student."

"That's only one possibility," Bostock said coolly.

She uncrossed her arms and looked at him.

"But can you give us the name of a student who would resort to murder?"

Fred looked down at his feet.

"No," he said. "But there could be. Remember Jack the Ripper? He was a doctor."

Ah, James' Jack the Ripper theory again, Coswell remembered. A rogue in a respected profession.

Bostock pointed to the door frame of the elevator.

"There are some serious scratches here and I doubt that you made them, Fred. You take such good care of everything, and I'm sure you're a better gurney driver than our killer. I see him as frantic to complete his deed and banging the gurney into the sides. He probably wore gloves, but maybe he scraped his wrist in the process and left some DNA."

Coswell was speechless. He had really underestimated this lady.

"In short," she said. "We badly need forensics help. Motives are nice, I agree, but hard facts and physical findings make for convictions."

Coswell was so used to James' babbling that he missed the opportunity to praise her.

"Interesting," was all he could say.

"And," she continued, "the cleaners who were working Sunday night should be interviewed soon—one of the jobs assigned to James, I understand."

"Now yours," Coswell said. "We'll go upstairs and get the company name from Dietrich's office. I also want to have a word with Dr. Montgomery's secretary."

"Is that all you need from me?" Fred said.

Coswell had wanted to ask him something but for the life of him couldn't remember what.

"Unless Corporal Bostock has questions for you?"

"Not at the moment," she said. "But I imagine that you get to know the students fairly well over the term, Fred. They are under a lot of stress and true personalities are often exposed under those circumstances. Would you let us know if Jack the Ripper reveals himself?"

Coswell pulled a card out of his wallet and handed it to him.

"Use the cell number," he said. "That will get me any time." And, turning to Bostock,

"Get Jane, Ward's secretary, to have some cards printed up for you. I assume you have a cell, too."

"Not set up here yet," she said.

"Do it soon."

"Yes, sir."

They made their way back up the stairs to the main floor. Fred punched the keypad and returned to the lab.

Coswell noted her watching him. 2613. Damn.

Fred was quite correct about Dr. Montgomery's secretary. He was gay all right, and not the least bit shy about revealing it. He had the same motor mouth as James. His name was Francis.

"With an i, but an e is okay, too," he said. "Whatever turns you on."

Also, like James, he was dressed immaculately—suede loafers, fawn chinos, a bright coral shirt left open at the neck, and hair perfectly gelled into a fashionable cock's comb. His only deference to conservatism was a single body piercing (at least visible)—a diamond stud in his right earlobe. He floored Bostock right after the introductions.

"You are just sooo gorgeous," he said to her. "I can't believe you are a policewoman."

Definitely a reaction from her—cheeks turned a McIntosh apple-red and her neck almost sizzled.

Francis remained seated behind his desk looking somewhat officious despite his flippant remarks.

"You'll want to speak to Dr. Montgomery," he said, "but I'm afraid she's at a conference in Edmonton."

"And she will be back when?"

"Wednesday, late morning. She is, by the way, aware of Dr. Kelly's death. One of your officers informed her yesterday."

McMorran, no doubt. Get right in there with the VIPs.

"Have you spoken to her?"

"Yes. She called me this morning. Apparently the officer who contacted her was rather abrupt in his insistence that she return to Vancouver immediately, but she plans to keep her commitments in Edmonton."

And then a thought occurred to him.

"You can't force her to come back, can you? They've been divorced for some time now. Surely she's not a suspect."

"We will need to interview her," Coswell said, "but it can wait until she's back."

"You could use Skype if you wanted."

"Not quite the same as in person," Coswell said.

"Oh, body language and all that. How clever, and of course, there's the security thing. Just anyone can hack into anything these days it seems. Foolish suggestion."

"But you're trying to be helpful," Coswell said, "and we appreciate that. You could be really helpful if you would answer some questions yourself."

Francis gave a little shiver.

"Oh how exciting. Just fire away. I'm at your disposal."

Coswell knew he'd have to be careful. There was such a thing as being too helpful.

"Did you have any dealings with Dr. Kelly yourself?"

"Did I? You can say that again. And 'deal' with him is right. One mustn't speak ill of the dead, but Dr. Kelly was a real pest—a belligerent one. He made life very unpleasant for Dr. Montgomery. Wouldn't make appointments, he'd just barge in."

And then, realizing what he was saying, he stopped suddenly.

"Now don't get the wrong idea," he said. "Dr. Montgomery is an absolute sweetie and so patient with that awful man."

"Do you know what was said in some of those meetings?"

Francis sat up straight.

"I'm no keyhole snooper, sir."

"Of course not,"Coswell said, "but perhaps you overheard some snatches of conversation?"

A smile.

"Not a word," he said. "This building has amazing soundproofing."

Bostock joined in.

"When was the last time Dr. Kelly came to this office?"

"Two weeks ago, but fortunately Dr. M was giving a lecture to the students and he didn't wait around."

"How did he appear to you?"

"Agitated, angry, pretty well normal for him."

Coswell's turn.

"Could you, to the best of your memory, give us the times and dates he came here over the last month or so, how long he stayed and anything else you think relevant."

"I record everything that happens in this office," Francis said and then pointed to a large daybook.

"Right in there. Much better than a computer."

He flipped the pages and then turned the book around for them.

"I don't see Dr. Kelly's visit recorded," Coswell said.

"It's there. Look in the margin at ten fifteen."

"AH in. Dr. M out."

"AH?"

"My personal code," Francis said.

Coswell chuckled. AH. Asshole.

A flicker of a smile from Bostock. She got it, too.

CHAPTER NINE

When they returned to the parking lot, a marked RCMP cruiser was pulled alongside theirs. As they neared, an officer got out on the passenger side—McMorran. He closed the cruiser door and leaned against it, one elbow on the roof—a casual, insolent pose. Coswell couldn't see the driver but assumed that he was the corporal who had stopped him and was now collecting Brownie points for leading his master to the enemy.

"I hear that you created a bit of a fuss with one of my officers this morning," he said. "But I quite understand. None of us is perfect, eh?"

"And you're not going to report it to show me what a

fine, tolerant person you are," Coswell said.

"I think a little tolerance goes a long way toward keeping up morale. Don't you?"

His smirk grew even more nauseating, but before Coswell could reply, McMorran turned his attention to Bostock.

"And you are—"

"Corporal Bostock, sir," she said and reached out to shake his hand.

He took it and held on noticeably longer than necessary, rubbing his thumb over the top of her hand.

"You don't have to 'sir' me," he said. "Only the lofty level of Inspector merits that."

He let go of her hand finally and said to Coswell, "And where is the good Corporal James, by the way? You and he are usually inseparable."

"Reassigned," Coswell said. "Corporal Bostock has taken his place."

A coarse laugh.

"Well, well," he said. "That certainly follows a pattern."

Coswell could barely contain his anger.

McMorran again regarded Bostock.

"You are definitely an improvement. I like your uniform. Very attractive."

Bostock blushed again. although Coswell thought it might have been from anger, but she seemed flustered.

"Uh, thank you," she said.

"I hope you've been properly welcomed to our local ranks," McMorran went on. "If not, I can offer my services ... both professionally and socially if there's no significant other in the picture."

This was too much for Coswell.

"For Christ's sake, McMorran. You sound like some overly hormoned teenager. Now get back to whatever useless job you were doing and let us get on with our investigation."

"Of which I am part, as you know," he said. "Hardly useless."

"Right. We'll keep you informed of our every move."

"Please do."

He was still standing beside his cruiser when they drove away.

Coswell pulled onto Westbrook Mall and headed north, planning to stop at the Gage Towers where McMorran's eyewitness lived. He looked over at Bostock. Her jaw was set hard.

"McMorran is one of Francis' AHs," he said. "Don't let it bother you."

She continued to look straight ahead.

"I'm more concerned about it bothering you," she said.

What to say? It did bother him, but why? His primal urge to protect a woman? That's probably what she was thinking, and in part that was true. But it wasn't just that.

"It bothers me that McMorran attacked my *partner*," he said. "If he'd done the same with James, I would have been just as angry."

"I appreciate that," she said. "But you shouldn't have to fight either of our battles."

God, he thought, what a difference from James. He would have skewered McMorran with some of his rapier sharp wit. She was right, though. Concern for her and her feelings was affecting his ability to function at peak level, although his peak level, he had to admit, was in a state of flux lately.

The Gage Towers are appropriately named after Dean Gage, a beloved math professor who eventually became university president. And they do qualify as towers—three of them, each seventeen storeys high. They dominate the skyline and to Coswell, remembering his years there when the tallest structure was the single clock tower in front of the library, the Gage Towers appeared incongruous to him.

Bostock appeared to agree.

"My goodness," she said. "These are really student residences? They look like hotels. Nothing like that at the University of Manitoba."

"Fifty thousand students at last count attend UBC," Coswell said. "And close to a third of them live on campus. Going up saves space, I guess."

He had no problem finding the visitors parking, but when he got out of the cruiser, he realized that all he had was a name—Gladys Sawatzky. No room number. Looking up at all those windows and seeing students coming and going everywhere, he realized he should have gotten more information from McMorran.

"You know," he said. "I've changed my mind. Chances are our witness will be in classes. Better we set up a time with her."

"There must be a residents' list somewhere," she said. "We could take a moment to check."

Without waiting for him to reply, she stopped the first student who walked by, a young man. "We are trying to find one of the residents here," she said. "Can you tell us how to go about doing so?"

"Sure," he replied. "Just go over there. That's the Commonsblock. Ask at the desk."

"You go," Coswell said. "I want to make a few calls."

The autopsy on Dr. Kelly had already started by the time James made his way to the morgue at the Vancouver General Hospital. To his surprise, Dr. Lockie, his coroner's office liaison partner, was among the large group sitting in the viewing seats. He assumed that anyone at her level would simply read the autopsy reports, but there she was, on the aisle of the very back row, and beside her was Charlotte, whom he had been trying to reach all morning. Most of the seats were filled with white or green uniformed individuals. There were places available in the back row, one, fortunately for him, next to Charlotte.

"Excuse me, Dr. Lockie, Charlotte," he said, squeezing past. Both acknowledged him with a curt nod. When he'd settled into his seat, Charlotte leaned over and whispered.

"Where's your chubby partner?"

"Tell you later," James said. "It's a long story."

The pathologist performing the autopsy was a man in his sixties, reading glasses perched half way down his nose and wisps of white hair peeking out from under his head cover. A senior pathologist, James concluded, Dr. Kelly's corpse worthy of his attention. He spoke into a microphone dangling down from the ceiling.

Most of what the man said was routine—condition and weight of organs, stomach contents (Professor Dietrich's dinner) and so forth. A few comments were of interest to James: "The skin shows a fine horizontal laceration at the level of the thyroid cartilage. The cartilage itself has been crushed and partially severed along a very fine line. This is consistent with a thin wire drawn posteriorly with considerable force. The major blood vessels, however, were not lacerated."

"Have you seen cases like this before, Doctor?"

The question came from Dr. Lockie.

Her interruption seemed to startle the man for a moment, obviously unaccustomed to people speaking before he had finished his dictation. He recovered quickly, however, and answered.

"No I haven't, Rowena," he said. "But I am quite versed in the subject. I've always been fascinated by the various devices humans use do one another in. Garrotting with piano wire or its equivalent has been and probably still is a useful method, particularly for clandestine individuals—professional assassins and the like. Silent, and unless the big vessels are cut in the process, it's virtually bloodless. I have many references with pictures if you'd like to see them."

A white coat from the front row spoke up.

"The killer must wear awfully thick gloves not to cut himself in the process."

"Indeed," the doctor said, "although the real professionals use grips attached to either end of the wire very similar to our neurosurgical Gigli saw."

James intended to look up Gigli saw. It sounded fascinating.

Dr. Lockie spoke up again (or Rowena to members of her inner circle, the pathologist obviously one of those).

"Would you say that in order to exert this degree of damage the killer was a person of considerable strength?"

The pathologist smiled.

"Not necessarily. Someone familiar with the technique and perhaps the anatomy could accomplish this with only moderate effort."

Man, woman or husky teenager, James thought.

"Bruising of the skin at the base of the thoracic spine would go along with the findings—a knee in the back—also in the assassin's manual."

James remembered Coswell throwing out the possibility that the killer could have been a woman. Still sharp, the old inspector and he had probably thought through the knee-in-the-back explanation as well. It felt good, though, that he, James, got to say it first.

The rest of the autopsy wasn't of any great interest to anyone, it seemed. There were no more questions, and as soon as the pathologist finished and put down his tools, everyone got up and filed out. Charlotte and Dr. Lockie started up a conversation the second they got outside the autopsy room. James stood beside them, wondering how he would corner Charlotte as Coswell had wanted him to.

"What did you think of that, Charlotte?" Dr. Lockie said.

"Pretty routine, I thought."

"Nothing that makes you wonder?"

"No, but you've had a lot more experience than me. What did you notice?"

Lockie turned to James.

"How about you, Corporal?"

James shrugged his shoulders.

"The partially severed larynx," she said. "A momentary tracheotomy, don't you think?"

The light went on for Charlotte. Not so for James.

"The victim could get some air in through the cut portion," Charlotte said.

"Right. He wouldn't pass out immediately."

James understood.

"He fought for his life," he said. "Probably clawing at his assailant's arms and hands. So strength then would have been a factor; Kelly was a big, powerful man."

"Right," Lockie said. "But he wouldn't have fought for long. Carotids compressed, blood and tissue blocking off his breathing. He would have passed out and then died quickly thereafter."

Charlotte joined in.

"I have samples from under the victim's fingernails. They are on the list for DNA analysis."

"Go for it, Charlotte," Lockie said, and to James:

"The killer may not have thought of handles for his garrotting wire. With all the force he had to apply, his hands would be badly marked."

She smiled and James again thought of his favourite aunt—a wonderfully wise lady.

"Well, I must be off," she said. "Prudhomme needs me, although I have to confess that I need him, too. I hate politics."

"Wish you were back in forensic pathology?" Charlotte said.

Lockie sighed.

"Many times, but I'm getting on, the pay's terrific, and the time off is wonderful. I've actually bought a timeshare in Mexico."

With that she marched off down the hall swinging her purse. James and Charlotte stood speechless for a good half a minute.

"I'll be damned," James said.

"It's really too bad," Charlotte said. "She was one of the best."

James' cell phone rang.

"You answer that," Charlotte said. "I'm off to the lab. See you later."

"But, but—"

She wiggled her fingers at him and walked quickly away.

James looked at the call display—Coswell.

He pushed the talk button and received a terse, "Well?"

James knew Coswell's moods. Something had made him grumpy. Clash with Bostock, maybe?

James related the pathologist's findings.

"So our killer is likely a man," Coswell said. "And what did you get out of Charlotte?"

"She didn't have time to talk to me, but we're meeting later at the forensics lab."

"Good. Call me right after you talk to her."

"How's it going with you?" James said.

"It's going. Now don't forget—right after you talk with Charlotte—call me."

And he was gone.

Coswell tucked his cell phone back into his jacket pocket and waited for Bostock to return from the Commonsblock building. She was right about forensics being their best hope in solving the case. There were just too many names that could be on the suspect list and that included women, despite the report James had just given him. Rage gave prodigious strength to even the weakest individuals. Add to that the fear of Kelly managing to break free and that strength could have doubled. No. Females were still on the list. And then he thought: Why is this word *"female"* coming up so often?

Bostock reappeared in less than ten minutes. Coswell watched her walk briskly toward him, a confident walk but very feminine. He could appreciate McMorran's interest in her. And then he chastised himself. He had to suppress his sexist thoughts. She was his partner, simple as that.

"I've found her, sir," she said when she got back to the cruiser. "She's in her room in the North tower. The receptionist called up and told her we were here. She'll meet us at the front door."

"Good," Coswell said. He should have said "Good work" or "Way to go," or something to that effect, but he was still annoyed that she had probably seen through his dodge about the girl's address.

When they got to the North tower, no one was in the lobby to meet them and the entrance door was locked.

"What's her room number?" Coswell said. "We can slide in when someone comes in or goes out."

"They wouldn't give it to me, even after I showed them my badge. 'Policy' I was told, which I find amazing. I didn't see anything like that at U of M."

"You haven't been listening to west coast news obviously. Women have been attacked on and near this campus recently at an alarming rate."

"I see," she said, frowning.

At that moment the elevator doors opened and a young woman appeared. She was dressed in jeans and a bulky, oversized sweater that almost reached her knees and hid much of her body's shape.

She walked across the lobby to the door and let them in.

"Sorry to keep you waiting," she said. "But I got stuck on the phone."

Coswell wondered at that. Didn't cell phones give people total mobility?

Her room was on the tenth floor. After introductions and while on the way up in the elevator, she carried on a constant chatter.

"My friend," she said. "The girl who was on the bus with me when I saw the guy walk into the parking lot by the Dental building. We both come from Grand Forks. Her room's in the West tower. She called me for the umpteenth time to tell me I was out of my mind getting involved in a murder investigation and that I should just hide."

"Well I'm glad you didn't," Coswell said. "We need more public cooperation like yours."

"More like my Mennonite mother's doing. 'Always be helpful to others,' along with 'Always tell the truth' and stuff like that. My friend's a Doukhobor. They've got a thing about police."

Especially the RCMP, Coswell reflected ... with good reason. In the early 1950s, the Doukhobors disobeyed the provincial compulsory school law, which prompted the government to order the RCMP in to enforce it. This involved separating children from their parents. The Force, naturally, were instantly branded villains and remained so for decades.

Gladys' room was a short distance down a nicely carpeted hallway. "Yeah, dumb, eh?" she said pointing to the door lock and having to use her key to open it. "But there are notices up all over the place to keep our doors locked, even if we're away only for a few minutes."

Another frown from Bostock.

Her room could easily have been an upscale Vancouver West End studio apartment. Just inside the the entrance door and to the left was a complete bathroom with toilet, shower, and vanity, the latter with a sink and an enormous well-lit mirror. A short hallway opened into the bed sitting room. There, a large window gave a panoramic view of Burrard Inlet. A small but fully equipped kitchen was tucked into one corner, the remaining space occupied by a desk, a floor-to-ceiling closet, and a low table upon which sat a Bose sound system. The bed, operated by a Murphy mechanism, was down.

"This is very nice," Coswell said. "When I lived in the Shrum residence way back, our rooms were like monks' cells. The communal bathroom facilities were half way down the hall."

"There are units like that here, too," she said. "But my father sprung for this. All I have to do in return is pass all my exams ... not so easy. In fact, I'd trade the luxury for a little less pressure from dear old dad."

"Hard to do it on your own," Bostock said. "Not many good paying summer jobs for women."

"You got that right, sister."

Coswell felt a twinge of guilt. Money had never been a problem for him in his student years, but even if he didn't have a rich father, any number of good summer jobs would have been available to him.

Seating in Gladys' room was a problem. The only chair was the one at her desk.

"Guest seating, I'm afraid, is the bed," she said, "but you can sit here, Inspector." She pulled the chair out for him.

Deference to my age, Coswell thought.

"No," he said. "Corporal Bostock will do the question-asking. She can sit there. I want to stand and look out at the wonderful view."

Bostock looked surprised but didn't hesitate. With everyone in position, she sitting the desk chair, Gladys on the bed, and Coswell standing at the window, she began.

"I know you told Sergeant McMorran everything

when he had you over at the station, but the atmosphere in a police station can cause witnesses to become confused."

Gladys sat up straight, and once again, got her mouth into gear. "Too true," she said. "That hard chair, those guys in Mountie suits standing around, looking down at me, and that Sergeant guy—whoosh, what an intense Alpha male he is. I'm not easily intimidated, but I was no match for him."

She rattled on.

"By the time he finished, I was close to saying that I saw pimples on the killer's face and the smoking gun in his hand."

"He led you?" Bostock said with genuine surprise.

"Like a lamb to the slaughter," she said. "Those car silhouettes he made me look at were the last straw. I pretty much picked one at random. I really have no idea what the car I saw looked like. I don't know cars from Adam."

"But you did see someone walking quickly from the anatomy buildings to the parking lot and getting into a vehicle?"

"Yes. That I did see. It's why I called after hearing the request on campus radio. Figured it was about time some of the violent jerks hanging around this place got caught."

"I'm not pressing you in any way," Bostock said, "but I'd like you to just close your eyes for a moment, pretend we're not here, and replay in your mind what you saw."

Gladys gave a big grin.

"Like self-hypnosis and truth serum without the serum?" she said. "I should be good at this. I'm a psych major."

She closed her eyes and remained silent for a full half minute, an effort for her, Coswell thought, but she was obviously enjoying the exercise. Without opening her eyes, she started to speak.

"Lydia, that's my friend, and I are sitting on the left side of the bus. I'm closest to the window. We've run out of things to say so I'm looking out and thinking how quiet everything was on campus at that time of night."

"Did you by any chance look at your watch when you had that thought?" Bostock said.

Eyes still closed, Gladys answered.

"Yes, I did. Like I told the sergeant. Eleven o'clock."

"Go on."

"Everything was so still that I guess it was the movement that caught my eye—the figure coming out of the dark into the lighted parking lot. I only watched him for a few seconds. He got into the car quickly and our bus moved past so I lost sight of him. I did notice his lights come on, though. He swung out real fast. Must have floored it."

She opened her eyes.

"But I really didn't see any details, so I'm probably not much help to you."

"You are being very helpful," Bostock said. "Now just a few questions."

"Shoot. I'm ready and a ton more relaxed than last time."

"You said 'he' and 'him.' What made you think it was a man?"

"Female bias?" she said, glancing over at Coswell and then laughed. "Just kidding, Inspector."

She turned back to Bostock.

"It was the stride and the swing of his arms. No femininity there, for sure, and when he got into the car he moved like an athlete—a male athlete."

Coswell knew he should let Bostock carry on but she'd drawn him into her interrogation. His question popped out before he could stop it.

"Sergeant McMorran told me you thought the man was over six feet tall, hatless, and wearing a seaman's type coat. By that I assumed he meant a Pea jacket."

"I'd lost it by then," Gladys said. "He asked me if the

man was wearing a coat and what length it was—full, three quarters, half. Good god, all I saw was a figure. I just guessed and he seemed happy with the three quarters. I didn't say anything about a Pea jacket."

"And the man's height?" Bostock said, seemingly unperturbed by Coswell's interruption.

"He said, 'How much of the man's head stuck up above the roof of his car when he got in?' Right, like I really had time to make a long-distance measurement. He got to the car and then into it in one motion. I made another guess to make the sergeant happy and said, 'his whole head.' Does that interpret as over six feet? I have no idea."

And then another thought.

"He might have worn a hat, too. A baseball hat, I think. I forgot to mention that."

"Just one last question," Bostock said. "Were you curious enough to look and see if the car passed your bus?"

"I was actually. We'd just seen one of those old crime movies at the Ridge and I had 'thief' stuck in my mind when I saw him. The car didn't pass us and I'm sure of that because our bus had shifted over to the curb lane so I would have seen him coming up on the inside."

Bostock looked over at Coswell.

"Do you have anything you'd like to ask, sir?" she said. "I'm through."

"No," Coswell said. "You've given us a very good account, Gladys, and again, I thank you."

He took one last look across to the North Shore mountains and turned to leave.

"Don't let us interrupt your studying." he said. "We can find our way out."

Gladys got up and followed them to her door, holding it open for them. Coswell let Bostock go first, and as he passed by Gladys he stopped and turned to her.

"If Sergeant McMorran calls upon you again for any reason, I want you to refer him directly to me. Tell him

Inspector Coswell gave you firm instructions to do so."

He handed her one of his cards.

"Should you have any problems with him, call my mobile number."

CHAPTER TEN

On the walk back to the cruiser, Coswell decided to clarify his antipathy towards McMorran.

"I guess it's pretty obvious that I have no great love for Sergeant McMorran," he said, "but I can assure you, it's based on good reason."

"I'm sure it is, sir."

"You looked surprised when Gladys described how he questioned her."

"I was. Leading a witness is not something I'd expect from a man of his rank."

Coswell nodded in agreement and then said. "Let me put the man in simple perspective for you and I do that not just to bad mouth the guy but to give you warning."

He could sense her ears perk.

"Sergeant McMorran, for want of a better description, is a buccaneer who wants to be captain of the ship, and he'll go to any lengths to achieve that.

And then, feeling that he'd said too much, he changed the subject.

"Now let's go find that first-year med student, Frank, uh—"

"Hoffmann," she said. "He was near the top of James' suspect list."

"Right."

Bostock likely wanted to hear more about McMorran, but Coswell was not about to be forthcoming and questioned himself as to why he even bothered to explain. Wouldn't it have been better to just let her form her own impressions? James certainly wasn't shy about digging the whole story out of him, but this woman just let it drop. What was she thinking?

When he drove the cruiser into the Dentistry building parking lot, he had another change of mind.

"Interviewing Gladys in her residence seemed to work well. I think we'll do the same with Frank Hoffmann. You go to Professor Dietrich's office and get them to give us his address. I'm going to call James and see if he's met with Charlotte yet."

"Not yet," James said over their phone connection. "She's in with Marie D'Allarde. I'm cooling my heels in the waiting room."

"Damn that Charlotte," Coswell said. "We won't get a thing out of her. It'll have to come from Marie."

"Is that so bad?" James said.

"No, but it'll mean my coming down there. Marie likes her performances."

True. Marie D'Allarde, the head of the forensics unit, liked to amuse herself by personally doling out the findings of her crew in face-to-face meetings with investigating officers.

"Okay if I attend, too?" James said.

"I'd be disappointed if you didn't."

A brief pause and then:

"Not going so well with your new partner?"

"She's okay."

"But not as much fun as me, I'll bet."

"Lot of baggage there. Doesn't look like it's going to unload any time soon."

"Patience, sir, patience."

"Just get us a time to meet with Marie and call me back when you've got it."

"Right."

"And...."

"And what?"

"See if you can dig out some information on Bostock. When Ward's gone to the golf course, bring Jane coffee and donuts or something. Maybe she'll let you peek at that file the Chief's got stowed away."

"Sir! I am shocked."

"Oh never mind. It was just a thought."

It took Bostock longer to come back from her errand than he expected—almost fifteen minutes.

"What was the problem?" he said when she slid back into the passenger seat.

"I can't believe the lack of cooperation around here," she said. "You'd think I was some peon messenger."

A little show of anger, Coswell noted. That's good.

"Dietrich's secretary sent me over to the Dean's office, which, fortunately, is just in behind the anatomy building. The signage, however, is terrible. It took me a while to find the place."

She took a deep breath, slightly winded from hurrying back.

"And then I had to stand, cap in hand, until they found some underling to go find the address for me."

"Maybe if you had cap on your head and full uniform they would have jumped to more quickly."

She gave him a soured look that said "That's not funny."

"Just joking," he said. "Your badge should have done it. But don't fret, we'll jerk more than a few academic chains around here before we're finished."

This seemed to pacify her.

"He lives in Robson House. That's one of the residences in Place Vanier. I have everything including his room number and his roommate's name—Wing Chu."

"Robson House!" Coswell said. "That's where I stayed when I was a student. Don't tell me it's still standing after all these years."

"Appears so, sir. I have a map if you've forgotten where it is."

He looked at her but there didn't appear to be any ridicule in her eyes.

His cell phone buzzed. It was James. Marie would meet them at two o'clock in her office. Charlotte had to leave immediately on another case so once again he had gotten nothing from her other than a quick "Sorry."

"All right then," Coswell said. "It's on to the VGH. We'll meet with Mabel, the ward aid. Did James tell you about her?"

"Yes. The hospital gossip."

"Let's hope she's more like an interested observer."

They lucked out with Mabel. She was just about to start her lunch break.

"I like the early time," she said. "I have a six o'clock breakfast so I'm starving by eleven."

She was a grey-haired, matronly lady with a cheery smile and a rosy face. She would have been a natural to play Santa Claus' wife.

She held up her lunch bucket.

"Ugly, I know," she said. "It was my late husband's but it feels good having something of his with me over lunch. Practical, too."

She led them outside down a flight of stairs to Heather Street and then across to three unoccupied benches adjacent to a courtesy bus stop. A city trash bin completed the seating area.

"I like to come here on nice days," Mabel said. "No one ever uses these for some reason or other."

She opened her lunch kit and took out a Thermos. "I'm sorry, I don't have extra cups or I'd offer you some tea."

"No matter. We're off to lunch ourselves soon," Coswell said. "You go ahead and eat yours. We just have a few questions for you."

They felt a bit strange interviewing in what was really a very public place—people walking right by them, cars close on the narrow street, taxis, bicycles, but no one appeared to pay any attention to them.

"I get kind of peopled out over the day," Mabel said, "and I find it very private here despite all the bustle. I know at least half of the people who work at the hospital, so lunch in the cafeteria is definitely not private."

She carefully unwrapped a sandwich, and was about to take a bite when she stopped and looked at them shyly.

"And I like to talk to George sometimes. He's been gone a year now, but I still feel he's close by."

That stopped Coswell for a moment. Grilling sweet old ladies was not his forte. He preferred hard-nosed criminals. Bostock, however, seemed to have no compunctions.

"Quite understandable," she said. "I was the same when my father passed away, but we truly need to disturb you only for a few minutes."

"That's okay," Mabel said. "You go right ahead."

Coswell gave Bostock the nod to proceed. She returned his nod and began.

"You've heard by now I'm sure, that Doctor Kelly was murdered out at the university."

Mabel laughed.

"Word of that went through the hospital like wildfire."

"With mixed feelings, we understand."

Mabel looked at her as though trying to read Bostock's mind.

"If you mean he wasn't loved by one and all, you are correct."

"Could you elaborate on that for us?"

"Well, in my opinion, and it's only my opinion, Dr. Lord Kelly should have stayed in Britain where lords get away with being high and mighty. Dr. Struthers is such a nice person and to be replaced by the likes of that man? Ugh!"

She accentuated her disgust with a deep frown before continuing.

"I didn't have much to do with him, of course, being on a medical ward, but I've heard terrible stories."

"Such as?"

"Molesting the nurses and female students, shouting at people in the OR, snubbing some of our most respected doctors. And his night life—disgraceful behaviour for the Head of Surgery in the biggest hospital in BC."

"Disgraceful? How?'

"I've heard, and again it's only something I've heard—he caroused into the wee hours at some Irish pub downtown, making a spectacle of himself, singing and carrying on."

Coswell thought that such behavior in an Irish pub was probably normal.

"Can you give me some names, strictly confidential of course, of the people who told you that?" Bostock said. "We are trying to get a picture of this man and information like yours is very helpful."

"No harm, I guess," Mabel said. "It was one of the surgical fellows that told me about Kelly's shenanigans. I've forgotten his name. He only came the once to my ward to do a consult. All I remember is that he had really red hair."

Coswell remembered the red-haired white coat who was one of the Xs on James interview list, although he, too, couldn't remember the man's name. James would, though.

Since Bostock seemed to have run out of questions and he couldn't think of any, he got up from the bench.

"Thank you so much for your help, Mabel—?"

"Pucket," she said. "Mabel Pucket."

Bostock got up as well, but just as they turned to leave, Coswell had a thought.

"Does Dr. Montgomery ever come to your ward?

She has something to do with neurology. That's medical, correct?"

Mabel smiled.

"Yes, neurology is a medical specialty, but it has its own ward, one floor up from mine. And Dr. Montgomery is a neuropathologist. She sees them after they're dead—in the morgue."

"Oh I see," Coswell said.

Mabel picked up on his disappointment.

"But my best friend Judy Sim is the ward aid up there and she keeps me informed."

Mabel put her fingers to her lips.

"Confidential again, eh? But Judy tells me she thinks there's a thing going on between Dr. Barrett and Dr. Montgomery."

"And Dr. Barrett is...?"

"A clinical neurologist. He sees live patients."

"What is he like, say compared to Dr. Kelly?"

"Like night and day," Mabel said. "Dr. Barrett is a nice, dignified man, a sharp dresser, and always a bow tie."

Coswell couldn't see how bow tie and sharp dressing went together but then he was no fashion expert. He'd ask James. Perhaps a character message there.

As they turned to walk away, Mabel had one last comment, that gave credence to her reputation as a gossip.

"Shame about Dr. Barrett's poor wife, though. She has multiple sclerosis, and him a neurologist."

On the walk back to the cruiser, Coswell concentrated on where to have lunch. But he was in a quandary now—how to ditch Bostock for a couple of hours and enjoy a break from her.

He looked at his watch.

"Damn, I almost forgot. I have a meeting with my

accountant at twelve fifteen today," he said. "Let's see what James is up to. Maybe you can do lunch with him and go over what we've gathered this morning."

Before she could reply, he had his cell phone out and speed-dialed James, who was back at headquarters. He said he would be delighted to have lunch with Bostock.

"Settled then," Coswell said. "I'll drop you off and pick you up again at one thirty. That will be plenty of time to get us to Marie D'Allarde's office."

He glanced over at her. No reaction, but then he didn't expect one, his excuse too smooth. He congratulated himself.

Now, where to have lunch? Somewhere to spoil himself a bit. The Vicinage on Fourth? Why not? Lord knows he had been there often enough for dinner; they should find a table for him.

James was standing in the headquarters parking lot waiting for Coswell to drop Bostock off. Ward was in his office, barking orders to Jane, his long suffering secretary. He sounded like he was in a particularly bad mood for the day and James had no wish to be caught meeting with Bostock, hence the parking lot.

As she walked towards him, he suddenly felt a wave of compassion for her. She looked so sad. He gave her his brightest smile.

"We're having lunch," he said. "How wonderful. A pleasant change from lunch with the boss. He can be such a grump at times."

He took her arm and turned her around, noting the stiffness he felt when he first took hold.

"We'll do the exotic Gino's again, if you don't mind. It's handy and they do have healthy choices. We'll go Dutch, so no fumbling for the check. I get enough practice at that with the inspector."

He felt her arm relax and she smiled.

"Gino's is fine," she said, "and I read the choices while I held the table for you and the inspector. There are some good ones."

He released her arm and off they went.

Gino's was packed when they arrived but they did manage to get stools side by side at the long window table. Both ordered the sesame shiitake and smoked tofu with hoisin and sriracha. It came too, with a generous portion of five-spice yam chips in a paper cone. To drink—herbal tea, times two.

James set the rules.

"No shop talk until this is all gone," he said. "Agreed?"

"Agreed," she said.

And it did get all eaten, with relish, and only then did they start up a conversation between sips of their herbal tea. James first.

"Not like our Inspector Coswell to miss out on lunch," he said. "That accountant meeting must have been important. Maybe he's getting audited by Revenue Canada."

She looked out the window, seemingly gathering her thoughts.

"It was forced, that accountant thing," she said. "I have a gift, if you want to call it that. I see through subterfuge very quickly. He just wanted a recess from me."

James' eyes widened.

"Are you sure? He's not in the habit of lying, even little white ones. Did something go wrong out there this morning?"

"Nothing I can point my finger at, but I couldn't help feeling I was a ball and chain he had to drag around."

James took a sip of his tea.

"May I offer something to you?" he said. "And it's a genuine offer from someone who knows what it's like to be an outcast in this wonderful Force of ours. And as a gay man, I can say this with all sincerity—let's be friends."

She held his gaze for a moment and then her eyes softened. "Accepted," she said. "And you may be the first and last so far as work is concerned, but I appreciate it."

"That's a girl," he said, and then catching himself, "Oh my, am I being politically incorrect?"

She smiled.

"Only one proviso to the friend agreement," she said. "Promise we won't ever worry about political correctness between us."

"Promise. Now tell James what happened this morning."

And she did, in great detail. When she had finished, James was astonished.

"You did a terrific job—both of you. Coswell should be jumping with joy. What is wrong with that man?"

She looked at him—resigned.

"I really don't know. If I had to guess, it would be because I'm not you."

"That's ridiculous."

"I'm not so sure. Every person I've spoken to about the man extols his self confidence and keen mind. I didn't see that today and I think it's because of me."

James thought for a moment.

"You know, when you're with someone day after day, subtle changes do go unnoticed. If I force myself to compare when I first started with him and how he's been the last few months, I have to say that he has lost something."

He frowned but then continued.

"No. Damn it. I think he puts on a lot of that memory loss business. Don't be surprised if he comes from way out in left field and solves the whole thing in a flash. You wouldn't believe how often just that has happened."

"I hope you are right," she said. "And I'll stop being so sensitive. If he wants me to shut up, all he has to do is say so."

James chuckled.

"You might consider actually saying that to him. Between you and me—he's intimated that he really wants to get to know you."

"Really?" she said, stunned.

"Really."

Coswell was not happy. When he got to The Vicinage, the place was not only full; there was a lineup at the door. He could have squeezed by and Nina, his favourite hostess, would have found him a corner somewhere, but being a bully was not in his nature. He opted instead for Le Boeuf D'Or Restaurant in Gastown.

En route to the restaurant, he decided that Le Boeuf D'Or was actually a better choice, and lunch there could be considered work related since it was just across the street from the Auld Sod Pub. He had managed to Google Irish pubs in Vancouver on the cruiser's inboard computer. Most were in the upscale hotel district downtown, but the Auld Sod was much more East Side. It was not all that far from his condominium in Chinatown. He reasoned that Kelly would feel more at home doing his carousing there and it did advertise itself as Vancouver's top Irish pub.

Coswell had never been inside the place.

He was not, however, a stranger at Le Boeuf D'Or, one of Vancouver's finest gourmet restaurants. Despite his loyalty to The Vicinage on Fourth, occasionally he had a craving for beef, and Le Boeuf D'Or's steak Diane was to die for.

The restaurant is located on the site of Vancouver's first jailhouse and Coswell was seated in a room that originally might have been part of the prisoners' exercise yard. Tables are closely set along one windowed side and opposite is a two-storey brick wall with faux peeling plaster. The ceiling is so high it is almost out of sight, but hanging down from it and hiding long heating ducts is the most extraordinary chandelier made up from a tangle of driftwood branches.

Coswell's Steak Diane was excellent as always, and the charred onions and potato fondant that accompanied it were perfect. He'd always felt that beef dishes should not be complicated by a salad or exotic vegetable creation.

He didn't need the sommelier to advise him on the appropriate red, but he listened anyway. The man spoke with a dignified authority. The '11 Côtes du Rhône, they decided, would be the best choice to go with his meal.

He was tempted to have the warm chocolate and caramelized banana tarte with lime ice cream for dessert but opted for a cappuccino instead. Sugar, it seemed, was tending to make him sleepy lately, although he could usually offset the effect with strong coffee.

When the waiter brought him his cappuccino, Coswell went into expense justification mode. He flashed his badge and told the man that he was investigating the recent murder of a Vancouver surgeon who may have dined at Le Boeuf D'Or. The waiter, whose name was Carl, responded with surprising enthusiasm.

"Dr. Kelly," he said. "I heard about it on the news, and yes, he has been here—once."

"Only once?"

"Yes and it goes back almost a year now. He came in late with two or three of his rowdy friends. We'd almost closed for the night, but he used the 'I'm a VIP' routine to bully our poor hostess. She seated them, but I was their lucky server or I would have been if it wasn't for Alain, our sommelier. He's Swiss."

"You don't bully the Swiss I take it."

"Darn right. Alain told them they'd had too much to drink. He refused to take their liquor orders and right-fully so; one of the party was almost ready to keel over. Kelly was loud but seemed to be in control, although he was furious when Alain wouldn't bend. He cursed him something awful but eventually they all got up and left."

"Over to the Irish pub across the street, do you think?"

"Yes and that's probably where they came from in the first place. We watched them stagger across the street and go in. I guess it was noisy and busy enough in there they could still get service, although I wonder how long that lasted. The Auld Sod I'm sure is as sensitive as we are about getting sued because some drunk they served gets in an accident."

"Yes. I've read some of those decisions."

"Not fair. If you can't hold your liquor, you shouldn't drink, or at least do it at home."

"I totally agree with you."

Coswell paid his bill, adding on a generous tip, and left the restaurant feeling doubly good: the meal had fired up his energy again, along with his mood and best of all, he had gathered useful information. The Auld Sod, he felt, was worthy of a full scale visit—going incognito and at night when Kelly's crowd would be there.

But it was getting close to one thirty. He had to pick up Bostock and head over to the forensics lab to meet with Marie D'Allarde. James could make his own way over. Best to keep an arm's length facade going, although he hated tip toeing around Ward.

CHAPTER ELEVEN

Marie D'Allarde, MA, PhD, was chief of the RCMP forensics unit, a civilian on a contract that was virtually renewed automatically whenever it came up. She was brilliant and had run the unit for over fifteen years. She was the same age as Coswell, but her round face was wrinkle free and she dyed her hair the second a bit of grey appeared among the black. Her French accent was as strong as ever.

As usual she was seated at her desk, her laptop

computer set up in front of her. She stood up when the three of them entered and came around to their side.

"Ah, Coswell and James, le duo dynamique—but who is this with you?"

Bostock stepped forward and extended her hand.

"Janet Bostock, Dr. D'Allarde. I'm new."

"Corporal Bostock," Coswell added.

D'Allarde took Bostock's hand in both of hers and smiled broadly. "Now le trio dynamique, n'est-ce pas?"

Coswell managed to grasp the word "trio," but before he could reply, James, who spoke fluent French, answered.

"No. I've been reassigned. I'm now the liaison officer with the coroner's office."

Her surprise was only momentary.

"Is that up, down, or sideways?" she said. "But never mind. I won't pry. You are here to get a boost up in your investigation of this terrible murder. Forensics comes to the rescue again."

She turned around and gathered up her computer.

"Let's go down to the boardroom," she said. "Much more comfortable there than peering over my shoulder here."

Coswell was hoping that he wouldn't have to do a lot of peering at anything. Marie's summations were enough—complete and to the point.

The boardroom was small and almost filled with a large, oblong hardwood table and eight chairs. There were large windows on the street side which were covered with gauze curtains filmy enough to filter the view to the outside and reduce distractions during boring meetings, Coswell supposed.

Something different from Marie's usual report this time was a projector on an arm which she pulled out and plugged into her computer. They were going to peer whether they liked it or not.

Screen after screen flew by, projected onto the end

wall. Marie gave a running commentary, which James and Bostock seemed to follow with interest. Coswell soon got lost in the minutia and waited for her summary.

Finally, it came.

"In short," she said. "We have a killer who left very little trace of himself—almost professional I'd say. The bits of cloth fabric we got just outside the fire door came from disposable booties. He also obviously wore gloves, which explains the absence of fingerprints and as you saw, we fingerprinted absolutely everything. A sample from an elevator door jamb has proved difficult to analyze. Charlotte is still working on it."

She turned off the projector and closed her computer.

"Now," she said. "Let's have those brilliant investigator questions."

No one spoke for a moment as all three tried to assimilate the findings. Coswell started off.

"I see on the path report that time of death was eleven p.m., give or take thirty minutes. Can you really be that accurate?"

She gave a short huff.

"Of course. This is the twenty-first century and we have the best forensics crew in Western Canada, maybe even all of Canada. In fact, I think the thirty minutes is a bit overdone."

She turned to Bostock. "How about you, young lady? Women, I think, have a perceptive advantage over men. Men, of course, eventually get it, but not so rapidement."

Bostock blushed.

"Er, I was wondering about the victim," she said. "Am I correct in saying that aside from the high alcohol content in his blood, there was nothing to suggest drug use—needle marks, nasal mucosal changes?"

Marie smiled.

"Definitely not. We are quite used to dealing with dead drug addicts in Vancouver, but you are thinking. Very good."

Still blushing, Bostock risked one more question.

"Under the victim's fingernails. I've been told that he was a large, powerful man. I would have expected him to claw away at his attacker."

"I thought as you did," Marie said. "But Charlotte tells me she was very thorough in her collection and those specimens were analyzed to the nth degree—some of his own skin cells, that's all."

"Knee in the back," Coswell said. "The killer kept him away even if Kelly did fight back. The only thing he got hold of was the skin of his own neck trying to grasp the garrotting wire."

Marie leaned over to Bostock, and said in a low voice, "See. The brilliant investigator."

Coswell's turn to blush, but not enough for anyone to notice. He felt more like a nap than working all of a sudden and this bothered him. Normally, the challenges of a murder investigation kept him going all day. Too big a lunch maybe? No, that was nothing new. Depression? Marie D'Allarde's forensic report was a big disappointment. So far as he could tell, it pointed nowhere. But two young, bright minds might have caught something.

"I feel like some exercise," he said when they returned to street level. "Let's all go for a walk. Fresh air in the lungs and blood pumping to our brains, eh? Help us get a perspective of just where we are with this case."

James was astonished.

"Exercise? My, my, is this the new Inspector Coswell?"

"Don't be cheeky, James. That walk home from the office yesterday was truly stimulating and I plan to do a lot more of it. Now let's hear your views on what's gone on so far and where to go next."

Coswell didn't know Burnaby well, but he did know that Central Park was just a couple of blocks from the building that housed the forensics lab. His sore feet could manage that far and he was certain that Central Park would have plenty of benches.

Bostock immediately dropped behind the two men as they walked along the narrow sidewalk. Convenient, Coswell thought. He really wanted to hear James' view.

And James didn't hesitate.

"The word 'professional' has come up twice now—me at the beginning and Dr. D'Allarde in her summary," he said. "Although stripping the body and laying it butt side up in a coffin does not sound professional to me. I suppose someone could have hired the killer and gave him instructions to do that. Either way, the motive is hate, no doubt about it."

To Coswell's annoyance, James turned his head and spoke to Bostock.

"What do you think?"

"I agree," she said. "The only other reason I can think of is a gang thing, and they did that as a message to someone."

Coswell almost turned around. That had not occurred to him and it should have.

James continued.

"Good suggestion," he said. "But who would get the message? A medical student? Someone on the staff? From what we've heard so far, Kelly didn't have much to do with anyone out there."

"Right," Coswell said, relieved. "And no description in the press about the bare ass presentation, so it wouldn't serve as a message to anyone outside the anatomy lab."

But she was right. Out of a hundred medical students and a dozen plus staff, there could be a rotten apple or two who did something to trigger such a message; drugs were the likely cause and that meant organized crime. He would keep that in the back of his mind but meanwhile, James' suggestion seemed the most logical.

"Okay," he said. "Let's go with the hate motive. Who

did he anger so badly that it got him killed."

"The list so far is pretty pathetic, I'm afraid," James replied. "Frank Hoffmann, the failed student, is the only one we know of so far who could be in that category, but he has an ironclad alibi—studying with his roommate, Wing Chu, on the night of the murder. There's the wife, of course, an unknown at this moment. She could be the key to the whole thing."

"And she's back tomorrow," Coswell said. "A most important interview."

"Yes," James said. "And you and Bostock will no doubt wring the solution from her."

Bostock. Coswell almost cringed. No help from James.

They had nearly reached the park and its welcome benches but Coswell stopped.

"That's far enough," he said. "We've got some loose ends to tie up before tomorrow. Back to the horses."

By the time they returned to the parking lot, Coswell's feet were killing him. He headed straight for the cruiser.

"I'd better go back to headquarters," James said, "but I think I'll stop in for a few minutes first at the coroner's office and see if Dr. Lockie has some make-work for me to do."

What Coswell was sure he meant was—"get back to working with Bostock, your new partner." The rat.

He dropped Bostock off at headquarters with a long list of tedious research: background checks on Kelly, Frank Hoffmann, and as many of the staff and medical students as she could get through on James' campus list.

"And as much as you can get on Dr. Montgomery, the divorce proceedings in particular," he said. "We want to be well prepared when we meet with her tomorrow. You can set that up as well. I'd prefer the morning, but the doctor is just getting back from Edmonton, so better make it the afternoon."

She responded to the tasks with surprising enthusiasm.

THE EXTRA CADAVER MURDER

"I'll get in touch with that cleaning firm as well," she said. "James didn't have time to get around to it."

"Good," he said. "Now, I have to be off to the Justice Institute. One of those coordinated police services be-buddies affairs. I'm knocking off after that and going home, so we'll meet again here tomorrow at eight o'clock. Okay?"

"Right, sir," she said. "Have a good evening."

Coswell took off in the cruiser and headed south on Main Street, his mind filled with angst. These little lies were catching up with him. He couldn't mention the information he had gotten about Kelly and the Auld Sod Pub; supposedly he was meeting with his accountant over the lunch period. But Bostock's gang suggestion intrigued him. He thought of the Mafia and how they stuck a bird in a stool pigeon's mouth after killing him. Kelly's nude posterior could have been a similar message.

Marie had ruled out the kinky sex as a possibility with a quick "Negative for any signs of recent sexual activity, either anterior or posterior." Nicely put.

He pointed the cruiser down Main Street and drove leisurely. When he passed the Vancouver Pacific Train Station where he had caught a cab back to his condo the previous evening, the distance he had walked seemed disappointedly little. He continued down Main, past the old Carnegie Centre on his left. He chuckled to think that old Carnegie would probably not be amused that the wonderfully elegant building he donated ended up in the downtown eastside surrounded by less than elegant bars, one star hotels, and pedestrian traffic consisting of the homeless, the addicted, and the lost.

A little further along he passed the Main Vancouver City Police Station on his right, which brought back memory of his meeting with PC Constable Wilkinson and their united concern over McMorran's drug unit tactics.

He turned left on Powell Street and again on Carrall,

both one-way streets, a boon to sensible vehicular traffic but not to street parking. There was nothing in front of The Auld Sod Pub but he did manage to duck into a spot around the corner on Cordova. As reasonable insurance, he unlatched the inboard computer and tucked it under the seat.

The happy hour crowd was just beginning to form in the pub but there were still seats at the bar. He walked to the very end and sat down. Two burly men and one woman were behind the bar. The woman came to take his order. She was wearing a large, fuzzy green leprechaun hat that dwarfed her thin face and made her look top heavy.

The wine list was quite reasonable for a pub. He ordered a glass of New Zealand Sauvignon blanc which he thought would avoid disappointment after the wonderful red he drank at lunch.

When the leprechaun lady returned with his wine, he took out his wallet and held it open, being sure that she could see his shield.

"I'm only having this one glass," he said. "I'll pay for it now."

"Eight dollars," she said.

He handed her a twenty.

"If you answer a few quick questions for me," he said. "You can keep the change."

She hesitated.

"We're getting awfully busy," she said. "But if it's quick, okay."

"Doctor Kelly was a customer here, probably many times. What can you tell me about him, who he drank with, his behaviour?"

She leaned over, arching her neck to keep the hat from falling off. "He was a pig and I'm glad he's dead."

"That's a good start," Coswell said.

"Sat over there," she said, pointing to a corner. "A reserved sign on it after ten."

One of the male bartenders was calling to her.

"Margie. For Christ's sake, move around. We can't handle it all."

"Got to go," she said. "I'll bring your change. I need this job."

"Keep it," Coswell said. "Just tell me the best time to come when the people Kelly was drinking with will be here."

"Pretty much any night after ten," she said. "I think they use this place as their office."

"Thanks," he said, pulling out another twenty and slipping it across the counter to her. "And I'd appreciate it if you kept our little conversation confidential."

The bill disappeared quickly into her pocket.

"You got it," she said, and then moved off swiftly, first to the till, and then she started taking orders from the growing number of demanding patrons.

Bostock decided that life was beginning to look up for her. She was glad Coswell gave her plenty to do while he was off at his meeting, and she thought she had done pretty well over the day. She was half way through the background checks and hadn't found anything of note—not even a DUI, which was a surprise in Kelly's case. He was supposed to have been a heavy drinker.

The two anatomy lab assistants were at the top of the list. One, a Dr. Debas, was of Ethiopian descent, but turned out to be a British citizen. The other, Dr. Tynan, was from Ireland. She debated extending her checks into the databanks of their home countries, but that would be time consuming and Coswell seemed particularly keen to get all the information on the Kelly-Montgomery divorce—a time consuming task on its own.

She was about to start on the second half of the list when James walked in.

"Deserted by the inspector again?" he said.

She told him about the Justice Institute meeting.

"So what did he leave for you to do?"

She caught the millisecond pause before his question, the Justice Institute meeting seemingly a surprise to him.

"Is that meeting a regular event?" she said. "I got the impression that it was. A 'coordinated police services be-buddies affair' is how he described it."

James pulled over a chair and sat beside her.

"It may have been a last-minute directive from Chief Ward. He does come up with these things every so often. Good PR and all that."

"No," Bostock said. "He would have said that. I think he wanted another recess."

James sighed.

"You could be right. Now let's try to think why, and don't tell me it's because you're not me. I think you've taken over my position beautifully. You got right into the discussion with Marie D'Allarde."

"With a couple of weak suggestions. You really lead the way."

"Now stop putting yourself down. You got into the Force as a woman—not easy, and you made corporal—even harder. I know. I worked my lovely butt off to rise above the pack. You obviously did the same."

"My lovely butt so far has caused nothing but problems, but that's a long story."

"Which I hope you'll tell me some time."

She smiled.

"Maybe. But right now I'd like some advice on how to make myself more acceptable to your former partner."

James leaned back and looked at her for a moment.

"I think you scare him."

"What? You've got to be kidding."

"No. Now let's just think about that. I've gotten along with him by being facetious as hell most of the time. I think he looks at my suggestions, the good ones at least, as flukes. You, on the other hand, come across as a deep-thinking person, deadly serious, and when you offer a suggestion, he knows it's been thought through with care and he'd better take notice. Somehow he finds that threatening."

She laughed.

"I'm about as threatening as a marshmallow and you don't fool me. There is nothing fluky about your thought processes. You're sharp."

James gave her a limp hand drop.

"I'll bet you say that to all the boys."

She reached across and punched his shoulder.

"You sound like my big brother," she said. "He loved to call me Joyless Janet."

"That's better. Now doesn't a little humour brighten the day?"

"It does, James, it does, and thanks."

He got up and pushed his chair back against the wall.

"I'm glad to be of help and if there is anything else I can do for you, let me know. In fact, I really hope there is, because I'm getting SO DAMNED BORED!"

"Did Dr. Lockie not find anything for you to do?"

"Let's just say my new post is in its formative stages. So far it appears that my role will be to follow Charlotte around and be the Force spokesperson for the media. That means back in uniform. In fact, I'm off to my apartment to find the wretched thing and get it dry cleaned."

"I think you'll make the perfect media rep. We need our image spruced up a bit."

Another hand flop.

"Now just stop it. You're making me so puffed up."

He started to leave but at the door he stopped and turned back. "Oh, I almost forgot. Let him do all the driving. Our inspector suffers from extreme motion sickness and hates to admit it."

When James left, Bostock felt her mood start to slip

again. She had overreacted to the driving incident. She quickly returned to her list. Work is what she needed.

Wednesday

Coswell didn't make it into the office until almost eight thirty; another night of too much wine and reading those disturbing books on Alzheimer's disease. He had actually moved on from the signs and symptoms tome to the book that the librarian had suggested, *Living with Alzheimer's*. He hadn't intended to read it but since he was now convinced that he was in the early stages, he might as well find out what his life would eventually become.

Bostock was alone in the office, working away on her computer. He desperately needed a coffee again. He barely had time to shave, let alone eat any sort of breakfast, and he had told Bostock he would meet her at eight.

"Sorry, I'm late," he said. "The cruiser was a bitch to get started this morning and the traffic up Main was dreadful."

The traffic *was* heavy and it took him a while to get the cruiser going because he forgot the keys on his kitchen table and had to go back for them. Also, the resident only parking was jammed as usual and he had to park two blocks away from his condo. So all in all, not much of stretch, although he shouldn't have used the word "bitch."

"No problem," she said. "I needed a little extra time this morning to get my report ready for you."

He was not anxious to hear any report until he had coffee and something full of calories for his stomach.

"Why don't you print it out and bring it along to Gino's? That way we won't be disturbed and I can concentrate without being interrupted by the desk phone, or worse, Chief Ward. He's about due to call me into his office again."

"Fine, sir. It'll just take me a few minutes. I did get a

time, by the way, for us to interview Dr. Montgomery—
two thirty this afternoon. I hope that's okay with you."

"It is," he said. Lots of time to get his brain into full
gear. He also hoped that her few minutes would really be
few because he was beginning to feel light headed.

CHAPTER TWELVE

They managed to hit one of the rare lulls at Gino's, only
two people ahead of them. Coswell quickly cut off the
argument over who was to pay.

"You've been working while I've been doing nothing
so far this morning. Besides, I'm having more than coffee
and I presume you had a very good breakfast again."

To his surprise, she didn't object.

"Thank you," she said. "I'll just have a coffee, black
please, and I see an empty table. I'll go over and hold it."

She said that with a smile. More surprise. But the
no-nonsense girl behind the counter was waiting for his
order and she wasn't smiling.

"A large cappuccino, a cinnamon bun, and a date
square," he said. "Oh, and a coffee for my partner, black.
Medium, I guess."

All but the cappuccino came up immediately. There
were two lattés ahead of him and so he took Bostock's
coffee and his breakfast over to the table she'd reserved.

"I bought you a date square," he said," but if you don't
want it, okay."

"Thank you. It looks delicious. My mom used to make
these."

He went back for his cappuccino, slightly disappointed,
but her cheery mood more than made up for the date
square and once he got into the bun, and the caffeine hit
his bloodstream, he thought he might feel cheery himself.

She had the good sense not to speak while he drank

the cappuccino and made it half way through the cinnamon bun. Finally, he spoke.

"Okay," he said. "Why don't you give me your report."

She opened a manila folder and, to Coswell's horror, pulled out a considerable stack of paper.

"Uh, perhaps you could summarize that," he said. "Just give me the pertinent material."

She pulled the first sheet off the pile.

"I've done that," she said.

And summarize she did. Coswell had to admit that James couldn't have done it better. She had gone through every name on the list and then some.

"The victim, Dr. Kelly, is clean. No priors in Canada, but I'll follow that up with the people in Ireland."

He wasn't sure how she was going to do that but it showed initiative; a move he hadn't directed, or even thought of.

She continued.

"Nothing came up on any of the students or any of Professor Dietrich's dinner guests. In fact, the only positive in the whole bunch was Dr. Montgomery's secretary, Francis DeBouvier. He was involved in an altercation six months ago at a downtown bar. The incident was described by the investigating officer as 'a gentleman of other sexual persuasion' being in the wrong bar at the wrong time. His birth name, by the way, is David Silverstein, son of a Montreal Rabbi."

She put the sheet back in the folder.

"I haven't quite finished. A number of the students as well as the two anatomy lab assistants are from foreign countries. It will take me a while to check that out."

"Okay," he said. "Now where does that leave us?"

She hesitated for a moment and appeared a bit confused. Coswell wondered if she had taken his comment as subtle sarcasm.

"It doesn't help much," she said, pointing to the

folder. "I guess all I can say from the information I got is that the likelihood of a criminal element is slim, and the only person with a violent tendency is Mr. DeBouvier."

"Negative findings are just part of the investigative grind, Bostock," Coswell said. "We don't often get the flash of insight that instantly solves the case, but add Francis to James' suspect board. Who knows what evil..."

She finished the quote.

"... lurks in the hearts of men."

Coswell almost choked on his coffee.

"You are way too young to know anything about *The Shadow,*" he said. "That's old-time radio."

"My grandfather. He loved that quote."

At last something in common with her, weird as it was.

She continued her report.

"I checked with the cleaning firm that does the anatomy lab. Their people finished just after nine on the night of the murder. I managed to get through to the crew supervisor, who fortunately was also the floor polisher. He said no one came or went when he was doing the basement floor."

"And upstairs?"

"They didn't start until seven and according to him, they had the building all to themselves and that's the norm on Sundays. He was the last one to leave and personally turned off all but the hallway and stairwell lights."

She opened the folder again and pulled out another page.

"The grounds stated for the Kelly-Montgomery divorce were adultery. Usually that speeds up the process, but it was slowed down by Dr. Kelly demanding half his wife's assets. The judge, however, ruled that Dr. Montgomery had accumulated those assets on her own, with no contribution from her husband, and so were hers alone. He also ruled that since there were no children and both were professionals with secure positions earning equal amounts of money, no special settlement was warranted."

Coswell thought that over for a moment.

"Left him hanging out to dry," he said. "But the adultery factor is interesting. Did you get the name of the corespondent?"

"Yes. The name on the divorce document was Hilda Balanchuk, also known as Renée Lafleur. I traced her to an escort service called Pleasures of the Pacific. I thought I'd better wait for your okay to press them for a home address."

"Permission granted. She rates an interview," Coswell said. "If Kelly had money problems, he wouldn't want a quickie divorce. Keep the wife paying the bills. So hiring a corespondent doesn't make sense. He was probably caught in bed with the woman by a private investigator."

"Would you like to do that this morning, sir? I suspect that this would be the best time of the day to find her at home."

"Good suggestion. Give them a call."

"Here?"

"Why not. I doubt that anyone is listening, and the staff knows we're cops."

She got nowhere on her cell phone. Completely stonewalled.

"Let me try," Coswell said.

She handed him her phone.

"This is Inspector Mark Coswell of the RCMP," he said to the unfortunate soul on the receiving end. "My partner, Corporal Bostock, has just made a very reasonable request to you. If you are not immediately forthcoming with Miss Lafleur's home address I will send two squad cars over to your establishment with uniformed officers who will make themselves hugely visible and repeat our request face-to-face. Now let's hear it."

It wasn't immediate, but it took less than two minutes.

He motioned to Bostock to write the address down.

"Thank you," Coswell said when he had finished. "Your cooperation is much appreciated."

He pushed the end talk button and handed the phone back to her. She was looking at the address she had written down.

"That's Dr. Kelly's residence," she said.

"Yes it is. You've been studying our reports. Good. Now let's head over there. Miss Lafleur will be expecting us."

"A phone call from her employer?"

"With a threat, I'll bet. Like 'don't say anything that will harm the business or else.' Prostitution is a dangerous vocation in this city."

Renée Lafleur answered the apartment buzzer seconds after Coswell released his finger from the button, and the moment he identified himself, the electric door latch opened. No sign of the manager.

Her apartment was at the very end of the second floor, next to the staircase. Convenient, Coswell thought. She could slip clients in and out through the fire doors.

Renée, dressed in a white terry cloth kimono, unlocked the door and let them in; a tall, generously proportioned woman. She had high, Slavic cheekbones, brown eyes, and black hair roughly piled up on top of her head. Obviously she had still been in bed when her agency called and had done nothing to beautify herself. In Coswell's estimation, however, with minimal effort and the right makeup, she would likely be gorgeous.

"Try to keep your voices down, please," she said. "My roommate's asleep. We've both worked late."

Probably to the very early hours of the morning, Coswell mused.

Their apartment did not look like a bordello, despite the manager's suspicions. It was nicely furnished in the

Ikea mode and showed no signs of empty liquor bottles, overflowing ashtrays, or clothing strewn about.

"Have a seat," she said, pointing to two California-style chairs before sitting down herself on a small chesterfield facing them. Bostock sat on the edge of her chair with her knees together and back straight, a pose, Coswell estimated that required musculature that he didn't have. The only way to sit in a California chair, from his point of view, was to give in to its design and settle back. Renée crossed her legs and let the kimono fall open across her thighs, but then quickly pulled it closed.

Once again, he gave Bostock the nod to start and this time she didn't hesitate.

"We are investigating a homicide—Doctor Kelly. I believe you have had some dealings with him?" she said.

Renée smiled.

"Dealings? That's cute," she said. "But, yes, he was a regular customer, and a good one. We did our 'dealings' in his apartment, which was really convenient for me. Saved taxi fare home."

"What fee did you charge him for your services?"

"Standard two-fifty an hour; a thousand for a complete sleep over."

Coswell had to put his hand to his face to hide his grin when he saw Bostock's startled expression. Prostitutes she dealt with in Winnipeg obviously didn't command anywhere near that price. Welcome to Vancouver.

Renée caught her reaction as well.

"I don't get to keep it all, unfortunately," she said. "In fact, I get to keep damn little of it considering I'm the product."

She sighed.

"But that's the price of marketing. Impossible to go it alone these days. Too much competition."

"How often did he call on you?" Bostock said.

"It varied. Sometimes as often as every other night;

other times maybe as little as twice a month."

Coswell was impressed. The man was a middle-aged pistol.

"Did he employ your roommate as well?"

"Keri? Never."

"And why not do you think?"

"Keri's from New Zealand. Kelly wasn't into foreigners, especially black. God knows he went on about it when he was into his booze. I wondered if he was analed by some black priest when he was a choir boy or something."

And then, seeing Bostock's shocked expression, "Sorry. It was just a thought."

"Did you ever have trouble collecting your fee?"

"No. He always paid, but he was no tipper and he hardly ever took me out anywhere. Just once as a matter of fact, to that Irish pub he liked."

"How did he behave when you were alone with him? Was he ever a bad date?"

"If you mean beat me up or something, no, but he was a lot of work at times. No problem with the first blast, but he always wanted as much as he could get for his money and I had to work hard for the repeats."

Bostock's red face prompted another, "Sorry, I didn't mean to be so graphic, but you did ask."

Coswell took over.

"During the breaks," he began, "did Kelly ever mention problems, names of people out to get him, anything you can think of that might have led to his getting killed?"

She laughed.

"I don't think he considered me anyone worth having a conversation with, especially anything personal like that. During the breaks, as you called them, he usually switched on the TV to the sports channel and worked away on a bottle of scotch. Never shared either."

"How about when he took you to his Irish pub?"

"That didn't go well. A couple of the guys at the table

were customers of mine. I think it was one of them who gave him my name in the first place. They started to kid him about me." She looked across at Bostock. "Comparing notes and that kind of thing."

"And Kelly didn't like it?" Coswell said.

"Got really hostile. I thought there was going to be a fight but Mr. C cut it off quick."

"Mr. C?"

She looked him in the eye.

"If you don't know Mr. C I'm sure as fuck not going to tell you."

She turned back to Bostock.

"Sorry again," she said. "I try to control my potty mouth but sometimes it takes off on me. Growing up in the Eastside does that to you."

A door opened and a woman came into the room.

"What's up, Renée?" she said. "Who are these people?"

She was stunning—taller even than her roommate and more slender, skin the colour of flawless ebony and a face that could be on the cover of any fashion magazine. She had on a full-length satin robe that clung to her body and shimmered in the room light. If Kelly turned that down, Coswell thought, he must have been nuts.

"Police, Keri," Renée said. "Looking into Kelly's murder. You know, Dr. Kelly, that client of mine down the hall."

And after a momentary pause, "They're not vice, so relax."

"Yes," Coswell said. "We're not vice and anything you've told us will be used only for our homicide investigation. It won't be passed on, I can assure you."

Keri looked relieved. Renée just nodded.

"We'll be off now," Coswell said, "and let you both get your rest."

Renée saw them to the door. Coswell went out first. Bostock followed, but just before she stepped into the hallway, Renée spoke to her.

"Keri and I aren't going to do this for much longer," she said. "We've saved up enough money to start our own business. Real estate, buying and selling."

"Good luck," Bostock said. "And I really mean that."

"Thanks. And good luck to you, too. Tough job you've got, especially for a woman, eh?"

When they returned to the cruiser, Coswell was pleased to see Bostock go directly to the passenger side. He had no desire to keep racing her to the driver's seat.

"We may as well head out to the campus," he said. "We've got a few hours until we meet with Dr. Montgomery. Maybe we can find Frank, the disgruntled student. He might be studying in his residence."

Bostock shook her head.

"I checked the first-year medical students' class schedule yesterday," she said. "It's quite intense. Their only time off during the day is from twelve to one thirty, and according to Dr. Dietrich's secretary, many of them come to the lab then for extra study."

"Surely they don't eat their lunch there beside those smelly cadavers," Coswell said, aghast.

"I guess they do, and since Frank Hoffmann failed last year, he's probably one of the ones doing just that."

Coswell thought this over as he drove slowly up Ash Street toward Twelfth Avenue.

"We'll have an early lunch then," he said. "I don't want preservative fumes coating my taste buds before I eat. We'll do the Pit Pub again. It will be a working lunch so save your receipt. They add up, I can tell you."

And then he wondered why he had said that. She wasn't his auditor.

He did, however, hope she had forgotten about her "my turn" compulsion. Worrying about cost to her would dampen his choices of what to order and he was starving.

It amazed him how quickly a cinnamon bun wore off. Maybe he was becoming diabetic.

They parked in front of the Student Recreation Centre which Coswell had noted was a shorter walk to the Pit Pub than from the Dental parking lot.

The place was almost deserted when they went in, classes still in progress at eleven forty-five. Coswell led the way to the same table that he and James had shared with med school class president Sally Chetwynd and her entourage.

"With a little luck," Coswell said, "you'll get to meet one of our most productive interviewees from day one in our investigation. Maybe she's thought of something else that might help us."

He really didn't need to say that. Bostock likely had memorized the names from James' report, but he thought it would reinforce his working lunch statement.

They had barely sat down when a waitress came over from the bar to take their orders. She was a pretty girl, blond, with no makeup and not a single part of her body pierced, including her earlobes. For a moment, Coswell took his mind off food.

"Don't tell me," he said. "Let me guess. You're from the Kootenays, right?"

Big grin.

"No," she said. "You're way off. I'm from Sointula."

Coswell wracked his brain. Where the hell was Swan-whatever?

Bostock was looking at him.

"It's an old Finnish community on a little island just off the North East coast of Vancouver Island," she said.

Damn! The woman knew everything. But why should that annoy him? James knew everything, too, but he was never irritating about it. He shut the thought quickly off and gave the girl his order.

"I'll have the Fully Loaded Poutine and a sleeve of Okanagan Pale Ale," he said.

Bostock looked slightly pained.

"Do you have anything fairly light? A salad?"

"No, Ma'am. I guess one of the sandwiches is as close as we've got to that—turkey and tomato on multigrain."

"That will be fine, toasted if you don't mind, and just water to drink, thanks."

Worried about her figure, Coswell guessed. But water? Maybe she was against drinking alcohol on duty. Well, tough titty, he was not going to alter his habits to conform to any such attitude.

Bostock, surprisingly, was the one to break the painful silence that followed the waitress heading off to get their orders.

"I only know about Sointula because of Bill Gaston," she said. "He wrote a novel about it which was very good. He grew up in Winnipeg."

How very, very uninteresting, thought Coswell, although it was nice to know she wasn't a geography genius. He had never been a novel reader, preferring non-fiction, but he certainly was not about to discuss the subject of his recent reading—Alzheimer's disease. What on earth could they talk about other than the case? Nothing.

Fortunately, the waitress returned with his sleeve of beer plus Bostock's water—and a worried expression on her face.

"I've been told that this table is actually reserved," she said. "Would you mind moving to one of the others? There's lots of choice right now."

"Don't worry," Coswell said. "We're part of the group that has this table reserved. We're early."

She went back to the bar, the worried expression still in place. Coswell watched her confer with an older man tending the bar; probably her superior. He looked their way and frowned, but just then, down the ramp to the bar, came Sally Chetwynd and her fellow female students. The barman stopped her momentarily and spoke to her. Her response echoed all the way across the room.

"No problemo. Nice change from listening to boring old anatomy."

She marched across the room to join them. She cast a momentary glance at Bostock as she plunked herself down beside Coswell. The rest of her group wriggled into place, almost pushing Bostock off the end of the bench.

"Where's the handsome hunk you brought last time?" Sally said, and then aside to Bostock, "No offense to you, sweetie."

"He's been reassigned," Coswell said. "This is Corporal Bostock, his replacement."

"Lucky for you, Inspector, but a bit disappointing for us girls," and aside to Bostock. "Hormones. Curse the bloody things, eh?"

The Sointula waitress arrived at the table and stood beside Sally intuitively, knowing she was in charge.

"You're new," Sally said. "Did they finally chuck Chuckee? He was a bit slow."

Without waiting for a reply, she ordered nachos and a pitcher of beer. Coswell marvelled that future health professionals would have that as a regular lunch.

"And bring the tab to me," he said to the waitress.

"Again?" Sally said. "That's really not necessary. We should be treating you this time."

"No. We're fishing for information on the Kelly case so it's on me."

"Well, go right ahead and fish."

She regarded her flock. "Sit up and pay attention, girls. The Inspector's going to ask questions."

They all stared at him, which took him completely aback. He hadn't yet formulated any questions and Bostock had become mute.

"Er, uh, just a general one to start," Coswell said. "Has anything occurred to you since our last meeting that might have some bearing on our investigation? Even the smallest bit of information can be helpful."

They exchanged glances with one another but nothing said.

Coswell turned to Sally.

"I don't see that Frank fellow here today. Did he stay in the lab?"

Sally called down to an Asian girl sitting at the end of the table. "Amy, Frank's in your group. Do you know where he is right now?"

"Wing didn't show up for class this morning," the girl answered. "Frank had to go back to the residence to get some notes he forgot and said he'd check on him."

"Wingie is Frank's roommate," Sally explained.

Coswell felt his cell phone buzz. He pulled it out of his jacket pocket and looked at the call display—McMorran. He switched off the buzz and returned it to his pocket, ignoring Bostock's obvious curiosity. Speaking to McMorran was at the bottom of his priority list.

"What did you think of my roommate, Marilyn?" Sally said. "She's really something, eh?"

"I agree," Coswell said. "I think she'll make a wonderful surgeon."

His cell phone buzzed again. He took it out to shut off again, but the buzz wasn't McMorran's name on the call display this time, it was James. He pushed TALK.

"I just got a call from McMorran," he heard James say. "Said he couldn't reach you but there's been another death on campus—Wing Chu, Frank Hoffmann's roommate. Hoffmann actually found the body and made the call. McMorran says it's a clear case of suicide."

Pause.

"Frank's the angry student who Kelly faile ... remember?" James said.

"Of course I remember," Coswell said. "We're on our way."

"You have the address, right?"

Coswell cut the connection.

He spoke quietly to Sally but loud enough for Bostock to overhear. No need to keep the news confidential, he decided.

"That call was about your classmate, Wing Chu. He's dead. Found in his room by his roommate just a short while ago. Suicide according to the attending officer."

For a second Sally was too stunned to speak, but she recovered quickly.

"Wingie's killed himself," she announced to everyone present.

Everyone began to talk at once … everyone except the girl, Amy, apparently frozen in a state of shock. Suddenly she stood up and virtually ran to the exit. Coswell motioned to Bostock but she was already on her feet and followed the girl out the door.

"Amy and Wingie were a twosome," Sally said. "She's going to be devastated by this."

Coswell had thrown decorum to the wind at that point and was busily shovelling as much of the poutine into his mouth as he could. Between swallows, he quizzed Sally.

"Can you think of a reason he would do this? Were they not getting along? Breaking up?"

"I don't think so," Sally said. "They've been going together since undergrad. This is so stupid. Suicides aren't rare in med school but they're usually from exam stress. Couldn't be in Wingie's case. The year just started."

Reluctantly, Coswell pushed his lunch aside, took one last swig of his beer, and got up to leave.

"I'll settle the tab on the way out," he said. "Finish your lunches, but when you go back to the anatomy lab, tell Professor Dietrich what's happened and that Frank likely won't be back today."

"Got it and thanks. You can call on any one of us at any time. Eh, girls?"

They all nodded, their faces grim. Such contrast to just a few minutes earlier. Even Sally sat staring silently at her hands folded on the table in front of her. In their stressful world, none of them needed this.

CHAPTER THIRTEEN

Bostock and the girl, Amy, were nowhere in sight when Coswell rushed up the ramp and out of the pub, but he knew where they would be—Bostock would use their cruiser as a private haven.

They were both sitting in the backseat. Bostock had her arm around the girl's shoulders. He stopped in his tracks for a moment. Should he leave them alone? Would Bostock's role as a sympathetic female override the need to really grill the girl who most likely had the answer to why Wing Chu had killed himself?

His debate was unnecessary. Bostock saw him through the back window, and after a quick pat on Amy's back, she got out of the cruiser and walked up to him.

"Sounds like a suicide situation all right," she said. "They had a quick dinner together last night at the Commonsblock cafeteria. Apparently the incident with Kelly's body really upset him. Their group was the one that got the coffin with Kelly in it."

"But he was a medical student, for heaven's sake," Coswell said. "He should have been able to handle that."

"A brand new medical student who maybe wasn't so keen to be a doctor in the first place."

"Did she say that?"

"She suspected it, but, as she said, 'there's so much pride in a Chinese man that to admit weakness is unthinkable.'"

"So she's whipping herself for not being his confidente."

"Something like that."

Coswell thought for a moment.

"It does all seem to add up to suicide," he said. "But we haven't ruled out murder."

Bostock's eyes flew open.

"Murder?"

"We need to get over there before McMorran messes up the scene. See if you can persuade the girl to go back to the pub. I think that's where her best support is right now."

"Yes, sir."

"I've told them to keep your sandwich warm. Do you want to go back and get it?"

"No, I'm fine," she said.

It occurred to Coswell that she was just like James in that regard—able to function on a low tank of fuel, a quality that Coswell had never possessed.

She walked over to the cruiser, opened the back door, and spoke to the girl. Whatever she said worked, and in seconds the two of them were heading back to the pub. In less than five minutes, Bostock returned, and two minutes after that Coswell pulled the cruiser into the parking lot of Robson House.

Just inside the front door of the residence and off to one side was a large common lounge. McMorran was sitting there with Frank Hoffmann. No sign of the other officers. When he saw Coswell and Bostock enter, he got up and came out to the foyer.

"This one won't take you long," he said. "Suicide without a doubt. Nice technique, but I won't spoil it for you. My corporal is upstairs guarding the body. Third floor."

Coswell looked into the lounge. Frank was sitting in

an armchair facing the large windows that looked out into the courtyard. He appeared to be in a trance, paying no attention to the goings on in the foyer.

"What have you got from him so far?" Coswell said.

"He came back here shortly after noon to check on his roommate and found him dead. Phoned 911 immediately. Used his cell."

"Did he disturb anything?"

"Felt the guy's neck for a pulse and turned off the drip."

"The drip?"

"You'll see. Very cool way to go."

"What else did you get from him?"

"He's in shock right now so I was letting him settle down when you came in. So far he's untapped."

"All right," Coswell said. "We'll get at him now."

He was tempted to leave Bostock with McMorran to do the interview but then thought better of it. McMorran would put her off and likely dominate the questioning.

"Don't you want to see the body first?" McMorran said.

"No. He's not going anywhere."

They went into the lounge. Frank Hoffmann appeared to have recovered somewhat. He got up from his chair and stood facing them.

Coswell told him to be seated.

Frank nodded. They all sat down, Bostock on the chesterfield facing Frank's chair, and to Coswell's annoyance, McMorran quickly plunked his ass down right beside her. That left a chair for him to Frank's left, equally annoying—better to be face-on with a subject.

McMorran had enough sense not to start the interview himself. Coswell gave a nod to Bostock. Let her start. A corporal over a sergeant. That should piss him off.

She gave a fleeting glance toward McMorran beside her but then looked straight at Frank Hoffmann. She leaned forward and gently touched his arm.

"You've had a real shock," she said, "but we'd appreciate it if you would start from the beginning and tell us what happened."

Her voice was soft, soothing, and her touch radiated empathy. Frank responded almost immediately. Bostock sat back with a subtle wiggle of her buttocks, away from McMorran.

"I only spoke to him briefly when he came back to the room last night. He was having dinner with Amy, his girlfriend. I was pounding the books and didn't want to get into any conversation. I just asked him how dinner went. He said 'fine' or something like that, and then 'don't let me disturb you.'"

"What was the tone of his voice?"

"Flat, but that was normal for Wing."

"The inscrutable East," McMorran said.

Coswell glared at him.

"What did he do then?" Bostock said.

"He just lay down on his bed."

A deep frown and then a shake of his head.

"I completely missed it," he said. "He was obviously depressed. I should have said something to him, talked him out of it, but this anatomy crap has me scared as hell. I'm not good at rote learning and that's what you have to do to pass the stupid course. I've got to go over and over everything a thousand times before it sticks."

"Was Wing as worried as you about the subject?"

"I doubt it. He was a year behind me in pre-med but I heard that he was a top student."

McMorran, seemingly bored by the questioning, leaned back in his seat and spread his arms across the back of the chesterfield, his right hovering behind Bostock's shoulders. She stiffened slightly but made no effort to move forward.

"Carry on," she said to Frank. "How long did he

lie on his bed?"

"I don't remember exactly. He got up at one point, though, and went out. He didn't say anything and I just assumed he was going over to the commons. But again, I should have twigged. Even people blessed with a photographic memory have to at least cover everything once and that takes time at your desk. He should have been at it like me."

"When did he return to the room?"

"I don't know. I gave up studying around eleven and crashed. Five or ten minutes maybe in the washroom first. I do remember thinking Wing was keeping kind of strange hours during a school week."

"And what happened this morning?"

"He seemed okay, almost cheerful. We had breakfast together over at the cafeteria. When we came back to the room to get our classroom stuff he told me to go ahead and he'd see me there. Wanted to get something out of the lockers, he said. And that's the last I saw of him until now."

"Just one last question," Bostock said. "Do you have any idea why he did this?"

Frank shook his head.

"Not a clue," he said. "I knew very little about him other than he was from Hong Kong and did all his premed at UBC. I didn't even know about Amy until I saw them having lunch together one day at the commons."

"But you were roommates."

"That wasn't by choice. Computers do most of the matching for the residences but I know they try to room foreign students with locals, so that's likely why we got paired up here plus we're both in first-year med."

He thought for a moment.

"We didn't have much time to get to know one another. Most of the first week is taken up in orientation sessions, medicals and stuff like that. Wing also had to get all his books. I do know that he had a Masters in Pharmacology, which is a pretty awesome ticket for pre-med. I just did the minimum—BSc popcorn degree."

He closed his eyes and shook his head, apparently overcome again.

"Such a waste. I should have done something to stop him."

"When someone gets that down, I doubt if anyone could have stopped him," Bostock said.

He opened his eyes, looked into hers, and then nodded.

Coswell stood up.

"That will do for now," he said. "I'm afraid it will be a while before you can take over your room again. I'd suggest you go back to the anatomy lab and catch up. Nothing like work to take your mind off bad things."

"Okay," he said. "You're probably right."

They all stood up at the same time. Coswell motioned for McMorran to lead the way out, followed by Bostock. But he held back, effectively blocking Frank's exit.

"Could money worries have been a problem for your roommate?" he said. "Medical school must be a costly affair."

"I don't think so," he said. "Wing always dressed well and it's not cheap staying in this residence with the meal plan added on."

"How do you manage?"

"An indulgent father," he said. "But I work during the summer break."

"Doing what?"

"I've got my first responder's ticket. I work with the BC Ambulance Service."

"Good for you," Coswell said, standing aside to let him by. "Now off you go. Sounds as though you'll make an excellent doctor."

A smile.

"Thank you," Frank said. "All I have to do is pass first-year anatomy."

Bostock and McMorran were waiting at the bottom of the stairs.

"Go ahead, McMorran," he said. "We'll follow you." Coswell was certain that the lecherous bastard was about to do the "ladies first" routine and ogle her all the way up the stairs. He followed immediately behind McMorran and let Bostock come last. He thought he caught an understanding look as he stepped in front of her.

McMorran then proceeded to vault up the stairs two at a time. Macho jerk, Coswell thought. Ape mentality impressing the female, no doubt, showing up the older, fitness-challenged male.

By the time he managed the six flights to the third floor, Coswell was breathing heavily. He hoped that Bostock didn't notice.

Fortunately, the dead student's room was at the very end of the long corridor, which gave him time to catch his breath. McMorran and his corporal were standing in the hallway.

"You can both wait out here while we check the scene over," Coswell said.

"Mind if we hold the door open?" McMorran said. "It's a learning opportunity, watching two homicide detectives at work."

"Just don't touch the door handle," Coswell said.

The room was exactly as Coswell remembered from his student days—small but efficiently designed for two students. Facilities matched on either side—clothes closets just inside the door, next a series of dresser drawers, single beds and finally desks with a long book-shelf above. Roommates would be back to back when they were studying.

One look at the scene and Coswell had to concede that McMorran was right; it had suicide written all over it. But from the moment James passed on to him the sergeant's cocky summation, he wanted to object. He'd thrown the murder possibility to Bostock more in spite than reality.

Wing Chu was lying supine on top of the bedding, fully clothed in a long-sleeved white shirt, black trousers, and matching socks. On the floor beside the bed was a pair of expensive looking loafers and a three-quarter length white lab coat. Lying on the latter was a rubber tourniquet. Both the shirt and the trousers were creased as though he had slept in them. His black hair was tousled but his eyes were closed and his face serene. He had found a mop from somewhere and wedged it against his bed, and on it hung a half litre bottle labelled normal saline. Attached to that was IV tubing leading from the bottle down to a needle taped to his right arm, the shirt sleeve rolled up. The drip chamber was still, the flow turned off. A professional job, Coswell thought. He walked over to the two desks and glanced down at each, aware that Bostock had moved up behind him. When he turned around, he saw her bending over the body, looking carefully at the dead man's neck.

"That's enough for now," Coswell said. "We'll leave everything untouched for forensics."

"I did call them," McMorran said. "They should be here shortly, unless they had a real Homicide to deal with elsewhere."

"Every death is a homicide, Sergeant, until proven otherwise," Coswell said. "You want to learn? That's covered in homicide 101. Ask any rookie."

No hiding McMorran's anger this time.

"And any rookie will tell you this is an obvious suicide," he said, and then turning to his corporal. "Let's get out of here. We've got more important things to do."

Getting to McMorran felt good to Coswell at first and then embarrassment began to creep in as they listened to the two march down the hall, the sound of their boots echoing like storm troopers on parade. Bostock turned to him, a questioning look in her eyes.

"I know, I know," he said. "I shouldn't let the man get under my skin, but he does, damn it. Now, what did you see in there?"

"I can't be certain because of the shirt collar, and I didn't want to disturb it, but I thought I saw evidence of bruising or a rope burn."

"A rope burn?"

"Yes, she said. Also, his hair is messed up and his clothes are rumpled, Looks like some kind of struggle took place."

Coswell's heart took a leap. She had something here.

"Good thinking. Someone committing suicide this way has no need to struggle. In fact, they usually try to ensure that their corpse looks good. I've seen women who actually had their hair done prior to doing themselves in."

He continued. "Anything else?"

"No suicide note. But maybe he didn't have time to write one. Worried that his roommate might return and stop him."

Their conference ended abruptly when James appeared at the end of the hallway and came striding toward them.

"Charlotte and her crew are unloading their equipment," he said. "McMorran just breezed by me. He didn't look happy. Not even a hello."

"He has more important things to do," Coswell said.

"Like what?"

"I don't know. Maybe there's a traffic jam on campus that needs him."

James grinned.

"Oh, how the mighty have fallen," he said, and then to Bostock, "Your homicide experience is going up in leaps and bounds, I see. A stiff a day almost."

The arrival of Charlotte and the rest of the forensic unit cut off further conversation.

"Inspector Coswell. We meet again," she said. "Almost

too soon, wouldn't you say?" Then without waiting for a reply, "McMorran just told me that you're fussing over an obvious suicide. Fussing how?"

"There's enough in there to raise suspicion," Coswell said. He was going to add a derogatory remark about McMorran but thought better of it. Let the man's stupidity look after itself.

Charlotte raised one eyebrow.

"Well, well," she said. "A little challenge for us. That sounds a lot more interesting. Now let us get to work. Anything special we should know?"

"He was a first-year medical student with a degree in pharmacology. Also, Corporal Bostock noted signs of struggle and a suspicious mark on the neck."

Give her due credit, Coswell thought. It might soften Charlotte up a bit.

But Charlotte merely nodded and then waved her crew into the room.

Coswell turned to James who was about to follow her.

"We'll hang around for a bit," he said. "See if you can get time of death pinned down, or at least tell us whether it was closer to when his roommate left this morning or when he returned. And most important—was he murdered?"

"I'll try," James said. "But we still haven't gotten very close. My charm doesn't appear to be working."

Students were beginning to appear in the building, having finished their lunches in the commons cafeteria. The few that came up to the third floor gave them curious glances but then disappeared into their rooms.

"Should I start collecting names?" Bostock said. "Someone may have seen or heard something."

"In a minute. But let's see first if James is successful. It really shouldn't take long to at least answer the murder question."

He was right. The door opened a crack and James

stuck his head out. He mouthed "murder" and pointed to his neck. The door closed.

Coswell looked at Bostock.

"Makes you wonder about our boy, Frank. One of the few Shakespeare quotes I can remember—'He doth protest too much, methinks.' Do you agree?"

She shrugged her shoulders.

"He fooled me then. I thought he was genuine, but I can see your point about time of death. We should be able to confirm that Chu was alive at breakfast and Frank's alibi after that will be his presence in class all morning. Killing his roommate, especially setting it up with the IV and all that, makes me wonder when he could have done it and why."

"A puzzle, I agree," Coswell said, feeling slightly squelched by her logic. "The window of opportunity is narrow … but possible. And motives sometimes are hidden deep."

There was no disguising the look of doubt in her eyes, and he deserved that look. Jumping to conclusions was so unlike him. James was always the conclusion jumper and he the voice of reason. So why did he do it? If he was trying to impress her with his brilliance, he had failed miserably.

The door opened again and this time James came out into the hall. He carefully closed the door behind him before speaking.

"Her ladyship has allowed me to give you an approximate time of death. She did stress 'approximate,' but in this case, with the body at room temperature, I think her estimate is probably within minutes. The man went his heavenly way at eleven-hundred hours, give or take very little. His demise was expedited by either what's in that IV fluid or whatever made the mark on his neck or both."

He spotted the glance that went between them.

"Is this not fitting well into your thinking right now? I thought you would be overjoyed—another murder to solve."

"Murder is not a joyful occasion, James," Coswell said, the sharpness in his voice embarrassing to them all.

Bostock spoke up quickly.

"Shall I start the door-to-door now, sir?"

"Yes," he said. "And I'll go over to the cafeteria and see if any of the staff remember serving Frank and Chu breakfast. We'll meet back here. Maybe Charlotte will give us a few more words of wisdom then."

She turned to go.

"Oh," Coswell said. "And see if you can find out whether the man was left or right-handed."

She looked puzzled, but only for a second and then nodded. A moment later she knocked and then entered one of the rooms.

"What?" James said.

"Pretty hard to insert a needle into your right arm if you are right-handed," Coswell said. "I suspect the procedure requires some dexterity."

James smiled.

"Dexter or sinister," he said. "Love the Romans. Now how about I join you at the cafeteria? I'm one too many bodies in that cubby hole. There's enough bumping into one another as it is."

Coswell was more than happy to say yes. No point waiting for Charlotte to finish. The results of the autopsy and the chemical analysis were what he needed, and if she had found anything like a fingerprint that shouldn't be there, it would all be in her report. A head to head with James might be more immediately useful.

CHAPTER FOURTEEN

Lunch period was over at the cafeteria but the deli there offered good coffee and cinnamon buns. Coswell had both. James stuck with green tea.

"I'm not sure all those cinnamon buns are good for you," James said.

"Cinnamon, I'll have you know," Coswell said, "has great beneficial effects. I've been researching this. It has anti-diabetic properties and it offsets the negative effects of high fat intake."

The same article mentioned that it also reportedly inhibited the development of Alzheimer's disease, but he decided not to mention that.

Most of the tables were unoccupied but Coswell headed straight for one that was being wiped down by a young woman. She looked up as he approached with his coffee sloshing in a cup in one hand and the cinnamon bun on a plate in the other.

"Good afternoon, young lady," he said. He remained standing until she finished wiping the table. "Just about done for the day?"

She gave him a big smile.

"Yes, thank goodness. I started at six and it's been busy, as usual."

Coswell set his plate and cup down on the table.

"I guess you can go home and have a nap now."

"I wish," she said. "Unfortunately I have a class at three and one this evening."

"Oh dear. That's harsh."

"You said it."

She was about to move on to another table but Coswell stopped her with another question.

"You must know a lot of the students who come here for breakfast. Do you happen to know Frank Hoffmann?"

"Frank, the grump?" she said. "Yeah, I know him. This is his second year in residence. A real complainer." And then, thinking she might have made a faux pas, "Friend of yours?"

"Definitely not," Coswell said. "And we appreciate the

information but could I ask you one more question?"

She glanced at James who obediently had donned his uniform for the day.

"May I ask you one first?" she said. "I've heard that something big has happened over at Robson House. Squad cars in the parking lot and Mounties going into the building. Can you tell me what happened?"

"A student suicide, it appears. A young man named Wing Chu. Do you know him?"

"Was he the Chinese guy with Frank this morning at breakfast? No, I don't know him. He's new to residence."

"Could you tell the mood at their table? Were they laughing it up, serious; you know what I mean?"

"Funny you should ask. I was quite surprised when they sat together. Frank never sits with foreign students. I heard he put in a request again to change rooms. He did that last year, too. Friend of mine works in placement. He's got to be as bigoted as he is grumpy."

She paused.

"I'm no snoop, but I couldn't help watching them. Frank looked his usual sour self but it was hard to tell the other guy's emotions. If I had to say, his body language spelled upset. He didn't sit with Frank long, either. In fact, when I cleared his tray, he'd left most of his breakfast untouched."

A voice shouted out to her from behind the cafeteria counter. "Rosy, we need you back here."

"Whoops, got to go," Rosy said. "Mrs. Legree calls."

James looked over at Coswell.

"Our Mr. Hoffmann sounds like an interesting character," he said. "But going from bigotry to murder in this country is a big stretch. There has to be a lot more than that if he's the killer."

Coswell bit into his cinnamon bun—not the best he had ever had, but not bad. Needed more icing.

"You're right, of course," he said, "We've got a long

way to go on this. Not much different than the Kelly case in that regard."

"You sound discouraged. Out of sorts for you. Anything wrong that I might be able to do something about?"

"You could be a sounding board for me on the Kelly murder," Coswell said. "This one's too fresh to get into a knot about yet, and you were in at the beginning of the Kelly thing."

"And pretty well out of it now, which, on reflection, I think is good. Bostock did the rah-rah-team thing, but deep down she has to feel that I'm imposing. I know I would be. Why don't you open up to her more? She's no dum-dum."

Coswell sighed.

"You are absolutely right," he said. "But this female thing has got me befuddled. I feel like I'm walking on eggshells half the time."

No use admitting that he was coming to realize that her femininity was merely an excuse. She was cool, logical, smart—and young. It was the threat of her showing him up that was the problem.

"I will try," he said. "Unfortunately, I've told her a couple of little white lies that will embarrass me if she finds out but I've got a lead that needs following up. Maybe you can help."

"Okay," James said. "But then I think you should invite her over for a coffee conference. You could probably use another cinnamon bun."

Coswell then proceeded to relate what he had discovered at the Auld Sod Pub, concluding with, "I think there could be a gang connection to his murder. Someone needs to be a fly on the wall in that pub and find the connection."

"Wow," James said. "That does sound promising, especially that Mr. C fellow, but let me think for a moment."

It was a short moment.

"If you are suggesting I be your fly on the wall, I have a better suggestion. You and Bostock go there as a couple. You've said many times that the criminal element can spot me as a cop a mile away. You, if I might say so, do not radiate policeman, and certainly Bostock in civvies could pass anywhere."

"You're kidding," Coswell said. "Bostock and I?" And then it dawned on him.

"Hooker and john, eh?"

"Exactly," James said. "If Mr. C is involved in the local prostitution business, a new girl with customer in tow walking into his territory should attract interest."

Coswell swallowed the last few bites of his bun, took a couple of sips of coffee, and then stared out the window, coffee cup still in hand. He appeared to be deep in thought, but shortly set the cup down with a bang and looked hard at James.

"Okay. I'll do it," he said. "You go back to the residence and send her over."

James got up immediately.

"Yes, sir," he said. "I'm off and I just know you won't regret it."

Coswell watched him hurry out of the cafeteria. That only gave him a few minutes to think up a good lie to tell her.

But he got a reprieve when Bostock came into the cafeteria pointedly looking at her wristwatch.

"It's two twenty," she said when she approached his table.

The appointment with Dr. Montgomery, Kelly's ex-wife! It had completely slipped his mind.

"Don't worry," he said draining his coffee cup. "We're just five minutes away from her office." Like he had planned it all the way.

They walked briskly back to the cruiser despite Coswell's feet still bothering him. He wondered if age-related arthritis began in the feet. Another topic to research on his computer.

"Anything come out of your door-to-door?" he said.

"There were only a few in their rooms," she said. "But one of them, a graduate student, during a pee break thought he saw Chu duck into his room carrying something. He gave an exact time—ten o'clock. He'd just checked his watch."

"Thought he saw?"

"He couldn't be sure it was Chu. I gather he meant the word 'duck' literally. He admitted that it could just as well have been Frank. They both have black hair."

"Or someone else entirely," Coswell said.

"Not likely. Everyone keeps their doors locked, apparently. Whoever went in had to have a key."

Upstaged again, Coswell thought, but then found a comeback.

"The don has a master key. Did you speak to him?"

"He wasn't in, but I left him a message to call me on my cell. I have it set up by the way, but Jane hasn't got my cards made up yet."

"When we get to the cruiser, I'll give you my phone and you can input your number. I presume you have my number in yours."

"I do," she said.

There was enthusiasm in her voice, which touched Coswell. Was this the new symbol of bonding—being on someone's cell contact list? Actually, he had a practical reason for asking her to do the inputting. He detested donning his reading glasses in public. The optician had talked him into half frames so he could look over the top of the lenses for distance without removing them, but they made him look old. He had his cell phone call display set to the largest font, but punching in numbers was a lot easier with his glasses.

Francis appeared to be in a total tizzy when they arrived at Dr. Montgomery's office. He almost leapt upon them when they arrived.

"I'm so glad you're on time," he said. "I'm just up to here (hand level with his nose) with things to do. The doctor's been back for just a few hours and I'm so snowed under."

He appeared to be on the verge of crying.

"I'll tell her you're here, and please, please take lots of time. I so need a break."

He didn't even go into the doctor's office; he merely opened the door and announced them in a very loud voice.

"The fuzz to see you, Dr. Montgomery."

She came out to meet them, giving Francis a quick frown on her way by him.

"You'll have to excuse Francis," she said. "He struggles for the right noun on occasion."

Coswell had to struggle himself—to keep his jaw from dropping. He had expected a Madam Curie type: a tiny, mousy woman with frumpy clothing and grey hair done up in a bun. But Doctor Montgomery was the exact opposite, except for her height, no more than five two. She was probably in her fifties, but one would have to look very closely to see that.

Her hair, a brilliant auburn, hung down to her shoulders, and as she moved towards them, the highlights danced like fire. Her eyes were a remarkable shade of green. She wore little makeup—some eye shadow and a bit of lipstick but had made no effort to cover the freckles that ran across her nose and just onto her cheeks. She wore a white lab coat left unbuttoned. Beneath was a tight-fitting, black, knee-length dress with a generous V-neckline that showed off her stunning figure. Coswell was totally smitten.

"I'm Kay Montgomery," she said, extending her hand toward him. "You are Inspector Coswell, I presume."

Her Irish accent sounded like music to him.

He took her hand and felt the warmth and the softness.

"Yes," was all he could get out. He had to tell himself to let go of her hand when she turned to Bostock.

"And you are—?"

"Corporal Bostock, Dr. Montgomery."

"I'm pleased to meet you," she said. "Nice to see our gender working in the front lines."

Coswell saw Bostock's professional face soften. Dr. Montgomery knew how to make people feel at ease. And pretense, Coswell decided, did not exist in this woman. She was just so perfect.

"Come into my office," she said. "Francis will get us a pot of coffee ... or would you prefer tea? Never mind. Francis, bring both, and some Peek Freans."

Francis rolled his eyes, threw up his hands and gave a big sigh.

"I'll try," he said.

"He's so dramatic," she whispered, and then out loud, "And a couple of chairs for my guests, s'il vous plaît."

They heard Francis groan.

Unlike the tidy, minimalist office of Marie D'Allarde, Montgomery's office was filled to overflowing—books, file folders, X-rays, journals. On the few areas of wall space that weren't covered by shelving or file cabinets hung framed photographs of scientific-looking individuals. The only colour in the room was a vase of yellow roses perched precariously at the edge of a totally cluttered desk.

"I hope you're not allergic," she said. "Fresh flowers are a habit I got into when I was at the Montreal Neurological Institute. That city can be so grey in the winter, not like the year-round green here, but I think they brighten up any room."

"Toot, toot." Francis called out as he pushed two chairs into the room, one in front of the other, causing Coswell and Bostock to jump aside. Montgomery had already found refuge behind her desk.

"You grab the first one, Inspector," he said, and when Coswell did so, he slid the other beside Bostock.

Thank you," Bostock said, a smile tugging at the corners of her mouth.

"De rien, belle dame."

Coswell wondered if Bostock spoke French. James was fluent in the language, having grown up in Ottawa. A momentary feeling of being out of place passed over him.

When Francis left and closed the door, Montgomery started the interview for them.

"You have probably dealt with more than your share of grieving widows, but I can assure you, my grief over Patrick's death is fleeting. Feel free to ask me anything that might help your investigation."

She was looking into his eyes. The warmth in them added to her smile and both jammed his cerebral circuits. He forced himself to look away from her and speak to Bostock.

"Why don't you lead off?"

And she did, no longer surprised by these sudden shifts from Coswell.

"Perhaps a short history of your relationship with Dr. Kelly would be a good start," she said.

"It's short all right and initially quite sweet. Patrick could be a real charmer when he put his mind to it. We met in Dublin two years ago. I was working at Queen Square in London at the time, but I'd flown over to Dublin to attend a neuropathology conference at St. James' Hospital. Would you believe, our first romantic meeting was in a pub close by."

From what Coswell had gleaned about Ireland, there were pubs close by no matter where you went.

"I'd gone out for a run with one of the local researchers," she went on, "a charming individual in his own right, but when we ducked into the pub to cool off, the poor chap was no match for the effusive Patrick Kelly. The man literally swept me off my feet."

She paused for a moment and looked down at the flowers on her desk.

"Funny now, looking back, I had plenty of warning that marriage to him wouldn't be a bed of roses. My running partner told me later that Patrick was not exactly what he appeared. 'Arrogant, selfish, hot-tempered, a bully'— words he used that I just attributed to sour grapes."

A hint of a blush flashed in her cheeks.

"My colleague and I ... what shall I say ... had been on intimate terms at previous conferences. I think in his own mind he parlayed that into more of a relationship than I intended."

A fox? Was this lovely creature a fox? But instead of shocking Coswell, it merely added to his fascination.

"Patrick and I had a whirlwind romance. He went back to London with me and we did the circuit—fine dining, a weekend at Brighton, walks along the Thames, theatre and the Cocksford Club."

A frown appeared.

"Ah, the Cocksford, London's poshiest gaming house. Our evening there should have rung a very loud bell. Some old surgical resident mate of his got us in as guests. I thought the dining room was the attraction—one of the best in London and we did have a magnificent meal, but it was the gambling, the bloody gambling that drew him there."

Bostock's eyes opened wide as though she had just experienced an epiphany. "Dr. Kelly had a gambling addiction?"

"Yes and I should have seen it. I blamed his behaviour that night on the amount we had to drink at dinner, added to what he imbibed at the card table. I had a dreadful time getting him to leave."

Coswell and Bostock exchanged glances. That would

explain his living in that old apartment block on Ash Street and his contesting the divorce. He was probably broke.

Bostock pressed on.

"I'm afraid that so far in our investigation, Dr. Kelly has not come across as a nice man. Carousing at night in an Irish pub downtown, abusing hospital staff at work—"

The smile returned.

"And womanizing, spending like there's no tomorrow. Yes, he was all that and more."

"Did he abuse you?"

"Only my pocket book. Otherwise he satisfied my needs very well so long as we stayed in the bedroom."

Bostock's turn to blush.

"Such a shame, really," Montgomery said. "He was a gifted surgeon—good hands, superb clinical acumen, and excellent judgment. Those qualities don't always go together, I'm sorry to say. I've seen a lot of mistakes in the autopsy room. His only professional weakness was a total lack of tolerance to anything or anybody less than perfect."

Coswell finally managed to switch into interview mode.

"We've heard that his lack of tolerance extended to racial bias. Did you observe any of that?"

She laughed.

"Oh yes. Get a few drinks into him and the only people he had a good word for were card-carrying Irish Catholics. In fact, he called me 'Lady Montgomery' during one of his snits but he did that only once."

She saw the puzzled expression on both their faces.

"My family background is Protestant. We're both from County Armagh, but Patrick was from the other side of the tracks, so to speak—Roman Catholic territory, and very anti anything that smacks of British aristocracy. Viscount Montgomery is a very distant relative."

Coswell was surprised. He thought the Irish hostilities

had disappeared decades ago.

"Could you elaborate on your pocket book comment?" he said.

"Yes, and it could have some bearing on the reason he was murdered. In fact, that's why I came back immediately after my conference—to pass on my suspicions to you."

Bostock leaned slightly forward in her chair.

Montgomery continued.

"I must have had a sixth sense about money problems right after we were married. Would you believe that he actually hit me up the first time for money to pay the priest who performed the ceremony? I insisted that we keep our finances separate. We worked out who would cover rent, food, insurance, etc., but it didn't take long before he couldn't keep up his end of the bargain."

"That must have created a lot of friction."

"You'd think so, wouldn't you? But love does strange things to the mind. He always had the most wonderful excuses. He fooled me for a long time by telling me he was investing in various schemes—real estate, shipping containers, gold market. Always needed just 'a little longer.'"

"What ended it all?"

"The gold market."

"The gold market?"

"Yes. When it went sky high I assumed we would be rolling in cash and told him so. That's when he finally admitted that gambling debts had eaten away all his assets."

"What did you do then?"

"Moved to Canada and accepted the teaching positions here. Unfortunately, it didn't work. Just weeks after we got here, he started on me again. But it wasn't just that. And this is what I think you want to know—he was being threatened."

"By whom?"

"I don't know. Organized criminals I presumed. Gambling people to whom he owed money. Hard people. And it wasn't one of his clever ruses. Patrick was genuinely frightened. I did give him money for a while, but eventually I said goodbye and arranged for a divorce."

"You paid for the corespondent?"

"Yes. He found her; I paid. Actually, she was a bargain compared to the divorce lawyer."

Coswell was silent for a moment, wondering why Renée Lafleur hadn't mentioned Kelly's wife in their "dealings." Perhaps it might have been bad for business—clients worried about being set up by their wives.

Bostock took advantage of the pause to take over the interview again.

"Did he leave you alone after that?"

She shook her head.

"For a while, he did. But I knew it wouldn't last. His disease was too chronic. He started pestering me again, usually over the phone. I wouldn't let him into my residence. Eventually he started coming here, to my office. I saw him a few times and, I'm embarrassed to say, wrote out a check for him each time, but finally I stood my ground and forbade him to ever cross my threshold again."

"And did he cross the threshold again?"

She smiled.

"My guardian wouldn't let him. Francis may not look it, but when provoked, he can be an intimidating presence."

Just then, as if he'd know what they were saying, Francis opened the door and stuck his head in.

"You are aware that you have a class waiting for you in lecture hall B, Dr. Montgomery? I think they're getting restless. I just spoke to their leader, Sally the Garungous."

Montgomery looked at her wristwatch.

"Oh, how time flies," she said. "We will have to continue this at another time if you think another time is necessary."

"It may be," said Coswell. "But thank you for talking to us today. We'll be in touch."

They all stood up. Coswell gestured for Montgomery to go ahead. He followed her out of the room, entranced by her hair glistening in front of him and the erotic swing of her hips. He had almost reached the door when he realized that Bostock wasn't behind him. He turned and saw her leaning over Francis' desk.

"May I look at your appointment book again?" she said. "I didn't really get a chance to go over it when we were in last time."

"For you, pretty police lady, anything. Be my guest," Francis said, turning the book so that she could read it.

As she was doing that, Coswell regarded Francis and thought back to his days as a rookie constable. His old sergeant liked to say, "If there's a fight that you have to break up, pick on the big guy. He'll go down like a sack. It's those feisty little buggers who'll squash your balls." Francis qualified. He was little and Coswell had no doubt that he was feisty. He would get Bostock to check on that bar fight in which Francis was written up. Apparently he was not a man to have angry at you.

Bostock took only a minute to scan the book before turning it back the way it was.

"Thank you," she said, "And just for our records, could you tell us your whereabouts Sunday night?"

"Oooh, am I a suspect? How thrilling. Which is more than I can say for my Sunday nights. That's when I do the week's laundry. Nine to ten at the Jiffy Clean on Main Street without fail. Absolute best time to go. You can always get machines then. And when the wash is done and I have it all in the driers, I go next door to Fong's Heavenly Chinese Food and have a bowl of noodles. Then home to early bed—alone. I'm between romances right now."

Coswell almost moaned. There was such a thing as information overload but Bostock appeared to take it all in stride.

"Thanks again for being so cooperative," she said.

"Any time, pretty lady," he said and as she turned to leave, "Your ensemble is excellent, by the way. But maybe a bit of colour? A neck scarf, perhaps?"

They took the stairs down to the main floor.

"We'll go back to the pub so you can have your lunch," Coswell said. "And we'll do a debriefing, but first let's peek into the anatomy lab and see if Frank Hoffmann is still agonizing over his dead roommate."

When they got to the door of the lab, Coswell stood back and motioned her forward. He still couldn't remember the lock code.

"You do it," he said. "And make it quick. Just a peek and then tell me what you see."

She had no problem with the code even though she had seen it punched in only once. I used to be able to do that, too, Coswell lamented.

Her peek took longer than he would have liked, but he knew she wanted to be accurate in her assessment, especially after her misjudgement of Frank during the residence interview.

Eventually she came back out and closed the main door quietly behind her.

"His group is at the station just inside the second doors," she said, "But he had his back to me. They're all totally engrossed in the cadaver. He did look up a couple of times, so that I could see his face in profile. He appears to be over his trauma; I saw him smile at one of the women working with him."

"Could you see Amy?"

"No, and I had a good look for her."

"I'm not surprised," Coswell said. "Chu's death must have hit her very hard."

Silence.

Coswell looked at her.

"What?" he said.

"My impression was that she is another example of 'The lady doth protest too much.'"

Damn. He had the quote wrong. It was about a *woman*. Who he couldn't remember, but it was definitely about a woman, not a "he." She was right.

"I think she held something back when we spoke," she said.

"That's interesting. If you're right then we're even. I never doubted that she was genuine, rushing out of the pub and all that. So she's all yours. You can get her address from the Dean's office after lunch."

"I have it. She lives in Ross House. That's in Place Vanier as well. They kindly gave me the whole class list when I went over there to get Frank Hoffmann's address."

Maybe she wasn't so "cap in hand" when she went there or at least with the underling who eventually got the addresses for her. The thought crossed his mind that Bostock on her own could be a much more effective investigator than she was trailing after him. But what would he lose if he turned her loose too often? A quandry.

CHAPTER FIFTEEN

The Pit Pub was almost deserted, again not surprising at mid afternoon, with most still in classes. Coswell told Bostock to pick a private corner while he told them at the bar to heat up her sandwich and have the waitress bring it over to their table, along with a glass of water for her plus another sleeve of beer for himself.

When he joined her at the table, he sat down opposite

and said, "Are you sure you wouldn't like something other than water to drink?"

"No, thank you."

Whether or not it was the mention of water or that coffee he had just drunk at the residence hitting his kidneys, he felt a sudden urge to urinate. Aside from the embarrassment of having to rush to a bathroom, the suddenness alarmed him. This had become an increasingly common event over recent months. He figured it was likely due to an enlarged prostate and hoped it wasn't cancerous.

He looked at Bostock. Surely she needed to have a "powder break." Didn't all women do that with great frequency? He looked longingly at the men's room door, which he could see just past her head.

"Well," he said, fighting the urge. "What did you think of our session with Dr. Montgomery and did you see anything interesting in Francis' daybook?"

"I think it was a good beginning," she said. "We got a lot of the story, but we didn't get her to tell us where she was at ten o'clock on the night of the murder."

Coswell felt the colour rising in his neck. That should have been one of the very first questions. No doubt she would have had a ready answer, but it was the way parties responded that told the story, the look in their eyes, the tone of their voice, how quickly.

"I thought we'd take it easy on her," he said. "Let her open up and I think she did that pretty well." Pure rationalization. He hoped Bostock wouldn't notice.

"She certainly pointed us toward the gang killing possibility," she said.

"Your theory, as I recall," Coswell said, hoping a bit of praise might take her mind off his negligence.

"Not a terribly serious one," she said. "I just threw it into the pot."

"But it does sound plausible from what she said, does it not?"

Another pause.

"Unless she was steering us that way," she said.

To Coswell's great relief, the waitress arrived and set down the sandwich and their drinks. She was the same girl who had served them earlier. He reached for his wallet.

"The beer's been paid for," she said. "The big girl you were sitting with said you'd be back and to tell you it was on her. There wasn't much of the poutine left so I dumped it. That okay?"

"Quite okay," he said. "Reheated poutine is not fit for human consumption."

"Whatever," she said. "Let me know if you want anything else."

And away she went with an air of nonchalance that wasn't there when she first served them. A veteran now after only a few hours. Amazing the adaptability of the young.

He had barely turned his attention back to Bostock when his cell phone buzzed. Like the water, it sent off his bladder and this time he knew he couldn't fight it. He quickly pulled the phone from his pocket and glanced at the display.

"Uh-oh," he said. "I'd better take this in private. It's personal.

With that, he pushed talk, held the phone to his ear and spoke into it as he hurried to the washroom.

"Just hold on a minute," he said.

He burst into the men's and went straight to the urinal, struggling to hold onto the phone and undo his fly at the same time. He just made it. When all was directed and flowing, he used his free hand to put the phone back to his ear. James was speaking.

"What is that noise?" he said. "It sounds like Niagara Falls."

"I'm having a gigantic piss. Now what's up?"

"That must be awkward."

"Never mind. Give."

"I'm afraid that I made a teeny assumption that I shouldn't have."

"How teeny and what assumption?"

"The marks on the neck. When Charlotte turned back the vic's collar the marks looked to me like he'd been strangled."

"So?"

"I should have asked Charlotte before blabbing to you, but you know how she is. Doesn't say a damn thing while she's working. I eventually got up the nerve to ask her and she said she didn't think that the marks represented anything fatal. Then she wouldn't elaborate. Gave me the usual 'wait for the autopsy results.' Maybe if you spoke to her."

His stream slowed to a dribble, but the amount he had urinated cheered him. Men with enlarged prostates tended to put out small amounts more frequently, according to the Mayo Clinic website. He set the phone down to put everything back in place before picking his phone back up and resuming his conversation.

"Did you remember to zip up?" James said.

"I'm not that senile, yet."

"Where are you by the way?"

"At the Pit Pub. Bostock missed her lunch."

"Ah. I see you've taken my advice. Be nice to her and, by the way, have you broached the subject of your date yet?"

"Don't nag. I plan to. Right after I get off the phone with you and yes, I want to talk to Charlotte. Don't let her leave until I get there."

"Hurry," James said.

When he emerged from the men's room, Coswell noted that Bostock had finished her sandwich and half the glass of water. Nice to see that she got hungry like everyone else. Maybe she would go to the Ladies' while he drank his sleeve of beer and he could get the waitress to bring over some nuts. But she didn't budge. Must have a bladder the size of an elephant.

"I have to go back to Chu's room and talk to Charlotte, but I'd like you to get that interview done with his girlfriend, Amy. You can take the cruiser if you like."

She shook her head.

"Ross House isn't far from Robson House, according to the campus map. I'll walk over."

"Okay, and when you're done, come back to the lounge in the CommonsBlock."

They were just out the door when he remembered the second part of his question to her.

"You were going to tell me if you found anything interesting in Francis' daybook."

"It *was* interesting. The actual time slots were primarily meetings, lectures, autopsies, clinical rounds, but there were very few names, yours being the latest. Drop-ins were never recorded in one of those spaces. They were printed in the margins, opposite the times. Dr. Kelly's name appeared of course, but there was another name that was noted much more frequently—Dr. Barrett."

Coswell did a quick rack of his brain but nothing came.

Bostock obviously noted the lights out.

"He's the neurologist who Mabel, the ward aid, told us was rumoured to be having a thing going with Dr. Montgomery," she said,

"Oh, yes, him. Well, I wouldn't put too much in that. She's a neuropathologist. One would expect them to collaborate."

But why so often? She had a point.

James was pacing outside Chu's room when Coswell puffed his way up to the third floor of the residence.

"Thank goodness you've finally arrived," he said. "They're packing up to go. I'd have had to throw myself at Charlotte's feet to keep her here for you."

"She would have just stepped over you."

Coswell took a deep breath, pushed the door open—and banged into Charlotte, bent down packing her kit. The door caught her mid derrière.

"Good God, Coswell," she said. "Couldn't you have knocked first?"

"Sorry. I just wanted a good look at those neck marks before the coroner's crew gets here."

"Be my guest," she said. "We're through."

"Uh, I was hoping you would give me your expert opinion."

She waved her two assistants out, and as they squeezed by Coswell, she held Chu's collar open for him to see.

"Superficial," she said. "Botched attempt before the IV? Certainly not typical of someone strangling him, and no bruises elsewhere. I'll know for sure when I autopsy his trachea."

Coswell had to agree. He had seen many hanging victims as well as strangulations. This was neither, but what did startle him was that he noticed the watch on Chu's right wrist. How had he missed this? No wonder Bostock looked puzzled when he told her to find out if Chu was right or left-handed. She probably didn't miss the watch. People wear wristwatches on their non-dominant side. Chu was left-handed, hence the IV into his right arm.

"But it looks like a suicide," Charlotte said, and then seeing the downcast expression on Coswell's face,

"You shouldn't be disappointed. That surgeon's murder should be enough to keep you busy."

She bent down and picked up her kit.

"Okay," she said. "Move along you two and let me out. I've got work to do."

Coswell turned and almost bumped into James, who

had been standing right behind him.

They stood outside the room, watching as Charlotte distanced herself from them.

"I missed it, too," James said. "The wristwatch."

But James had an excuse. He would have been looking over everyone's shoulders and his view of the dead man's wrist obscured. Coswell had no such excuse, and James' comment didn't cheer him one bit.

"Bostock is interviewing the girlfriend right now," he said. "I'm meeting her over at the commons. Can you join us?"

James frowned.

"Don't tell me you haven't set up the Irish pub gig with her yet."

"No time," Coswell said. "And I might need your support."

"Oh, all right then, but I have to wait for the meat wagon."

"And the press?"

"No, not the press. Suicides don't rate. Only bare-assed murdered surgeons are worth their coming way out here."

The coroner's crew arrived as they were talking—two men dressed in dark clothing, their jackets police-type with BC CORONER SERVICE across the backs. They worked quickly and had Wing Chu's body bagged and on a gurney in just minutes. Getting it down the six flights of stairs was a challenge, but the men handled it with practiced ease.

"They're just so big and strong," James said.

The residence don still hadn't returned to his room when they checked.

"No note or cell phone number," Coswell observed. "How would anyone get in touch with him in an emergency? Poor show, I'd say."

"I'll get his number from the students' services

office," James said.

"Or just ask Bostock," Coswell said. "She's probably got it."

The commons sitting lounge was deserted except for a young man practicing at one end on a baby grand piano. He barely looked up at them when they entered. Coswell led the way to a comfortable seating area at the opposite end, where they settled into two big armchairs facing one another.

"Bostock shouldn't be long," Coswell said. "I'll bring you up to date."

James listened carefully to Coswell's summation of the Kelly case, for once not interrupting but when he finished, the comments began to flow.

"If Chu's death was suicide," he said, "it does downgrade Frank Hoffmann on the suspect list. I'd still have his alibi checked out, though."

"No doubt that's already on Bostock's list of to-dos ," Coswell said with a hint of resignation.

"No, of all the possibilities," James went on, "I guess I have to agree with the gang theory, even though I didn't back it at the start. The professional garrotting, the hooker's comments regarding the mysterious Mr. C, the gambling addiction. It would all fit."

"My thinking exactly," Coswell said. "So the sooner Bostock and I do our surveillance at The Auld Sod Pub, the better."

James nodded and then shot him a mischievous look.

"But that only covers one of your three motives—greed—i.e., the gang wanted to send a message to welchers. There's still the hate possibility, though; Kelly was definitely a candidate for that—a bully and a bigot. And, of course, Bostock's "love" motive. That Dr. Barrett sounds interesting. Maybe he felt compelled to get rid of a great millstone around his beloved's neck."

"And now, I suppose, you're going to add "fear" to confuse the issue further," Coswell said.

"Can't really ignore it, although so far the only person who might have feared him enough to kill him would be his ex-wife."

That suggestion barely registered in Coswell's mind before he ruled it out. Impossible.

"More likely the gang connection again," he said. "Maybe he threatened to blow the whistle on them and get his debts erased that way."

At that moment, they saw Bostock enter the commons through the main doors. She glanced first in the direction of the cafeteria but then saw James stand up and wave to her from the lounge. She turned and headed their way. Coswell had no intention of standing. The chair was too comfortable, and at his age, he deserved some consideration.

"She really is quite lovely," James said as she smiled at the pianist and continued towards them.

Coswell looked at him.

"Don't confuse yourself, James," he said.

She sat down on an adjacent chesterfield rather than a chair, again keeping her back straight. Coswell wondered if the woman ever relaxed.

"How did it go with Amy," he said.

"Very well. Easy, in fact. I think she probably wanted to open up when we first talked."

And I didn't give her enough time to do that, Coswell lamented.

"She had actually just called it off with Wing Chu," Bostock continued. "Apparently he'd been coming on too strong with the Chinese culture business but she's Canadian through and through. Her great, great grandfather helped bring the railroad to BC back in the eighteen hundreds. But Wing wanted her to learn Chinese and even started asking her to wear more oriental-style clothing."

"That's ridiculous," James said. "From what I read, the young in China want the opposite—the more Western, the better."

"Chu's family is old school ... literally," she said. "Generation after generation of teachers and scholars. If he got serious enough about Amy, and they contemplated a more permanent arrangement, she would have to fit in."

Coswell nodded.

"And move back to China with him."

"That was what did it," Bostock said. "Amy didn't get into medical school by being a meek and mild female. She has a life planned for herself right here in Canada and wasn't about to abandon it to go starry-eyed to a foreign country."

There was an edge to her voice, almost as though Amy's story was her own, but she caught herself and quickly reverted to her police voice. "She told me that he didn't create any kind of fuss. He seemed to accept her decision as something he expected and simply needed to hear. They parted quite amicably after dinner. At least she thought so, which added to her shock when Sally announced to everyone at the Pit Pub that he had killed himself."

Coswell crossed his arms over his chest and sank back even further into the soft backrest of his chair.

"It all piled on," he said. "Reality hit the poor fellow like a giant hammer. He starts into a profession that he doesn't really want; his roommate is a bigot; Kelly's body shocks him; his girl friend gives him the kiss-off."

Bostock picked it up from there.

"So he decides to kill himself," she said. "And the lack of reaction to Amy's rejection, his cheerfulness at breakfast with Frank—all typical of a suicide who's made up his mind."

Coswell smiled.

"You really stayed awake in those psychology lectures,

didn't you?"

Bostock blushed.

"I did find them interesting," she said.

Coswell chastised himself for putting her down. The only reason he could think of for his doing so was that McMorran, the blockhead, had been right and it rankled him. But taking it out on her wasn't fair and he saw James frowning at him.

"Okay," he said. "Now, unless something comes up, I think we can turn all our attention to the Kelly case. James has come up with a suggestion in that regard which I'd like him to present to you."

James choked back a cough. Coswell suddenly appeared to take interest in the arm of his chair.

Bostock showed no hesitation whatsoever when she heard the plan and mercifully didn't ask how the information had been obtained.

"Of course I'll do it," she said. "I haven't done any undercover work before. It will be a good experience for me."

I hope so, Coswell thought. He was having trouble seeing himself as a john and Bostock as a hooker.

"When would you like to do this, sir?" she said. "I might need to pick up something appropriate to wear."

James sat up.

"Clothes shopping. Now that sounds like a lot more fun than this dull police work," he said. "Do you need help?"

Coswell cut off her reply.

"She still has some dull police work to do today," he said, "And surely to God you have something more important on your slate."

"Not really," James said.

"You can tag after Charlotte then. The minute she finds out what was in that IV bottle, I want to know about it. I'm still puzzled about how rumpled our corpse looked.

Maybe those neck marks weren't self-inflicted."

He turned to Bostock.

"We'll do our undercover business tomorrow night."

She nodded enthusiastically.

"Meanwhile, I want you to go back to headquarters. James can drop you off. We need to know Kelly's financial transactions over the past few months, checks he wrote, credit card accounts, ATM withdrawals. You'll need a warrant to do that but no problem. Call Judge Bentley's office and tell him I requested it. He and I have a long history."

"What are you going to do now?" James asked.

"I'll clean up around here. I want one last go-around in Chu's room, and I should check out his locker before everything gets moved out. I'll also look for good places to hang one's self. Might even find the actual rope. We do get lucky sometimes."

"And the don?" Bostock said.

"Yes, him, too. He can't have gone far and he'll need to pack away Chu's belongings until he finds out what the parents want done with them."

It took Coswell fifteen minutes to do all that. He stopped first at the don's room. Still no one home. Wing Chu's room revealed nothing worth noting. In the basement, there were a few good sites to use for hanging but no visible evidence that Chu had used any of them. He could see through the wooden slats into the locker well enough to know it wasn't worth the bother of getting the key to open it.

This done, he went back to the cruiser and drove to the anatomy building. The student day was almost done; Dr. Montgomery would either be back in her office or soon returning to it. He would be waiting for her.

Francis had been told to leave early.

"She is just so nice," he said after dutifully printing

Coswell's name in the margin of his daybook. "I've worked for others who had no appreciation of just how hard their assistants work. I'm going home and have a long, hot soak in the tub. Sitting at a desk all day just raises hell with my back."

Before leaving, though, he pushed a chair again into Dr. Montgomery's office, complaining all the way. "I wish she would let me get rid of some of the stuff she has in there. It's ridiculous that I have to move chairs in and out when she has visitors."

Francis had barely left when Montgomery swept into her office carrying a sheaf of notes. Seeing Coswell sitting there startled her.

"Inspector Coswell," she said. "I wasn't expecting to see you so soon."

He stood when she came into the room, but that created an awkward situation. She had to brush by him so close that for a brief instant her perfume and the slight touch of her body made him slightly giddy.

She threw the folder she was carrying onto her desk, pealed off her white lab coat, and draped it over the back of her chair before sitting down. As she did so, her breasts swelled forward.

"Please be seated," she said.

He knew she had noticed his helpless ogling, but there wasn't a trace of modesty in her gaze; more that of a temptress, or at least that's what he thought he saw.

"We did have more questions for you earlier, and since we would like to move along as quickly as possible, I thought we might finish up before you went home today."

She held him with her gaze.

"I have a better idea," she said. "If you are free, why don't we have dinner this evening? I'm about to head over to the Recreation Centre. I teach a class there on Wednesdays."

Dinner? Alarm bells were ringing in Coswell's head,

but he paid them no attention.

"I *am* free this evening," he said. "And dinner sounds good, but only if you come as my guest and we go to my favourite restaurant, The Vicinage."

"Oh my," she said. "Isn't that ironic. Patrick said it was the best restaurant in Vancouver. But the prices? Are you sure?"

"Absolutely. Fine dining is my one vice," he said

Again that bemused smile.

"How about I pick you up at seven?" he said.

"Perfect. I should be really hungry by then, so I might be a costly date."

"My pleasure. I'll see you at seven."

It wasn't until he got back to the cruiser parked in the Dental lot that he came back to earth. What in God's name had he done? Dating a suspect? Insane. Where had this rush of hormones come from? Testosterone was supposed to diminish with age. What to do?

And then he calmed down and began to rationalize. What better way to interview a suspect than in a relaxed atmosphere where they would loosen up and, hopefully, be free with their answers. A good vintage wine would help. Why bloody not? But guilt nagged at him.

He didn't want to go back to headquarters. Good to let Bostock work alone, and James could get him on his cell phone if he got anything worthwhile from Charlotte. But he didn't want to be disturbed. He took out his phone, scrolled down to Bostock's number, and punched it in.

"This is taking me longer than I thought," he said to her, "and I've about had it for the day. Not feeling so hot. Would you phone James and tell him not to bother calling me tonight. I'll meet with both of you tomorrow morning and we can go over everything."

"I hope you aren't coming down with anything," Bostock said.

"No. I'll be fine tomorrow, I'm sure. I just need a good night's rest."

"Fine, sir. I'll pass on your message to James."

He hadn't really lied all that much. It *was* true that he didn't feel so hot, if raving guilt could be classified as such. And then he had an awful thought—he hadn't gotten Dr. Montgomery's home address. It was too late to go to the Dean's office and he definitely wasn't about to phone Bostock and ask for it. And then he cursed his stupidity; the answer was obvious—just ask her.

He expected that she would drive her car to the Rec Centre, and so he waited in the cruiser for her to appear. When she didn't show after fifteen minutes, it was obvious that she had walked there taking the very route he and James had used to get to the Pit Pub two days before. No problem then, he would find her there.

But when he walked into the centre, his nerve began to waver. The place was enormous. It didn't exist when he was a student there. Where could she be? She didn't say what class she was giving. He assumed Yoga, or maybe dance but possibly she was just giving a lecture.

Students were coming and going from a large reception area; signing in he presumed. When there was a brief gap in the line he went up to the desk. It was manned by a muscle-bound young jock in a Tee shirt so tight his nipples stood out. He wore a name tag that simply read PAUL.

"Dr. Montgomery is giving a class here this afternoon," Coswell said, "Can you tell me where it's being held?"

Paul gave him a look that said "How does a flabby guy like you have anything to do with such a gorgeous creature?" But he answered the question with a pleasant smile.

"She's giving the Krav Maga Defense course," he said. "The Dojo is on the second floor. We are so lucky to have her as a volunteer. The women on campus are signing up for her course in droves. She's a black belt from Montreal, you know."

"I didn't know," Coswell said.

"The class has just started. I hope I don't need to interrupt her. Those women are very intense."

"No," Coswell said. "I'll see her later, but can I have a peek in? I'm curious. I know nothing about Krav Maga."

"Certainly. Just go up those stairs," he said, pointing. "Near the end of the hallway you will come to a couple of big glass doors on your right. That's the Dojo."

CHAPTER SIXTEEN

He could see the whole room through the doors. The class was in session and there was Kay Montgomery in a judo outfit. In just seconds, Coswell knew what Krav Maga Defense was—how to street fight. It wasn't called that in his basic training, but a brutal RCMP sergeant taught the same thing to all recruits. Coswell swore he had permanent bruises from the sessions.

She was giving a demonstration using a male student who had her in a bear hug. It was difficult to follow exactly what she did, but it all seemed to happen in one motion. Her elbow flew back, catching the man on the side of his head, and at the same time she hooked her foot behind his knee sending him twisting backwards. He landed face down on the mat. In a blink she was on him, with her knee pressed on the base of his spine and one of his wrists pushed up so high his shoulder looked ready to pop.

Coswell turned away from the door and made his way back to the cruiser. He would use that People Find thing of James' on the inboard computer to get her address, something he could have done in the first place. Logic blocked out by the opportunity to see her again? But the violence of what he had just seen had dampened his ardour—Kay Montgomery was quite capable of killing someone if she so desired. Too late to call off the dinner, but sadly he would go now in a different frame of mind—his policeman's mind.

Bostock turned off her cell phone and sat back in her chair. She had played along with Coswell's sudden malaise, but she knew he was up to something. But he could be just avoiding her again. She thought back over their day and couldn't come up with a reason. Other than getting a little too enthusiastic about the suicide business, she had been very careful to remain low profile. Did he think she wasn't capable of doing a good job finishing off the door-to-door or interviewing the residence don? Had she missed something that he wasn't sharing with her?

She wished James had hung around so that she could have discussed her concerns with him, but he had come into the office just long enough to find out that Charlotte had gone out to the forensics lab in Burnaby. "I have to go beard the lioness in her den," he said. "Wish me luck." With that, he left then without a backward glance. Not likely that he would return to headquarters later. It was almost five o'clock.

Getting the warrant Coswell wanted proved not as easy as he said. Wednesdays were Judge Bentley's golf afternoons and he was still out on the course. His secretary suggested she call a Justice Mackenzie, the judge on duty. That was, of course, the logical thing to do, but she hesitated. Coswell had specifically mentioned Judge Bentley. Was MacKenzie as amenable? Suddenly, she could feel herself spiralling down again into depression and crippling anxiety. *Corporal Bostock*—what a joke; she couldn't even make a simple decision.

Her purse beckoned, tucked under the desk. She had tried so hard not to take the pills during work hours, but knew if she didn't the spiral would soon hit rock bottom. Either way she would be useless at completing any task. She reached under and got the purse. It took her a minute to rummage through it and find the pills. Her pistol was in the way, so she took it out and laid it on the desk. She found the pill bottle, shook one out, and put it under her tongue, enough she thought to calm her so that she could at least get things in order before leaving the office.

She put the bottle back into her purse and snapped it shut before remembering the gun still lying on her desk. She looked at it, a heavy, ugly piece of cold metal—a Smith and Wesson 5946 semi-automatic with the RCMP logo on the barrel.

She remembered the thrill when it was first issued to her. It represented power, an equalizer, a unisex defender ... or aggressor. She practiced with it at the range by the hour, eventually getting her sharpshooter's certificate. Only once had she fired it in a lethal manner to bring down a knife-wielding assailant who unfortunately didn't die. The world would have been a better place without him.

When she put it back into her purse, she checked that the ten-round clip was still wrapped up in a tissue.

Jane, Chief Ward's secretary had gone home early. Wednesday afternoon was his golf day, too. There were a few constables still in the general office but they were getting ready to leave. Soon she would be the only one left. Her to-do list glared at her: finish the foreign student checks; contact the manager of Kelly's apartment to find out what bank the rent checks were issued on; get a dress for the Irish pub undercover job.

She got up from the desk, put a paperweight on the list, grabbed her purse, and headed for the exit. A minute later, she returned and got her sweater out of the closet. The day was so warm she hadn't needed it, but shopping for a dress might take a while and it did cool off in the evenings.

THE EXTRA CADAVER MURDER

Vancouver City Bus service, she discovered, was excellent. Waits were minimal, especially from headquarters to downtown. She caught one just minutes after she walked the short distance to the stop. And no problem getting a seat. The rush was coming out of downtown, not heading into it.

She felt better. Whether it was the pill or the prospect of dress shopping that did it she wasn't sure and cared less—the spiral had been broken. Now what should she buy? And then it dawned on her that she had no idea what a Vancouver hooker wore. Net stockings and a super short mini? But then Renée popped into her mind. At one thousand dollars a night that woman certainly didn't have to dress cheap. Best to buy something alluring and in good taste, something similar to the dress that Dr. Montgomery wore under her lab coat.

Back at his condominium in Chinatown, Coswell was also deciding what to wear. He usually went to The Vicinage directly from work dressed in whatever he had chosen for the day. The staff seemed to pay no attention to his wardrobe even if it consisted of his favourite windbreaker and full-fit trousers. He had observed, however, that most of The Vicinage clientele were more elegantly attired, and dinner with Kay Montgomery would demand his best.

Unfortunately, the least seedy of his wardrobe were items he had bought and didn't like. After much rummaging he came up with a pair of fawn chinos, which he had worn only once, a cowboy denim shirt left over from his session in the Chilcotin, and a lightweight blue Tilley travel blazer. He had bought the latter because of the abundance of pockets and the "touch more room in the back." But he needed more than a touch because it always felt constrictive to him. It did, however, go with his shoe collection—nothing but black oxfords.

He put it all on and looked at himself in the bathroom

mirror. Not bad, he thought, although it needed a bit of dash. An Ascot? He did have one from his student days, but it was an affectation then and would be even more so now. No. What he had on would have to do. Before turning away, he leaned closer to the mirror and wondered for a moment if he should grow a pencil moustache like Hercules Poirot. No. That would be an even bigger affectation.

He went into his living room to wait. It was almost an hour before he had to leave to pick up Montgomery. Everything was done— reservation at The Vicinage, table for two in a private corner upstairs, and her address obtained from Canada 411—Point Grey Road, an upscale neighbourhood for sure—a whole different scene than her ex-husband's surroundings on Ash Street.

A couple of fingers of good scotch appealed to him at that moment, but why? Had he not turned back into a cool headed investigator instead of a foolish old man with an erotic fantasy? He had no reason to be nervous, but the image of the Krav Maga had faded, replaced with that lovely, freckled face.

He cracked open a bottle of Glenlivet that he was saving for a special occasion and poured a glass. It worried him to think how long it had been since he spent an evening with a desirable woman. Did he have any functioning testosterone left, he wondered? Perhaps he had a pituitary tumour. Or more likely—his liver was packing in. The Mayo Clinic listed long term alcohol consumption as a leading cause of a dysfunctional libido.

James got more than he bargained for when he arrived at the forensics lab—three tough-minded women gathered in the boardroom—Sergeant Charlotte Jacobsen, the hedgehog of field forensics, Marie D'Allarde, the chief herself, and Dr. Lockie, the assistant coroner, his liaison contact. They were not having late tea as one would expect. Instead, they were drinking beer—no glasses, straight from the can.

He debated backing out of there but D'Allarde, seated at the head of the table, caught sight of him.

"Corporal James, mon beau garçon," she said. "Come join the party. Grab a beer out of the lab fridge. You might have to move a few specimens first."

James had never liked beer. In fact he drank very little alcohol, but he didn't want to be a teetotaller in front of this group. He opened the fridge. D'Allarde wasn't kidding; there were specimens on every shelf. The beer was contained in what, in a normal fridge, would be the crisper. He pulled one out and took it into the boardroom, noting that it was one of those awful, microbrewery things that was probably loaded with malt. He hated that taste, his aversion conditioned by his mother, the health nut, who mixed a teaspoon of Brewer's yeast in his orange juice each morning to boost his vitamin B level.

He was also taken aback by the picture on the can—a woman riding an old fashioned bicycle, her short skirt blown way back revealing stockings, garter belt, and panties. If that wasn't sexist, nothing was. A strange choice for the three women sitting in the boardroom.

Charlotte patted the back of the chair beside her.

"Drop your tush here, James," she said. "We are just about to give the facts to Dr. Lockie, so she can sign off on your Chinese suicide, and it was suicide, despite Coswell throwing me that 'enough to cause suspicion' bone."

"How can you be so sure?" James said.

She looked sideways at him.

"You have doubts?"

James just shrugged. Poking the lioness was dumb.

"Our dead medical student managed to set up an IV drip on himself with enough KCl in it to kill an elephant," she said. "God knows how he stood the pain at the injection site. That stuff is such an irritant. He would have suffered less if he'd been successful hanging himself."

So much for the rumpled clothing and messed up hair that Coswell had placed such significance on. The poor man had been writhing in agony.

"He tried to hang himself first?" Dr. Lockie said.

"Most likely. It would be consistent with the marks I saw on his neck, and one of his ears had what looked like a rope burn on it."

"And how did he get the KCl and the IV equipment?"

"He had a degree in pharmacology according to Coswell," Charlotte continued. "So presumably he had access to storage areas in the lab. Too bad he didn't also swipe some barbiturate to knock himself out and save all that pain."

James couldn't help wading in, despite telling himself to listen and not speak.

"It may not have been so easy for him," he said. "He had graduated, so maybe he didn't want to raise any suspicions when he appeared there for no valid reason."

"Could be, I suppose," Charlotte said. "But the bottom line is that he did and he killed himself. Case over."

James couldn't argue with that, but he hoped that Coswell would agree. The inspector had an annoying habit of wanting one hundred percent confirmation. Comments such as "most likely" and "presumably" did not fly with him.

"Now take a good sip of that beer, James," D'Allarde said, "and tell me what you think."

James popped the pull tab, put the can to his lips, and then stuck his tongue in the opening. He gave a few glugging sounds before setting the can back down on the table. Even the small amount he had got on his tongue tasted vile.

"Excellent," he said, and tried to think of a way to get rid of the can without anyone noticing that it was still full.

D'Allarde beamed.

"Bien sûr," she said. "Almost as good as les bières de

Québec. It was such torture those years I spent in Washington drinking that awful American stuff."

Dr. Lockie laughed. "I'll drink to that," she said. "But you could have substituted good wine. The Americans do know how to make that."

"My betz cells prefer beer," D'Allarde said. "Must preserve them, you know."

"A theory I've chosen to ignore," Dr. Lockie said. "But let's turn for a moment to the feature event of the week— Dr. Kelly's murder. Anything new on that? The press has given me a little break, but if nothing more spectacular comes up, they'll be back."

"Nothing, forensically speaking," Charlotte said.

They all turned and looked at James who threw up his hands.

"I've been replaced on that case," he said. "Totally."

He hoped that comment registered. Any continued involvement by him might be leaked back to Chief Ward.

"And by a female, no less," Charlotte said. "What's the word on her, James? I've heard rumours."

The other two women looked at him, obviously interested. Gossip, thy name is woman, James thought to himself, and then, recalling some of the parties he had attended, he squelched the thought. Gossip was unisex.

He smiled.

"Sorry to disappoint you, Charlotte," he said, "but I don't do rumours."

"How dull," D'Allarde said, picking up her beer. "Rumours are the spice of life along with a little sex."

Time to go. James put his hand on the pocket that held his cell phone and pretended that it had vibrated. He pulled it out and looked down at the screen, being sure that Charlotte couldn't see it.

"Whoops, duty calls," he said. "I've got to go back to headquarters."

"I thought you were off homicide," Dr. Lockie said.

"Yes, but there are other things to be done," he said. "Chief Ward does not tolerate idle hands."

"Too bad," D'Allarde said. "We were enjoying your company."

James grabbed the beer and headed to the door. He tilted the can to his lips for a moment before leaving the room, but once out and the door closed behind him, he made his way to the men's washroom. There he poured the beer into a toilet and watched the vile stuff disappear when he hit the flusher. Before leaving, however, he went back into the lab and set the empty can on a table beside the fridge. Wonderful brew.

CHAPTER SEVENTEEN

Coswell took a cab to pick up Montgomery.

The Point Grey Road address turned out to be a large condominium complex that consisted of two brilliant white, three-storey blocks joined in the middle by something that looked like a spaceship perched on four skinny pillars framing massive windows and an entrance door adorned with an arch of inset pebbled glass. The designer, Coswell mused, must have decided to make up for the boring wings by incorporating features of Roman, Mideastern, and even American Georgian (à la Tara in *Gone With the Wind*) architecture into the centrepiece.

No names again on the residents' board, but he had her unit number—319. She answered almost immediately.

"How did I know that you would arrive promptly at seven?" she said. "Come right up."

How *did* she know? Did he come across as an obsessive, or even worse, a bird dog on the scent? He fretted all the way up the stairs to the third floor. No elevator. The building was obviously older than it looked.

She opened the door and what little resolve he had made to stay in the police mode vanished. She was wearing an emerald green silk dress that clung to her body in all the right places and was a perfect offset to her auburn hair. On her neck, a thin silver strand supported a heart-shaped red jewel that matched her lipstick. Unfortunately, it drew his attention to her breasts again, which were barely contained by the dress. He quickly focused on the jewel.

"Is that a ruby?" he said. "It's quite lovely."

An enigmatic smile.

"Yes. I inherited it from my mother."

She motioned for him to come in.

"I'm almost ready," she said and pointed down to her bare feet. "Shoes. Always a big decision for a woman."

She hurried off and ducked into a room at the end of a short hallway. Coswell looked around. Everything stated expensive to him—the furniture, the art work, the carpets. He decided that she was probably renting the place furnished. Nothing in that neighbourhood sold for much under a few million. With a spendthrift husband and a professor's salary he doubted that she could actually own the unit.

He was looking at one of the paintings when she came back into the room.

"A Chagall," she said. "Patrick liked it for some reason. I plan to sell it. It reminds me of intestinal parasites."

Then she probably was an owner. Interesting. He wondered where the money came from.

She got a black shawl out of the front hallway closet and handed it to him. He stepped behind her and draped it over her shoulders as she held her hair up. That very action, and the sight of her perfect neck, were exquisitely erotic.

"Thanks," she said and let her hair cascade down over the shawl.

He followed her down the stairs to the cab, the driver having agreed to wait. Coswell noticed that she had chosen red pumps with high heels as her footwear but descended the carpeted stairs with confidence. And she made no comment about the cab waiting, taking it in as much stride as going down the stairs in high heels. She was used to all this.

Nina, the lovely hostess at The Vicinage, greeted them with an even bigger smile than usual. Since James was the only person he occasionally treated there, he suspected that Nina probably thought he was gay. To arrive with a beautiful woman would reset her perception, but he would have to be more cautious admiring her derrière, which he invariably did whenever she led him to his table; a rare bit of voyeurism on his part.

As they moved to the stairs that gave access to the mezzanine, Coswell saw Iain Pope, the owner of The Vicinage, talking to a group of diners at one of the large tables on the main level. One of them, a handsome, middle-aged man in a formal dinner jacket, had shifted his attention from Iain to them, and gave a big wave. Coswell had no idea who he was, and then he realized that the man was waving to Montgomery. He tapped her on the shoulder.

"Someone over there knows you," he said.

She turned and looked.

"Gordon Struthers," she said. "A colleague of Patrick's."

She returned his wave with a smile and a feminine one-handed finger waggle.

Doctor Struthers, Coswell remembered—the surgeon who was now Chief of Surgery at the VGH—Kelly's replacement.

Nina took the RESERVED sign off their table and pulled a chair out for Montgomery, who deftly unwound her wrap and draped it over the back before sitting down. Coswell slid into his chair and felt the chinos bind into his crotch.

Nina set menus in front of them and gave the wine list

to Coswell. She didn't do the "Would you like something to start off with?" routine. Waste of breath in Coswell's case; he always started off with something.

He flipped the wine list open and gave the first page a cursory glance. New acquisitions were always there; the rest he had long since memorized.

"We'll start with a split of Prosecco," he said, "while we peruse the menu."

He didn't have to look at that either. Anything new and Nina would tell him. As predicted, she did.

"For starters, we have fresh Fanny Bay oysters done Rockefeller style with Panko crumbs and grated Gruyère cheese. The special entrée is Gabriola Island herb-roasted pork tenderloin with root vegetables. We're told that the pigs are taken for processing in pairs so that they have companionship right until the end."

She paused to let that sink in, oblivious to the fact that death and dying, especially of pigs, held absolutely no sway with either diner. But she finished with a flourish.

"And for dessert, a sugar pumpkin crème brûlée in anticipation of Halloween."

Over a month away, but Coswell didn't spoil her performance.

Montgomery handed her menu up to Nina.

"Sold," she said. "It's a special evening for me all the way."

If Nina read anything into that comment she didn't show it and immediately turned her attention to Coswell.

"You can bring me the same," he said. "But I'll have the Fraser Valley duck instead of the pork."

He picked up the wine list still open in front of him and turned over a few pages. He didn't want Montgomery to think he was all that familiar with the grape.

"The Prosecco will do us through the oysters," he said, "but what shall we have with the entrée?"

Nina's eyes widened. This was new to her. Coswell

never asked advice for his choice of wine. The question proved rhetorical.

"Duck and pork are close, I think," he said. "How about a Mission Hill Pinot Noir, Nina? What do you think?"

"Good choice, sir," she said. "I'll see if we still have some of the Martin Lane."

He was about to expound on his choice. That very BC vintage shocked the wine world when it won a Decanter Award in London the previous year, but he let it go. Instead, he thought he had better establish that his entrée choice was not obedience to a religious doctrine.

"I like pork," he said, "but I haven't had duck in a while, and I think they harvest them in flocks so they *really* have companionship."

She smiled and then became pensive.

"Ah, death," she said. "I'm not totally numb to it, despite my profession. Patrick's death did upset me. Our marriage was short, but there were the sweet moments, and he didn't deserve to die that way."

For a brief second, Coswell wondered how she knew "that way" but then decided that Francis had probably told her all the gory details with relish.

He was about to get her to tell him more about their relationship when Dr. Struthers mounted the stairs and came to stand by their table.

"Good to see you out enjoying yourself, Kay," he said, and then turning to Coswell. "I'm Ken Struthers."

Montgomery interjected with an introduction.

"This is Inspector Mark Coswell," she said, "of the RCMP."

A flicker of surprise crossed the man's face but he extended his hand. Coswell shook it, not bothering to get up. He also noted Montgomery's use of his first name, not recalling that he had ever mentioned it to her. Had she done a James-type search on him?

"Ah, yes," Struthers said. "You came to the department office a couple of days ago. I hope Carol gave you everything you needed."

"She was very helpful," Coswell said. He was about to add, "and I'll be back to see you both," but thought that might be rather asocial under the circumstances.

An awkward moment passed as neither he nor Montgomery encouraged further conversation with Struthers.

"Well, back to the Mrs.," he said. "Enjoy your dinner."

As Struthers turned to go back downstairs, Coswell looked below at the main floor. There were women seated on either side of the vacated chair, one of whom was looking up at them, her face filled with anger. When she noticed Coswell looking at her, she quickly turned away and began talking to the man seated next to her.

Was her anger on the basis of a social gaffe, or had Montgomery provoked a spark of jealousy? The woman was certainly no beauty. She reminded Coswell of those horsey English types who tromp around in jodhpurs and high-top leather boots, speaking in deep voices. With such a handsome husband, jealousy would be a natural reaction. Or was there more to it than that?

Nina arrived with their Proseccos and set them down, interrupting his speculations.

Coswell picked his glass up and held it toward Montgomery.

"To your good health," he said.

She raised hers in response.

"And to yours," she said. "And to your success in apprehending Patrick's killer."

She delicately touched his glass with hers and they drank. But his thoughts returned to Struthers, and a possible relationship with Montgomery. Maybe his was another name to add to Dr. Bennett's, the neurologist who ward aid Mabel had linked with Montgomery. He recalled his "fox" impression when Bostock and he interviewed her. In addition to their sexual proclivity, vixens were predators.

Montgomery saved him delving into the subject.

"Kenny is such a nice man," she said. "He deserved a medal for tolerating Patrick's arrogance. They were such opposites in every regard."

Coswell wondered if that included sexual performance. Kelly was apparently triple A in that regard. Was Struthers "just a friend" kind of guy despite his good looks?

"We used to get together socially," she continued. "But Patrick could be such a boor, especially when he drank too much, and Kenny's wife couldn't abide him even when he was sober."

"I gather that Dr. Struthers would have been a popular choice for Chief of Surgery," Coswell said. "Your husband's appointment must have caused some ill-feeling."

"Not with Kenny. He never complained, even when he ended up so many times being Patrick's stand-in at multi-discipline department meetings. I had to attend those, of course, and it was downright embarrassing. Kenny used to make a point of sitting beside me, which helped a lot."

The knight in shining armour approach. Maybe Kenny's testosterone level was right up there, too. And maybe the urge to protect Montgomery was in the same league as her secretary, Francis. But a killer? Didn't sound like it but still worth checking his whereabouts on the night Kelly was murdered.

He was getting his questions further organized in his mind when their oysters arrived. Thereafter, interview changed to pleasant conversation. Marvellous food plus the company of the lovely Montgomery grabbed his policeman's mind and totally shut it down. And whether by design or accident, she led the conversation.

"I've always had a thing for the RCMP," she said. "My

parents visited Canada when I was a little girl and brought me back a genuine Mountie doll. I loved it. Almost wore the poor thing out. Tell me how you ended up on the Force."

And away he went—life story, interesting cases, humourous incidents. Any time there was a lull, she kept him going with her questions, of which she seemed to have an unlimited supply. Before he knew it the dinner was over and Nina was at their table asking if he would like to finish up with a cognac or port. Montgomery answered immediately.

"Now it's my turn to host," she said. "Patrick, unwillingly I must say, left a few bottles of very old scotch when he moved out. It's not cognac or port but I think it will do."

Nina gave him a knowing smile and headed off to get the bill. His head was floating and he didn't think it was the wine, although he did notice that Nina refilled his glass at least twice as often as she did Montgomery's. But an invitation back to her residence? Heaven.

And second heaven was the scotch Montgomery served him back in her condo: a twelve year old Cragganmore single malt that made his earlier Glenlivet pale in comparison. He leaned back in the massive leather chair and let the taste linger in his mouth. She left the bottle on a glass coffee table in front of him.

"Dr. Kelly had good taste in scotch," he said.

"He had good taste in everything," she replied. "Unfortunately cost was a reality he could never grasp."

She had kicked off her shoes and was sitting on the accompanying leather chesterfield with her legs tucked up, the hem of her dress pulled just above her knees. She passed on the scotch. "It gives me a headache, I'm afraid, but I'm so glad you are enjoying it."

The drink she made for herself was a clear, bubbly

something or other with a slice of lime stuck on the side.

"You probably want to know if I ever met any of Patrick's shady friends," she said. "But I never did. I presume he met them at that Irish pub he frequented downtown. In fact, that was the only place he was a regular so far as I know. I had no intention of every going there. I knew it would be full of his ilk—Republicans to their Catholic core. No place for a Protestant girl like me."

She looked over at his glass—almost empty. He couldn't believe he had downed it so fast but she swung her legs off the couch and quickly refilled it—almost to the brim.

"Whoops," she said. "I'd never make a bartender."

She set the bottle back on the table and returned to the couch, snuggling down even further and exposing more of her thighs.

"We did go out socially, Patrick and I," she said. "The symphony, opera, theatre, but our evenings were most often separate. Surgeons supposedly have those late night cases, but somehow Patrick had a lot more time free than I did. The reason for that was mainly my fault. I wanted to impress everyone on staff with my willingness to sit on committees, give evening lectures to medical students, and run research projects that were never nine to five."

"An exhausting schedule," Coswell said, catching himself slurring the s's.

"Yes," she said. "It probably explains why I had a blind eye for so long. Maybe if I had paid him a little more attention he wouldn't have gone as far astray as he did."

Coswell was getting confused. Somehow Kelly had gone from boor and financial drain to poor boy. Where was this woman coming from? Suddenly he felt very warm. He had drunk the scotch too fast and the restaurant wine hadn't even begun to leave his bloodstream. In short, he could feel himself getting very drunk and he wanted out of there before he made a fool of himself.

Montgomery seemed to sense his concern.

"I have an early lecture tomorrow," she said. "Would you mind terribly if I called it a night?"

"Not at all," he said, avoiding words with s'es. He set his glass down on the table, concentrating hard on not spilling the ounce or so he hadn't drunk. He stood up just as carefully and made his way to the door. Mercifully he didn't tip over.

"I'll call you a cab," she said.

"No. I think I'll walk for a bit," he said. "I'll have no trouble hailing a cab on Point Grey Road."

At the door, she leaned forward and kissed his cheek.

"I had a lovely evening," she said. "You are a truly fascinating person. We must do this again."

He made it to the street level only by virtue of a death grip on the stair banister. Luck was with him, however, because he almost immediately managed to flag down a Yellow Cab returning from a drop-off in Kitsilano. A walk was the last thing he wanted. Crashing in his own bed was the priority.

CHAPTER EIGHTEEN

Thursday

Coswell's bedside alarm wakened him with a jolt at 6 a.m. He couldn't remember setting it but was glad that he did. He swore after his previous hangover, when he didn't get into the office until eight, that he would never again let that happen. He was losing his touch fast enough without his juniors labelling him an alky.

He staggered into the bathroom and stood over the toilet to empty his bladder, but nothing happened. Pressing on his lower abdomen didn't help and he had no sensation of fullness. Was he dehydrated? Had the previous night's alcohol dried him out? Or had it sucked the fluid out of his system and deposited it in his brain? That would explain the pounding in his head.

After a minute or so, he gave up and went over to the sink to brush his teeth and shave. His image in the mirror was not a cheery sight—a haggard old man. It wasn't until he had slathered shaving cream on his face that he began to replay his evening with Montgomery.

What had he accomplished? Certainly not anything worthwhile so far as the Kelly case was concerned. Struthers as a possible suspect could hardly be taken as a great breakthrough. And what had he gotten out of talking with her? Less than nothing. He hadn't even established her alibi. Bostock's admonishment about that nagged. And then a chill went through him. Would she and James find out about the dinner evening? He might be able to con James into thinking it was a deliberate probe for information on Kelly's murder but somehow he didn't think that would wash with Bostock.

But then the memory of that kiss at the door, the waft of her perfume and the image of her entrancing face came to him. To hell with them all, he decided. Life was going by fast enough for Mark Coswell and he deserved a little romance ... as unrealistic as it might be.

A shower, switched to cold at the end, an ibuprofen washed down with a giant glass of orange juice, and two black, double-strength coffees from his ridiculously expensive Scandinavian automatic machine put new life into him. This also included his excretory functions, much to his satisfaction.

He phoned for a taxi and went outside to wait for it. The sun was just rising and the eye-watering, downtown morning automobile exhaust smog was still an hour away.

The only glitch in his euphoria was finding Bostock hard at work in the office at seven-ten.

"Good heavens, Bostock," he said. "You aren't being paid by the hour, you know."

He wasn't sure how to take the slightly pained expression on her face.

"I haven't managed to get very far with the record checking of the foreign students," she said. "Early morning is the best time to phone overseas."

Coswell had actually forgotten that she had taken this on and felt a little guilty that he had let her do so just to keep her out of his hair.

"I wouldn't waste too much of your effort on that," he said. "Any student with a criminal record isn't likely to get past the university's screening process."

He thought this would be a relief to her but she seemed disappointed.

"I did get a couple done," she said, "the surgical residents—"

He cut her off.

"You can put that on my desk, but Dr. Kelly's financial records are first priority. How far have you gotten on that?"

Now she looked decidedly uncomfortable.

"Judge Bentley was unavailable when I called his office yesterday," she said. "I did leave a message for him. His secretary told me he would be in his office today around ten."

"Who was the judge on call? Did he drag his feet on issuing a warrant?"

She blushed.

"I didn't contact him," she said. "I thought that Judge Bentley—"

"Never hesitate to use all your options, Bostock. The on-call judge could have been a pussy and given you the warrant, thus allowing us to get going on the trace first thing this morning. Bentley might very well have a stack of higher priority items on his desk when he gets there today."

"I'm sorry, sir. I'll remember that next time."

God, why did he feel like he had just kicked her? James would have gone into one of his "Please don't hit me, sir," routines, completely defusing the reprimand.

"Okay," he said. "But put his number on your speed dial and keep bugging his secretary. I'd prefer not to go begging myself."

"No, sir. I'll definitely get it done ASAP."

"Good. Now are you all set for tonight?"

"Yes. I have an outfit that I think will be appropriate."

"Not too expensive, I hope," Coswell said. "That might catch the bean-counter's eye."

"I won't claim it as an expense," she said. "I can always use it for other occasions."

"Do you have any questions about your role?" he said.

"No, sir. James gave a very clear outline of the plan yesterday."

"Very well, but remember, If things look like they're going to get rough at any time, I want you out of there in a flash."

"I can handle myself," she said. "You needn't worry."

He frowned at her.

"I worry. So remember—out in a flash."

In two quick blinks, the look in her eyes went from annoyance to what could only be interpreted as mischief.

"If the men at that table really are murderous gangsters, you will actually be the one closest to the danger, won't you?" she said. "But I'll have my service pistol. That should even the odds—two weapons against whatever they have."

"Bostock. If I thought there'd be gunplay, neither of us would be going on this scouting mission and I don't carry a weapon."

"Oh," she said.

He tried to read her expression but it had gone blank. Something had happened there but he couldn't tell if it was good or bad.

He took the sheet of paper she had given him over to his desk, but before he had time to read it, his intercom buzzed. Only one person ever did that—Chief Ward, or more specifically Jane, his secretary. Another of Ward's bad habits was arriving at headquarters each working morning at seven sharp.

"He wants to speak with you—now," Jane said.

For once, the old war-horse was in a good mood or seemed to be.

"I've had some good news regarding Corporal Bostock," he said. "It appears that she hasn't furthered her threat to leak her sexual harassment complaint to the press. I suspect that's largely due to your efforts in taking her under your wing."

Praise for doing nothing? But Coswell wasn't about to disillusion him. Being in Ward's bad books was more the usual. The change, even if brief, was to be enjoyed.

Ward continued.

"I realize that reassigning Corporal James was not popular with either him or you, but I hadn't planned to make it permanent. I assure you that when Corporal Bostock settles down and we find a mutually agreeable position for her, you and James will be reunited."

Coswell's mood shot up to the sky but just as quickly it fell back to Earth. Great for him and James, but what was going to happen to Bostock? And then he thought why should I care? But he did care. She was a full corporal in one of the greatest police forces in the world, not some faceless soul in a typing pool. She deserved to have as much pride and satisfaction in her work as the rest of them. Somebody needed to go to bat for her. Might as well be him.

"I'm impressed with Corporal Bostock," Coswell said. "She has a quick mind and she's taken to homicide like a duck to water. I would hope that ultimately the position you find for her is coincident with her talents."

Ward looked surprised at that but quickly moved on.

"Whatever," he said. "Now on another matter—"

Here it comes, thought Coswell. The party's over.

"Pressure is building again over this Dr. Kelly case. The media is adding it to the muggings in the University Endowment Lands and painting the whole institution as a haven for violence. Dean Brockhurst has spoken personally to me now on two rather uncomfortable occasions. What can you give me that will make him feel better?"

"Progress is being made in the Kelly murder," Coswell said. "We have a list of plausible suspects and we are in the process of narrowing it down."

This sounded good, but he knew that it wasn't fooling Ward. The man had dealt with cons far more subtle than this one from his chief homicide inspector. Their suspect list was growing, not shrinking.

"I want that process speeded up," Ward said. "Do you need more manpower?"

He was going to ask for James to be allowed to join them, but then surprising himself, he decided not to.

"No," he said. "Corporal Bostock and I can handle the Kelly case. The muggings, of course, are being dealt with by Sergeant McMorran, since so far none of the attacks have been fatal. Perhaps you should speak to him about those."

Ward narrowed his eyes.

"Yes, I'll do that," he said. "And I've warned him off speaking to the media. That task is now in the hands of Corporal James."

And that very Corporal James was sitting in Ward's outer office when Coswell emerged from his meeting.

"Next," Jane said.

James got up from his chair.

"I hope you haven't riled him up," he said.

"See me after," Coswell said.

Bostock was on the phone when Coswell returned to his office. With her free hand she was jotting something down on a notepad and hung up just as he sat down.

"That was the manager of Dr. Kelly's apartment," she said. "I thought he would be an early riser. He gave me the name of the bank that Kelly used. It's on Broadway, right by the General Hospital."

"Good," Coswell said. "It's always better to deal with people directly than over the phone, especially when institutions are involved. I want to do another tour of VGH this morning, so as soon as the warrant comes through we can walk over to the bank."

"And we don't have to wait for it here, sir," she said. "I'll have it downloaded on my phone so it can be printed anywhere, at the hospital or even at the bank if necessary."

Another should-have-gone-to course that Coswell turned down. The same super geek who gave the computer sessions returned to give a one day course on cell phone capabilities. James had attended and that was good enough for Coswell, but the few basics he personally had mastered obviously weren't going to cut it any longer.

"Of course," he said to her, and then got busy with the mess of papers on his desk. The sheet that Bostock had given him lay on top. He glanced at it.

The first name he read was a Haile Dubas, Born in London, England, 1982. FRCS (Gensurg) St. Marks Hospital, London, 2011. Unmarried. Grandson of Princess Aida Desta.

Princess who?

Coswell called over to Bostock.

"This Dubas fellow sounds like some kind of royalty."

"He is," she said. "His grandmother was Emperor Haile Selassie's granddaughter."

James had just walked into the room and heard her answer.

"A famous lady for sure," he said. "She refused to flee Ethiopia when Selassie and anyone connected with him were imprisoned. Ended up in prison herself. Great story. You should check out the documentaries done on her life. Fascinating."

"I'll add that to my list," Coswell said. "Now how did you make out with our intrepid Chief? You weren't in there very long."

"Long enough to get a short lecture on dealing with the media, plus a long list of reporters, TV people, and such to whom I'm to offer myself up like some Incan slave. And I'm to get my hair cut. Apparently my lovely curls aren't the image he has in mind."

He turned to Bostock. "And speaking of image, how did your shopping go?"

He held his hand up,

"Now don't tell me. Let me guess," he said, finger to his temple. "I see a cocktail dress, black, lots of knee showing, generous neckline and deeply scooped back."

"You can discuss fashion later," Coswell said. "I want to hear what Charlotte had to say yesterday."

"Not nearly as interesting," James said. "But if you insist."

He then recounted Charlotte's report, ending with "She was one hundred percent certain that Wing Chu's death was a suicide."

"Hmm," Coswell said. "One hundred percent, eh? And before the autopsy, no less. Tsk, tsk. Not like Charlotte to jump the gun like that. Maybe she's getting overworked."

"Maybe," said James. "Which is not the case with me, however. He put on his hat and started for the door.

"I must be off. My first appointment of the day is with a TV news journalist by the name of Wendy Carruthers who I'm told starts work at five thirty in the morning. Hopefully by the time I meet with her she's half asleep and we can have a short session."

As he passed Bostock's desk, he leaned over to her and said in a low voice, "You'll knock them dead tonight, Bostock. I just know you will."

The work day also started early in the Department of Surgery offices at the Vancouver General Hospital. The secretary, Carol, Dr. Struthers' secretary, was at her post when they arrived. Coswell asked to speak to her boss.

"He's in surgery all day today," she said. "Taking on Dr. Kelly's cases has doubled his work load."

Obviously he and Bostock were going to be an intrusion, but Coswell too, was under the gun, and interviewing Struthers was important. Professionally it appeared that he was the closest to Kelly, hence a vital source of information.

"He must take some kind of a break between cases," Coswell said. "What about lunch?"

"The change-over times for his surgeries are usually no more than ten or fifteen minutes. He has lunch in the cafeteria, but it's a working lunch with the residents and interns. Dr. Tynan is the non-scrubbed surgical ward resident this morning and he will be giving Dr. Struthers a report on inpatients and cases he's seen in the outpatient's clinic."

"Oh my," Coswell said. "It does sound like a full day for the doctor. When does he finish?"

She sighed.

"I can't say," she said. "He's also on emergency call, which could mean a continuum of cases well into the evening."

"And tomorrow?"

"No change, including the emergency call which Dr. Kelly was supposed to have done."

"That takes us to Saturday."

"I'm afraid so," she said.

"Well, thank you for your time," Coswell said. "I'm

sure you have extra work to do as well. We'll let you get back to it."

But before he left the office, he turned and asked, "Is Dr. Debas the scrubbed-in resident today?"

"Yes," she said. "He's first assist with Dr. Struthers all day."

Back out in the hall, however, Coswell wasn't about to abandon his plan to interview the surgeon. Debas being with him was an added bonus. Despite the gang killing theory being up front at the moment, the hate motive was still a considerable possibility. He remembered Kelly's aversion to Kiri, the gorgeous black hooker, Renée Lafleur's roommate. Ethiopians were black so far as he knew, and since Kelly was such a jerk in the OR, he probably made life miserable for Debas.

"We'll go over to the operating rooms," he said. "I'm sure as hell not going to wait until Saturday to see Struthers."

"Do you really think they would let us in there?" Bostock said.

"No harm in trying."

It was easier than he expected. He had dealt only with Emergency Room nurses in the past and they were no pushovers, badge or no badge. But the head nurse in the OR suites was a pleasant, accommodating lady who reminded Coswell of the kindly sisters who ran the Catholic Hospital in the community he grew up in.

"You can wait in the surgeons' lounge, Inspector," she said and then looked at Bostock. "It's not co-ed, but if you don't mind seeing the odd surgeon in his under shorts you can wait with him. I'll get a message to Dr. Struthers that you are there. Come, I'll show you the way."

The surgeons' lounge was accessed from the main hallway through an unmarked door. "Lounge" was a peculiar term for it since the space was taken up mainly by lockers and benches. There were a few easy chairs and one huge chesterfield that looked as though it had accommodated more than its share of dozing surgeons. Greens were neatly folded and stacked on shelves labeled TOPS and BOTTOMS, but a significant number were also scattered about on the furniture and on the floor. Three dispensers containing masks, booties, and hats were adjacent to another unlabelled door that presumably led directly into the surgical area. A cart covered with a white cloth held a coffee urn, cups, spoons, sugar, cream packets, and a tray of donuts.

Before leaving them, the nurse perused a list posted on a corkboard beside the door.

"Oh dear," she said. "You could have a bit of wait. Dr. Struthers is just about to start his next case. But unless you're happy here, you might find it more interesting to watch him from the observation deck."

"That would be excellent," Coswell said, although if Bostock hadn't been along he would have been quite content to wait in the lounge with the coffee, donuts, and nap couch. But case-wise, observing Dr. Kelly's professional milieu was probably the better idea.

The observation area was a glassed off balcony overlooking the operating table. There were three steeply sloped rows of theatre-like seats. None were occupied. Bostock was all set to go to the very front but Coswell had other ideas. He had quickly taken in the whole scene— surgeons and nurses masked and gowned; an anesthetist busy with his equipment at the head of the table; all apparently ready to go. But the sight that sent a shiver through him was the figure lying on the table almost completely covered with green drapes leaving only the abdomen exposed.

He had seen more than his share of gore and dead bodies in his long career, and none had really upset him. Even the autopsies, with the cutting, the bone saws, the opening of the skull hadn't bothered him. But this naked rectangle of living skin awaiting the surgeon's knife made his own skin crawl.

"Perhaps we should sit in the back row," he said to Bostock. "We would be less of a distraction to them."

She gave him an odd look but followed him to the upper seats. Coswell took his time, hoping the first incision would have been made before he got there. He thought he could handle it after that, but no luck. It was almost as though they were waiting for him to settle before they started.

He stared at that vulnerable patch of flesh as the nurse passed a scalpel to the surgeon who, without a moment's hesitation, took it and laid the skin open in one long swipe.

A wave hit Coswell so hard he knew he was seconds from passing out. In desperation, he fumbled for his cell phone and dropped it at his feet. He bent over to retrieve it, hanging his head as far down as he could.

"Damn," he said. "Where is that thing?"

Bostock bent over to help him.

"It's okay," he said. "I think I've got it."

He knew he had just enough blood left in his head to get out of that room before another wave hit him. Still bent over, he said to Bostock, "They're going to be a while, it looks like. I should have taken a pee break before I left the surgeons' lounge. You stay here. I'll be right back."

He put all of his concentration on lifting his head carefully and visualizing his escape route—hold on to anything—seat backs, banister, door frame, wall. Somehow he made it and prayed that Bostock had returned her attention to the surgery. His exit was anything but dignified.

The second wave hit him just as he stepped out into the hospital corridor. Quickly he knelt down and busied himself tying and untying his shoes. In a few moments, it passed.

Slowly he stood up grateful for the handrail that ran the length of the corridor. A few deep breaths and his pulse slowed, the crisis over. But what to do now? Certainly not go back to the observation room. And then inspiration hit.

He walked back to the head nurse's office. She was on the phone and signalled for him to have a seat. He hoped that the colour had returned to his face.

And when she hung up the phone, he immediately made his request.

"My partner is more interested in the surgery than I am and I'd like to make the best use of our time. There is a Dr. Tynan I would like to talk to. I understand that he's the non-scrubbed resident for the day. Would you be so kind as to see if he is available?"

"Certainly," she said. "I'll call through to the ward first. It's just on the next floor."

She got through immediately. Dr. Tynan was on the floor.

"Would you ask him to meet me in the surgeons' lounge?" Coswell said. "That way I'll be there when Dr. Struthers finishes his surgery."

CHAPTER NINETEEN

He remembered Tynan as the red-haired fellow in the lecture hall who spoke up about hospital duties and was one of the Xs on James' list, along with his partner, Debas, the Ethiopian royalty. They had both been on duty at the hospital the night of the murder. Neither had said anything worthwhile during the interview, citing what a good teacher Kelly was. They had obviously left out a lot. Time to loosen them up.

While Coswell waited for him, he tried to remember all he knew about the man, aside from the lecture hall interview. He hadn't read Bostock's report on him, but he did recall that Mabel, the ward aid, mentioned the surgical fellow with shocking red hair who had told her about Kelly's Irish pub carousing. Presumably he had observed it first hand.

When he came in, it was obvious that Tynan's most striking feature *was* his hair. Otherwise, he looked like some Pickwickian character: thin face, deep set eyes, and a sharp nose. There was nothing cheerful or welcoming about him. In fact, he gave off the aura of a busy man who didn't take kindly to being interrupted at his work.

"You wanted to see me?" he said, glancing at his wristwatch.

Coswell took a moment to decide what approach he would use and since he smelled arrogance, he selected the hard line.

"Yes," Coswell said. "We've discovered that you weren't exactly forthcoming during our brief session on the campus. Now, have a seat. This is a brutal murder being investigated and we need all the information we can get."

Tynan sat on the arm of the chesterfield. He didn't appear the least intimidated by Coswell's statement. If anything, he looked more annoyed.

"I answered all your questions," he said. "Not my fault if you didn't ask the right ones."

Coswell congratulated himself for accurately picking up on the man's arrogance. Nothing he liked better than a hostile witness. A worthy challenge if the subject had a brain to go along with it.

"True," he said. "So this time I'll be more specific. Let's start out with your assessment of Dr. Kelly as a person, not as a teacher."

Tynan appeared to relax. He slid down onto the chesterfield and leaned back but his eyes had taken on a sly look about them.

"He was a bastard," he said. "Simple as that."

"In what way?"

Tynan looked up to the side as though measuring his response. "Bastard probably sums it up best, but let me elaborate for you," he said, "Dr. Kelly was an overgrown lout of a man who treated people like dirt. He was blessed with a marvellous pair of hands and good diagnostic ability. Otherwise it wasn't worth being in the same room with him."

"But you're Irish, too," Coswell said. "I'd think he would have taken it easier on you."

"He did, but I despised how he treated others."

"Can you give me some examples?"

"Haile Debas, my fellow resident, is probably the best example. Haile is the complete opposite of Kelly, except for his surgical abilities, which are superb. He's kind, dignified, and should have been praised, not bullied."

"Bullied how?"

"His name, for one. Kelly called him Rastus, a derogatory term for an Afro-American, I understand. The man was probably too stupid to realize it, but it's also an insult to Rastafari, the movement that worships the Emperor Haile Selassie. A double insult therefore to Haile Debas who is a descendent of the emperor."

"Why do you suppose Dr. Kelly did that?"

"Thought he was being funny, I guess, or frustrated that he couldn't find anything to criticize."

"You seem to know a lot about Debas. Are you friends as well as fellow residents?"

"I'd say so. We've both been saddled with this compulsory year in a residency program before we can get our licenses to practice in your wonderful country. That despite the fact that the Royal College of Surgeons proclaimed us specialists some time ago."

Tynan made no real effort to hide his bitterness. Sarcasm dripped from "your wonderful country."

Although Coswell was tempted to ask why the young surgeon had chosen to come to a country that was making life difficult for him, he wanted to know more about Debas.

"How did your partner take the ridicule from Dr. Kelly?"

Tynan smiled.

"If you mean was he mad enough to garrotte the ass? Possibly, but Haile keeps his emotions well under control and besides, he and I were working the night Kelly was killed—i.e. no opportunity."

"You sound like a police detective," Coswell said.

"I read a lot of crime fiction. It relaxes me."

Coswell heard the lounge door open and a moment later Bostock appeared.

"I wondered what had happened to—"

She stopped abruptly when she saw Tynan sitting on the chesterfield.

Coswell introduced him.

"One of the names on Corporal James' list," Coswell said.

"Yes, I remember," she said and gave the young resident one of her unnerving blank stares.

Tynan looked again at his watch.

"I must get back to the ward," he said. "There are some serious cases that need my attention."

He got up from the chesterfield, his casualness gone.

"By all means," Coswell said. "If we need to speak to you again we'll be in touch. But just one quick question before you go. Have you ever been to The Auld Sod Pub?"

Tynan gave a coarse laugh.

"Because I'm Irish?" he said, and then. "I did once, but never again. That buffoon Kelly was there. He had the audacity to chat up my girlfriend. Now I really have to get back to work."

They both listened for the door to close before

speaking. Coswell started off.

"Sorry to worry you," he said. "But this Tynan fellow just kind of fell into my lap. I didn't want to pass up the opportunity to interview him. Everyone is so busy around here."

"No problem," she said. "The surgery was quite fascinating. That Dr. Debas is really something—not a wasted motion. Dr. Struthers stood and mainly watched. A nurse did most of the assisting. They're just finishing up."

"Good," Coswell said, "because the gist of what I got out of the angry Dr. Tynan is that Debas was being significantly harassed by Kelly. I wonder if there's a little of that mid-eastern hot blood temperament in him."

"Ethiopia is in Africa, sir."

"Close enough. We need to interview him."

But that wasn't to be. The lounge door opened again and the head nurse rushed in.

"I'm sorry," she said. "But there's been an emergency on the ward. One of Dr. Struthers' cases from yesterday fell trying to get out of bed and ruptured her wound. They've all rushed off to deal with it."

"Not a good time for us to be around?" Coswell said.

"True. Best you come another day."

The ring of Bostock's cell phone solved the question as to where they should go from there.

"The warrants have come through," she said.

"Warrants plural?"

"Yes," she said. "James didn't have time to request one for Kelly's cell phone records. I just added it on."

"Good move. I'll let you follow up on that this afternoon but meanwhile we'll go over to his bank."

The bank manager wasn't nearly as accommodating as the head nurse in the OR. He double checked everything: their IDs and the warrant which Bostock had gotten printed out in the hospital library. Coswell suspected he had never dealt with anything like that before. Finally, although the man still looked pained about the whole thing, he led them to a small office which virtually hummed with computer equipment.

After introducing the two officers to the young woman who apparently ran the whole show he left, closing the door firmly behind him. Her name was Laurie. She looked about sixteen to Coswell, face heavily made up, the eye-shadow liberally applied and lipstick that was almost black. She was probably quite pretty under it all.

The only chair in the room was the one she was sitting in.

"This is terrific," she said. "I've never worked with the police before. What is it—money laundering, tax evasion?"

Coswell elevated her enthusiasm even further.

"Murder," he said, "And you could give us the key to solving it."

Her eyes lit up.

"Wow! Bring it on."

Bostock handed her a slip of paper with Kelly's name and the account number on it.

"Aw, that's too easy."

And it obviously was because the entire account appeared on her screen in seconds. She pivoted the monitor so that they could see it.

"Shall I go back month by month for you?"

"Yes," Coswell said but when he saw how small the letters were he told Bostock to take over.

"My back's really bothering me," he said. "I'll go have a seat outside."

"You could sit in my chair, if you like," Laurie said.

"No. You stay there. You're running the computer."

He had his reading glasses with him but they didn't work worth a damn for the computer screen, and of the two pairs he had for that, one was at headquarters and the other in his condo.

"I'll get print outs," Bostock said.

If the RCMP didn't work out, Coswell mused, she could always get a job in an old folks' home. She appeared to have a great understanding of senile frailties.

"Anything interesting?" Coswell said as they walked up Willow Street from Broadway back to the hospital.

"He was a big spender, no doubt about it," Bostock said. "His credit card was maxed out—restaurants, liquor outlets, specialty stores, and the like. Very few personal checks. He did most of his banking online. Aside from rent, the only others were to a car mechanic and to the escort service that Renée Laflame works for."

"Those must have added up," Coswell said.

"They did, but what I find most striking were the frequency and amounts he withdrew from the automatic teller machines. Each time, the daily maximum of five hundred dollars and often several days in a row."

"Goodness. That must have dropped the old balance fast. But those are all the outs. What were the ins?"

"Direct deposits of his university salary, a few checks from some private clinic, and, of course, the checks from Dr. Montgomery."

"Did those add up to much?"

"Not in the beginning; a few hundred at a time and spaced quite far apart. The last six months, though, they shot up to two thousand a crack—four of them."

She let him mull that over for a second before continuing.

"The majority of his gambling then must have been strictly cash. He did have some big credit card payments to casinos, but those stopped a few months back, probably when the card maxed out."

"What was the bottom number?"

"He was flat broke," she said. "No safety deposit box and no sign of any stock broker dealings."

Although it was only two short blocks back to the hospital, the first was rather steep, forcing Coswell to slow down. As he did so, he looked ahead to see where it would level out, but what he also saw was Kay Montgomery and a man come out of a building on his left, both wearing white coats. He got only a brief glimpse of the man but to his dismay, he looked like a mature male model in a clothing ad—salt and pepper hair styled to perfection, a nice tan, broad shoulders, and a confident, athletic gait.

As he watched, neither of them looked back as they turned left toward the hospital.

"I wonder who that is with her," Bostock said. "Maybe he's one of the names on our list."

"Maybe," he said.

"Do you want to catch up with them?"

"No. We won't have to. They're turning left. Probably going to the Heather Street entrance, and you know who will be parked across the street right now having her lunch."

"Mabel Pucket."

"Right. Now slow down, no need to rush."

By the time they reached Mabel, Montgomery and the man with her had gone up the steps into the Heather Pavilion.

"Well hello again, Inspector ... and Corporal Bostock, isn't it?"

"Hello, Mabel," Coswell said. "Mind if we join you again? I could use a rest. We've just walked up from Broadway."

"Those hills just get steeper with age, don't they?" Mabel said.

Coswell regretted using his rest excuse. He didn't need to be reminded of his age.

"I notice Dr. Montgomery just ahead of us. Do you know who that was with her?"

Mabel gave a self-satisfied grunt.

"I certainly do. That's Dr. Bennett, the neurologist I told you about. Ever since my friend, Judy, filled me in about them, I've sort of kept my eyes and ears open. Those two are together a lot—coffee breaks, lunch. They're a regular cafeteria twosome and don't seem to give a damn, pardon my French, who sees them."

She took a sip from her Thermos cup.

"I know you didn't take much stock in it, but I tell you, it's more than just professional interests. Judy swore she saw them hold hands once when they were alone in the nursing station."

Coswell's interest was piqued.

"And," Mabel said. "They go sailing every week. Just the two of them. Poor Dr. Bennett's wife stuck at home in her wheelchair."

"Did Dr. Bennett have much to do with Dr. Kelly?" Bostock asked as Coswell to be momentarily at a loss for words.

Mabel turned to her, almost annoyed having seen the effect of her revelation on the inspector.

"Not in the hospital," she said. "Neurology and General Surgery are worlds apart. I don't know socially, of course, but I could probably find out if it would help you."

"Every bit of information about Dr. Kelly is useful to us," Bostock said. She opened her purse and pulled out one of her cards.

"Here," she said. "I meant to give you this last time we met. Feel free to call me if you have anything more to tell us."

Mabel took the card and looked at it.

"Lovely," she said. "Nice colours, and I really like the Mountie on the horse."

Coswell got up from the bench.

"We must be off," he said. "Enjoy your lunch, and thank you for all the information."

"You're very welcome," Mabel said. "Delighted to help."

When they were out of earshot, Bostock said, "I hope you didn't mind the card thing. It occurred to me that I might have been a little too enthusiastic about Mabel's participation, and it would be better she pester me than you."

Coswell chuckled.

"I appreciate that. Now if you could only field all of Chief Ward's calls to me, my life would be rosy indeed."

Bostock sat at her desk and tried to get a handle on her roller-coaster association with Coswell. There were times when she was sure he had come to accept her, but then it would fall apart like the latest repeat of his solo lunch hours. This time it was a meeting with a Vancouver Police detective in the vice squad. "He and I go way back," Coswell had said. "We're having lunch at his favourite greasy spoon so I'll spare you that and our boring conversation." He told her to take the afternoon off once she had checked out Kelly's cell phone records and rest up in preparation for their night at The Auld Sod Pub.

James came in at that point and brought her ruminations to an end.

"You've got to stop frowning like that, Bostock," he said. "Or if you must, I'll loan you some of my wrinkle cream."

She laughed.

"That's better," he said. "Now what has the inspector run off and left you with this time?"

"Dr. Kelly's cell phone records. Not much of a job. I got it all through the marvel of cyber-communication. Didn't have to leave my desk."

"Wonderful. That was a task I was supposed to do but never got around to it. Anything interesting?"

She turned the screen so he could see it.

"Not a heavy user, was he?" James said. "I don't see anything worth noting."

"Me neither. You'd think that he would have a bookie or two at least on the speed dial. I don't even see his hooker lady Renée Laflame, and I know he had regular visits with her."

"He could be a Luddite, or paranoid about being traced on so-called smartphones. Probably did all his business using a land line at the hospital."

"Or face-to-face," Bostock said.

"Yes, and tonight's the night to find out what faces. Are you a little nervous?"

"No," she said, "I'm a *lot* nervous and it's not the danger, though the inspector seems to think there could be some. It's fear of blowing a chance to look good in front of him."

"Oh, oh. There's that frown again. Now put fear of failure right out of your mind. You look good just standing still. I'd be more worried about Coswell. He's never done anything like this before. He could end up being a bull in a china shop."

He thought for a moment.

"Or a lamb in the tigers' den. There have been a number of nasty shootings lately in public places like The Auld Sod. Better take your weapon. Coswell never carries one."

"I plan to."

James' turn to frown.

"I was kidding," he said. "I wouldn't want you having to shoot at anyone."

"It wouldn't be a first."

"Oh my God. You've shot someone? You, the harassed one?"

James looked genuinely shocked.

"I didn't shoot my harassers," she said. "Although I sometimes wonder if maybe I should have. Not to kill, but maybe to neuter a bit."

James pulled over a chair and sat beside her.

"You have just shattered a precious image that I had of you," he said. "Please restore the quiet, obedient, nice Corporal Bostock that I have come to know and love."

He put his hand over hers and stared into her eyes like a kindly priest giving solace.

She began to giggle and then dissolved into laughter.

"It's all so stupid," she said, wiping the tears from her eyes. "My fault really. Getting corporal stripes went to my head. I thought respect went along with them, but I was wrong and I should have known that, played it much different."

"Different how?" James said. "I could use a few pointers myself."

"I don't think so. You do very well using the best method of all—humour. Hard to be a bully if your potential victim has everyone laughing. Bullies need fear to satisfy their warped minds."

"But sexual harassment is different than gay-bashing."

"Is it? How do you deal with the bashers?"

James cocked his head.

"I usually question their sexuality. The old 'takes one to know one' attack. Worked in the schoolyard and still seems to be effective."

"And that's exactly what I should have done. Challenged them, not go whining to the boss, which, by the way, was a big mistake."

"And then you got mad."

She got up and went over to check that there was adequate paper in the office printer. When she returned to her desk, she continued.

"Yes, I got very mad, and the threat I made in Winnipeg to go public was, in my mind, the only option I had. But look where it got me—transferred out under a cloud, wedged in here like some unwanted relative, and absolutely nothing done at the source. I'm probably just some boardroom joke back there."

She could feel her face flush as the anger grew again.

"The harassment was both mental and physical," she said. "I could handle the physical, but the innuendos, the snide comments. and the frank propositions on duty were soul destroying."

"I find it hard to imagine that senior officers wouldn't have put a stop to it. You did go to them, I presume."

She looked hard at him.

"*They* were the problem. Some sort of entitlement notion, I suspect. The ranks I could live with, but when a couple of the randy types from above took more than a professional interest in me, my life became a hell. 'Boys will be boys' was the excuse I got. And the advice? 'Ignore it,' they said."

James sighed.

"And I thought I was hard done by. But are you going to give up the fight?"

She picked up a pencil and began doodling on a piece of paper. "I've decided to fight another way, as unrealistic as it might be in my present position," she said. "I want to rise up the ranks so I can be eye-to-eye with the lot of them, or better still, one notch above."

James whistled.

"Whoa. First you drop the gun bit on me, now it's your ambition to kick some ass. How is that nice Corporal Bostock I used to know going to do that?"

"I wish I was as resolute as I sound, James. Some days I just haven't got it, and I know there are a lot of strikes against me, but that's the goal. I figure if I can get Inspector Coswell on my side, it could be a big step forward. Anyone making a name for themselves in homicide is promotion material."

"And if your plan fails?"

"I'll go to the media. The Force needs women members and they deserve respect. I'm not going to let the bastards get away with it."

"Oh God, Bostock," James said. "You'll be crucified if you

do that."

"At that point I don't think I'll care. My heart will be broken anyway. You know, I've dreamed about being a Mountie since I was nine years old. There's nothing in this world that I want more than keeping this job, but not if I have to abandon justice in the process."

James sat back in his chair, put his hands behind his head for a moment, and then crossed them over his chest.

"All I can say, Bostock, is that you have come to the right place. Coswell is a straight shooter. He's in a bit of a snit right now, but it's melting, I can assure you."

"Still dodging me at lunch, though," she said.

He leaned forward.

"I doubt it. More likely he has gone back to his condo for a long nap before lunch. I think he's been doing that for some time now, long before you arrived. I'm actually worried about him. He's taking his age way too seriously and I think his alcohol intake is catching up with him."

"He did look hungover this morning," she said.

"Be patient and keep up the good work. He's noticing it more than you think."

James got up, pushed the chair back to where he got it from and started for the door.

"I'm having lunch with Allan Q. McIver, the shock jock of CXRM. Please don't tune it in. Bye."

Bostock gave him a wave and blessed the warmth he had brought with him.

Tonight she was going to be a star, or die trying.

CHAPTER TWENTY

Coswell barely made it back to his nest. He couldn't remember ever being so tired. It took all of his concentration to drive there after dropping Bostock off at headquarters. Fortunately, a car pulled out from in front of his condo just as he turned onto his street.

A parking space in Chinatown midday. Thank God for little miracles.

He didn't even make it to his bedroom. The chesterfield just inside the front door accepted his frame like a warm embrace. In seconds, he was fast asleep.

Two hours later, he opened his eyes. It took him a moment to focus on his wristwatch.

"Damn", he said. "Two thirty."

He had been truthful to Bostock, or almost truthful. Lunch with Jack Ryan of the Vancouver PD Vice Squad was what he had planned, although he hadn't told Jack. Never mind, he thought, I'll arrange it now. He dialed Jack's cell phone.

"Jack, old buddy," he said. "Long time no talk. How about lunch today?"

"What do you want, Coswell? I've had lunch."

"Oh dear. Is it really that late? I've been working my butt off. Time just flies by."

"I repeat, Coswell. What do you want?"

Jack Ryan's crustiness had always appealed to Coswell. His kind of cop. No bullshit.

"I need some information on a Mr. C who hangs out at The Auld Sod Pub. There's a chance he's involved in illegal activities, i.e. vice and since you are the king of vice in this town, I've come directly to you."

"Wait a moment. I'm just having an orgasm over that compliment."

Pause.

"Mr. C is Conor Bonahan," Ryan said. "He runs the local Irish Mafia. You name it, he's into it—drugs, gambling, prostitution, the usual. If you're trying to implicate him in a homicide, however, you'll have a tough job. Conor is a very sharp lad."

"There's always dirty work to be done. I presume he has some hired muscle."

"He does. Most of them have just stepped off the boat from Ireland, but there's one who's a former biker named Larry Kearney. A nasty piece of work. An Irish name but he's Canadian, from Montreal."

"Former biker? That's pretty rare, isn't it? I thought once a biker, always a biker."

"True, and the suspicion, of course, is that he's still a member and serves as a liaison between his gang and Bonahan's mob. We're working on it."

"Has the name Dr. Patrick Kelly crossed your blotter?"

"Not in a criminal way. He's one of the hangers-on. There's a few of those, too. Irish ex-pats who seem to get a charge out of associating with criminals."

"The Ryans got over all that?"

"Three generations ago and all cops. No sympathy for any kind of criminal, Irish or otherwise."

"Thanks for the info, Jack, and we'll really do lunch one of these days."

"Right. I'm holding my breath. Bye"

The mention of lunch brought Coswell's own situation into focus. He was starving and couldn't even remember his last cinnamon bun. But where to go? Lunch at The Vicinage was over. It was a beautiful Vancouver afternoon. Why not a place with view? He had always meant to try the restaurant at the Jericho Sailing Centre and this was a perfect time to do so.

There were a surprising number of people at the Centre and its restaurant, the Galley Patio and Grill. The place was busy and he actually had to line up to give his order much like Gino's at morning coffee. The burgers listed all looked good but he decided on the beer-battered cod and chips. He added a sleeve of Galley Special Lager to his order, paid, and took the number he was issued out to the patio. A table freed up just as he stepped outside and he quickly took a seat, happy that he was within easy earshot of whoever called out the numbers.

The patio was really a balcony connected to the sailing centre buildings and literally gave a bird's eye view that was simply magnificent—the beach in front with a myriad of sailboats pulled up on the sand; the Jericho pier with a few patient fisherman dangling lines into the water; casual walkers and a few souls just sitting peacefully doing nothing. And then English Bay itself, with not only sailboats of every size but tugs and freighters, cruise ships and float planes. Across the Bay the North Shore high-rises, and behind them the majestic Lions and surrounding peaks.

His number was called almost too soon as he enjoyed the view, but his hunger soon switched his attention to the food set down in front of him by a cheerful young man in a black T-shirt that said I LOVE MY DINGHY. Thank goodness for proofreaders, Coswell thought to himself.

He squirted the brown malt vinegar supplied at the table over his chips and followed it with a liberal application of salt. To hell with his blood pressure. The first chip he tried was perfect. The cod was even better. Finally, the lager—excellent as well. Gastronomic serendipity.

It took him a minute or two before he could slow down his eating; it was that good. When he managed, however, he looked down at the beach. There was very little activity and he assumed he had arrived during happy hour for club sailors. No boats were headed out and only one or two just coming in. But then he heard laughter coming from below him, and a moment later, two people appeared pulling a sort of wheeled apparatus supporting a sailboat. The individual doing the pulling was turned facing the other who pushed from behind. Both wore skin-tight neoprene suits, but the red hair of the pusher and the laugh were immediately recognized by Coswell—Kay Montgomery. Another look at the man and he, too, registered—Dr. Barrett.

Coswell lost interest in his food. What were those two doing out on a working day together? He had seen them that very morning at the hospital. And then it occurred to him—time together at work, or a daytime tryst, would spare Bennett's multiple sclerosis afflicted wife. Mabel and her friend were right. There was a thing going on between them, no doubt about it.

He watched them unload the boat at the water's edge and hoist the rigging. When they pushed off, Bennett hooked up to a trapeze and Montgomery took the tiller. All was done with practiced expertise. In minutes they were well out into the bay.

He looked down at his half-eaten fish and chips, pushed the plate away, and picked up the beer glass. He sipped slowly and started to think. What had Bostock said about Montgomery's checks to her ex? Eight thousand dollars worth in the past six months. That didn't sound like charity; it sounded like blackmail, and what better reason for blackmail than a cruel, adulterous affair behind an invalid wife's back.

Bostock regarded herself in the mirror. To use Coswell's term, her face didn't look "hookerish" enough. She applied a brighter red lipstick and brushed on more eye shadow. Better. No point making her eyelashes any longer, they were more than long enough naturally. She tried a couple of come-hither looks. That only made her laugh.

There was a full length mirror behind the closet door in her bedroom. She went in, pulled the door open, and did a critique. Not bad. She had her mom's boobs. The perfect size according to a comment she had overheard once—"not too big, not too small, just right—a nice handful." Obviously a sexist jerk, but at the time she was rather pleased by the comment.

She was also pleased about her new upbeat mood, and thankful again to James for getting it there. Butterflies flittered about in her stomach, but they were good butter-flies, just like the ones before her hockey games. She prayed that the feeling would last even if just for this one night.

Her gun was tucked neatly in the little black purse she had chosen and, ignoring the rules, she had loaded it. Nothing in the breech, but racking it would take less than a second. Snapping open the purse would take a bit longer, but not much. The only part of her ensemble that bothered her was the four-inch heel shoes. She really couldn't remember the last time she wore anything like that. But if need be, kicking them off and running in stocking feet would be no problem. She was ready.

Coswell's enthusiasm was at the other end of the scale compared to Bostock's. The incident at the Jericho Sailing Centre had really upset him. It made him realize how silly his infatuation with the woman had been. She was a murder suspect, first and foremost, nothing more. To add to his gloom, he had to admit that The Auld Sod escapade would likely turn out to be a waste of time and wondered why he had let James talk him into it.

Nevertheless, he had made a commitment and so at ten o'clock he pushed open the doors to The Auld Sod Pub and went in. It was even busier than the afternoon he had come before and definitely noisier. He glanced over at the "reserved" table. A half dozen men were sitting at it and two women. There wasn't an empty table anywhere near them. In fact, there wasn't an empty table anywhere.

There were a couple of stools free at the far end of the bar nearest to the reserved group. Better than nothing, he thought, and hoped Bostock would spot him quickly. He looked around and was happy to see that the waitress he had interviewed at his daytime visit to the bar was nowhere to be seen. Night off, he hoped.

One of the bartenders came to take his order.

"I'm expecting someone to join me here," Coswell said, "but there's not a table to be had. Could I put a reserve on this stool beside me?"

"Only if you buy an extra drink to put there."

Coswell looked up at the drink list.

"No problem. I'll have a pint of Guinness Pale and for my friend a glass of your Pinot Grigio."

He felt a twinge of guilt ordering the cheapest wine on the list. There was an excellent New Zealand Sauvignon blanc and only two bucks more. But maybe she didn't drink wine at all and it would be wasted. The Pinot Grigio would do.

He had no problem fending off the seat seekers.

"Wife's in the can," he told each one. He deliberately kept his gaze away from the reserved table, focusing his attention on the door instead. Bostock arrived at 10:10—exactly as planned. He leaned back on his stool and turned his head to make himself more visible. After a few seconds scanning the crowd she spotted him but gave him only a millisecond glance. Instead she stood for a moment as though sizing up her options. She continued looking around as she proceeded in his direction. Coswell was impressed by her performance—a hooker on the prowl—beautifully done.

He turned his back to her, pretending to be interested in one of the huge TV screens above the bar, and waited.

"Is this seat taken?" she said.

He turned, feigning surprise and gave her a big smile.

"Yes," he said. "Just for a lovely lady like you and, surprise, there's a drink for you."

She slid onto the stool ignoring the fact that her skirt retracted up her thighs a good eight inches. She looked at the glass of wine.

"I hope you can do better than this," she said, and gently slid the glass away from her. She looked up at the bar list. "This is an Irish bar. I see that you're into the right spirit with your Guinness. I'd like a tot of Connemara. That's a single malt Irish whiskey. More appropriate than Italian plonk, don't you think?"

Coswell almost moaned. It was the most expensive of the Irish whiskeys. But she played her role perfectly. If the men sitting around the reserved table had any hormones at all, her arrival had to have stirred something. He noticed that she had positioned herself so that her every move was broadcast to them.

He called over to the bartender in a loud voice, emphasized by standing and waving his hand in the air. The man responded immediately.

"My friend wants a real drink," Coswell said. "Take this away, please, and bring her a Connemara."

The bartender gave Bostock the once over but didn't comment. He picked up the full glass of wine and went to wherever the good Irish stuff resided to fetch her whiskey.

Coswell's next jolt was feeling her knee pressed against leg and her head turned and tilted toward his.

"If you look just over my shoulder," she said, an intoxicating smile on her lips, "you can see them all. Have they noticed us?"

Her perfume wafted over him, and for a second he almost forgot why he was there. But he quickly came to and did as she suggested. Three of the men facing them had indeed noticed. Two were commenting to one another and the third, a thin, hawk-like man was staring intently their way. And then two good things happened: the bartender arrived with Bostock's whiskey, and the couple sitting at a table for four adjacent to the reserved group got ready to leave. Before the bartender could deposit the whiskey in front of Bostock, Coswell had a twenty pulled out of his wallet and waved it in front of him.

"If you can get us that table over there," he said to the man, "This is for you."

In mid-motion, the bartender halted and then called

out to the nearest waitress.

"Carly. Hold that table for these two folks. I'll bring their drinks over."

It was that simple and Coswell knew that the taxpayer would think the money well spent.

They made their way to the table, Bostock ahead. She stopped at the chair facing the reserved group. Coswell pulled it out for her and pushed it under as she sat down. Very gallant. He took the chair immediately to her left, which put him eye-to-eye with the three men who had been watching them. The two women at the table, he noticed, couldn't light a candle to Bostock look-wise. They were definitely not wives, however. They had "hookers" written all over them.

The thin man was still staring at them. Coswell took the opportunity to nod to him. No response. He started talking to Bostock, loud enough, he hoped, to be overheard.

"I'm glad you came along," he said. "For a Montreal man, Vancouver's deadly dull. Christ, there isn't even a place downtown to make a few bets. I like a little action for my money, including you, eh?"

"Can't help you with any gambling," she said. "But I'm sure we can work out an arrangement just between the two of us."

"Name your price," Coswell said. "I'm good for it."

Out of the corner of his eye he saw the thin man make a barely discernable nod to a man directly across from him.

"A grand would keep me warm for the whole night," Bostock said.

Coswell was aware of movement behind him and then a man's voice at his shoulder.

"Couldn't help overhearing. Maybe I could suggest something that would interest you."

Coswell turned his head and looked up—way up. The

man could have been a basketball player he was so tall. He was also black, had a shaved head, earrings, and arms covered in tattoos. Despite the cool fall weather, he was dressed in jeans and a T-shirt stretched across a massive chest. Had to be the biker guy.

"Maybe your little lady could take a powder break while we talk, okay?"

The two women had also moved from the reserved table. Coswell could see them heading, he presumed, to the ladies' room. They would be there if Bostock left at that point. Alarm bells rang in his head.

"Well, I don't know—"

"It's okay, Sweetie," Bostock said. "I could use a tinkle but watch my drink, eh?"

And before he could object, she pushed back her chair, grabbed her purse, and was off. The giant took a seat across the table from him.

"You're a gambling man, non? You just dabble, or are you a serious player?"

The accent surprised Coswell—not Jamaican, as he expected, but French.

"Serious as they come," Coswell said.

"You're from Montreal. Me too. What is your favourite casino there?"

Coswell cursed himself. He should have done some online research about Montreal including the casino scene before deciding that he would use the city as a lead in.

"I don't do casinos," he said, thinking fast. "Private wagering is my bag, but here it looks like casinos or nothing. And to make matters worse, I fly in and discover my old buddy, Doc Kelly, has been offed. Patrick Kelly. Did you know him?"

Coswell caught the slight frown when the man heard Kelly's name, but carried on with his spiel.

"He was going to get me into some good action here,"

he said. "We talked just a couple of weeks ago, on the phone. Bummer he's dead."

That brought their conversation to a complete halt. The man made no attempt to disguise his confusion; he turned his head sharply to his right, obviously seeking instructions. Finally, the hawk man spoke, his voice cold and his eyes never leaving Coswell's face like a snake staring down a mouse.

"I smell cop," he said.

There was no doubt in Coswell's mind that he had just been spoken to by the infamous Conor Bonahan and now had to make a quick choice—either abandon the charade and just grill the hell out of the bugger, or continue the act. He chose the latter.

"Then you need your nose fixed," he said. "What in Jesus' name makes you say that?"

"Cops ask questions. You just asked one in a bit of a coy way, I might say."

Coswell remembered Jack Ryan's comment "Conor is a very sharp lad." Might be hard to outwit this one, but worth a try.

"Well, that just went way over my head," Coswell said. "The only question I need answered is where to get some action for my money. If that ruffles your feathers, then to hell with you. I've got a live one already, a little poker in bed, eh?"

The black man leaned ominously across the table and said "No one tells Mr. C to go to hell." His biceps bulged and for a second Coswell regretted his choice of words, but he also saw a change in Bonahan's attitude.

"It's okay, Larry," he said. "Any friend of Dr. Kelly's is welcome here. We all miss him, don't we lads?"

They all nodded like a bunch of parrots—all except Larry, who continued to look at him with a menacing stare.

"Yeah, Pat was a lot of fun," Coswell said. "Only fault

was betting over his head. Still owes me a bundle, but he was always good for filling a seat. Kind of like a cover charge having him along. Who did he find to back him out here? That wife of his still spotting him?"

Larry appeared annoyed that he had suddenly been left out of the conversation. He clenched his hands together and cracked his knuckles. "Nobody owes us bundles," he said. "It's pay up or goodbye."

Bonahan shot him a look that said "Shut up."

"Larry likes to play the tough boy," he said. "Actually he's a pussy cat, aren't you Larry?"

Larry looked away. "Yeah, a pussy cat," he said.

Bostock made her way slowly to the women's washroom, letting the two from the reserved table enter well before her. She was surprised when she went in herself to discover that the three of them were the only occupants. Unusual in a pub that served mainly kidney-flushing beer. One of the women was using a stall, her feet and panties visible below the door. The other was leaned close to a mirror carefully reapplying lipstick. When she saw Bostock's reflection, she stopped and turned toward her.

"You got to be new around here," she said. "Probably don't know that this territory's taken, like one hundred percent."

Bostock had no need to use the facilities but she moved to one of the mirrors over the four sinks and checked herself out, completely ignoring the woman. She heard the toilet flush and out of the corner of her eye she saw the second woman appear.

"She ain't talking, Eileen," the lipstick applier said. "Pretty snooty if you ask me."

"I heard," the other one said. "Maybe she needs a little lesson, eh?"

They now had Bostock's complete attention.

"Yeah," the lipstick one said, stepping toward her. "A

little messing up might just help her on her way."

In a flash, the woman's hand shot out, grabbed a handful of Bostock's hair, and yanked her to one side. At the same time the second woman, Eileen, with surprising quickness, positioned herself at Bostock's back and grabbed her shoulders.

This could have ended badly for Bostock, but in addition to her shooting prowess, she excelled at another element of her rookie training—defensive tactics.

Instead of jerking back to pull her hair free, she lowered her head a few inches and drove it into the woman's neck. At the same time she kicked off her high heels so that she could use the power in her legs to keep driving the woman backward. Eileen, still holding onto her shoulders, had no choice but to either stay on for the ride or let go. She chose the latter, which added to Bostock's propelling force all the way back to the tiled wall where the back of the lipstick lady's head smacked with a sickening thud. She slid noiselessly to the floor.

"You've hurt her, you bitch," Eileen screamed and lunged toward her, but too late. Bostock had spun around. Her second move came from her brother. "Never risk getting busted knuckles," he had said. "Use the heel of your hand. Drive it straight into their beak. Works every time."

And Eileen was the sad recipient of that advice. Bostock just managed to jump back before the blood spurted. Eileen staggered over to a sink in an unsuccessful attempt to keep the blood off her dress. Not a good night for her to have worn yellow.

The lipstick lady was beginning to show signs of life and so Bostock merely slipped her shoes back on, glanced briefly in the mirror to rearrange her hair, picked her purse off the counter, and left. She hoped that Coswell had had time to establish a good rapport with the black guy.

But then all went wrong. Bostock no sooner had sat

down at the table with Coswell and Larry when the lipstick lady came rushing toward them, circled the table and then whispered something into Bonahan's ear. Only Bostock noticed the blood trickling down the back of the woman's dress from her scalp wound. Black a much better colour.

A smile slowly formed on Bonahan's face and he looked directly at Bostock.

"My nose is at it again," he said. "I think Bunny here just fixed it." His smile didn't waver but the humour was leaving his voice. He turned his attention to Coswell.

"A truly wonderful performance, officers," he said. "Much more entertaining than the vice patrol that sneaks in here from time to time. You are homicide, right?"

Larry's eyes opened so wide they looked about to pop out of his head.

"Cops! Shit!"

He pushed his chair back and jumped up as though the whole table had become contaminated.

"Calm down, Larry," Bonahan said. "I'm sure it's just a question or two these fine people want to ask although I'm a wee bit puzzled. Why not just be up front with us?"

Coswell returned the smile.

"We thought it worthwhile to create a friendly atmosphere," Coswell said. "Interviewing with our uniforms on sets such a bad tone."

"Albeit an honest one," Bonahan said.

"But not conducive to honest answers."

The smile was gone now.

"All right. Game's over. If it's about Kelly's passing to the angels, we had nothing to do with it. He was a drinking companion. A fellow Mick. That's all."

"He was a compulsive gambler," Coswell said. "That usually goes along with impossible debts."

Bonahan's eyes narrowed.

"What's that got to do with me?"

"Rumour has it that you run the action around here.

Kelly spent a lot of time in this pub—ergo the suspicion that he owed you money."

Finally a laugh from the man—or at least a semblance of a laugh. "Ah, but I love the word 'rumour.' To quote an old Irish bard: it means, fact-wise, you haven't got a pot to piss in. Patrick Kelly owed me absolutely nothing. If truth be known, I probably owed him a drink or two. He was very generous when it came to covering the tab."

Bostock looked up at Larry still standing beside her.

"Where were you last Sunday night at ten o'clock?"

Larry didn't get a chance to open his mouth.

"I can answer for him," Bonahan said. "He was right here, knocking back a pint with the rest of us. Isn't that a fact, lads?"

The parrots nodded again.

"And that, I'd suggest, brings down the curtain on your little show. Enjoy your drinks."

Jack Ryan was right. Conor Bonahan was one smart cookie.

Conversation started up almost immediately beside them—innocuous subjects. Larry returned to his seat. The lipstick lady headed back to the ladies', presumably to help Eileen clean herself up.

Coswell looked at Bostock and was startled to see her looking downcast.

"I thought that went very well," he said. "Don't you? And what the hell happened in the ladies?"

"I blew it," she said. "They attacked me and I overreacted."

"What do you mean, 'overreacted'? What were you going to do? Stand there and get beat up?"

She looked down at the table.

"I should have talked my way out of it," she said. Her eyes were beginning to well up with tears.

Coswell knew he had to say something, but nothing came to him. *Women*, was all he could think of. But what would he have done if she were James? Changed the subject, of course.

"If you're not going to drink any of that wonderful whiskey," he said, "I could help you out."

To his astonishment, he had chosen the right words. She blinked a few times and then smiled.

"I'm going to drink the whole fucking thing," she said. "I need it more than you do."

They took separate cabs. Coswell offered to share one and see her to her apartment but she declined.

"I'll be okay," she said. "I'm a little out of practice with alcohol but one drink won't disable me. Thanks anyway."

He did wait until her cab pulled up and opened the door for her. She slid in, again ignoring how far her skirt came up.

Before he shut the cab door, he said, "You did good, Bostock. Sleep well."

His words hung in the air like a warm breeze for her until the door to her apartment closed behind her. Did he really mean that? She cursed herself for getting all teary at the pub. Some tough cop behaviour that was. And she *had* blown it. When the lipstick lady first started talking to her, she could have defused the whole situation. Pleaded ignorance. Said she was just a hick from Winnipeg trying to make a few bucks. Asked for advice. There were a dozen ways she could have handled the situation better.

The buzz from the whiskey was fading. Her shrink had said no alcohol with any of the meds. So okay. He didn't say anything about adding alcohol to alcohol. She pulled a raincoat out of her closet and put it on over her hooker dress. The miserable high heels got kicked off and replaced with a pair of Nike runners. There was an all-night beer and wine store just around the corner.

As she descended in the elevator, it occurred to her

that she now looked the part of a wino. Just needed the paper bag. Janet Bostock, Supergirl. Hooker to wino in the blink of an eye.

CHAPTER TWENTY-ONE

Coswell, back in his condominium, was having no such bad feelings. Everything had gone more or less as he had planned. He wanted to get a sense of that crowd, Bonahan and Larry in particular. If Kelly's murder was a gangland killing, they were the obvious gang to do it.

And the undercover manoeuver was worthwhile. Although brief, it brought out two points that he doubted would have been revealed in a routine interview. One, Larry was a loose cannon and probably not too bright and two: portraying Kelly as a generous, fellow Mick drinking buddy was a smokescreen. The man was a compulsive gambler; easy prey for an organization like Bonahan's. They would have cleaned him out for sure, and when that moment arrived and Montgomery had ceased to bail him out, what would they do? Charity would be highly unlikely. But did he owe them enough money to be killed over it? Did they need his murder as an example to others? Despite Larry's knuckle-cracking, Coswell doubted it.

No. Kelly must have threatened them somehow. Expose the gambling and the prostitution? He certainly knew both of those subjects well. But maybe there was a third illegal activity that he might have known about— supplying prescription drugs. As a medical person, Kelly may have gotten wind of something like that. Perhaps he was approached to participate.

Yes, Kelly could very well have been snuffed by the Irish Mafia and this added to his euphoria. It was much more logical than suspecting Montgomery. To the former, murder was just part of the business, whereas the latter was a respected member of the healing profession. And he just couldn't bring himself to believing a gorgeous creature like her could be capable of murder.

He leaned back in his easy chair and poured himself another round of his special Glenlivet. The bottle was open, so might as well work on it rather than the cheaper stuff that was his house supply. He took a sip and held the nectar in his mouth for a moment before letting it slide down his gullet. Wonderful. The Guinness was okay, but nothing like the Glenlivet. He wondered what Bostock's Connemara had tasted like.

And then his thoughts turned to her. The whole gang theory was hers from the start, even though he and James had squelched the idea when she brought it up.

Another sip.

She continued to be a puzzle to him. One minute she's super efficient, smart and a step ahead of him; next minute she's as meek and mild as the downstairs maid or worse, on the verge of tears over making some imagined mistake. In reality, her breaking up the party came at a perfect time. God knows what he would have done if a gambling session been arranged. Vice was Jack Ryan's job, not his.

But he had to admit that her tears somehow made him feel more in control. And then he chuckled to himself. What a chauvinist thought that was.

Living with Alzheimer's beckoned to him, his bookmark at page eighty-nine. He reached for it and then sank back in the chair. Not tonight.

Friday

Coswell marched into headquarters at seven forty-five feeling better than he had for weeks. Chief Ward, he knew, would have preceded him by fifteen minutes and with a little luck would actually have something with which to occupy himself before his secretary, Jane, arrived.

Bostock's report on Kelly's cell phone records was front and centre on his desk. He started to peruse it when James walked in.

"Don't waste your time reading that," he said. "I've seen it. Nothing that will help."

He looked at Bostock's desk.

"Not in yet? That's unusual, but then she had a late night, eh? How did it go? I'm dying to hear what happened."

Coswell related the entire adventure, ending with, "It's definitely worth pursuing further."

James was more interested in Bostock's role and especially her encounter in the ladies' washroom.

"How did she look? Black dress, right? Simple strand of pearls, I'll bet. Hem length?"

"She's a cop, James. I don't pay much attention to how cops dress and as for the washroom incident; you'll have to ask her."

"Oh, you're such a spoilsport," he said. "Or partially blind. I'm sure she was stunning."

"She looked like a hooker—an expensive one."

And at that moment, the expensive hooker came into the room looking almost funereal—pale, dark circles under her eyes and when the office door shut with a sharp bang, she winced.

Coswell instantly empathized. He recognized a giant hangover and he knew it wasn't just from the one glass of whiskey she had at the pub. Bostock was a drinker. Her "*I need it more than you do*"came back to him.

James was much more sympathetic.

"Bostock! You look like cold death slightly warmed over. You should have phoned in sick."

"No," she said. "I slept in this morning. That always makes me a bit groggy."

Groggy, my ass, Coswell thought, but he knew the

appropriate remedy.

"And I'll bet you missed breakfast," he said. "So over to Gino's we go. A double espresso and some carbohydrates will perk you up."

She gave him a look of eternal gratitude.

Gino's was the usual morning zoo when they walked in.

"You do the table again, Bostock," Coswell said. "James is treating this morning. It's only fair. He had last night off. I'll have the usual."

"Thank you," she said. "I'll go with your suggestion: a double espresso, and maybe a cinnamon bun."

Coswell and James joined the lineup, almost six deep.

"She's hungover," Coswell whispered. "Be nice."

"I noticed. Her perfume didn't quite cover the odour of alcohol trying to escape. Couldn't you have prevented that?"

"She only had one drink in the bar. That's all from homework."

James glanced over at her as she staked out a table for them.

"Oh dear," he said. "There's more to that poor girl's story than we've been let into. Maybe I *will* do a little snooping in Jane's file cabinet."

"Please do," Coswell said. "And don't feel the least bit guilty about it. Ward made us part of her therapy and we need to know all the facts."

James was held up at the cashier. For some reason his credit card wasn't working. Coswell quickly abandoned him and went over to collect his and Bostock's coffee from the barista.

When he made his way over to the table, Bostock eyed the espresso like a starving puppy.

He put it in front of her and sat down, his own cappuccino in hand. "James is right," he said. "I have no problem with your taking the day off."

She didn't reply until she had downed half the strong drink in a single tip. "I'll be fine. What do you want to do today?"

James was on his way over, having commandeered a tray to carry his coffee, two cinnamon buns, and a date square.

"I've just had breakfast," he said, setting it down, "but that square looked so good. I decided to risk a wee bulge to my perfect figure. Now, what are you two sleuths up to today while I hold back the journalistic hordes?"

Coswell noticed his sparing Bostock the telling of her Auld Sod Pub washroom affair.

"I haven't decided yet," he said. "We've got that Ethiopian resident at the hospital to interview, and maybe Dr. Struthers, Kelly's successor. He's the only person who seems to have had any personal relationship with him. In a hospital that size there are surely some fellow gambling addicts. Maybe Kelly hooked up with them—Misery loves company, eh? Struthers might be able to give us some names."

James shrugged.

"Seems to me that the ex-wife would be a better source in that regard."

Bostock, who had been warily picking at her cinnamon bun, joined in.

"Yes," she said. "Our first interview with her was rather brief. She had a class waiting for her."

"That, too, of course," Coswell said. He tried to put as much as he could into *of course,* but he dreaded that interview. Somehow he had to do it without Bostock present. He debated whether or not it was worth his contacting Montgomery in advance and asking her not to mention their evening out, but that would be admitting intrigue. Not a wise move.

Bostock was showing more interest now. Her queasy stomach had obviously tolerated the first nibbles of the cinnamon bun because half of it was gone and life was re-entering her body.

"And check out Larry's alibi for last Sunday night with the servers who were on duty then," she said. "Maybe one of them will talk if we promise confidentiality. Probably best to interview them at home, though."

Her enthusiasm spread to James.

"Good stuff," he said. "Just three days into the investigation and you're zeroing in. Blow the goon's alibi and you can really put the screws to the whole gang."

He sat back in his chair and gave a theatrical sigh.

"I am a tiny bit disappointed, though," he said. "I had my heart set on a crime of passion—love or hate or whatever, not just some gangland execution. That's so unromantic."

Bostock quickly spoke up.

"I don't mean to imply that that's the only route to follow. We will certainly continue to look into other possibilities," and then, embarrassed at her forwardness, "If you agree, sir."

"Of course," he said, wondering why he kept using those words. He didn't feel very *of course*.

They started off their hospital visit again in the Department of Surgery. This time their reception was even chillier. Carol, the secretary, had not been amused.

"I understand that you almost ambushed Dr. Struthers in the surgeon's lounge yesterday," she said. "I certainly hope that you won't try that again today. There was a tragic event on the ward while you were waiting there. The patient, one of Dr Struthers', died from a complication."

Coswell was going to object to her insinuation that he and Bostock may have been partly responsible for the death, but the secretary was on a roll.

"His case load today is even heavier than yesterday. Add that to a three a.m. call to emergency and we have a very tired surgeon. He doesn't need any more stress."

"We are not ogres," Coswell said. "And after what you've just said, you can be assured that we won't bother him today. We would appreciate, however, your letting us know when he would be available to us."

This calmed her down, although her body language spelled "I'm not sure I believe you." A reasonable suspicion considering that "ambush" was the right word.

Bostock sensed the animosity towards Coswell and took over.

"Do you think that Dr. Debas might be available for us today?" she said. "We would really appreciate talking to him and that would tie up a loose end. We did manage to interview Dr. Tynan yesterday."

It looked as though a cloud had just passed over Carol's head. "And how did that go?" she said.

"He doesn't exactly project a warm and fuzzy feeling," Coswell said. "Seems a bit on the angry side. Understandable, of course, having to go back to school before being allowed to practice in Canada."

She paused, measuring her response.

"It's a good rule," she said at last. "Some of the foreign training is not up to our standards and so it gives us here time to adequately assess those who apply for staff positions at the VGH."

She cut off further conversation by picking up her phone and punching in a number.

"I'm calling through to the ward," she said. "It's Dr. Debas's non-scrub morning. He should be making rounds."

Momentarily that was confirmed.

"I'd suggest you go over there right now," she said. "He's just finishing rounds, and since he was up all night with emergency cases, I'm sure he wants to get some sleep over at the Doctors' residence."

If Dr. Debas needed sleep, he certainly didn't show it. He was waiting for them in the patients' lounge looking bright and alert. Coswell recalled Kelly's prejudice regarding blacks and Debas certainly qualified in that regard, but unlike Tynan, his demeanour was pleasant and respectful. When they walked into the lounge, he stood up from the chair he was sitting in and gave them a big smile, revealing dazzling white teeth. He extended his hand to Coswell first. Whether sexist, simple recognition of authority, or deference to age, Coswell couldn't decide, but he wondered what Bostock thought.

"I am pleased to meet you, sir," he said and shook hands with a surprisingly firm grip. Coswell expected something softer from a surgeon's hand, a sense of don't injure this delicate instrument of healing.

"Inspector Mark Coswell," he said.

Debas turned to Bostock and again extended his hand.

"And this is my associate, Corporal Bostock," Coswell said, noting that he didn't actually shake her hand but seemed more to caress it. Bostock's usual blank expression broke into a broad, unprofessional smile.

The patients' lounge was on the east side of the building and the light streamed through the large windows, giving a cheery atmosphere to the place. The chairs and sofas were red vinyl but somehow they fit, and when Coswell sat down in one of the chairs, it felt almost as comfortable as his condo recliner. Bostock chose a two-seater across from him. Debas sat down beside her and unlike being forced to share a seat with Sergeant McMorran, she showed no objection whatsoever.

They were the only people in the room.

"Where are all the patients?" Coswell said. "If I were stuck in hospital, I'd want to get out of my room and in here as soon as I could."

"Right after rounds is hand out meds time," Debas said. "But they will be filing in here soon."

"Then we'd best get on with it. Dr. Struthers' secretary told us you've had what sounds like an all-nighter in emergency. You must be exhausted. Does that happen every night you're on call?"

"Pretty well," he said. "The VGH is the referral hospital for the whole province. The case at three this morning was a gunshot wound flown down from Prince George."

His face clouded over for a moment as he continued.

"And, unfortunately, there are the post-op complications on the ward."

"Like the one yesterday," Coswell said. "I gather that didn't go well."

"It didn't."

Since it was obvious there would be no more talk about that, Coswell pressed on.

"Can you think back to last Sunday, around ten p.m.? You told us that you were on call but were you in the hospital at the time?"

He laughed.

"There's no point leaving the hospital when you're on first call. I stayed in the Doctors' residence."

He thought for a moment.

"Last Sunday was actually an unusually quiet day. I probably could have gone home, but I went over to the library and got in some study time. My BC licensing exams are coming up, which contain a lot of general medical questions. It's been a long time since I did any of that."

"The library's open at that time of night?"

"The hospital library is open twenty-four-seven. Has to be. One never knows when a quick brush-up on a procedure is necessary. And after hours is generally the only time residents and interns have to study. Too busy during the day."

"Was your partner, Dr. Tynan, studying with you?"

"No. Kevin wanted to spend the evening at home with his girlfriend. He carries a pager, so no problem contacting him. His flat is just a few blocks away."

"Did you have to contact him?"

"No. As I said, it was a quiet day. We did have an early supper in the cafeteria, though. He wasn't getting together with his girlfriend until later."

"You're friends, I gather."

"Yes, thrown together by similar circumstances," he said, smiling. "We share common stresses."

"Like Dr. Kelly?"

His smile grew broader. "Especially Dr. Kelly."

"Dr. Tynan has told us about the rough time he gave you in the operating room. Insulting remarks, I gather."

An outright laugh this time.

"You mean the Rastus tag? He had another good one, too: "Emperor." My first name got him going. I don't know whether he actually knew that I am one of Haile Selassie's descendents."

"That must have made you very angry."

"Not at all. In fact, I found it rather amusing, and in a way, complimentary."

"Doesn't sound very complimentary to me."

"It meant that he couldn't find anything in my surgical performance to criticize, and my how he loved to criticize."

Bostock suddenly interjected.

"I watched you from the observation deck yesterday. You are very good."

Coswell was startled. What kind of interview question was that?

"Thank you," Debas said, turning to her.

Bostock blushed.

"I'm sorry to have to be so picky," Coswell said. "But to back up for a moment, what was the time interval that you spent in the library?"

Debas seemed surprised for a moment but then answered.

"I understand," he said. "You must eliminate suspects, much like we do differential diagnoses, although I hope I am well down your list."

"The list is rather horizontal at the moment," Coswell said, "unless you can help us in that regard."

"Who killed Dr. Kelly? No, I can't think of anyone with that sort of violence in them. But to answer your question, I went to the library shortly after supper with Kevin, probably around five thirty. I took a break at seven and went over to the cafeteria for a coffee, which turned out to be a lengthy affair."

"You met someone?"

"Yes. Marilyn Hawthorne. She's a fourth-year medical student who plans to be a general surgeon and haunts the department. I swear she lays in wait for any surgeon passing by."

Coswell wondered about that. If Bostock's reaction was any example, Marilyn might have had more than surgery on her mind. Debas obviously had sex appeal.

"We must have talked for the better part of an hour before I could get away."

"Back to the library?"

"Yes, but I faded after an hour's worth. Studying something you're not really interested in is very sleep-inducing. I gave up and went back to the residence intending to have a short nap, but I totally passed out and didn't come to until midnight. And then, of course, I couldn't get back to sleep. Bummer."

Coswell looked over at Bostock.

"Do you have anything to ask? I'm finished."

"Yes," she said. "Can you give us the name of Dr. Tynan's girlfriend and tell us how we might contact her?"

"Her name is Sofie Kovac. She's an instructor in the Dental Faculty at UBC. You could reach her there, or just get her cell phone number from Kevin."

Coswell abruptly stood up.

"We'll let you go now," he said. "Thank you for being so cooperative."

"No problem," he said, getting up from the sofa along with Bostock. Again the handshake with Coswell and for Bostock, but she was the only one to receive the additional finger caress.

"I'm so pleased to meet you."

They had no opportunity to discuss their interview on the way back to the cruiser. The hospital seemed to be at maximum activity—mobile patients out in the hallways, nurses returning med trays, and aids clearing up breakfast debris. As they walked along, however, Coswell had a nagging thought. There was something in that interview that he was missing, but for the life of him he couldn't think what it was. Recent memory loss, again. He shifted instead to baiting Bostock about her obvious attraction to Debas.

"Handsome fellow, that," he said when they got into the cruiser.

"Certainly much more pleasant than his friend."

Nice dodge he thought.

"Doesn't quite have a clean alibi, though," he said.

"No, but it seems highly unlikely that he would leave the hospital while on emergency call."

"True, but he had backup. Dr. Tynan was on second call."

"But if Dr. Tynan were called while Dr. Debas was busy murdering Dr. Kelly, he would want to know why his friend wasn't there to take the call. And since Dr. Tynan seems to believe that Dr. Debas had reason to hate Kelly, he would surely have suspected his friend might have killed him."

"And kept that from us, risking a charge of concealing evidence in a murder investigation? Hard to imagine that their friendship is that close."

No comment.

Coswell put the cruiser in drive and pulled out of the hospital parking lot.

"We've got a couple of things to do out on the campus—finish questioning Dr. Montgomery and tracking down that girlfriend of Dr. Tynan's so why don't you do the girlfriend and I'll see if Dr. Montgomery is available."

She nodded and for a few minutes remained silent but later she spoke up.

"Are you happy with Frank Hoffmann's alibi?" she said.

He looked over at her. The wheels in her head were obviously turning.

"Are you implying that James and I might have glossed over our interview with Wing Chu, his roommate, when we did that initial mass lecture hall session?"

The words were no more than out of his mouth when he regretted it.

"Oh no," she said. "I'm sorry. It's just—"

"No apologies needed," he said. "We had to cram in way too many interviews that day and we might have slipped up on Wing Chu. Thinking back, I'm not exactly sure of our wording when we asked him what he was doing on Sunday night. When he said that he and Frank were studying in their room, I can't remember whether he specified times."

"I can check with James," she said.

"Good. His memory is a lot better than mine these days."

Another regret. He had told himself not to whine to her about his frailties. She was intimidating enough without.

CHAPTER TWENTY-TWO

Francis was fuming when Coswell stepped into Dr. Montgomery's office.

"Police, police," he said. "This is harassment. One

Mountie leaves and five minutes later another one arrives."

McMorran! He must have taken another staircase down to the foyer. But why had he come?

Francis' rant ended abruptly when Montgomery stepped out of her office.

"It's okay, Francis," she said. "I'm glad Inspector Coswell is here. Please come in, Mark." Coswell noted Francis' arched eyebrows at Montgomery's use of his first name.

He beat Francis to the punch this time by quickly grabbing a chair and hauling it into Montgomery's office. She closed the door behind him and began speaking before they had even sat down.

"That Sergeant McMorran is an awful man. If he wasn't a policeman I'd have had Francis throw him out on his ear."

Her pretty face was red and distorted in anger.

"What happened?" Coswell said.

"He as much as accused me of murdering Patrick, for heaven's sake. He found out from one of the security people that I was in my office at the time he was killed. Of course I was in my office. I was gathering my material for the Edmonton conference."

She took a deep breath before continuing.

"And it's not a pleasant feeling thinking that Patrick was being choked to death just two floors below me while I was blithely rummaging about."

Coswell mentally kicked himself. He was being punished again for not putting the routine "Where were you exactly between ten and midnight?" question to her at the first interview. First, the embarrassment with Bostock; now, even worse, McMorran had asked it.

"Surely that answer satisfied him," he said.

"You'd never know by the look he gave me."

Coswell tried to repress his concerns, rationalizing that it was really McMorran who upset her and not the question.

"Don't let it bother you," he said. "McMorran's a jerk, if you'll excuse my unprofessional assessment of the man."

Her colour returned to normal and she gave a sheepish smile.

"I guess I did overreact," she said. "Thank you for that."

He should have then put the whereabouts question to her but he chose another topic instead.

"We have a witness who spotted a man getting into a car in the Dental Building parking lot Sunday at eleven p.m. apparently in a big hurry. He could have been Dr. Kelly's killer. Her description of the vehicle was very hazy. 'Small' was about the best she could do. Did you notice anything like that when you left? I presume you park there, too."

"All of the anatomy staff park there," she said. "It's the closest lot to the building. I remember remarking to myself how deserted it looked compared to normal. Patrick's sports car was there and, yes, one other—a blue Volkswagen Golf. I drive a Golf, too, only mine's that mundane steel-grey colour. You don't see many blue ones. It was still there when I left, along with Patrick's car."

"Was anyone else in the building besides you, lights on in another office or the lab?"

"No, and I think I would have noticed. I exited out the front door, so I pretty well covered everywhere except the basement. I didn't see anyone outside, either, but I was long gone by ten thirty."

He didn't have a chance to continue. She changed the subject.

"I really enjoyed our dinner the other night," she said. "You are very good company."

"My pleasure," he said.

"You know, I have a teaching session with the neurology residents this evening, but I'm going to go for a bit of a sail right after work. I have joint ownership of a Star dinghy with Doug Bennett. He's head of Neurology at the VGH. We're both sailing nuts. He's going to the theatre with his wife tonight so I don't have a crew. Would you like to take his place?"

Coswell's heart soared. So they own a sailboat together. That sounded like a Platonic affair, and she did mention Bennett's wife. Why shouldn't he accept?

"That sounds like fun," he said. "What time should I meet you?"

"Is five o'clock too early?"

"No problem. I can arrange it."

She got up from her desk.

"Wonderful," she said. "I'll see you there."

Francis took over, pushing the chair back to its place in the waiting room.

"Well at least you people don't take a lot of the doctor's time," he said to Coswell, and then turning his head back to Montgomery, "I've just fielded a call for you from Dr. Dietrich. I promised you would call him right back."

She gave Coswell a smile.

"Academics," she said. "They never leave you alone. See you later."

Another arching of Francis' eyebrows.

Coswell ignored him and quickly left.

But out in the hallway, a lot hit him at once. She never mentioned the Jericho Sailing Centre. It could very well have been any one of the others—The Vancouver Yacht Club or the Kitsilano Yacht club, all three were close to her condo. She must have seen him having lunch on the patio when she and Bennett hauled out their boat but why didn't she mention it?

And a second date with a suspect? Go out in a sailboat? He had to be crazy.

He made his way down to the main floor intending to see if Frank Hoffmann was in the anatomy lab, but half way down the stairs his cell phone buzzed. He pulled it out of his pocket and checked the call display—Charlotte.

"I don't believe it," he said into the phone. "A direct call from the elusive Pimpernel of the forensic unit. What earth-shattering information do you have that has moved you to do such a momentous thing?"

"Don't be sarcastic, Coswell," she said. "I've called you lots of times."

Charlotte was never one to use the word "sir" and he liked that.

"I've managed to extract enough DNA from that swab off the elevator door jamb to do mapping. I can tell you that it was one helluva fiddly job, but unless someone else put it there, your killer left his mark."

"Fantastic! You've just made my day."

"Now don't get too carried away. DNA analysis isn't like ordering a bag of popcorn. I don't want to hear that I have to analyze mouth swabs of half the UBC medical faculty and students."

"Of course not," he said. "Although that would be nice."

"Just get me your big three, or at most six," she said. "We can move on from there if it's indicated."

Coswell's mind raced. Big three? Six? Who? Fred, of course. He might have bumped the door carting up the ten bodies. Who else? Larry the biker for sure, Frank Hoffmann, and—Kay Montgomery.

"Your victim, by the way, aside from a blood alcohol reading of point one, was clean—no drugs, no toxins. He did have a very nice dinner, though, and some fine scotch."

"I'm so glad you get such joy from your work, Charlotte. I'll have those DNA swabs over to you as fast as I can get them. One or two might be a problem."

"Good luck. Over and out."

Coswell punched his contacts button and scrolled down to Bostock's number.

She answered after the second ring.

"Yes, sir," she said.

"We've just got a break. Charlotte's found DNA on the elevator door swab. Where are you right now?"

"I'm still in the Dental Building. Dr. Tynan's girl-friend is giving a class which should finish in another ten minutes. I can interview her then."

"Just leave her a message to contact you and set some-thing up for later. I want you to meet me at the cruiser. We need to get DNA samples to Charlotte right now."

"Right," she said. "I'm on my way."

"Now what's the best way to go about this," Coswell said as they sat in the cruiser. "Charlotte's put a maximum of six on what we can send her. Three will be priorities, I gather. Who do you suggest?"

She answered immediately.

"First off, any of the staff who might have used the elevator. It could have been just an innocent smudge. If none of them match, I'd start with Larry, of course, and then I'd have to think about it."

She paused for a moment.

"Just names really after that—Dr. Montgomery, Frank Hoffmann, maybe Dr. Struthers, Francis—"

"Dr. Debas," Coswell added. "Tynan, but I'm getting a weak feeling. Our suspect list is just too damned flimsy."

"It seems that way, sir."

"Oh well, didn't some sage mention that police work was mostly a lot of routine plodding? Just keep collecting names and rule out the innocent?"

"Yes," she said. "And we haven't finished checking out alibis. Maybe that will eliminate some of those names."

"True, but a positive DNA would be a lot quicker."

"How will we go about getting Larry's DNA?" Bostock said. "He's not likely to be very cooperative."

"You're right about that, but it shouldn't be too hard to out think him. I'll take on that job. What I would like you to do is corner Fred, explain the DNA on the elevator and the need for samples, but to keep it to himself. I think it would be a bad move for us to go on open attack with mouth swabs in hand. We don't want to spook our killer."

He turned the key in the ignition and started up the cruiser.

"We'll go back to headquarters," he said, "and see if we can find you a vehicle. You'll need to drive out to Burnaby and get some collection equipment. Fred's sample has to be a good one. I don't want Charlotte moaning about a poor specimen. If Fred says there were others who might have touched that part of the door, then I'll leave it up to you to get their DNA as surreptitiously as possible."

"And then get it to Charlotte, I presume?"

"You presume correctly. Now there's no need for us to meet up later today. We both have lots to occupy us so let's say eight a.m. tomorrow—report time—okay?"

"Got it," she said.

Coswell's third trip to The Auld Sod Pub wasn't entirely work related. It was lunch time and he had noticed the Jameson Irish steak on the menu when he and Bostock were there. Anything with an Irish whiskey glaze had to be good. He sat at the end of the bar well away from the few other patrons who were sitting there. He was served again by the skinny waitress with the floppy hat. He gave her his order, which included a pint of Guinness up front.

He started to turn around on his bar stool to survey the crowd, but a familiar figure coming through the front entrance made him turn back quickly—Larry, preceded by two individuals as ugly as him—biker types. They went directly to the reserved table which actually had a RESERVED sign on it. Coswell kept his back to them.

"Is Larry doing lunch here now?" Coswell said to the waitress when she brought him the Guinness.

"Yeah," she said. "He damn near lives here."

"Were you on duty last Sunday night?"

"I wish. Weekends are big tip days. No, I just work Monday to Friday. Boring and piddly tips—not that I'm fishing, mind you. Just facts."

She glanced down the bar toward the bartender who was changing one of the kegs under the taps. Satisfied that he wasn't paying any attention to her, she turned back to Coswell.

"You looking for more information? Checking up on Larry? He's a biker, you know."

"The answer is yes, yes, and I know. But I've got a twenty for you if you can get me the names and how to contact the staff working last Sunday night."

"No problem," she said. "The list is up on the corkboard beside the office. It even has the table assignments."

"Good. And you can have two more twenties if you get me Larry's empty glass when he's downed it."

She backed away from him.

"Jeez. I don't know about that. I don't want any trouble with Larry. He's a bad dude."

"Don't worry. I'll have that glass off your tray and into my pocket so fast nobody will see it, trust me."

"I'll think about it," she said, and then hurried off to the kitchen to put in his steak order.

He took a few healthy swigs of his Guinness while he waited. There was a lot of noise and loud laughter coming from Larry's group, although he couldn't quite make out what they were saying.

His food order arrived fifteen minutes later along with a large napkin.

"I got what you wanted," she said. "It's folded in the napkin."

"Good job," Coswell said. "Now how about the glass?"

"Okay, I'll do it, but get ready. His glass is almost empty. Use the napkin to cover it."

She set everything in front of him.

"And chug-a-lug your beer so I have an excuse to stop by and pick up your empty."

"No problem," he said, "But he wasn't a chug-a-lugger normally and so he barely managed to empty his glass when she rounded the end of the bar and came toward him with Larry's empty glass on her tray. He put up his hand to flag her down, palming the open napkin as he did so. She leaned over as though she couldn't quite hear him. He used the napkin to hide the switch. It went perfectly, his glass for Larry's.

When she left, he attacked the steak, which proved heavenly and when she brought him the second Guinness, it tasted even better than the first. There was a lot to be said for food pairing.

When he finally called her down to settle his bill, he got the three twenties to her just as efficiently as the glass switch—rolled up under his credit card. He also took care when he left to keep his back to Larry and exited via a circuitous route around the perimeter of the pub.

Rather than go directly to the forensics lab, Bostock decided to take a short detour back to the VGH. She thought another session with Dr. Debas before he got sequestered again in the operating room was warranted. Coswell hadn't really delved into reasons why Kelly would have been hated to the point of getting himself murdered. There had to be others.

It was just after noon. She decided that the likeliest place to find Debas would be in the cafeteria, having lunch. She was correct, although it took her a few minutes to spot him in the long lineup of hospital staff filling their trays from a surprisingly varied selection—healthy and unhealthy.

She waited until he was almost at the checkout before she walked over and spoke to him.

"Hi," she said. "May I join you?"

His smile sent a wave of pleasure from her breast all the way to her toes. She remembered the touch of his hand on hers when she and Coswell interviewed him in the patients' lounge. It had been a long, long time since she felt anything like that. Her job, her career, had been too all-consuming.

"What a pleasure to see you again," he said. "Of course you may join me but have you had lunch? It's all free to me so I'll just back up and get you something. Any preference?"

"Oh, you really don't have to do that," she said. "I—"

"No problem. How about a bowl of their bouillabaisse with a French roll? That's what I'm having."

"Well,—"

"Done," he said. "And I'll get us a couple of teas ... or would you prefer coffee?"

"Tea would be perfect."

The eating area was filling up fast but he led her directly to one of the few tables for two tucked away in a corner of the room.

"My favourite spot," he said. "I usually pull out a book and look as engrossed in it as I can. Quiet time is a rare commodity in a big hospital."

"And I've butt in," she said.

"You are immensely better company than any book," he said. "I am truly glad to see you but, of course, you are here on business."

She blushed.

"It can wait," she said, tasting the bouillabaisse. "This is really good. I always thought hospital food was bland."

"A well fed staff is a happy staff," he said. "A universal axiom, I think."

"I'm curious," she said, breaking the roll in half. "Have you applied to go on to surgical staff here?"

He smiled.

"Ah, the questions." and then seeing her frown. "No,

that's quite all right. You are doing your job."

"Actually, I am truly interested," she said. "You have such talent. Our gain, of course."

"And Ethiopia's loss, you mean?"

Another blush.

"I'm four generations from Ethiopia," he said. "My family has been English for a long time. In fact, I'll bet I'm more British than you are Canadian. There are a lot of Bostocks in northwest England. When did your ancestors come to this country?"

She had hit a nerve.

"You are absolutely correct. My grandfather came out from Manchester right after the Second World War, but no way did I mean to imply that you should go back to Ethiopia. I know your English background. The gain I was referring to was your choosing Canada over England." A white lie. She had been thinking Ethiopia.

"Oh dear," he said. "My sincere apologies. I try hard not to let colour rule my mind, but there have been a lot of Dr. Kellys in my world who think I should be with my own kind."

Bostock pressed her advantage.

"I don't think like that," she said. "People should be judged on their merit, not anything else—skin colour or gender."

He looked deep into her eyes.

"Gender. Of course. A woman competing in a trad- itionally man's field. You must suffer prejudice, too. But Canada is not Dr. Kelly. I've been treated very well here. Much less prejudice than I experienced in Britain."

He held out his hand.

"Let's shake on this," he said. "Fellow warriors in the fight for equality."

She felt the warmth and the happiness that went with it. Beats hell out of pills and alcohol, she thought.

"Now ask me anything you want," he said. "It would

be great if you were the one to solve the case, eh?"

He chuckled.

"Practicing my Canadian," he said. "Not bad, eh?"

"That's very good," she said, and resumed eating her lunch. He did the same, although he had no problem speaking between mouthfuls.

"But I haven't answered your first question," he said. "Yes, I have applied for a staff position here. Dr. Struthers, I know, is desperate to get help with the teaching, and doubly desperate now that Dr. Kelly's gone."

"There must be a number of surgeons on staff in a hospital this size. Don't they all teach as well?"

He sighed.

"The Hippocratic Oath? It's not even part of the graduation ceremonies now. Everyone does the bare minimum and very few allow decent hands-on experience. Fear of lawyers, I guess. That was something else I had to get used to in this country."

To her embarrassment, Bostock polished off the soup and her roll before Debas was half through his.

"You really were hungry," he said.

"Bad habit," she said. "I eat too fast. I have a brother who liked to compete at the table. But don't mind me. I'll have some tea."

She poured herself a cup and for a second wondered if they had cinnamon buns. Coswell's eating habits were rubbing off on her. She took a sip of tea and then got on with her so-called reason for being there.

"I'm finding it hard to understand Dr. Kelly's attitude in the operating room," she said. "We've been told some nasty stories. If new blood is so badly needed, surely the head of the department would feel obligated to create an atmosphere that would attract people, not put them off."

"He didn't seem to care. Poor Dr. Struthers had to mend a lot of fences."

"Well I expect your application will be accepted

without a hitch, now that Dr. Kelly isn't around to stick his prejudice into the mix."

"I hope you are right," he said. "The job's to kill for, eh?"

He almost caught her, but couldn't suppress his laughter.

"Just kidding," he said. "Don't look so serious."

"Comes with the job," she said. "And if I'm to be the shining star on this case, I need to be serious. The word "'kill" is the operative one. Do you have any idea? I promise everything you tell me will be held in strictest confidence."

He pushed his bowl away and poured himself some tea. There was still half the roll left. Her brother would have pounced on it.

"Dr. Kelly angered a lot of people here, but I don't see any one of them as a murderer. The medical profession doesn't tend to attract that type of individual."

"True, but historically there have been rogues— sadistic, murderous ones," she said.

"Psychopaths? Yes. Get any significant population together and you'll find one or two, I suppose, even in the heady world of academics. But as you well know, a psychopath is a true chameleon. Hard to spot."

"And commits his crime not in a fit of passion but in a cool, calm, well planned manner and everything we've found so far points to that. Whether the killing was direct or contracted is a moot point. We are considering an organized crime element."

"That would seem more likely to me," he said. "Dr. Kelly mixed up in something like that wouldn't be out of character. I've heard that he liked to party with gangsters."

"Dr. Tynan tell you that?"

"Yes. Kelly's behaviour embarrassed Kevin, a blot on the homeland's reputation. Kevin is very straightlaced— more English than Irish that way."

He took a sip of his tea and regarded her with a twinkle in his eye. "Now, how about I get to ask you a question?"

"Go right ahead. That's certainly fair."

"Is there a significant other in your life and if not, would you let me take you out to dinner some evening?"

Bostock was surprised by this. It took her a moment to answer him.

"Uh, I really would," she said. "But—"

He threw up his hands.

"What an insane question I've asked," he said. "I'm sure it is totally forbidden for you to go out with someone who is part of your investigation. But maybe when the case is solved?"

She extended her hand.

"Deal," she said, but just as he reached for it, a call came over the PA.

"Dr. Debas. Code four on D ten. Code four on D ten."

"Oh no," he said. "Not another one. I have to run."

And he actually did run—right out of the cafeteria.

She sat stunned for a moment by the abruptness of it all but she recalled a similar event had occurred when they were interviewing in the surgeons' lounge. "D ten" was the surgical ward and "Code four" was obviously something bad.

She took a few more sips of tea and then, after looking around to see that she was not being observed, picked up Debas's half-eaten roll, wrapped it in the serviette that he had crumpled up, and put it into her purse.

She was certain that Charlotte would have no difficulty isolating his DNA from those. Clearing his name had moved well up on her priority list.

CHAPTER TWENTY-THREE

Coswell didn't feel like driving all the way out to the forensic lab to deliver Larry's beer glass and so pulled into headquarters, hoping to find James there. He was the liaison person; let him liaise.

"Just caught me between vital assignments," James said. He was sitting in Bostock's chair. In front of him was a sheet of paper covered with doodles. Coswell glanced at it.

"Good to see that you're working on a new vocation—graphic artist," he said.

James picked up the sheet and surveyed it.

"Not bad. But my talents are more toward creative writing. I should be working on the Great Canadian Novel while I sit here with nothing to do."

Coswell pulled the beer glass out of his pocket and handed it to him.

"Here's an exciting job for you," he said. "Take this to Charlotte. Leave it in the napkin and be careful not to smudge the fingerprints; they're Larry's. We could have the Kelly case all wrapped up when she's finished with it. She found some DNA in a sample from the anatomy lab elevator door."

"Wonderful. Now there's an errand I don't mind. Gives me a chance to put the screws to Charlotte and Charlotte is so rarely screwable."

"James," Coswell said, "I'm beginning to wonder about you. First Bostock's appearance and now Charlotte's screwability. Are you on something that's affecting your hormones?"

"I am surrounded by the gender. Maybe it is affecting me but what have you got Bostock doing this afternoon? Wild goose chase?"

"Not at all. She's on a DNA field trip. If Larry's sample doesn't match the elevator door DNA, we'll need to keep looking."

"True," James said. "Well then, I'll be off."

Coswell saw Bostock's reports under James' doodle sheet, but all the talk of sex and hormones had turned his mind to another matter—his sailing date with Kay

Montgomery. How was he going to handle it? Should he take a chance and hope that the open sea air would keep his nausea in check? A horrible picture popped into his mind—him barfing and the wind carrying the vile stuff straight back striking the woman at the tiller. No, he couldn't risk that. What to do?

Be honest, he decided. Tell her about his motion sickness. Maybe another sailor would be available to go out with her and he could simply wait in the patio restaurant, convince her to have supper there with him before her teaching session.

But then he thought further on the subject. He could get the same result by faking an emergency call and arrange to meet her later. That would maintain his dignity and still afford another chance to spend time with her. Yes, that's what he would do.

He debated phoning Bostock, to see how far she had got in her DNA mission but then decided to just leave her alone. She would no doubt get it all done with great efficiency. It was too late in the day to start on a new project and he had to find something to wear to the sailing centre. Since there were definitely no sailing type clothes in his wardrobe, he needed to pick something up. Mountain Equipment Co-op was where all the jocks in the Force went to get stuff and it was handy—just a few blocks from headquarters.

As he left his office, he had a nagging feeling that had forgotten something important and something that he had just thought of. He tried to track it back, cursing at how fast his short-term memory was fading. It was a job for Bostock, and not much further back was something he missed in the interview with Debas. But thoughts of Kay Montgomery kept pushing everything else away. By the time he got to the cruiser, his only thought was trying to picture himself in a sailing outfit.

Lunch with Debas, pleasant as it was, had put a dent in Bostock's self-imposed schedule, and the traffic on Kingsway was brutal. She was tempted to turn on the siren but that would be an abuse of power. Nothing to do then but grit her teeth and endure the crawl all the way to the forensics lab in Burnaby.

When she finally pulled into the parking lot, she was delighted to see James just getting out of his vehicle. She gave the horn a couple of taps to get his attention. He stopped and waited for her, Larry's wrapped beer glass in his hand.

She rushed over to him.

"James," she said. "I'd really like to stop and talk to you but I've got to get out to the campus. Would you be a dear and give this to Charlotte? Tell her it's from Dr. Debas."

"No problem," he said, holding up his bundle. "Coswell got this one from Larry. He tells me that it's priority number one. Where would you like me to tell her to put Debas?"

"She might as well run his with Larry's. I don't think it's adding too much."

James gave her a suspicious look.

"Think you might have a hot possibility, too?"

Bostock almost blushed at the word "hot."

"Nothing like Larry," she said. "But why not get a jumpstart on the rest?"

"Good thinking, assuming that the sample on the elevator door isn't just good old Fred's," he said. "Well off you go and shall I tell Charlotte you'll be back today bearing more samples?"

"That's the plan."

She made much better time out to the campus via Marine Drive and arrived at the Dental Building parking lot a few minutes after four. Getting Fred out of the anatomy lab was no problem. She got his attention by waving through the second door window.

"Help yourself," he said, opening his mouth to receive her swab. He had readily agreed to keep the tests confidential and enthusiastically volunteered to get a sample from Frank.

"They're wearing rubber gloves now when they work on the cadavers, the wimps," he said. "There was a time when students got in there bare-handed. They're almost finished for the day so I'll get his for you."

He had also answered her question about the possibility of someone else making the smudge on the door.

"Nobody but me ever uses that elevator," he said. "The few people who come down to the basement go by the stairs. The elevator is slow as mud."

"What about the cleaners?"

"Oh, yeah," he said. "I forgot about them. They probably do use it to get their big floor polisher to the basement. I've seen the monster and it would be a bugger getting it up and down stairs. Bad enough that they have to haul it up to the second floor."

Damn, Bostock said to herself. Another DNA to collect.

"But I doubt if the guy would have any trouble getting the polisher in and out of the elevator. Hard to imagine that he'd whack his hand on the door. Maybe you can just phone and ask him."

"Good suggestion," she said, and pulled out her notebook. "I think I still have his cell number."

She flipped over a couple of pages.

"Yes. There it is," she said. "Varsity Cleaners. The guy's name was Marko Ilic."

"Marko Ilic?" Fred said. "Nah, it couldn't be. Can't imagine Marko cleaning floors."

Bostock felt her antennae rise.

"You know this fellow? I thought you were gone when the cleaning crew arrived."

"I was, but I remember there was a Marko Ilic in last year's anatomy class. He flunked out same as Frank Hoffmann but Marko didn't have a daddy who's CEO of a corporation that donates big bucks to the university."

"No second chance for Marko, I take it."

"Nope. Flunk first-year anatomy and you're out of med school on your ear. Too bad. He was one of the nice ones."

Bostock felt herself focus.

"Was Dr. Kelly one of his examiners?"

"He was. Hoffmann, Ilic. Everything alphabetical. They were lab partners as well."

"What happens to people like Marko? I presume they switch over to another faculty."

"I guess so," he said. "But it's got to be hard on them. They spend at least four years in pre-med and then get the big news—accepted into the wonderful Faculty of Medicine at UBC. Whoop-de-do—for him and his family. Lot of pride gets bruised, I'm sure."

He gave her a knowing look.

"Figure he might have done it, eh? Could be. It comes to me now that he was Serbian, and from what I see on TV, killing is pretty common over there."

Bostock comtemplated that she was having a morning of ethnic prejudices, first Dr. Debas and now Fred, but she had no time for a discussion.

"I'm going to make a quick trip upstairs," she said. "Can I meet you back here in say ten or fifteen minutes?"

"No problem."

Marko Ilic was a sudden diversion in her plan to collect as many DNA samples as she could. Francis and Dr. Montgomery were on her list, and she wanted to get those before phoning Coswell about Ilic. Going ahead with an inquiry that promising on her own would risk the inspector's ire.

Francis was at his desk when Bostock arrived.

"Oh, it's the lovely Corporal Bostock again, minus the less than lovely Inspector Coswell. To what do I owe this pleasure?"

"I've misplaced the notes I made when I went over your daily record. Would it be too much to ask if I could see it again?"

"Not at all. I'm glad to see that my little jottings are of such interest."

He handed her the book, which she took over to an adjacent chair and began going through it page by page, notebook in hand. A few minutes later, she was rewarded for her patience. Montgomery called Francis into her office.

The moment the door was closed, Bostock jumped up and went over to Francis' desk and replaced the daybook. In someone as obviously vain as he was, she was certain a comb at least, or maybe even a brush, would be at close hand. She didn't have to look far. A comb was just inside the top drawer of his desk. She quickly used a tissue to wipe through the teeth and then tucked the sample into her pocket.

When she first visited the office with Coswell, she had noticed that Montgomery hung her coat on a rack in a corner by the hall door. She managed to go over it, extract a few hairs from the collar and gather a used Kleenex from one of the pockets before Francis returned from Montgomery's office.

"Done so soon?" he said, seeing her standing at the door.

"Yes. And again, thank you so much for your help."

He waved his hand.

"Anytime," he said and just as she opened the door to the hallway, "That dark blue is lovely, but have you ever tried ash grey? With your black hair it would be stunning, especially if you added a coral necklace."

As promised, Fred had the medical student's rubber gloves for her. She thanked him and then went outside to phone Coswell. She was about to tap his number on her cell when she saw Sergeant McMorran walking briskly toward her. She put the phone back in her pocket. Bad luck.

"Why don't you come along, Bostock?" he said as he mounted the steps. "And watch me question a suspect the way it should be done. No namby-pamby psychology stuff."

"Who—?"

"Just follow me, gorgeous, and all will soon be clear to you."

She almost had to run in an attempt to keep up with him. He marched down the hallway past Dietrich's office, the anatomy lab, and then went up the stairs to the second floor, two steps at a time. She was half a hallway behind when she saw him go into Montgomery's office.

"Now see here," she heard Francis say. "You can't just barge in—"

She made it to the office just in time to see McMorran's back disappearing into Montgomery's office and Francis desperately trying to get out from behind his desk to stop him.

"Whoa, Francis," Bostock said. "Let me go in and referee. You'll just get in trouble."

He looked at her with fire in his eyes but it quickly faded.

"Okay," he said. "But I'm right here if you need me. That big bully doesn't scare me."

"What in God's name—?" was all that Montgomery got out before McMorran started in. He put both hands on her desk and leaned forward, his face just a foot or so away from hers.

"You've not been entirely truthful to us," he said. "That was a very foolish thing to do."

"What do you mean?" she said. "You are being ridiculous."

"Am I? Then let's just go over what you told me at our last meeting. You said that you went directly home after the staff dinner on Sunday."

Montgomery seemed totally unaware of Bostock's presence in the room, McMorran had her total attention.

"I thought we cleared that up," she said. "I told you I stopped briefly here at my office to get some material I needed for a conference in Edmonton."

McMorran stood up, took a few steps back, and leaned an elbow on top of a filing cabinet. Montgomery finally noticed Bostock but said nothing to her.

"And then you went straight home to your condominium, which would make it around ten thirty, correct?"

"Yes. I had an early morning flight booked and a long day in Edmonton."

Uh-oh, Bostock thought. Too much information. She just dug herself a hole if she was lying.

McMorran's smile was maddening.

"What would you say then if I told you that one of your neighbours, a man out walking his dog, saw you drive your car into the underground parking of your condo building at eleven thirty?"

Bostock watched Montgomery's face. Fear for sure, and maybe guilt?

"He must be mistaken," she said.

McMorran stood up and glared at her.

"I don't think so," he said. "And to add further to our information, another neighbour, whose balcony is next to yours, was watching a late TV show and saw your lights come on five minutes after the dog walker saw you."

The look changed to pure panic.

"That's enough," she said. "I don't like your attitude and if there is any further questioning to be done, I wish Inspector Coswell to be present."

"Probably wiser to call your lawyer." McMorran said. "And have him or her meet you at the station. We'll continue with our little talk there."

"I don't need a lawyer," Montgomery said. "I've done nothing wrong."

Bostock was already on her cell phone.

Coswell was pacing up and down at the entrance to the Jericho Sailing Centre when Bostock's call got to him. He answered it on the second ring.

"Can't talk to you at the moment," he said. "Call me back in fifteen minutes, okay?" By then, he reasoned, Montgomery would have arrived and he'd have the perfect excuse to leave.

But Bostock stopped him dead in his tracks.

"Dr. Montgomery has just been taken into custody by Sergeant McMorran," she said. "We're going over to the campus precinct building."

His first reaction was one of relief, the sailing venture was off, but then—apprehension followed by deep anger.

"What's that airhead done now?" he said.

"Can't talk. They're leaving. How long will you be?"

"Five minutes."

Bostock wondered where he was that was only five minutes away.

It took him seven minutes, siren blaring, but only because some old fart on Blanca was either deaf or too stupid to pull over. When he drove into the precinct lot, he noticed that Bostock's vehicle wasn't there. McMorran likely commandeered her to be the chaperon on the drive to the precinct in his cruiser.

The desk officer was the constable whom James had dressed down for smoking on duty.

"They're in the conference room," he said, pointing to a short hallway. "Second door on your right."

Coswell didn't bother to knock. Instead, he gave the door a great push so it swung wide open when he stepped in. This had the desired effect. Whatever had been going on before he arrived came to a complete halt. He fixed McMorran, sitting at the head of the table, with the most malevolent glare he could muster.

"This had better be good, McMorran," he said. "You interrupted some very important police work I was doing."

If McMorran had been startled by the abrupt entrance, it didn't last. He remained seated and responded with an indifferent shrug.

"If your police work involved Dr. Kelly's murder, I doubt that it's more important than this."

Coswell looked over at Montgomery. She was seated at the very end of the conference table. She had her head turned toward him and the pleading look in her eyes went right to his heart. Bostock, her police face on, was standing beside her.

"Okay," he said. "Let's hear it."

McMorran described how he had acted on his suspicion that Montgomery was not telling the truth when he first interviewed her. He had literally done a door-to-door inquiry at her condominium complex. He finished with, "You have to think that someone who goes to the extent of lying to the police has something serious to hide—like murder."

"Brilliant," Coswell said. "You've gone from A to B with linear thinking that only you could be proud of."

McMorran looked ever so slightly less confident.

Montgomery finally interrupted the sparring.

"Please, gentlemen," she said. "I didn't tell the whole truth and there was a reason: I am having an affair with a married man. I intended to go straight home after the staff dinner, but he called me just as I was getting into my car. We arranged a brief meeting at a private venue. I didn't mention this to you because a marriage and possibly a career could be ruined. I'm truly sorry that I've caused so much trouble."

"What's his name?" McMorran demanded.

Coswell quickly cut him off.

"I think you have traumatized Dr. Montgomery sufficiently, Sergeant," he said, "She has confessed and expressed remorse."

He turned to Montgomery.

"Corporal Bostock and I will drive you back to your office."

McMorran jumped to his feet.

"What the hell—?"

"We'll take it from here, Sergeant," he said. "And a little reminder to you. *I* am the chief investigating officer here. Don't do anything like this again without consulting me first."

He gestured to the two women.

"After you, ladies."

As he followed them out into the hall, the hair rose on the back of his neck as he imagined daggers shooting from McMorran's eyes.

He drove quickly back to the Dental Building parking lot and prayed that the sailing date subject wouldn't come up. Bostock was sitting in the passenger seat and Montgomery in the back.

His worry was for naught because Montgomery remained silent until they arrived at the lot, and even then didn't comment until she got out of the cruiser.

"Unless you need more from me right now," she said. "I'd like to shut down things in my office and go straight home. I'm suddenly very tired."

"Quite understandable," Coswell said, twisting around to speak to her. "We can talk again tomorrow."

She closed the door and started to walk toward the anatomy building but after a few steps she stopped and turned around.

"I think she wants to say something more," Bostock said.

Coswell held his breath, but all Montgomery did was throw a kiss in their direction and then continued on her way.

"That was meant for you, sir," Bostock said. "You really saved her day."

Coswell didn't miss the innuendo.

"I know what you are thinking," he said. "I should have let McMorran push her some more but I never could stand seeing a witness badgered. We're supposed to be more intelligent than that."

No comment and that bothered him more than if she had just come out and said he had let the woman off too easy. Time to go on the offensive.

"Now tell me what you've managed to accomplish this afternoon."

She related all her DNA sampling, glossing over her conversation with Dr. Dubas and then told him of her new lead, the floor cleaner, Marko Ilic.

Coswell was truly impressed and said so.

"But the same rule goes for you as McMorran—never leave me in the dark. You've handled this well and I applaud your initiative with the DNA. James couldn't have done it better."

Damn, he thought. There I go again, using James as the benchmark for her.

But she didn't seem fazed by it.

"Thank you," she said. "That's a real compliment."

"And this Marko lead is yours, but I'd like to be around when you talk to him."

She was surprised.

"Of course, sir, I—"

"And let's get him on the job," Coswell said, "when his co-workers are present. Makes it easier to verify times and all that. Are you into some more overtime tonight?"

"Certainly. I have nothing else planned. I just have to drop the samples off at the forensics lab."

"All right then. What time was it that the cleaners started work?"

"Seven o'clock," she said. "But that was a Sunday. They may start later on a Friday."

"I doubt it. Weekends start on Friday, even for professors."

He looked at his watch.

"It's past five thirty. I tell you what. Let's meet back at headquarters. I'll get us a reservation for dinner at The Vicinage. And don't object. You deserve a reward for your fine work today."

CHAPTER TWENTY-FOUR

But the gourmet dinner was not to be. They were two blocks from the restaurant when the central dispatch came through on the cruiser radio.

"10-96 University Endowment Lands, 10-96"

Bostock grabbed the mike and pressed the send button.

"Unit 783 responding. Give exact location of 10-96. Over."

The radio crackled.

"Huckleberry Trail—"

Another transmission cut off the speaker.

"Sergeant McMorran, UBC detachment. We've got it, dispatch. No assistance required."

"The fool," Coswell said. "If the body's still warm, that park needs to be surrounded and he can't do that with his manpower. Find out where that trail is, Bostock."

He had already switched on the cruiser's siren.

"I know it," she said. "It starts at Sixteenth Avenue and Imperial Drive."

He held the steering wheel in one hand and with the other fished his cell phone out of his jacket pocket.

"Here," he said. "Go to my contacts and find Wilkinson. He's head of the city PD's homicide. Get him on the line for me and put the thing on speakerphone."

She managed to do so, despite being jerked fore and aft as Coswell sped up the hill through the upscale neighbourhood on Trimble Street, braking and then accelerating through the many stop signs.

"He's finally killed someone," Coswell said. "Not happy just mugging anymore."

Deputy Chief Constable Wilkinson was virtually walking out the door of the Vancouver PD main precinct when he received the call but he had no problem understanding Coswell's shouted instructions.

"Don't worry," he told Coswell. "My men will have that area surrounded. If the perp takes one step out of the Endowment Lands, he's in our jurisdiction. Keep me posted, though. I don't want to waste their time if your dead body isn't a fresh homicide."

That settled Coswell down with a thump. 10-96—report of a body found. The Endowment Lands had seen its share of suicides, dead derelicts, and victims dumped from elsewhere, domestic and gang related. That should have been his first thought as well. Why had he jumped to the mugger conclusion so quickly? Was it his aging brain unable to process more than one thought at a time, or was it a knee-jerk reaction to McMorran's name? Either way, he was slipping.

He glanced over at Bostock but all he saw was excitement.

Trimble dead-ended at Sixteenth Avenue. A quick left turn and a mere block away was Imperial Drive. Parked at the trailhead was a single cruiser with an occupant in the back seat. Standing beside it was an officer who turned out to be McMorran's corporal. He walked over to their cruiser when they pulled up.

"That was fast," he said. "We just radioed for back up. That lady in the back seat over there is the one who called in the 911. She was standing right here when we arrived, shocked to hell. She was walking her dog, a big rottweiler. The dog actually found the body. She insisted that it stay with her in the cruiser. Hope he has quiet bowels."

"Who is with the victim?" Coswell said.

"Just Sergeant McMorran. I'm to be here to direct everyone and look after this lady. Oh, and to call forensics."

McMorran, alone at a possible crime scene. Coswell almost shuddered.

The constable rattled on.

"She's in there about a hundred metres, just off the trail. Young woman, a jogger, obvious rape."

"ID?"

"None. It was probably in her shorts but I couldn't see them around. Killer probably kept them as a souvenir." and then, apologetically, "I didn't get to see much. Sergeant McMorran ordered me right back to the cruiser. He didn't want our 911 lady to take off, I guess, although we did tell her to stay here."

"Okay then," Coswell said. "You can remain with her until someone comes to relieve you."

He then phoned Chief Constable Wilkinson.

"It's the real thing," he said, and reported what the corporal had told him, adding, "I'll let you know how fresh it is as soon as forensics gets here but meanwhile every male exiting the Endowment Lands needs to be identified and interrogated."

Assured that the city officers would do so, he signed off and signalled to Bostock.

"Let's go," he said, and when he got out of the constable's hearing range, "Before McMorran screws up the crime scene."

He led the way along the path. It was well used and

he knew why. The Endowment Lands were essentially a forest in the middle of the third largest city in Canada. Just a few paces into it and the city disappeared. Even the traffic noises seemed to fade into the background.

To Coswell's great annoyance, the crime scene was marked, not by McMorran's presence, but by his service hat at the side of the trail.

"Where the hell—?"

Bostock walked gingerly to the edge of the trail and looked down into a small depression.

"She's there," she said, pointing.

Coswell came over and they both gazed at the woman's body. She was lying supine, her head lolled to one side, dark brown hair pulled back in a pony tail, a long-sleeved sweatshirt tight over her breasts, the hem up above her navel. From there she was nude all the way down to her feet, still clad in runners and short socks. Her legs were spread wide apart.

Coswell knelt down, ignoring the dirt on his trousers, and placed the back of his hand on her leg.

"Cold," he said. "She's been here a while."

Next, he looked closely at her neck.

"Where have I seen this before? Garrotted with a wire, it appears."

He then looked carefully at her pubis.

"But what don't I see?"

"What?" said Bostock, seemingly unperturbed.

"No bruising and no semen smear. Even if he killed her first, you'd expect some sign but Charlotte will tell us for sure."

"And that position," Bostock said. "It looks posed; arranged post mortem."

"I agree," Coswell said, standing up. "But where is McMorran?"

"He must have seen someone suspicious and went after them."

"That would be just like him," Coswell said. "No waiting for backup. He should have at least radioed his corporal. Looks like he's back in his narcotics gunslinger mode. I hope he doesn't shoot some innocent citizen."

Bostock was shocked.

"You really don't think an officer—"

"I wouldn't put anything past that cowboy." He looked down at her shoes.

"You seem to know these trails. Do you think you can catch up to him in those?"

"Yes, sir."

"Okay. Off you go, and tell him I want him back here immediately. I'll stay here."

She stepped back onto the path and started to jog. Coswell called after her.

"Be careful and make lots of noise," he said.

He watched her and admired how effortlessly she ran, her arms swinging rhythmically despite holding her purse in one hand.

And then he waited ... and waited. His first puzzlement was: where in hell was the backup McMorran ordered? Out there talking to the corporal? Ridiculous. The city boys, of course, would be patrolling the perimeter, but if McMorran really saw someone suspicious, a proper search should be organized using his whole staff.

And as the minutes went by, he began to worry about Bostock. He had virtually sent her to get McMorran on impulse without considering that the killer could jump her like he did that poor woman lying just a few feet from him. Add that to trigger-happy McMorran and she could be in real danger.

He pulled out his cell phone and called her, praying she would answer it. She did, but it took three rings.

"Yes, sir," she said, breathing heavily. "I haven't seen him yet, but there are so many trails branching off Huckleberry, he could have taken any one of them. I have called out to him numerous times."

Coswell gave thanks to whatever god and then, "Bostock, I want you back here as fast as you can come. I was wrong sending you out alone like that."

A moment of silence.

"You don't need to worry, sir I can—"

"Bostock!" he said. "That's an order."

"Yes, sir."

He broke the connection and looked at his watch. If she wasn't back in five minutes he planned to call in the cavalry.

He looked down again at the body and noticed something black just a few feet away almost obscured by a big sword fern. He carefully knelt down again and stretched forward on his hands to get a better look. But a noise distracted him. Something off to his right, crashing through the bushes and moving toward the trail—fast. An animal? The killer?

Before he could stand up, a figure suddenly burst into view twenty metres down the trail—McMorran with pistol in hand! He first looked to his right, away from Coswell, but then turned and faced him, pistol raised and the barrel pointed directly at Coswell's head.

Another prayer and again it was answered by Bostock.

Her voice came from behind McMorran, steady and determined. "Put the weapon down," she said. "Or I'll blow your head off."

McMorran froze and then slowly turned toward her, holstering his gun in the process. She had her Smith and Wesson pointing at his chest, and then deliberately lowered the barrel and pointed it at his crotch.

"For Christ's sake, Bostock," he said. "Put that thing away."

Coswell stood up and brushed the dirt off his trousers, a stalling tactic to allow his heart to slow down, and make sure his first comments wouldn't come out as squeaks.

"Yes, Bostock," he said. "Put it away. I'm sure Sergeant McMorran has a good reason for running through the forest with his sidearm waving about."

McMorran was still facing Bostock and didn't turn around until he saw her remove the clip, eject the round she had in the breech and put them, along with the gun back into her purse.

"I had a very good reason," he said walking up to Coswell, his confidence apparently back to normal. "Like you, I was kneeling down beside the body when I heard somebody running away from me, down the trail. I shouted for whoever it was to stop, but that just sent them away faster."

"What did you shout? 'Hey, you?'"

"Of course not. I identified myself."

Coswell was seething.

"I'm going to tell you something, McMorran. I want you to go back to your cushy campus office and write a full report on what's just happened here. I'd suggest that it be the best report you've ever written because mine will have terms like 'incompetent,' 'disregard for procedure,' and a recommendation for immediate demotion."

McMorran stood for a moment, blinking rapidly, and then brushed past Coswell with long, angry strides.

Coswell looked at Bostock, limping towards him in stocking feet.

"Do you think he would have shot you, sir?" she said. "I wasn't sure."

He had an overwhelming urge to hug her but held back.

"You stay here," he said. "Where did you leave your shoes? I'll go get them."

While they waited for Charlotte and her crew to arrive, Bostock quickly identified the black object that Coswell had been looking at when McMorran burst onto the scene.

"It's a thong," she said. "Likely fell out of the shorts or whatever she was wearing over it when the killer stripped her."

"If he was a collector, though, like the constable suggested, why wouldn't he take the thong as well as the shorts?"

He thought for a moment.

"It is black and awfully small," he said. "I didn't see it at first. Maybe the killer was in such a hurry he didn't have time to look around."

Bostock nodded, but then had a thought of her own.

"I wonder about the ID though," she said. "Do you think he might have taken the shorts for that reason alone? No time to rummage through the pockets so he just grabs them and runs."

"But why would a rapist care about his victim being identified?" Coswell said, "and besides, someone is bound to report her missing very soon. She isn't some street person."

And then he got her point.

"The killer isn't a mugger or a rapist, you mean. He's a cold-blooded murderer and he had a reason for doing this. Delaying her identification gives him time to set up an alibi. Certainly something to think about."

James was the first person to come down the path toward them, talking a blue streak.

"You would think that the official spokesperson for the RCMP would be notified well ahead of the media when a dead body is found in the Endowment Lands. But oh no, and who is it they've glommed onto when I finally get parked behind the traffic jam out there?"

"Ward promised me that he'd warned McMorran off doing stuff like that," Coswell said.

"Well it didn't work. They virtually packed up their cameras when I arrived and showed no interest whatsoever in an official statement, which come to think of it, I couldn't have given anyway because I don't know what's going on."

"McMorran's mouth sells papers. That's all they're interested in."

James looked down at the body.

"Who is she?"

"Don't know," Coswell said. "No ID on her."

Bostock, who had remained silent up to this point, spoke up.

"I'm trying to visualize how the killer approached her. If he jumped out of the bush, you'd think she would have heard him and fought back but I didn't see any sign of that. I think he came up from behind her on the trail. Another runner."

They both looked at her and then at their feet.

"Charlotte is going to be sooo mad," James said.

All three backed up a step.

"That makes perfect sense," Coswell said. "The trail's single file. He's behind her; waits until there's no one to see him, and swish—wire over her head and drags her off the trail. Seconds. And no chance for her to fight back."

"Stripping her wouldn't take much longer and then he's off," James said. "With any number of escape routes. I think I read somewhere that the Endowment Lands are like one thousand acres."

Further discussion was cut off by James' radiophone, strapped to his uniform—a hiss of static and then McMorran's voice.

"I've got him," he said. "Hunt's over, folks. Next stop, lockup downtown."

They were all too stunned to speak. James ultimately broke the silence. He unclipped the radio and gestured with it to Coswell.

"Care to comment?" he said.

Coswell took it and pressed send.

"To all units. This is Inspector Coswell. That is not a stand down order. I repeat—not a stand down order. Hold positions until further notified."

He had barely handed the radio back to James when his cell phone buzzed. It was Chief Wilkinson.

"I heard all that," he said. "What gives? It was one of my units that apprehended the suspect at a bus stop. Your Sergeant McMorran tried to take over, but the alleged perp was on our territory and quite rightly they've taken him downtown. Now, can I let the rest of my men get back to business? They're having to ignore all kinds of calls while they sit around out there."

"Chief," Coswell said. "I'm sorry but at this point I don't know—"

"Then you'll have to make do with your own men," he said. "There is a limit."

"I understand," Coswell replied, "and thanks for stepping in so quickly."

"Good luck then," Wilkinson said and terminated the call.

"McMorran probably cleaned out the men at headquarters with his backup call," James said, "but that's not nearly enough to cover the perimeter of an area this huge."

"You're right," Coswell said. "Okay then. Tell them to stand down but keep their eyes open."

With that he started back to the cruiser. Bostock fell in step behind him. When they got to the trail head, theirs was the only cruiser parked there, along with the forensic unit. Charlotte and her crew were unloading their equipment.

"Scooped on this one by the dashing Sergeant McMorran, eh?" she said when they walked up.

Coswell ignored the jibe.

"James will fill you in," he said said, and then walked directly to the cruiser. Bostock held back.

"Touchy, touchy," Charlotte said to her. "So where is the body? It would save me beating the bushes."

Bostock told her and then added that James was at the site.

"Thanks," she said. "Now you'd better hurry after Inspector Grumpy."

CHAPTER TWENTY-FIVE

Coswell was quite familiar with the inside of the Vancouver Police Station at Hastings and Main. He had been given a temporary office there during the West End Murders affair. Despite its clean lines from a distance, on closer inspection it was showing its age.

"It's looks old," she said when they mounted the stairs and entered the front door. "How long has it been here?"

Coswell didn't answer her. He was actually older than the building, erected in 1953, a fact he didn't wish to share.

The desk sergeant told them that McMorran was with Inspector Marsden in his office on the second floor. Marsden was the number two man in the Vancouver PD homicide unit. He had worked with McMorran on many occasions and was secretly sympathetic with the younger man's tactics. He was not so fond of Coswell, who had been given seniority over him in the West End investigation."

"I'll let them know you're here," the sergeant said, reaching for his phone.

"No hurry," Coswell said. "They're probably talking over old times. Give them a few more minutes. I know the way to the interview rooms. Tell them to meet us there. The corporal and I want to get a good look at the suspect before the interrogation."

McMorran's corporal was sitting outside the room. He jumped up when he saw them.

"Why don't you take a break, Corporal," Coswell said.

"No need for you to be here now."

"But Sergeant McMorran—"

"*Sergeant* is correct," Coswell said. "And I'm an inspector, so I repeat—take a break. I'm sure the desk sergeant can point you to their coffee machine."

They took a moment to observe the captive through the one-way glass. He was young, scruffy, and nervous. A homeless drug addict was the first impression that came to Coswell's mind. So many just like him walking around the downtown Eastside.

As they watched him, he got up from the chair he had been sitting on and began to pace about the room.

"Okay," Coswell said. "Let's go in and get his story before the troops arrive."

The man looked relieved to see them.

"Finally," he said. "Someone comes. I shouldn't have been left alone in here."

Coswell got him to sit down again facing the two of them across a table, bare except for a recording device. A nod to her and she switched it on, giving the date, time, and those present after the suspect's name was determined—Derron Sweeny, age nineteen.

"Tell me what happened in your own words, Derron," Coswell said.

"Shouldn't I have a lawyer or something?"

"Do you need a lawyer? You haven't been charged with anything yet, have you?"

"No, but that sergeant is awfully sure I killed the woman in the park."

"Why would he think that?"

Silence. Bostock spoke up—in a voice that was soft and sympathetic—a woman's voice talking to an upset child.

"Take your time, Derron," she said. "We're really here to help you."

He looked at her and saw something that got him

going—in a rush.

"I was just having a toke in the bushes with a couple of kids from the high school when we heard the siren. They hightailed it back to the school. I cut through the bush to the nearest trail and that's when I saw her lying there. I stopped for a second, thinking she needed help, but then I could see she was dead, her legs spread apart."

He took a couple of swallows. His Adam's apple bobbed up and down.

"I just panicked," he said. "Got off the trail right away and ducked into the bush."

"Why?" Coswell said. "You could have gone back and led the police to the body. You didn't kill her, right?"

"No! I'm not a killer, for God's sake."

And then silence again. He bowed his head and stared down at the table.

"I got a record," he said at last. "Got caught over the possession limit—once, so I'm a pusher, eh? And look at me. Do I come across as your typical good citizen? I knew they'd think I did it and all I wanted to do was hide."

"The sergeant heard you in the bushes."

"Yeah, and I could see him whip out his gun. I ran like hell. He was fast and damn near caught me, but I managed to double back a bit and hide under a bunch of salal. He came barrelling right past me with that ugly gun."

"Did he call out to you at any time?"

"No, but he didn't have to. I could see he was a Mountie."

Coswell wonder whether McMorran was listening outside.

"And then what happened?" he said.

"I waited until I heard him talking to someone and then worked my way far enough in the opposite direction until I came out on Sixteenth, near a bus stop. Figured I could hop on one and get back downtown. That's where they got me. Just my luck the cops were parked across the street."

At that point the interview was interrupted.

"Sergeant McMorran has just come into the room," Bostock said into the recorder and gave the exact time.

"Stop it," McMorran said, "and hit replay. I want to know what's gone on so far."

"That was Sergeant McMorran," Bostock intoned, "requesting the interview be halted."

"And this is Inspector Coswell refusing that request," Coswell said. "The interview will continue as soon as Sergeant McMorran leaves the room. He has obviously upset our subject."

Which was true. Derron's pupils were hugely dilated, presumably from fear but possibly residual, from something more potent than a marijuana toke.

McMorran glared at the recorder as though it were some pest he needed to squash, but then turned and stomped out.

Bostock leaned forward and dictated into the machine. "Sergeant McMorran has left the room." She then looked up at Derron.

"You've done really well," she crooned. "We just have to ask you a few more questions, and then you'll probably be able to go."

Derron's jaw dropped.

"Really?" he said "Okay, for sure. Ask me anything."

"Did you see anyone other than the sergeant from the moment you parted company with the high school kids to when you came out on Sixteenth?"

"Not a soul, but then I didn't want to see anyone."

"We'd appreciate it if you would give us a sample of your DNA," she said. "Will that be a problem?"

"No. You go right ahead. I didn't kill her and I didn't touch her body."

Bostock took one of Charlotte's collector vials out of her purse. Derron opened his mouth without being asked.

Either he had experienced the sampling before this, Coswell mused, or more likely he had watched a lot of crime shows on TV.

"What did you have in your pockets when Sergeant McMorran apprehended you?" he asked.

"Nothing," Derron said emphatically. "Bit of cash in my wallet, that's all."

Coswell smiled. McMorran hadn't even caught him with the drugs. Nothing to hold him on. Too late for a plant. It was all on the recording.

He signalled Bostock to turn the machine off. She did so after announcing the fact and the time.

"Why don't you rustle up something for Derron to drink, Corporal," he said, "while I go out and speak to the sergeant."

"Certainly, sir," she said. "How about a coffee, Derron?"

"Much appreciated."

"I'll be right back," she said. "Don't go away." And then she laughed. Derron gave her a big smile. Buddies.

McMorran and Inspector Marsden were standing just outside. The former was livid, the latter amused.

"Haven't changed a bit, eh, Coswell?" Marsden said. "Everything your way."

"Seems to work if you recall."

McMorran couldn't contain himself.

"That's it? You're going to let a possible killer go after that piddling interview?"

"And what are we going to charge him with?" Coswell said. "Running away from a gun-waving policeman?"

If McMorran's face could get any redder, he could pass as a beet.

"Now, once again," Coswell said, his voice hard, "I'm telling you to go back to your precinct and write that report I suggested to you before." He turned to Marsden.

"As soon as my corporal gets back and Derron in there

has his coffee, we'll see him to wherever he's living now. That will free up your interview room. Our sincere thanks for letting us use it."

Marsden seemed to be enjoying the proceedings.

"Any time," he said. "Always a joy to watch you work."

Coswell couldn't be sure but he thought he detected a hint of sarcasm.

"Thanks, but I don't need a ride," Derron said after taking a bite of the donut Bostock brought him along with the coffee. "I can walk okay, and there are people around here who might take it the wrong way if they see me getting out of a cop car."

"I understand," Coswell said. "But if I were you, I'd lay low for a while. The sergeant, as you could see, is not a happy fellow right now."

There was a slight delay as Derron had some difficulty swallowing his second bite of donut.

"You mean he might come after me?"

"Let's say it would be worth your keeping that in mind," Coswell said. "But we don't want you to disappear from us. Corporal Bostock will give you one of her cards. Call her sometime tomorrow. We may need to talk to you again."

She took a card out of her purse and handed it to him.

"Use the cell phone number," she said. "You can reach me at any time with that."

He accepted the card and shoved it into his back pocket.

McMorran was nowhere to be seen when they went down to the main floor, where Derron retrieved his wallet from the desk sergeant, nor was his cruiser in the parking lot.

Coswell was worried, however. McMorran could be making a few passes before he went back to the campus, hoping to spot Derron alone somewhere.

"I'd advise you to use the alleys until you get well away from here," Coswell told him. They stood and watched as the young man took off at a trot and disappeared around the corner onto Cordova Street. From there he would have a choice of alleys going in all directions.

"You can bring up his rap sheet tomorrow," Coswell said. "But I don't think you'll find much. McMorran's probably had a look at it already and if there was anything like violence, especially against women, he would have pressed the point."

And then he remembered.

"Damn! I have forgotten something terribly important, and it's a first."

It took her a moment to get it.

"The dinner reservation," she said. "I forgot it too in all the excitement, but I'm sure they'll understand."

A brief call on his cell (The Vicinage was one of his contacts) confirmed that they did understand. Iain Pope, the owner, answered the phone himself. "One of our guests told us about the murder in the park," he said. "He saw it on the evening news. We knew you would have been called there."

Unfortunately there wasn't a table to be had, since as usual on a Friday they were booked solid after seven.

"We still have Marko the floor cleaner to interview," Bostock said. "And the food at the Pit Pub sounds pretty good to me right now."

"A girl after my own heart," Coswell said, and then quickly, "Not meant in a sexist way, of course."

"Not taken that way."

"We'll swing by the park first," he said. "Charlotte might still be there. You can give her the DNA swab."

The forensic crew was just packing up when they got there. James was talking to a reporter, one who must have missed McMorran's performance. Coswell parked well ahead and walked back using the forensics van as cover. Bostock gave Derron's DNA swab to Charlotte.

"A suspect already?" she said. "I'm impressed. We'll try to match it with some of the samples we've taken from our latest victim."

She placed the sample carefully in a tray filled with similar tubes. "And I've got some good news for you," she said. "Shoe prints, or should I say one good shoe print—no thanks to the troops who stepped all over the adjacent path. I'll show you."

She retrieved her digital camera from the front seat of the van, switched it on, and scrolled down a series of shots, finally stopping at one.

"Here," she said. "Have a look."

She had enhanced the image, which showed the distinct print of a track shoe completely at right angles to the path, the heel mark pointing to the bushes.

"Wow," Coswell said. "What a break. Now all we have to do is find whoever owns that track shoe and we've got him."

Charlotte smiled.

"Your job. I did mine pretty well. Time of the deed, I'd say roughly an hour before I got there. Your perp may still have been in the vicinity."

She scrolled a few more of her pictures.

"Cause of death, pretty obvious. Someone with snare wire running around strangling people?"

"Snare wire? In the city?"

"Just an example," Charlotte said. "I'm a prairie girl. Used to snare gophers when I was a kid."

"Why am I not surprised," Coswell said.

She turned off her camera and returned it to the front seat of the van.

"Okay," she said. "Always enjoy talking to you, but I've got to go and unload all this stuff. It's TGIF, eh?"

Coswell wondered what a forensic ghoul did for fun

on weekends but wasn't about to ask.

"Time to get out of here ourselves," he said to Bostock. "I feel sorry for James, but I don't want to get caught by that reporter."

They lucked out at the Pit Pub. Coswell worried that Friday evening would be as busy there as at The Vicinage, but the pattern, according to the waitress who served them, was a busy happy hour right after classes then a lull for a couple of hours until the real party began. Nine to two a.m.

Hungry as he was, Coswell decided to pass on another order of poutine. He decided on the beer and burger combo instead. To his surprise, Bostock ordered the same. So much for health food.

The beers came first. Coswell raised his glass to her. She responded with hers, looking a bit puzzled. Their glasses touched.

"Here's to living another day," he said. "And thanks. I wasn't sure, either, and from my vantage point, and knowing how much the bastard hates me, I was probably even less sure than you."

She smiled.

"I appreciate your saying that," she said. "When I replayed the whole scene, I was starting to feel very foolish about it. A Mountie shooting a Mountie—preposterous. Do you think he'll report me? Another bad mark could do me in."

"Not with me in your corner. You'd be amazed how I can interpret a scene. McMorran had buck fever, gun ready to fire. You had to bring him to a complete halt and you did so with great presence of mind. Nothing like threatening a man's family jewels. I saw you lower the barrel."

She couldn't suppress a laugh.

Coswell continued, "I'd counter any accusation he

makes and top it off by recommending you for a formal commendation."

He thought for a moment.

"Maybe I'll do that anyway. We'll see what he does."

To his surprise, she seemed horrified by the thought.

"Oh, please don't do that, sir," she said. "Only as a last resort. I'm on enough blacklists at the moment without adding Sergeant McMorran to it. I suspect that he has more than a few members on his side. That type always does. I've seen them in action."

Coswell was annoyed at himself for not having thought of that too. She was absolutely right. Even he had had to fight the rednecks off when James became his partner.

"Of course," he said. "Only as a last resort, as you say, and even then I'll do it quietly through Chief Ward. He has his prejudices, but he's absolutely straight when it comes to things like this. He'll take my word over McMorran's. Don't you worry."

She didn't look all that relieved and he wondered how badly she had been hurt by whatever went on in Manitoba. He wanted to ask, but, in truth, he was afraid to. James he could manage, but with a female, he was totally at a loss.

But something had happened in his attitude toward her. It started, really, at The Auld Sod Pub, when she downed the Connemara because she "fucking" needed it. Human. And the way she stopped McMorran. Tough. Yes, Corporal Janet Bostock was a decent person and a fine officer. He was damned lucky to have her as a partner. He only wished he could say that. Instead, he turned to a more comfortable topic—their cases.

"The obvious question, of course," he said, "is whether or not Kelly's murder and this poor woman's killing are by the same person. We can't ignore the MO, both garrotted with a wire. And if they are, what does it mean? A psycho killing at random? Both the victims just convenient to him? Wrong place, wrong time for both?"

"And likely to kill again," she said.

They were silent then, both contemplating that possibility. But shortly they were brought back to the present by Sally Chetwynd, the med school first-year class president, who came marching down the entry ramp. Coswell, facing the entrance, waved her over to their table.

"I'm just taking a short breather," she said. "Memorizing bumps on bones gets boring after a while. But now I'm feeling guilty. I don't see any of my class here."

"May I buy you a pint?"

"No, thanks, much as I'd love one but a coffee's more what I need. Too bad Ritalin's not on the menu."

Ritalin—an upper, popular on the street.

"You seem to have your pharmacology well in hand," Coswell said.

She held both hands up. Surrender.

"Not me, officer," she said, and then a broad grin. "I could probably get it prescribed, though. My mother was so sure I had ADHD. Now it's more like I've got narcolepsy. Open that anatomy book and boom, an overwhelming urge to go to sleep."

The arrival of their hamburgers cut off further discussion of drugs. Coswell ordered a coffee for Sally. She wanted nothing else.

"Watching my figure, eh?" she said, and then looked over at Bostock. "I'd kill for yours."

Coswell was about to bite into his burger when two young men entered and took a table facing one of the TV screens that showed a hockey game in progress. One of them Coswell recognized immediately—Frank Hoffmann. The other was a tall, lanky man dressed in dark blue coveralls, his hair cut short.

"There's someone I wouldn't have expected during study hours," Coswell said.

Sally turned in her chair.

"Frank Hoffmann and his buddy Marko," she said. "A couple of losers in the anatomy world. Yeah, you're right. Frank should be hitting the books. He won't get a third chance."

Coswell saw Bostock pause mid bite.

"Marko?" she said. "Marko Ilic?"

Sally's eyes widened.

"Yes. How do you know him?" she said and then, "Right. Good thinking. He had as much reason to hate old Kelly as Frank. Maybe even more."

"Tell us about him," Coswell said.

"I don't know him personally," she said, "but he hangs out here at the pub in the evenings. He used to go out with my friend, Jenny, when they were both in pre-med. Why they got together, God only knows. They're total opposites. She's super smart and he's just so-so. But Jenny's one of those stray-dog collectors and Marko qualified. She's a mothering type and he needs mothering."

"How so?" Coswell asked.

"He's a Serbian war refugee. Poor as the proverbial church mouse. It amazes me that he could afford to go to university. He's got a job as a cleaner but that wouldn't pay his fees."

She leaned forward and lowered her voice.

"I'm guessing he's getting money under the table somewhere."

"Desperation destroys morals?" Coswell said.

"Yeah, something like that," she said. "I guess when bullets start flying around it's everyone for themselves."

Coswell continued to work on his hamburger, washing it down with beer, but Bostock had stopped eating, completely focused on Sally's information.

"You said Marko used to go out with your friend, Jenny. Do you know why they broke up?"

"He had his off days—mood swings and all that but Jenny, the dear soul, tolerated them. Post traumatic stress disorder, she called it. She has a degree in psychology so you have to believe her."

Bostock nodded her head.

"The actual breakup came right after he failed out of first-year med. She'd been accepted, so it was Marko out and Jenny in. A Serbian male, it appears, doesn't tolerate coming second to a woman."

"Was he ever abusive to her?"

Coswell was now pausing to take in the conversation as well. He was getting a nasty feeling about young Marko.

"Like, did she show up with black eyes? No, not that I ever saw." She paused for a moment, thinking.

"You know, it was strange. Men bottle up stuff like that but women tend to talk it out. I was probably closest to Jenny, but she never said a word to me about it. I do know it was her that did the breaking."

"How so if she didn't say a word to you?" Bostock said.

"One of the reasons he hangs out in this place. You can see him mooning from across the room whenever she's here. Gives her the hurt little boy look."

Thoughts were buzzing in Coswell's head, and he suspected the same thoughts were going through Bostock's. Marko had been dealt two blows in addition to what he suffered in Serbia—his career ambition destroyed and his girlfriend lost—all due to one egotistical surgeon. Great motive for revenge, and he was in a perfect position to commit the crime.

And then another thought.

"Does he often come in here with Frank?" Coswell asked.

"Not as often as he comes here by himself. Frank can't afford to spend the time away from his books. But they're made for each other. The same ilk, I believe is the ancient expression."

Coswell almost winced. He thought "ilk" was still a commonly used word.

Bostock went back to eating her hamburger, but periodically she looked over his shoulder at the two young men sitting behind him.

Sally, as usual, kept up a running commentary—about classes, professors, university life, none of which was of great interest to Coswell. He just nodded politely. She finally finished her coffee, looked at her watch, and then got up to leave.

"Got to get back to it," she said. "Thanks for the coffee. It really helped. I'm wide awake now, but if your narc squad buddies ever have to clean out their evidence lockers, see if you can get me a few Ritalin caps, eh? One lasts all night, I hear. Great for cramming."

"I'll keep you in mind," Coswell said.

The waitress came by to take their plates and ask if they wanted another beer.

"Not for me," Bostock said. "I'll just nurse this one for a bit."

Damn. Coswell thought. He really wanted another but she had set the tone. They were at work and he was driving.

"I'm going to do the same," he said, and handed the waitress his credit card, feeling a bit foolish since his glass was almost empty.

He had managed to angle his chair so that his back was to the two men. It also served to block off their view of Bostock.

"I don't want to turn around," he said. "So let me know what's happening back there."

"Absolutely nothing," she said. "They're hypnotized by the hockey game—Canucks at Toronto."

"When will that end, do you think?"

"It's almost over. Canucks, three zip. Toronto needs some new forwards."

"I'm amazed that you can tell that. You've only been watching the game for a few minutes."

"Long enough," she said and then, "Hoffmann's draining his beer and getting up to go."

"Marko too?"

"No, he's ordered another drink."

"Perfect," Coswell said. "Lean forward a bit so Hoffmann doesn't notice you. When he's gone, we'll mosey on over and chat with Marko."

A few moments later, Bostock gave the word.

"I think we can mosey now. Hoffmann's gone."

Marko was still looking at the TV when they walked over to his table. Coswell had his wallet out. He flashed his badge.

"I'm Inspector Coswell," he said, "and this is Corporal Bostock, RCMP. We'd like to have a word with you." They sat down, one on either side of him.

Most people react with apprehension when a police officer confronts them, guilty or not, but Coswell observed that the young man was startled well beyond the norm. His pupils dilated like he had been injected with adrenalin. Marko had a fear of authority, no doubt about it.

"Bostock," he said. "You're the policewoman I spoke to on the phone."

"Yes," she said, "and that's what we'd like to go over again with you."

"What for? I answered everything you asked."

His pupils hadn't shrunk one iota. Marko was one scared fellow, but Coswell had to consider the man's background. Police where he came from were probably a whole different element. But then again, he had been in Canada for a few years and should have lost some of that fear by now.

Bostock continued to question him.

"I didn't ask you the exact time you left the anatomy building on Sunday night and where you went from there."

"We had two more buildings to do," he said. "Didn't finish till after midnight. That's the way job goes."

"No breaks?"

He was beginning to perspire.

"Yes, we have breaks."

"Perhaps then you could give us a more exact idea of your movements from say nine o'clock to eleven."

To Coswell's annoyance, the waitress arrived at that point, disrupting the flow of the questioning. She set a glass of beer in front of Marko and looked askance at the two officers as she did so.

He picked the glass up, which was a mistake. His hand shook so badly he almost spilled some but he managed to get it to his mouth and take a large swig. He shook almost as badly putting it back down.

"This is all about Kelly getting killed, isn't it?" he said. "Frank told me you were suspecting everyone but why me? I had nothing to do with it."

Bostock had turned to ice.

"I'd appreciate it if you would answer my question. Where were you from nine to eleven p.m. last Sunday night?"

He looked into her eyes, presumably hoping to see some compassion, but soon turned away and stared down at his hands.

"I hated the man," he said. "I got to admit it but I didn't kill him."

Time for a little good cop, Coswell decided.

"We're not saying you did but you could very well have been the last person in the anatomy building before Dr. Kelly and his killer arrived. Questioning you, then, is a matter of routine."

Marko looked up at him, a flicker of relief and his pupils returned to normal.

"I was last one to leave building," he said. "I send crew over to Chemistry building while I finish up floor polishing in basement. After lock everything up and get polisher back to van, almost ten."

"I guess you have to hustle to get everything done," Coswell said. "You used the anatomy lab elevator, I presume, to get your polisher up and down from the basement. Did you happen to bump into the door of the elevator either coming down or going up?"

"No. Done that hundred times. No big deal move polisher around."

Bostock moved in again.

"So when did you get over to the Chemistry building?"

Pupils back to fully dilated.

"Not go there right away," he said. "Drove van to Vanier Place. Girlfriend there in residence. Just want to see her for a minute."

"Are you referring to Jenny?" Bostock said. "Or is this someone new? We've been led to believe that you and Jenny are no longer a twosome."

Anger this time.

"Who tell you?" he said. "That personal."

Bostock leaned over, her face just inches from his.

"Nothing's personal in a murder investigation, Marko. Now explain yourself. I'm losing patience with you."

Coswell's turn.

"Best you answer her," he said. "We really don't want to haul you down to the station."

Resignation.

"It's Jenny still," he said. "My mind, anyway. Phone calls, my texts, she never answers. I just want private talk with her."

He paused—reminiscing it seemed.

"I ask don to call her room; tell her I am downstairs in lounge. He does but she say no."

"And then?" Bostock said, her voice sharp.

Embarrassment.

"I know her room so I go to side of building and call up to her. I even throw pebbles at window, but nothing.

So I give up and go away."

"Time?"

"Don't know. Too upset. Ten, ten thirty. I drive back to Chemistry building. Unload polisher."

"You checked in with your staff then, I assume," Coswell said. "We'll need some names to verify the time."

Marko reached for his beer glass but quickly put it back down. His tremor had gotten worse.

"I not check in then," he said. "I go to basement door and start polishing so they don't know I am gone so long. I am supervisor, but one of crew is owner's niece. Hates my guts. I give her hell once on the job. Dumb to do that."

Bostock threw up her hands feigning exasperation.

"Well when did you talk to someone?"

"Maybe eleven," he said. "They work top floors down. Greta was first person I talk to."

Coswell leaned back and gazed at him.

"Were you in the army when you were in Serbia?" he said.

"Yes. Every man over eighteen. Compulsory."

"A lot of killing over there from what we see over here on the news," Coswell said. "Must have been pretty bad."

The tremor stopped and he returned Coswell's gaze with a cold stare. "Long time past. Far away," he said. "I'm in Canada now five years. I don't kill anyone. Now I must go back to work. Break is over."

He quaffed the last of his beer in one long draft and slammed it down on the table. One quick glance at Bostock and then he was off, paying his tab at the bar before leaving.

Bostock quickly wrapped the empty beer glass in a napkin and put it in her purse.

"More work for Charlotte," she said.

"How many is that now?" Coswell said. "Six? That's her limit. I hope she clears them soon. We may be giving her more."

"Derron's doesn't count," she said. "Totally different case."

"You tell her."

CHAPTER TWENTY-SIX

Saturday

A full morning in the office on Saturdays was Coswell's habit, but lately his desire to do so had fallen to zero. Sleeping in, also a rarity, overrode any ambition to get moving early. This worried him since he wasn't staying up any later at night, and everything he had read on aging stated that the older one got, the less sleep required.

A thyroid deficiency seemed the likeliest cause according to Medline, which would go along with the fatigue he felt more and more. He added that to the list that he wished to discuss with his physician.

Still in his pajamas at ten thirty, he contemplated the weekend. Two unsolved murders, a ton of related paper-work to do, check Larry's alibi with the list he was given. But did it have to be done any sooner than Monday? Charlotte had all the DNA samples now including Marko Ilic's, delivered on the way back to headquarters from the university. He had also told Bostock that she more than earned two days off and was not to come in to the office until Monday. That ensured that she wouldn't be there to show him up.

The buzz of his cell phone sitting in its charger on the kitchen counter startled him. Who? He checked the call display—James.

"I'm in the office having just finished a very unpleasant session with the local newshound TV types regarding the

THE EXTRA CADAVER MURDER

dead jogger," he said. "I need a break with someone who doesn't want to ride on my back and thought you'd be here. How about it? I've also had a peek at our Corporal Bostock's file, naughty boy that I am. Impressive."

That did it.

"See you at Gino's in ten minutes. Bring the file. It's Saturday. Nobody will miss it."

It took a bit longer, since he thought he should at least shave before going out. Never know who he might run into.

Gino's was almost deserted compared to usual. James was sitting at one of the prime tables that looked out onto Main Street. Before joining him, Coswell ordered a small cappuccino and his usual cinnamon bun to temper the caffeine already in his system.

"This job is really starting to get to me," James said. "One minute I'm sitting on my lovely tush with nothing to do, and the next I'm frantically trying to beat off the media attacking me like a pack of starving hyenas."

He leaned forward and spoke softly.

"And you'd think this monkey suit would be a deterrent to Miss Overly-Hormoned over there, but oh no. She even told me that men in uniform really turn her on."

He pushed the file folder over to Coswell.

"And little Miss Bostock's file makes me feel even more uncomfortable. She is really quite something. You may never want me back."

Coswell quickly read through it. She applied to the Force almost the day she finished high school. Her references glowed to the extreme—the school principal, her church minister, and even the local MLA. She aced the police aptitude test and scored so high on the Six Factor Personality Questionnaire, which measures how conscientious the applicant is, that she could have been declared a saint. The results of her physical abilities requirement evaluation were equally outstanding. In fact, she could have passed the male requirements let alone the female ones.

James was watching him read.

"Did you see those physical ability results?" he said. "I must ask her if she played defense on her hockey team. She'd have been a bruiser."

Her final assessor summed it all up—"This is the most outstanding candidate I have ever had the privilege to interview."

The plaudits continued through her first three years. The words "model officer" appeared and even one "consider for promotion." Extraordinary for a neophyte ... and then the incidents that earned her the corporal stripes, the "lively affairs" that Chief Ward had mentioned.

The first was an "officer down" situation. Her senior partner out in the open had been shot by a hidden assailant. Bostock, gun in hand and firing repeatedly at the source of the gunfire, pulled the wounded officer to safety behind their cruiser. Backup arrived momentarily. The officer survived and Bostock received a commendation.

The second involved a raid on a bikers' haven led by an older sergeant who suffered a heart attack just before giving the order to go in. Despite two corporals being present, confusion reigned as to who was in charge. Bostock, occupying the flank, noticed movement at the back of the building where two vans were parked. Believing the bikers to be escaping, she took the initiative and called her unit to redeploy and launch spike belts across the driveway. The manoeuver was successful and the bikers apprehended. The two corporals were admonished and Bostock was promoted.

That appeared to be what led to her problems. Coswell read easily between the lines. The male members, all the way up the line, would feel threatened by her and use her gender to put her down. Comments like "some difficulties with command" appeared and "overly sensitive to traditional staff banter." The latter remark actually came from the district commander.

There was nothing specific anywhere in the file regarding her transfer other than the simple recording of the fact. Obviously the nitty-gritty was passed along verbally.

Coswell closed the file.

"Well?" James said. "What do you think?"

"If you believe in justice," Coswell replied, "she should have submitted a formal, written complaint giving all the facts, and made sure it was put in her file to offset the negative stuff."

"You think she didn't?"

Coswell shrugged.

"And it was removed?" he said. "That's certainly possible, but whoever did that would be taking one helluva chance legally. She's smart enough to have had copies registered somewhere."

"Ooooh, a ticking bomb for our sterling Force."

Coswell nodded.

"But I think, despite all her grief, she truly does revere the Force and given the chance and a better atmosphere, the bomb could get defused pretty quick."

James levelled his eyes on him.

"And do you think we've done that?" he said.

Coswell squirmed in his chair.

"Perhaps not as fully as we could have," he said. "As fully as *I* could have, but I've got the message loud and clear."

While Coswell and James were perusing her personnel file, Bostock was running the seawall. It was her first chance to do so since coming to Vancouver and she had looked forward to it. There were good running trails in

Winnipeg, but the views around the Stanley Park seawall were far more stunning. She started at the Vancouver Rowing Club and ran counter-clockwise. It had been too long since she had a decent run. It took her almost to the Brockton lighthouse before her breathing settled and her legs moved without conscious effort.

But the scenery wasn't enough to occupy her mind. As usual, work and personal life interrupted. She had made progress getting Coswell to accept her, but accept her as what? A competent officer probably, but as a full, trusted partner? Probably not. Her gender was in the way, as shown by his safety concerns for her. But was it really her gender? Would he not be the same to a younger, male colleague? Perhaps she was being too sensitive and then laughed at herself. That was precisely the comment that had made her so mad when she first reported the harassment.

But then her mind clouded over. The harassment in Winnipeg was real and not to be joked about. It was pointed and vicious. Worst of all, she had to suffer it alone without support. She was too embarrassed to mention it to her family or to any of her friends. Like rape, she thought, and remembered her own naive annoyance at victims who wouldn't report the assault.

Burrard Inlet with all its activity diverted her for a while—pleasure boats of every variety, tugs, freighters, and one very large cruise ship. Other runners nodded to her as they passed. Lions Gate Bridge loomed ahead.

She forced herself to think of the cases she and Coswell were working on. Larry, the biker was certainly a prime suspect in Dr. Kelly's murder, and hopefully his DNA would match that on the elevator door at the anatomy lab. She wondered why Coswell had not acted sooner on checking the his alibi. If iron clad, it would save Charlotte some work.

Investigating the young woman's body in the park

wouldn't get far until she was identified. Again, she was surprised that Coswell hadn't assigned her to monitor the missing persons' reports. Surely something would come in soon.

And maybe she was just being her old critical self again. A nagging female. Coswell was probably doing it all himself. He did that a lot, it appeared.

And she had things of her own to do—check Francis' alibi at the Foo Yong Cafe. Settling that would also have saved Charlotte some work. And if Dr. Tynan's girlfriend confirmed his alibi, there would be no need to get his DNA whatsoever. But who else? Dr. Montgomery's lover, Dr. Barrett, for sure. He certainly wasn't sitting at home with his invalid wife. And Dr. Struthers, the new head of surgery. They hadn't had a chance to interview him yet. His name wasn't on Dr. Dietrich's dinner list so where was he at the time of the murder?

Siwash Rock appeared. Her legs were beginning to feel tired but the rock brought back memories—her father reading Pauline Johnson's poems to her; the poet's ashes scattered there when she died. And another memory—brunch at the Ferguson Point Teahouse with her parents and brother, Tim. That was on her things to do in Vancouver list so why not tick it off now, she thought, and her legs were sending a much louder message. They'd had enough abuse.

She didn't want to go into the restaurant sweating, and so slowed to a walk. There was a short section of grass separating the seawall from the road in front of the Teahouse. She had barely stepped onto it when she heard the distinctive rumble of Harley motorcycles coming up the road on her left. When they came into view, she could see that there were three of them. Two of the riders wore full helmets and face shields, but the third only the useless Kraut helmet favoured by biker gangs. She recognized him immediately—Larry, Bonahan's muscle man.

She moved over to a big Douglas fir tree and stood behind it. Peeking alongside, she saw the three come to a stop and then back their bikes into two parking spots. They dismounted and began removing gloves, jackets, and helmets. Larry was closest to her, but beside him another face from The Auld Sod Pub appeared—Conor Bonahan the gang boss himself. The third rider she could see only in a glimpse, obscured by the other two, but she saw enough. When he walked with them to the Teahouse, Sergeant McMorran moved with his usual swagger.

Her mind filled with questions. What in God's name was an RCMP officer doing in the presence of two sleazy characters like that? Undercover? Impossible. He was too well known from his days with the narcotics unit. An innocent association? People who rode motorcycles were an unusual lot, she had to admit. Their common love of the noisy machines seemed to override all else. And the name McMorran was also Irish. Maybe the link was there.

But the bottom line, in Bostock's mind, was that McMorran was either a total fool or blinded by arrogance to think that being seen in public with Bonahan and his enforcer was not a very bad thing.

She quickly returned to the seawall. Her legs had recovered enough that she could go into a reasonable jog which she kept up to Second Beach before she was forced to walk again. Lunch had left her mind; a shower at her apartment on Chilco Street took priority but as she walked, the thought of telling Coswell what she had seen eased the feelings of discomfort in her legs. McMorran was of special interest to him.

Monday

James was the most expressive when Bostock told them about her sighting in Stanley Park.

"How wonderful," he said. "If he keeps that up there

should be a sergeant's rank come open soon. What do you suppose the man was thinking?"

Coswell had shown very little reaction to the news; a slight arch of his eyebrows but they both looked at him now, waiting for him to comment.

"He'll weasel out of it," he said. "You underestimate his talent. Believe me, he will snow the brass with one of his famous explanations. I'd advise you both to keep this under your hats.

He saw their disappointment.

But don't fret," he said, "It's registered, and if he continues to play with fire, he's ultimately going to get burnt. It has happened before and it will happen again."

It more than registered with Coswell. It set him to thinking. Conor Bonahan and Larry would stay as far away from policemen as possible, so what gave with McMorran? Purely sociable? Unlikely. Bonahan was all business. There had to be some gain in it for him. But what was the gain for McMorran? Was he contemplating a career change? Interesting.

James had a morning meeting scheduled with Dr. Lockie at the coroner's office.

"She doesn't seem satisfied with our long distance communication any more," he said. "I have to meet with her in person, and that's beginning to worry me."

"Well," Coswell said. "While you're having your tête à tête with our assistant coroner, see if you can hustle Charlotte up with those DNA samples."

James grunted.

"Charlotte looks upon hustle as hassle," he said. "And I've learned never to hassle her."

"Try," Coswell said.

Aside from Bostock's news about McMorran, the start of the day did not go well for Coswell. Chief Ward called him into his office for a debriefing, which ended with "I hope the DNA results do solve the Dr. Kelly case. You don't seem to have anything else and that young jogger murder needs to be cleared up fast. The Dean tells me the women on campus are living in a state of fear."

Bostock's questioning look when he went back to their office, almost caused him to snap at her but then he remembered his promise to change his attitude. He sighed instead.

"Not good," he said. "We need to hustle, and unlike Charlotte, backtalk is not an option with the Chief Inspector."

He had given her The Auld Sod Sunday night staff list before his meeting with Ward with instructions to contact them and set up interviews. She held the list in her hand.

"I started on this," she said, "but I don't think phoning them is going to work. I tried the bartender first and to quote him, 'I was too busy to notice who was there and who wasn't, but if Mr. C says Larry was, then he was.'"

"Did you—?"

"Definitely not. I didn't mention anything about Mr. C giving Larry an alibi. The guy came right out with it."

Oops. Dumb question. He deserved her sharpness.

"Then he's spoken to them all," he said. "Probably a waste of time for us to do any interviewing."

She frowned.

"But maybe face-to-face we could crack one of them. Threaten them with an obstruction of justice charge if they lie."

He smiled at her.

"You're a tiger, Bostock," he said. "But let's see what Charlotte comes up with first. If Larry's a match, then we'll go at the whole lot of them with a vengeance."

This appeared to mollify her and he thought his tiger comment had struck a good note.

"I had better luck with the Foo Yong restaurant," she said. "There was actually someone there this morning at eight o'clock. An older man with shaky English who apparently works from opening to closing. Francis sounds like one of their favourite customers and the old fellow confirmed his alibi for the night of Kelly's murder."

The only one hundred percent confirmed alibi of all their suspects so far, Coswell noted.

"Our list is really petering out," he said. "Who's left?"

She looked down at her notebook.

"I've got Dr. Tynan's girlfriend to see yet and there's still Dr. Struthers."

But that would be it so far as names were concerned. If the DNA results were all to come back negative, they would be back to square one. Their best bet then would be a psycho killing at random who got a tickle out of leaving his victims in some sort of degrading pose.

"Oh, and I got the time for the autopsy on the dead girl in the park," Bostock said.

"It's scheduled for ten o'clock at the VGH."

"We'll go," he said. "I don't relish seeing a young body carved up but we need to know the details and this isn't one to wait around for a report on. And, besides, Charlotte will be there so we can relieve James' hassle with our hassle."

That gave two hours to do some paper work. Coswell looked forlornly at the stack on his desk which he swore was growing by an inch a day. Bostock caught his look.

"A lot of that is from me," she said. "I took the liberty of writing up the reports on what we've done so far. Just pencil in your corrections and I'll redo them all."

"Very good," he said, quietly bemoaning the fact that James' was no longer writing reports for him. James never expected him to read anything he typed up.

"And while I'm doing that you can set up a session with the girlfriend," he said. "Her confirmation of Tynan's alibi won't do over the phone. You need to look her in the eye."

He thought for a moment.

"And I don't want to be chasing after Dr. Struthers. Tell his secretary he's to make a definite time to see us, preferably soon after the autopsy."

"Should I do the same with Dr. Bennett?"

"Absolutely."

Coswell knew what she was thinking. Bennett and Kay Montgomery had each other for an alibi, no one else, and they were in the vicinity at the time of the murder. Frank Hoffman's alibi died with Wing Chu, but Chu had virtually confirmed it at the screening interviews in the lecture hall. Marko's story had a gap in it but that could be filled by his girlfriend, Jenny, who would certainly remember her residence don's call Sunday night and the pebbles to the window. And Greta from his cleaning staff would have noticed how much of the floor polishing he had gotten done when she saw him at the Chemistry building. Both would narrow the gap to almost nothing. No, Bennett and Kay, much as he hated to admit it, were just under Larry on their suspect list.

He flipped the stack over so he could scan from oldest to latest. The first report he came to was Bostock's overseas research on the two residents, Debas and Tynan. He was about to put it aside, since he had already seen it, but the name "Tynan" in bold print stopped him. He hadn't really read that far; the information on Debas had taken up all of his attention. And then the nagging thought that had been stewing at the back of his mind for days came sharply up front. Two interviews with the man had not given a clear picture of his alibi.

The right question was put to Tynan when he was first interviewed on the campus—'Where were you on the night of Dr. Kelly's murder?' But both he and James had too quickly accepted his answer—'I was on emergency call at the General Hospital.' They had made the assumption that emergency call involved being cloistered at the hospital. But Tynan was not at the hospital; he was with his girlfriend, according to Debas. So why didn't he say so? Why the glib response? Was he so arrogant that he figured such a simple answer to two dumb cops would save him a lot of breath?

But what really bothered Coswell was the fact that he, the chief homicide investigator for the Vancouver RCMP, had not even asked the question when he and Tynan were one on one in the surgeons' lounge. A second chance to pin the man down—totally missed. Would Bostock have made the same mistake? Would James, if he had been present at the second interview? Probably not. Their brain cells hadn't been ravaged by age and alcohol.

He read the report carefully and came to an abrupt halt with Bostock's last note—"juvenile record pending."

She was talking on the phone and so he had to wait, but the moment she ended the call, he got up and walked over to her desk with Tynan's report in his hand.

"What's this about a juvenile record on Tynan?" he said.

She looked up, startled by the tone in his voice.

"I got that from the Garda Síochàna in Northern Ireland, their vetting unit," she said. "The lady I spoke to was very helpful, but she had to get a higher authority to okay passing on juvenile records. I'm still waiting on that."

"Good," he said. "It's worth looking into. Maybe we have another suspect to take Francis' place as someone with violent tendencies."

She looked doubtful.

"He's thirty-six years old," she said. "Whatever he did to get his name on the juvenile offender list was a long time ago. His record is squeaky clean since then and what would be his motive for murdering Kelly?"

What she meant was that he was clutching at straws—and she was right.

"You never know," he said, sounding like some old pedant. "Maybe they're on opposite sides of the Troubles?"

She almost choked trying to suppress a laugh.

"I think that ended a long time ago," she said and then realizing that he wasn't trying to be funny, quickly moved on.

"Dr. Struthers has agreed to meet us at eleven fifteen this morning, in his office," she said. "But I'm not having much luck with Sofie Kovac, Dr. Tynan's girlfriend. She doesn't hold classes on Mondays. The office did give me her home phone number, but all I've got so far is her answering machine."

"Do you have her address?"

"Yes. Seven hundred block Thirteenth Avenue. That's near the hospital."

"It is," Coswell said. "In fact it's just around the corner from Kelly's apartment. A long ways from her work. Odd."

And then a thought.

"I wonder if she and Tynan are cohabiting," he said. "Check on that, will you?"

One quick phone call to Dr. Struthers secretary gave her the answer.

"It's the same address," Bostock said.

Coswell nodded.

"Then we'll both interview her," he said. She'll undoubtedly back up her boyfriend's alibi but let's see if she needs to put on an act or not. We'll drive by on the way to the autopsy. Maybe she's turned her phone off."

CHAPTER TWENTY-SEVEN

The address on Thirteenth Avenue was an old up-down duplex conversion. Parked cars lined both sides of the street making it impossible for Coswell to double park the cruiser without blocking the whole street. He drove on by planning to come back after the meeting with Struthers, or even after lunch—but then he saw the car.

It was parked just in front of the RESIDENTS ONLY sign—a blue Volkswagen Golf. An unusual colour for that model according to Kay Montgomery, who had seen one just like it in the Dental parking lot the night Kelly was murdered. Could this be the same car?

To Bostock's alarm, Coswell accelerated, sped to the end of the block, did a 360 at the roundabout, and came back. He had also noticed a one-car parking space alongside the duplex. He pulled into it, ignoring the fact that the cruiser now straddled the sidewalk and blocked whoever owned the car parked there.

Someone did notice, however. An older woman dressed in housecoat and slippers appeared on the front step.

"You can't park there," she shouted.

Coswell got out and walked over to her. Bostock followed him, perplexed.

"Police," Coswell said to the woman. "And don't worry. My corporal here will move our vehicle if someone needs to get out."

She didn't look totally convinced and so he presented his ID to her.

"We are trying to contact Sofie Kovac," he said. "She's given this as her address."

The woman almost growled.

"Young people shacking up. No wedding rings," she said. "Disgraceful, and him a doctor."

Coswell took that as a peculiar yes, she lives here.

"Is that blue car over there hers?"

"Or his, I don't know," the woman said. "They both drive it. Mainly her, though. He walks to the hospital. She takes it to the university. Teaches dentistry out there, according to him."

"She's not answering her phone," Coswell said.

"Maybe they went away somewhere for the weekend," the woman said. "I haven't seen either of them since last Friday."

"And the car has been parked there all that time?" Coswell said.

"Yes. Hasn't budged, and that's a prime spot. Move out and there's someone just waiting to pull in. Thank goodness we have that space alongside the house. It's one of the advantages of owning the place."

Coswell could feel his excitement mounting. Something important was happening, he was sure of it, but he had to concentrate.

"We are investigating a homicide that took place out at UBC a week ago yesterday. You may have read about it. Dr. Kelly the professor of surgery?"

She was now showing signs of interest herself.

"Yes," she said. "I saw it on the TV news. What do those two upstairs have to do with it?"

Be careful, Coswell told himself.

"A car just like theirs was seen parked by the Dental building at the time of the murder," he said. "And since she works out there, we thought she might have seen something useful to our investigation."

He glanced at Bostock, standing beside him. Her interest now was obviously on par with his.

"I don't see an entrance for the upstairs unit," she said. "How do they get up there?"

The woman pointed to the door behind her.

"Porch," she said. "Inside's two doors—one for us and the other's to the stairs for them."

"It's a wooden building, I see," Coswell said. "You must hear them moving about. Doesn't that bother you?"

"It does, but we can use the rent, and I don't want to climb those bloody stairs anyway. Husband's a crock, too. Bad arthritis. The space would be wasted."

Coswell tried to sound as casual as possible.

"The Sunday before last," he said. "Were you at home in the evening?"

"No," she said. "Sunday's our whist night at the Legion."

Coswell's heart sank. Damn.

"Were your renters in their apartment when you left for the Legion?" Bostock asked.

The woman thought for a moment.

"I think so. Yes, they were. I remember him coming in about six. Had a coat over his white uniform. She was home, too, vacuuming. We left for the Legion at seven. Whist starts sharp at seven thirty."

"And when did you come home?" Coswell said.

She chuckled.

"Almost midnight, would you believe? Hubby likes his beer and when he gets together with those old vets, the war stories go on and on. Me and the girls do extra rounds of whist."

"Was their car parked outside then, did you notice?"

"Can't remember," she said. "Sorry."

So much for that, Coswell said to himself. Disappointing.

"We'd really like to know if she's in right now," Bostock said. "I could run up and see. Save you climbing the stairs."

"Be my guest," she said. "They only lock the door upstairs."

Coswell stifled a smile. She had obviously snooped at some time or another.

There was no answer to Bostock's repeated knocks.

Coswell thanked the woman and gave her his card with instructions to tell Sofie to call him.

"Shall I see if the car's unlocked?" Bostock said on the way back to the cruiser.

"No," Coswell said. "Our cooperative landlady is probably watching and we don't want her having anything more to gossip about."

The whole forensics crowd was at the girl's autopsy—Charlotte, Marie D'Allarde, Dr. Lockie, and James. The pathologist was a younger man this time, but he worked with a similar efficiency to his senior colleague.

Coswell had difficulty concentrating on the pathologist's voice, droning on for the most part with routine findings that boiled down to the fact that the girl was a superb physical specimen of youth—fit and healthy. Her stomach was empty, so she had gone for a run prior to her supper. The only signs of trauma were related to her strangulation. No bruising elsewhere, including her genitalia and as Coswell had noted, no evidence that she had actually been raped.

Dr. Lockie was the first to speak to Coswell when it was over.

"Still no ID on her?" she asked. "I'm surprised. The press got a very detailed description of her from Sergeant McMorran and I hear even the campus radio has been broadcasting regular pleas for information. The fear, of course, is that she was a student."

Ward's admonishment to McMorran had obviously fallen on deaf ears.

"We can only wait," he said. "But something will come up soon. She was definitely no dropped-out druggie."

"No," Bostock added. "Those shoes she had on were top of the line Nikes. One hundred and sixty bucks a pair."

Coswell was shocked, not by the fact that a girl living in a walk-up rental could afford to spend that kind of money, but that running shoes actually cost one hundred and sixty dollars. His fancy dress shoes were less expensive. And then, to his dismay, he realized that his dress shoes were probably as old as the dead girl.

Charlotte was waiting at the exit instead of charging off as she usually did.

"Got a preliminary for you on your DNA samples," she said, "and then only because I came in on the weekend to analyze them."

"God will reward you," Coswell said.

"I'd settle for a raise in pay, but here's the skinny. All negative. No matches and I sure as hell hope that means something to you because it represents a lot of effort on our part."

"Not even Larry's?" Bostock blurted out.

Charlotte smiled at her.

"Nope, not even the sample marked Larry," she said. "Had your hopes up on that one did you?"

Bostock blushed.

James had stayed behind as well and was listening in.

"Oh dear," he said. "That just blew a lot of theories. Now what? Maybe my 'crime of passion' again?"

Coswell had to admit that James was right but who's passion? They were running out of candidates. It gave him some satisfaction that Kay Montgomery's DNA had cleared. The thought of her still gave him a tingle even though she was having an affair with her colleague Dr. Barrett.

James for once had nothing on his agenda until the afternoon, and so Coswell called a conference.

"We don't meet with Dr. Struthers for a while yet," he said. "How about joining us for coffee in the cafeteria, James?"

Despite the risk of hurting Bostock's feelings, Coswell wanted James' thoughts on the two cases. He needed all the help he could get at this point.

"My goodness," James said when he was told about their latest revelations regarding Dr. Tynan. "Did we let him slip under the wire? Good work, Bostock."

"I just got the information," she said. "Inspector Coswell made the connections."

She would have made the connections, too, Coswell realized, and likely much sooner if, instead of him, she had been in on the two interviews with the man.

"Whatever," Coswell said. "The point is that this fellow, Tynan, needs to be followed up on. There are inconsistencies surrounding him and we don't have any DNA from him yet."

Bostock appeared to take this as criticism.

"He was on my list," she said, "But the opportunity to collect it surreptitiously as you said just didn't come up. And there's still Dr. Struthers and Dr. Barrett."

"Perhaps you don't need to be so surreptitious," James said. "If they are innocent, why object?"

"It is sort of an invasive procedure," Bostock said. "Much like insisting on a breathalyzer test. With everyone sensitive about their rights these days and stories about samples getting mixed up, you can understand why people would object."

"Quite true," Coswell said, even though his reason was to keep the suspects ignorant of the fact that they were being tested, rights or no rights.

"The problem with Tynan, as I see it, is motive," James said. "What on earth would be the provocation? He and Kelly were fellow Irishmen."

Coswell shrugged.

"Don't know," he said. "Kelly tried to come on to his girlfriend once but that's pretty weak. And his fellow resident, Debas, was the one who got all the hazing. Tynan apparently was spared."

Coswell thought back to his interview in the surgeons' lounge. He winced, remembering what he'd said: "You're Irish, too. I would think he would have taken it easier on you." That was a statement, not a question. Bad technique. Tynan effectively switched the whole conversation to Debas. Was it deliberate?

"Well, unless you two can think of something else," he said. "We're left with four possibilities: Tynan, who has no motive, Struthers, who sounds too nice to kill anybody, although becoming department head might be a motive and Dr. Barrett in some mad plot with Kay Montgomery, for whatever reason God only knows."

"That's three," James said. "Who's the fourth?"

"A whacko who could be anywhere and anyone."

Silence.

"In short," Coswell said. "We are far up the proverbial creek and our paddle is slipping away."

"How poetic," James said.

Dr. Struthers was actually amused that he was on their suspect list.

"Reminds me of the Inspector Morse series on the BBC," he said. "All those Oxford professors killing one another for positions, but I'm afraid you will have to scratch my name off. My wife and I were at the opera that Sunday evening—The Flying Dutchman—all three hours' worth. We didn't get home until after midnight."

He couldn't offer any suggestions as to who might want to murder Kelly.

"A difficult man, for sure," Struthers said. "But with considerable talent. I probably miss him more than most. I'm a general surgeon, but I do primarily peripheral vascular work. I referred all my complicated abdominal cases to him. Now I'm stuck having to deal with them myself. Not fun."

"Aren't there other surgeons on staff who do that kind of work?"

"None that are full time university," he said and then seeing Coswell's puzzled expression, added, "Economics."

Bostock spoke up.

"I understand that Dr. Debas has applied for a full time staff position when he finishes his year of residency," she said. "Did Dr. Tynan do the same?"

Coswell looked at her. He couldn't recall hearing that about Debas, but then again she probably told him and he forgot.

"No, Dr. Tynan has not applied," he said, rather brusquely, Coswell thought, and was sure he saw a slight frown. Worth persuing.

"Corporal Bostock was very impressed with Dr. Debas when we watched your surgery from the observation gallery," he said.

The smile returned to Struthers' face.

"He will be a wonderful addition to staff," he said. "In fact, I don't know what I'd do without him right now. I even had to steal him from Dr. Dietrich today. He was supposed to be at the anatomy lab."

"Just as a matter of interest," Coswell said, "Who chooses new staff? Is it done by a committee?"

"There is input from others, but essentially the opinion of the department head holds sway."

"I take it that Dr. Debas is a shoo-in now, with Dr. Kelly no longer making the decision."

Struthers looked surprised.

"Dr. Kelly approved Dr. Debas some time ago. In fact, his recommendation was absolutely glowing. I've just rubber-stamped it. I also let Haile know, on the QT, of course."

So much for Debas as a suspect—no DNA match and no motive.

"Could you tell us more about Dr. Tynan?" he said. "We gather that he had an easier time with Dr. Kelly and I'm a bit surprised that he hasn't applied for staff here, coming all the way out to the west coast as he did."

Struthers' guard went up again.

"I'm afraid I can't comment in any depth about that," he said. "I—"

Coswell interrupted before he could go on.

"This is a murder investigation, Dr. Struthers," he said, "and Dr. Tynan is a person of particular interest to us right now. Confidentiality does not apply."

Struthers took a deep breath and then sighed.

"Dr. Tynan proved to be a disappointment, particularly to Dr. Kelly, who twisted more than a few arms to get him the residency position. Tynan's CV, let us say, was less than stellar but he was trained in an Irish hospital and Dr. Kelly seemed to think that counted for a lot."

He leaned back in his chair and gave another sigh.

"I guess I might as well put it bluntly. Dr. Tynan is not a good surgeon despite his opinion of himself. He possesses only average technical skill and his clinical judgment has come into question a number of times. Add that to his callous treatment of patients and I, for one, regret not challenging Dr. Kelly more aggressively when the resident selection committee met."

Bostock interjected.

"If Dr. Tynan has such a high opinion of himself, why didn't he apply for staff?"

"Nothing I said to him, but I think Dr. Kelly eventually made it obvious that he wouldn't be accepted."

"Did you actually hear him do that?" Bostock said.

"No. But I got it second hand from the OR staff. And contrary to what you've heard, Dr. Kelly was brutal to Tynan, almost to the point of declaring him incompetent. He probably thought he could whip him into shape that way."

Another lie from Tynan, and a big mistake by Kelly. Slapping down someone with an ego like that would only lead to intense anger, as Coswell well knew, McMorran being a personal example.

Once again they were interrupted, this time by Carol, Struthers' secretary.

"The ward just called," she said. "They need you over there right away."

"Can't the resident handle it?"

"Dr. Debas and the assistant residents are scrubbed in the OR and Dr. Tynan has phoned in sick. Apparently the only one around is a fourth year medical student."

"I'm sorry," Struthers said. "I'll have to go."

"No problem," Coswell said. "We've finished anyway. You've been a great help to us."

"What do you think?" Coswell said when they went out into the hall. "Was Tynan in the apartment when we were there, too sick to answer the door?"

"I knocked loud enough to wake the dead," she said. "He could have been ignoring me, but you'd think he would at least have shouted to go away."

"We'll drop by again after lunch. Maybe the landlady will let us peek in on him."

"Do you want to try Dr. Barrett first?," Bostock said. "He's really the last on our hospital list."

"No. I need sustenance. We'll do the cafeteria. Maybe Marilyn Hawthorne, the fourth year eager beaver will be there and give us a little more on Tynan's treatment in the OR. She must have witnessed some of it."

But they were only half way there when Bostock's cell phone rang.

"Vancouver PD," she said, looking at the call display. "I asked them to call me if anything came up that might ID our girl in the park."

She listened for a couple of minutes without interrupting and then she ended the call with, "Inspector Coswell and I will take it from here. We'll notify the UBC detachment, but thanks for offering."

She said nothing to Coswell while she rummaged in her purse for her pen and notebook. She quickly scribbled something down and then turned to him.

"What?" Coswell said.

"I think we might have an ID on the murdered girl," she said. "Sofie Kovac, Tynan's girlfriend."

If a chair had been handy, Coswell would have collapsed into it.

"How?" he said.

"She was supposed to show up at a friend's place on Sunday night to go to a book club meeting. When she didn't show, the friend called Sofie's cell phone and when she didn't get an answer, she called the apartment. No answer there either so she just left a message."

"How close a friend?" Coswell said. "Why didn't she phone Tynan at the hospital?"

Bostock shook her head.

"I don't know," she said. "But when she saw the morning news with a clip of McMorran's description of the victim, it prompted her to call the police. Her name's Valerie Green and they gave me a number where she can be reached. I recognize it. It's the Dental faculty at UBC."

"Call right now," Coswell said, "and tell her to stay put. We're on our way."

CHAPTER TWENTY-EIGHT

The receptionist at the Dental faculty led them into a small conference room to wait.

"I passed on your message to Valerie," she said. "She's giving a class right now, but it will be over in just a few minutes."

She hovered for a moment, obviously bursting with curiosity, but getting no response from the two stone-faced officers, she left them.

They positioned themselves at the table—Coswell facing the door and Bostock at the end on his right.

Valerie Green arrived just five minutes later. They were expecting someone more Sofie Kovac's age, but this woman was middle-aged with grey hair and bifocals. She met them with formal handshakes and a worried look.

"They wouldn't tell me anything when I phoned the police," she said after sitting across from Coswell. "I hope you are not bringing bad news about Sofie."

Coswell nodded to Bostock. She had one of Charlotte's photos of the dead girl on her cell phone. Bostock brought it up and handed the phone to Valerie.

One glance and the woman burst into tears.

"It's her," she said, sobbing. "That's my Sofie."

"I'm sorry for your loss," Coswell said, noting the woman's use of "my."

More sobs. They waited for her to collect herself.

"A terrible loss," Valerie said, wiping away tears with a tissue she pulled from her uniform pocket. "Sofie was the daughter I never had. I kind of adopted her when she came on staff. Poor thing. She worked so hard to succeed."

More sobs. When she settled again, Coswell asked, "Can you tell us how to get in touch with her family?"

"There is no family," she said. "Slaughtered in the Bosnian crisis. Sofie was at dental school in Ireland when it happened."

"Is that where she met Dr. Tynan?" Bostock said.

Valerie's whole body stiffened.

"Kevin Tynan," she said. "Another trial in her life. Why she followed that arrogant creature to Vancouver and then stuck with him for so long, I'll never know."

And then her eyes narrowed and she looked intently at Coswell. "You suspect he killed her, don't you?" she said. "Not some crazy. Well, I can tell you, he *is* someone to consider."

Bostock looked like she'd just found gold. Coswell spoke up quickly.

"You've just implied that their relationship had ended. Was that so?" he said.

"Yes. I was Sofie's confidant. Things were not going well for Kevin at the hospital and he was taking it out on her. It took me a while but I finally persuaded her to leave him."

Suddenly she stopped.

"Oh my God," she said. "Do you think it could be my fault she's dead?"

Time to slow this all down, Coswell decided.

"Now, now," he said. "You're making huge assumptions. Dr. Tynan is someone we're planning to talk to but we have nothing to say he's a murderer."

That seemed to mollify her to a degree.

"I guess I am," she said. "When we had lunch on Friday she still hadn't given the word to Kevin. I told her to quit procrastinating."

"Is an after-work run a routine for her?"

"Yes. 'Have to keep up my miles' she'd always say. Long-distance running is her thing—marathons and all that."

"Did she usually run alone?"

"Yes," and then a sharp intake of breath. "But sometimes with Kevin when he's at the anatomy lab. He's a runner, too. Do you think—?"

"We will certainly ask him," Coswell said. "But may I make a request? Would you be willing to do an official identification of Sofie's body, seeing that she has no family? If you don't, we can ask Dr. Tynan of course."

"Don't let that evil creature anywhere near Sofie," she said. "I'll do it."

Bostock had been sitting back in her chair but now she leaned forward. "Was the book club meeting at your place?" she asked.

"No. It's held at the Dunbar Library once a month. We have a routine. Sofie would end her run at my place. I live on Sasamat, just off of Sixteenth. She would shower and change out of her running gear and then we'd go to Domino's Pizza for a bite before the meeting. I'd drive her home after."

"What did she do with her car? We understand that she drove it to work each day."

Ah, Coswell thought to himself. How did her car end

up in front of the duplex? Good question.

"Not on book club Fridays," she said. "Kevin drives her to work that one day. Normally he goes to the anatomy lab with one of his doctor friends. The guy drives a big Mercedes. I've seen him a few times. Handsome fellow. Charming, too, I've been told. Shame that Sofie didn't hook up with him."

The sadness deepened.

"I waited until the last minute Friday, but then I went to the book club meeting by myself. Figured something must have come up. Not like her though. I should have known something awful had happened. She didn't answer any of my calls to her. I even left a message on their apartment answering machine."

They offered to take her to the morgue in the cruiser but she declined.

"I'll take my car," she said. "You people have lots to do. Get the person who killed Sofie and put him away forever."

Coswell let Bostock deal with taking Valerie to the morgue. He always detested the job, and besides, he was absolutely famished. Bostock seemed to exist on some kind of energy bars she kept in her purse. She had offered him one but it looked totally unappetizing, more like a piece of asphalt than something edible.

The main lunch crowd had passed through the cafeteria; only a few sat around, but off to one side he saw Debas in his greens, sitting alone, eating a sandwich and washing it down with intermittent gulps from a coffee cup. He was obviously in a hurry. Coswell, hungry as he was, didn't want to miss the opportunity to speak to him and so went directly over to the table.

"If you don't slow down," Coswell said, "You're going to have indigestion."

Debas looked up and smiled.

"Better than passing out from hypoglycemia and falling face first onto the surgical site," he said.

A wave of nausea swept through Coswell. He hoped that comment wouldn't spoil his own lunch.

"Don't stop eating," he said. "I can imagine how pushed you are today, with your partner Dr. Tynan being ill."

"Yes," he said. "Len over at the doctors' residence told me he's been holed up in one of the rooms over there since the start of the weekend looking dreadfully ill."

"Why wouldn't he have stayed home?" Coswell said.

"Maybe he didn't want to give whatever he has to his girlfriend."

Coswell paused. Would he be doing a disservice to the poor souls that Debas would be working on over the day if he upset him with the news? And then he silently kicked himself. He was getting soft in his old age.

"His girlfriend, Sofie Kovac, was murdered on Friday evening. Attacked during a run in the University Endowment lands. Her body has just been identified by one of her work colleagues."

Debas froze. Coffee cup half way to his mouth. He put it down slowly and looked Coswell in the eye.

"A mugger?"

"Possibly, but there are some inconsistencies."

"You suspect Kevin," he said.

"The boyfriend automatically goes to the top of the suspect list in murder cases."

"Kevin has a lot of anger inside him but I don't see him as a murderer. I didn't really know Sofie. I met her only once, when the three of us went out one night for pub food."

He pushed his plate away leaving half of his sandwich. A Reuben, Coswell noted.

"A quiet girl," Debas went on. "She let Kevin do all the talking. In fact they were more like some old married couple than young lovers."

"Has he said anything to you recently that might indicate they weren't getting along?"

"Not a word, but now that I think of it, he rarely ever mentioned her."

"Odd, wouldn't you say? Most men talk about their significant others, even if it's only to bitch about them."

"True," Debas said. "But we medical types tend to shop talk when we're together and anyway, Kevin would be the last person I'd expect to discuss his personal life with anyone. He's really a bit of a closed book."

He took a last sip of coffee and put the cup on his tray along with the sandwich plate.

"I really have to go," he said. "I presume you are on your way over to see Kevin. Will you tell him, please, that I'll come over to the residence as soon as I can? He'll need someone, and I'm probably it now that Sofie's gone."

Coswell watched him put his tray on the dirty dishes conveyer belt and disappear out the exit doors.

Bostock arrived way too soon, from Coswell's point of view. He had been slow getting his tray loaded up. When she came into the cafeteria he hadn't even made it to the cashier. He waved to her and pointed to the end of the line, but she shook her head and pointed to the table where he had been talking to Debas.

"You're going to pass out from hypoglycemia if you don't eat something more substantial than those bars," he said, setting down his tray. *Hypoglycemia*. He liked that word. It had such a professional ring to it.

"There's 250 calories in each one of those," she said. "They're very filling."

He looked down at his tray: a full Rueben with extra mustard, side of chips and a large piece of lemon meringue pie. Probably a thousand calories, but his coffee was black. That should count for something.

THE EXTRA CADAVER MURDER

"Then you'll collapse from dehydration. At least go over there and get a drink."

She came back with a coffee—black.

"How did the viewing go?" he said. "You didn't take very long."

"Sofie wasn't a pretty sight. Valerie didn't wish to linger."

She sipped her coffee and watched him eat, much to his annoyance. He pushed the plate of chips towards her.

"Have a few," he said.

She looked at them for a moment and then daintily picked one up. "They go better with catsup," she said.

"Catsup's full of sugar. Bad for you. Better you eat them plain."

She began to nibble on it.

"I wonder what kind of fat they fry them in."

The doctors' residence was definitely on the seedy side from Coswell's vantage point, and the man at the reception desk fit right in: age sixty-five plus, plaid shirt with a frayed collar, and a messy head of white hair. He peered at them over his reading glasses.

"Dr. Tynan told me he didn't want to see anyone. He's sick."

"He'll see us," Coswell said. "Sick or not."

His shield quickly ended Len's resistance.

"I'll ring his room and tell him you're here," he said. "Give him a chance to make himself decent, what with the lady here and all."

But there was no answer to Len's call.

"Not surprised," he said. "He went out his morning to see if he could get something to stay in his stomach, but he came back looking worse than when he left. Told me he had to stay on fluids until whatever he had lifted. Couldn't you come back later? Maybe he'll be feeling better."

"Unfortunately no," Coswell said. "Maybe you could

take us to his room. I think I can persuade him to open the door."

"I can't leave the desk," Len said. "But go ahead. He's on this floor, room seven, last one on your right."

The dreary corridor reminded Coswell of an old hotel in the Cariboo—bare walls, old wooden doors, and a faint, musty smell.

He knocked on the door.

"Dr. Tynan," he said in a loud voice. "It's Inspector Coswell and Corporal Bostock. We know you are ill, but we must speak with you."

"The door's not locked. Come in."

The room was tiny: a single bed, a night table, a wall phone immediately above it, an open clothes closet, and a single chair on which Tynan was sitting. He was wearing dark slacks and a fleece hoodie, hands jammed in the pockets as though he were freezing.

"Sit on the bed if you want," he said. "I'd offer this chair but I don't feel like moving. What's this about?"

Coswell sat on the bed. Bostock remained standing.

"It is my sad duty to inform you of the death of your friend, Sofie Kovac."

Tynan jerked as though receiving an electric shock. His eyes flew wide open.

"Sofie? Dead? How? When?"

A normal response, Coswell thought. If he was acting, he was very good.

"Friday evening. She was attacked while running in the University Endowment Lands."

Tynan's head fell forward and he closed his eyes.

Coswell let the silence hang for a few moments and then began. "You'll understand that we need to ask you some questions," he said.

Tynan opened his eyes and looked at him. His eyes full of pain.

"She wouldn't return my calls," he said. "I phoned

and phoned. I left messages on her cell and even on the machine in our flat. I should have gone to see her but I felt so rotten."

"Your relationship was ending, we've been told."

Anger flashed.

"Valerie, that old bitch told you, no doubt. Sofie and I could have worked out our differences if she'd minded her own business."

Grief rather easily overcome by anger, Coswell noticed.

"Have you caught her killer yet?" Tynan said.

"No, and that, of course, is why we're here."

He glared.

"Surely you don't think I had anything to do with it?"

"Routine," Coswell said. "We start with those who knew the victim best and in this case, that's you."

Tynan just shrugged.

"Whatever," he said. "But let's get this over with. I'm feeling very nauseous and getting this awful news hasn't helped."

Poor you, Coswell thought. He's a lot better off than his girlfriend. "Basically we just need you to describe where you were last Friday."

With no hesitation, he began to recount. Rehearsed, was Coswell's immediate impression.

"I drove her to work that morning," he said. "And that's when she told me we were through. She wanted me to spend the night in the doctors' residence and said she'd move her things out of the flat Saturday morning."

"And then?"

"I did my day in the anatomy lab and then drove Sofie's car to the flat. I got my kit out of the bathroom, a change of clothes, and walked here. Gordon was on duty at the desk. You can check with him."

"And then you got sick."

"Yes. It came on very suddenly. I thought it was

something I ate but obviously it's a flu bug of some sort."

Suddenly he bent forward and began to retch. Bostock quickly reached under the night table and pulled out a wastebasket which she handed to him.

They watched as he vomited. The smell almost caused Coswell to do the same.

When Tynan finally came up for air, he sputtered, "I must really ask you to leave me right now. You can talk to me later. I'm not going anywhere."

Coswell jumped up from the bed.

"Of course," he said. "Let's go, Bostock."

They stopped at the reception desk just long enough to thank Len and find out that his replacement, Gordon, came on duty at five. Bostock had a single question.

"Is there another way in to the residence, or does everyone come through the main entrance and pass by your desk?"

"There's a back door, which is a bit of a shortcut, but the house staff usually come up here anyway for messages and to let me know they're here. That's a rule. Occasionally a doctor will call me from his room phone but that's pretty rare."

They were almost at the cruiser when Bostock spoke.

"I was a little surprised that you didn't challenge him about Sofie ending their relationship in the morning. Valerie said Sofie hadn't told him when she went off for her run in the afternoon."

"He would have said she was wrong," Coswell said. "His word against hers. It's best he thinks we're happy with his statement right now."

"I must say that he was convincingly sick, though," Bostock said.

"I'm not so sure," Coswell said. "Did you notice the amount of chunky stuff that he barfed up? From what Len said you'd expect nothing but liquid."

"Ipecac," Bostock said. "I should have thought of that. When Len phoned his room, after been told not to bother him, Tynan would have considered us the likely visitors. So he swallows just enough to cause him to vomit shortly after we come in. He'd know the right dose and it would be easy for him to get some from the emergency department."

"And even if it wasn't us and it was Len knocking on his door with some emergency instead, the performance would still help his alibi. You know, Bostock, I'm getting the feeling that we're close to getting two cases solved for the price of one."

They stopped briefly at headquarters. Coswell wanted to have a warrant before going through Tynan and Sofie's flat. Bostock got one in record time and printed it out. The only hold up was James, who was there and wanted to be brought up to date.

"Amazing," he said after hearing Coswell's summary. "A crime of passion times two—love and hate. But do you really think Tynan did them both? The girlfriend, maybe. Love lost and all that. But Dr. Kelly? I really don't see enough motive. Criticism by the boss? Goodness, if that were the case, there'd be bodies everywhere."

"True," Coswell said. "But Tynan is our hottest suspect at the moment."

"Well go to it then. But is there something I can do to help? I have absolutely nothing on my blotter for the rest of the day. Give me something—please."

Sympathy came from Bostock first.

"There's the background check on Tynan in Ireland," she said. "His juvenile record. I haven't heard back yet."

"Unfortunately it's in the middle of the night in Ireland right now," James said. "But not to worry. I'll fiddle away on the internet. Maybe I can find something. 'Armagh' you said? That's where he and Kelly came from. Right?"

"Right, and they were both working in hospitals in Dublin."

Coswell had only one suggestion for him.

"Maybe you could give Charlotte a call and tell her we'll be bringing her some DNA shortly, and this time we want it processed without delay."

"After the whole lot she just did for you came up with zero matches?"

"Tell her I'll bet the price of lunch on this one."

CHAPTER TWENTY-NINE

The landlady read the warrant, taking far longer than necessary. She was obviously dying of curiosity and miffed when they wouldn't give her any detail but she gave her pass key to Coswell.

"Lock it again when you leave," she said.

Bostock led the way and had the door unlocked and opened by the time Coswell wheezed his way to the top of the stairs.

"You go ahead," he said. "I'm just going to catch my breath for a moment. Those bloody stairs are so steep. I'll bet they're not to building code."

Bostock had donned disposable gloves and was poking around in the bathroom when Coswell finally entered. He was surprised to see how neat the apartment was. The only time his condo looked like that was just after his housecleaner had made her weekly visit. No clothes scattered about; not even dirty breakfast dishes in the sink.

For want of a better expression, the place looked totally sterile. There was nothing personal hanging about. The fridge was devoid of photos; no reminder notes, shopping lists; not even a calendar. And in the adjacent sitting area, no magazines. They did have a television set with a single remote.

"This place is about as homey as a twenty-five dollar a night motel room," he said.

Bostock had come out of the bathroom and was headed to the single bedroom, where Coswell could see through the open door that it was as neat and tidy as the rest of the apartment.

"Smartphones, sir," she said. "Everything in the palm of your hand. I'm surprised they even have a land line, and with an old fashioned answering machine no less. Must have come with the apartment."

Coswell looked into the small kitchen area and saw the machine tucked up against an automatic coffee maker, red light flashing.

He went into the bedroom. Bostock was going through the closet.

"The running stuff is all hers," she said. "Nothing of his and no running shoes."

She went over to a set of dresser drawers against a side wall and started going through it.

"Mostly her stuff," she said. "Just socks and underwear for him. Few T-shirts."

"Anything worthwhile in the bathroom?"

"No. He's totally cleaned his stuff out of there. No toothbrush, shaving supplies, deodorant, combs. There's even a brand new bar of soap in the shower and the shampoo is definitely hers. Flower-scented stuff. The laundry hamper has a few of her things in it, none of his."

"What you're telling me is there's nothing to get a good DNA sample from," he said.

"Exactly, and no runners to take a tread print off of."

"Don't worry about the DNA. He drove her car back. Unless he wore gloves, you should be able to get something off the steering wheel."

"I suppose," she said. "I also saw the keys beside the answering machine, but not as good a source as a toothbrush or comb."

"Have to make do but let's go out and listen to the messages. Tynan said he left some. The times of the calls will be on it, too. At least they are on my machine."

Only two people had left messages: A very short one on Saturday morning— "Sofie, it's Val. Please call me." The others were from Tynan. The first, at ten p.m. on Friday. "Sofie. Please answer your phone. I'm sorry for being such a jerk to you and I promise I'll make up for it." The second was at midnight. "Sofie, please, please, please call me." He made more calls on Saturday and Sunday morning but did not leave a message.

Further inspection garnered nothing for them.

"Amazing that there's no mail, no bills or flyers around," Coswell said. "Sofie must have been a neatness freak."

"All done online now," Bostock said. "Banking, bill paying, even shopping."

Coswell thought that over for a moment.

"But there is something that wouldn't be stored online—passports. Have a look through that dresser again."

She found them tucked under the paper lining the bottom of Sofie's underwear drawer.

"His and hers," Bostock said, leafing through them. "Both Dublin addresses, but not the same. Interesting."

"Put them back exactly as they were," Coswell said.

James was sitting at Bostock's desk, staring at the screen of her computer when they got back to headquarters.

"I hope your search was as interesting as mine," he said, and then not waiting for a reply, "Just for the hell of it, I ran Tynan, Ireland, rather than fiddling with any police stuff, and lo and behold, at the very top of Google's list was a Baronet Alfred Tynan, assassinated at his abbey in County Armagh in 1981. The Provisional IRA took credit for it. Tynan was a big name in the Loyalist cause, sworn enemies of the Republicans."

"Fascinating," Coswell said. "But I want you to take a break from your surfing to get these samples Bostock just took out to Charlotte. The ASAP ones—remember?"

"No. Listen," James said. "This is important. It brings us back to the hate motive, and if I'm right, and Tynan is your murderer, it's all here."

Bostock moved over to the desk and looked over James' shoulder at the screen. In a moment, she grasped the significance.

"A double murder," she said. "The Baronet's adult son, who was visiting with his two young children at the time, was killed as well and the abbey torched. The children were saved by a maid who hid with them in a broom closet."

She looked at James.

"You don't suppose?"

"I do. Our Kevin could have been one of the children."

Coswell struggled with the math. Bostock was well ahead of him.

"He would have been eight years old at the time. Old enough to be terrified and to remember," she said.

James scrolled down and pointed to a name.

"And the pièce de résistance," he said. "The chief suspect, according to the local media, was—ta dah—Kelly! Patrick Kelly of the IRA. Not our dead Patrick Kelly, obviously, but perhaps a relative."

Coswell laughed.

"That's thirty years ago. Ancient history."

"Not so ancient," James said. "I've done a lot more research and apparently the animosity between the two camps still burns and if you add that to the childhood trauma, a surgeon's ego and being ridiculed professionally by a hated name...."

And a social inferior. Coswell remembered Tynan

using the word "lout" in his assessment of Kelly. A snob term.

He went over to his desk and sat down. James and Bostock regarded him as he tapped the blotter with a pencil.

"It would tie everything together," he said. "The girl-friend somehow a threat and he had to shut her up. Hard to imagine that kind of hate, though."

But it existed he knew ... The Middle East, Asia, Africa, and obviously, Ireland. Blessing to be living in Canada, he thought.

"How are you going to handle this?" James said. "Confront Tynan? Get a warrant to search his room in the Doctors' residence?"

"No. Let's see what he does over the next twenty-four hours. If he's guilty, he'll run. That's my guess. He knows we're closing in and home must look pretty good to him about now."

"I smell a boring surveillance detail," James said.

Coswell turned to Bostock.

"How about we do the first shift?" he said. "Like now to say midnight?"

"Certainly," she said.

James put up his hand.

"I'll nab some unlucky constable and do the grave-yard shift," he said. "I've met Tynan, so it's best that I do the job."

"Much appreciated," Coswell said. "We'll relieve you in the morning."

Coswell parked the cruiser on Heather Street, at a spot that gave a view of both the main entrance and back door of the doctors' residence.

"You can start off," he said to Bostock. "I might as well clean up the last of our suspects while we're here—Dr. Barrett, the neurologist. He's the only one who hasn't been interviewed. I know that Tynan is our big number one, but routine is routine."

"I agree," she said. "And we haven't collected his DNA yet."

In truth, Coswell wanted to see if Kay Montgomery was in the hospital. She would be an excellent source to check out Tynan's motive. There was a good chance that the resident's name would have come up in conversation with her ex-husband.

Thoughts of her had also popped up frequently over Coswell's weekend, despite lecturing himself to forget her. But such pleasant stirrings were rare in his life and getting rarer. Why turn them off?

As soon as he was out of sight of the cruiser, he called the university and asked to be put through to her office. Francis would know where she was. But Montgomery herself answered the phone.

"I'm my own receptionist today," she said. "Francis phoned in sick this morning. What can I do for you?"

There was a formality in her voice that disappointed Coswell. Whatever gratitude she had for being rescued from McMorran had passed. She was on guard.

"Dr. Tynan has become a person of interest to us," he said. "I wondered if you could give us a better picture of him and his relationship with Dr. Kelly."

Pause, and then she spoke.

"Kevin Tynan?" she said. "Do you think—?"

"Just something that we're looking into."

Another pause.

"Yes," she said. "I can understand your interest in him. I've never met the man but I remember Patrick's remarkable change in attitude toward him. At first he was so enthusiastic. He actually fast-tracked Kevin's residency application, blinded, no doubt by the Dublin surgical background. But somehow the name didn't register with either of us, although it should have."

"Tynan? Yes, I'm aware of the Baronet incident back in the early '80s," Coswell said.

"You'll know then, that Kevin's background is everything that Patrick's wasn't—upper crust, Protestant, Royalist, and when Kevin arrived, his superior personality didn't help. 'A little snob,' Patrick called him and after a few sessions in the OR, 'an incompetent snob.'"

"And rode him unmercifully, I understand," Coswell said, "although Tynan himself said nothing to us about it."

"'Better an Irishman shouting than a quiet one brooding,' as the saying goes," she said. "For you, that whole scenario of Patrick's death must have seemed bizarre, but I can tell you—in Ireland, even today, that would have been written off as just another example of good old sectarian hatred."

Coswell couldn't help noticing how enthusiastic she had become on the subject of Tynan, but perhaps it was just her clinical mind at work. And then her tone completely changed. Did he detect relief?

"Now I hope you haven't taken me off your list of future dinner guests," she said. "I'll even offer to pay this time."

"Maybe when this is all over," Coswell said. "But thank you for your input on Dr. Tynan. That has been very helpful."

"Any time," she said, cheerily. "And I mean that. Bye for now."

He looked down at his cell phone for a moment, thinking, and then he quickly shut it off. Interviewing Dr. Barrett had just become more of a priority.

He had gotten as far as the main hospital pavilion when Bostock called him on his cell phone.

"He's moving," she said. "Out the front entrance and turning up Heather Street. I'm going to follow him on foot."

Coswell felt his chest tighten. Bostock on the tail of a suspected killer.

"Stay well back," he said. "And—"

"Got to run," she said. "He's crossing Twelfth and I don't want to lose him."

The connection ended. Damn.

Assuming Tynan was headed back to his apartment, Coswell debated which was faster—return to the cruiser or head off on foot? He decided on the latter, the apartment only a few blocks away.

He ignored the pedestrian crosswalk light on Twelfth, which unfortunately was red. A series of angry blasts from car horns when he rushed across merely caused him to increase his pace. When he turned left on Thirteenth, he was relieved to see that huge oak trees and parked cars lining the street would give him something to duck behind since Tynan would be coming toward him. This proved to be an unnecessary concern. The only person he saw ahead was Bostock standing in the middle of the sidewalk facing him half a block away. She waved as soon as he came into view and pointed to Tynan's apartment.

Coswell slowed to catch his breath and then stopped. Bostock circled behind a van parked on the street and hurried over to join him.

"He's just gone in," she said. "What do you want to do?"

Coswell looked at his watch.

"Give him five minutes. He should be in the middle of packing his suitcase by then. Hopefully the landlady's there to let us in the front door. I'm sure Tynan will leave the others open. We can surprise him."

CHAPTER THIRTY

And that's exactly what happened.

"Whaat?" Tynan said when Coswell pushed the door open. He was indeed packing a travel case.

"Feeling a lot better, I see," Coswell said. "Going

somewhere, are you?"

His shock at seeing them disappeared quickly. He returned to his packing.

"The answer to both those questions is 'yes.' I've had enough of this cursed country and I'm going home."

"Then I guess now's the best time to bring you up to date on the two murders we're investigating—Dr. Kelly and of course, Sofie Kovac."

He stopped then and looked at them.

"All right," he said, pointing to the chesterfield in front of the TV. "Have a seat, but you'll have to hurry. I have a flight to catch soon."

When they were settled, he pulled over a kitchen chair and sat in front of Coswell.

"Okay," he said. "Let's hear it. I don't give a damn about Kelly, the swine, but I hope you've found Sofie's killer."

Coswell tried to detect a hint of fear, or at least worry, in Tynan's eyes, but all he saw was disdain. Established over many years, he surmised.

"We believe we've solved both cases," Coswell said, "with one name—yours."

Finally, a flicker of unease.

"That's absurd," he said.

Coswell shook his head.

"Not really, and with your interest in crime novels, I'm surprised that you should say that."

He felt Bostock shift slightly beside him and out of the corner of his eye he saw her purse appear on her lap.

"DNA," Coswell continued. "The greatest advance in crime detection since the fingerprint. It's just so damned hard to do anything these days without leaving a trace and unfortunately for you, we've found such a trace."

"Where?" Tynan said, challenging.

"On the door to the elevator from the basement of the anatomy lab, for one. Pushing that gurney must have been a real struggle. You probably have a bruise on your wrist where you banged it on the door. And, because you likely weren't wearing gloves when you strangled Sofie, we'll no doubt have lots of opportunity to get your DNA from her."

Silence.

Coswell went on.

"Your reason for killing Dr. Kelly is obvious. Sofie was a bit more of a puzzle, but here's what I think happened there. She hadn't told you she was ending your relationship, although you suspected it. A change in her mood after hearing about Kelly's death, perhaps? At any rate, you started to panic, knowing that her confirming your alibi for Sunday night would be vital."

He paused for a moment to let that sink in before continuing.

"You went on your post workday run with her, letting her go ahead, and when the perfect moment came you slipped your wire over her head. She would have reached back in a futile attempt to release your hold and I'm sure gathered some of your skin cells under her fingernails in the process. That, by the way, is being analyzed as we speak."

Coswell prayed that Tynan wouldn't realize that he had time to burn. It would take two or three days for Charlotte to do the analysis.

Tynan's head bowed down for a second and then slowly he stood up. He turned to face the kitchen windows, put his hands on the counter, and stared out to the street as he spoke in a quiet, sad voice.

"It was supposed to be a new start," he said. "Coming to this country. No more hate. Sofie was the one who actually chose Canada. 'No Troubles there,' she said. But then Kelly, the Fenian bastard, spoiled the whole thing. He was as bad as the worst back home. Animals, all of them."

"And Sofie?" Coswell prompted.

Tynan's shoulders slumped and he sighed.

"Ah. Poor Sofie. I borrowed her car that night. To get some things set up at the anatomy lab, I told her. Haile was on first call at the hospital, so that just left me to do it. I knew Kelly was going to Professor Dietrich's party. He changed the call rotation so he could attend."

He paused, seemingly overcome with emotion before continuing.

"When Sofie heard that Kelly had been murdered, she became suspicious. I denied it, of course, but she just kept getting more and more agitated. I knew she would be a gift for any policeman interrogating her."

"And so you stopped her?"

"Yes."

The first indication Coswell had of anything about to happen was Bostock stirring beside him and then everything exploded in a blur of movement. Tynan reached forward and then spun around, a vicious-looking knife in his hand. Too late Coswell remembered the wooden block on the counter that held an array of knives.

Bostock jumped to her feet gun in hand. She quickly slammed the clip into place and racked a shell into the chamber. Her purse fell to the floor with a thump.

But she wasn't fast enough. In a flash, Tynan grabbed Coswell by the collar and, with amazing strength, jerked him to his feet. Coswell's next sensation was cold steel on his throat, and Tynan behind him.

"Drop the gun, lady," he said, "or your boss will be squirting blood all over this room."

Coswell looked at Bostock. To his dismay, she wasn't looking at him. Instead, her eyes were fixed on Tynan, and the look in them did not comfort him. He was hoping for fear and obedience but there was only resolve—steely resolve—and the gun pointed at Tynan's head didn't waver a bit.

"Yes," she said. "I suppose you could do that, but

maybe you should consider what's going through my mind right now."

The pressure lessened ever so slightly on Coswell's throat.

"If you add my inspector to your victims, you've moved up into a whole new murder bracket—the killing of a police officer. That will not go well for you in a court. But I suppose that's a needless point because, if you do use that knife, I plan to fill you full of nine millimetre lead slugs, starting with your balls and moving upward until I finally blow your brains out. It might take a while, though. Lot of pain. Think about it."

Tynan, fortunately, did think about it—taking very few seconds to do so. The knife clattered to the floor and he held his hands up.

"Okay," he said. "You've got me."

Coswell suddenly had an overwhelming urge to urinate. He bolted for the bathroom. When he came back out, Bostock somehow had managed to put cuffs on Tynan and had him sitting on the chesterfield.

"Shall I phone for backup, sir?" she said, and then, "To take him to the holding cell."

Coswell had to fight hard not to laugh; the whole scene was so bizarre—a woman who looked like the teacher every pre-adolescent school boy was in love with standing next to a cold-blooded killer who had just threatened to kill him.

"You do that," he said.

They were half way back to the cruiser when Coswell finally asked the question burning in his mind.

"How long were you going to keep up that bluff?" he said.

"I wasn't bluffing," she said. "And I expected you to jerk your head to the side at any second. He wouldn't have had enough brain left to do anything with the knife."

Coswell thought about that for a few more steps.

"Is there a scientific basis to that statement?" he said.

"Absolutely, sir."

He glanced at her. Sphinx again, looking straight ahead.

CHAPTER THIRTY-ONE

Tuesday

For once the call into Chief Ward's office was a welcome one for Coswell. Praise was due and he intended to be certain it was directed where it belonged.

The smile on Ward's face was such a rare thing, that when he entered the chief's office it confused him for a moment. The man was almost ebullient.

"I have to admit, Coswell, that I had my doubts you'd solve this case so quickly," he said, leaning back in his chair, also a rarity. He usually sat ramrod straight or leaned forward in a threatening manner. "You've earned a commendation and I shall record it appropriately."

Coswell had always wondered where his commendations were recorded and if they had ever meant anything. He still seemed to fall into Ward's barrels of doo-doo with annoying regularity.

"Thank you," he said. "But the truth is that Corporal Bostock deserves those commendations. She not only was the lynchpin in solving the cases, but on two occasions saved my life."

And then as an afterthought, since Bostock's penchant for threatening maximal force might be in question he added, "In a manner of speaking."

"Good for her," Ward said. "And that brings up another matter. Sergeant McMorran has just handed in his resignation."

That sent Coswell's pulse racing. He wasn't surprised

at the news, but no way would McMorran have done that without blaming someone, and that someone of course would be Inspector Mark Coswell.

"Yes," Ward said, returning to his normal upright posture. "I'm as shocked as you are, but it seems that being 'put out to pasture,' as he called his present posting, has become intolerable to him."

Coswell breathed a sigh of relief. So far, blame had not been directed his way. He quickly commented, "The sergeant is a man of action, sir. No doubt about that. Maybe if you offered him one of the northern posts, he might reconsider. Plenty of action up there."

Ward gave him a suspicious look but didn't continue the topic.

"We'll see," he said. "But right now I have to decide on a replacement for him. There really aren't any sergeants I wish to re-assign at the moment, and so I've contemplated following through on my promise to Corporal James—promote him to sergeant and give him the post. What do you think?"

Emotions whirled in Coswell's mind. He should have been unhappy about the prospect of losing James and he was ... to a point. But Bostock had made an impression. As an assistant investigator, she was definitely on a par, and with some hardening up of female sensitivity and more humour on her part, the loss of James wouldn't be so bad. Besides, he couldn't live with himself if he said anything to ruin this opportunity for his ex partner.

"I think that's an excellent idea," he said.

"Good. Now on a final matter," Ward said. "The liaison position I created has been a popular one both locally and with headquarters in Ottawa. Gracing that position with a female officer to replace James would be the perfect move, in my opinion. Corporal Bostock seems to have settled down thanks to you, which would make her the ideal candidate for the job."

Coswell was too stunned to speak.

Ward put up a hand.

"No. Don't thank me," he said. "And this time I'll find someone more normal for you as a new partner."

"What on earth?" James said when Coswell returned to their office. "You look like you've lost your best friend. I thought you'd come out wearing a medal."

Coswell forced a smile.

"You're next," he said. "Ward wants to speak to you."

"Oh shit," James said. "Please excuse my Dutch. What have I done to come under his radar?"

Bostock was sitting at her desk, hands folded in front of her.

"I've put Tynan's juvenile report on your desk, sir," she said. "It came through by fax from Ireland very early this morning."

This time, Coswell read it without pausing.

"Nasty crowd for a sixteen year old, eh?" he said after he had finished reading. "I wonder why they call them Orangemen. Orange is such a happy colour."

"Probably where he learned his garrotting technique," she said. "I don't think the report is any use to the crown prosecutor, but it does add to our understanding of the man, don't you think?"

"Psychology has never been my forte, Bostock," he said. "I think we all muddle through life as best we can. Some just make very bad choices."

James, to their astonishment, returned from Ward's office barely five minutes after he had left them. He stood in the doorway and crooked his finger at Bostock.

"Next," he said. "It's just like at the dentist's office." But as he held the door open for her and she went to go by, he whispered to her, "I've set it up for you. There's a promotion waiting if you push for it. Go get 'em, girl."

She looked at him, totally puzzled, but he just pointed

down the hall to the chief's office and repeated, "Go."

"What the hell was that all about?" Coswell demanded.

James smiled.

"I turned down the UBC post," he said. "Surprised the hell out of our revered leader, but I told him my burning ambition is to be your ultimate replacement as chief of homicide and I wished to wait until that opportunity arose."

"And he accepted that?" Coswell said, dumfounded.

"Yep. Just like the old saying, 'You can lead a horse to water but you can't make it drink.'"

"I think the quotation describes an ass, James, not a horse."

"Ah, a beast of burden. How appropriate."

Bostock's session with the chief took much longer. She didn't return for almost twenty minutes, and when she did, her expression gave nothing away but she preempted any remarks from them with one short statement.

"Let's do Gino's," she said. "And this time, I'm buying."

"He's actually a reasonable man," she said, scooping some of the foam off of her cappuccino. "Or at least one of the few who is willing to listen."

This was an image neither James nor Coswell recognized.

"I took your advice, James," she continued, "and pressed my advantage. I won't go into detail, but suffice it to say that Chief Ward has a much better picture now of my history and my ambitions."

Coswell was still contemplating her comment about the chief's willingness to listen.

"Working out his postings was easy," she said. "It turns out that McMorran's corporal was actually senior in service years to him, so he was the obvious choice for his successor."

"And James' liaison position?" Coswell asked.

"Me," she said. "With sergeant's stripes and a promise to be considered for further advancement if I do a good job."

James was ecstatic.

"Wonderful, wonderful, wonderful," he said. "A fairy-tale ending. No pun intended."

Coswell lifted up his cup.

"To Sergeant Bostock," he said.

James seconded the toast.

For once, Bostock didn't blush. She was one of them, and she was happy.

ACKNOWLEDGEMENTS

The characters in this work of course are fictional. The setting for the most part is not. I spent many years in those environs—the UBC campus, the VGH, the streets of Vancouver (and a number of the pubs and restaurants). I can clearly see Coswell, Bostock and James moving about them. This has made writing the novel easier ... once I got started.

The first scene I had early on—a true event (minus the victim) but then I was stuck. It took a most unexpected email to bring on the inspiration to get going again and to that person I am truly grateful. Writer's block can be so painful.

I try to keep the time in the present but often I slip back as images from the sixties take over. The Ridge Theatre for instance is long gone; the Hastings and Main police precinct is no more; and I'm sure the security system in the Anatomy Building is now state of the art. There are more examples but perhaps the reader familiar with today's Vancouver and the UBC medical school will enjoy picking them out.

I have others to thank: Don Kerr especially who has board edited me through three of these now; Andrew Wilmot who smoothed over so many bumpy spots; the wonderful staff of NeWest Press, Paul Matwychuk, Matt Bowes, and Claire Kelly who have been so helpful; and to NeWest Press itself for continuing to support Canadian writers.

And finally I want to dedicate this work to all of the Corporal Bostocks, wherever they may be.

ROY INNES
Gabriola Island
July, 2016

Roy Innes was born in Regina, Saskatchewan, but has lived most of his life on the West Coast. A retired eye surgeon, he turned his love of reading crime novels into writing them.

His Inspector Coswell of the RCMP series began with *Murder in the Monashees* (2005) followed by *West End Murders* (2008) and then *Murder in the Chilcotin* (2010); all with excellent reviews. *The Extra Cadaver Murder* is the fourth in the series. He lives with his wife on Gabriola Island, BC.